I0715552

TERROR BY NIGHT

TERROR BY NIGHT

THE SUPERNATURAL AFFAIRS OF MADISON CAVENDISH AND SUE SUNMOUNTAIN

James G. Goodridge

GRAVELIGHT PRESS | LOS ANGELES

CONTENTS

DEDICATION

This book is dedicated to the following: the Universe, everyone who didn't believe I could do this book and those who believed I could, Celeste Rita Baker, Jarvis Sheffield (Black Science Fiction Society), Lin Lucas, Valjeanne Jeffers, Doug Draa, Penelope Flynn, Cranston Burney, Roxanne Bland, Kevin Entwistle (Rollo Ahmed's grandson), Sonia James, my little but growing knot of fans, horroraddicts.net, Greta, Otto, Brian, Shae, Cedar, Kim, Cheryl, Lorraine, Kathy, Starr, my cuz (Larry), my sis (Brenda), my children (Montel, Baron, Adasia, Rosa), my grandson (MJ), the Keiler, Reliford, and Freeman families, and of course Dianne Pearce and David Yurkovich.

JGG

IVERSIDE DR.
107
ONE WAY
TERROR BY NIGHT

THE
CAVENDISH
AFFAIR

1914

Unlike other finance and brokerage houses in the Wall District, 112 Nassau Street is an odd, angled building, and though I dare say it is not in competition with the mammoth Singer Tower up on Broadway, it is nonetheless scraping the sky.

The building is fitted with a sub-basement, yet this contains no vaults for the protection of stocks, bonds, or other assets. Damp death-scented earth covering the concrete floor stretches out to the walls. One particular wall that, had it been on ground level, would be facing south toward New York Harbor was sledge-hammered away, exposing a dark void, a glow of magenta light not from this world, a light more similar to the hue commonly associated with Easter, yet sicklier.

On this night there are screams fighting with the sound of footsteps that echo down from above to the sub-basement. The screams amount to hysterical pleading from a woman in a summer dress that, once cream-colored, is now covered in soot. Her pretty strawberry-blonde hair is barely held together by the red candy stripe ribbons for which she is well known. The footsteps she struggles against belong to a man, he too of fair hair, in a dark morning coat.

A black cat silently hops down the steps behind the abductor and prey, hoping to pick up some type of souvenir to bring back to its cubbyhole, to add to its collection, part of a maze of secret rooms that would have made mass murderer H.H. Holmes envious of its design, had he not met his demise, twitching for fifteen minutes at the end of a hangman's noose, in a Pennsylvania prison sixteen years earlier.

"Why are you doing this to... me?!" the woman yells, hands raw from clawing at the brick walls as they descend down the stairway.

"This should shut you up, my dear!" bellows the morning-coat man as he slams her head against the stairway wall, causing her to black out, which is, in point of fact, a best-case scenario considering what will transpire next.

At the wall opening something large from below begins a hungry movement, a sticky sound of sloshing in the wet. Lest he get too close to the edge, the morning-coat man times his steps like a hammer thrower, raising the petit woman over his head. He takes a running start range of motion, pitching the young lady, who had so much Broadway theater promise, into the abyss.

In the blink of an eye, tentacles, long, magenta with purple seborrhea spotted and scarred, their widths the size of tree trunks, grab the unconscious female in midair like a rag doll and then pull her down for digestion.

"Rest you down, Father; may she serve you well," the man calls as he scrambles back. "Be gone, you!" he yells, kicking out at the dark feline that momentarily blocks his escape back up the stairs. The cat, which has a mutual hate for him, scampers to its cubbyhole with a prize between its fangs.

"Now that you're finished acting the maggot, what are we to do with the others?" asks a woman, standing behind the marble concierge's desk of the Beaux Art Building's lobby, her skin like ivory and cold to the touch. Long black ringlets of hair, favoring the right side of her face, help hide the absence of her right ear. A Victorian black dress, long out of fashion, gives her dour beauty, until she bares her fangs. "When do we drink *duine beag*?" she asks, as Cranston Vauxhall hurriedly bolts the access door to the basements, then slides over a large urn of alchemist extracts, the last line of defense should Father decide to slither up to street level.

"Now, now, Mary. We will step up to the bar and take our fill of our guest soon enough. Then we will give a new deed on life to the booley dog cop so as to assist us since you don't like dealing with Father. You know as well as I do that we must take care to have someone available for the next feeding cycle. Does that please you, you provincial left-handed whore?!"

"Go down to see Nicky, have a Devil's party while sitting on his pitchfork, Cranston!"

As Vauxhall raises his hand as if to strike a blow to Mary's face as he had done on numerous occasions, Mary flinches, but instead he focuses on adjusting his morning coat. Vauxhall wonders if it might be time to put Mary on Father's feeding cycle menu. He senses Mary feels mutual disdain for him as he's long held for her. Having previously rejected her mawkish feelings of love for him (such emotions were for the weak and living), he finds her a bore these days and nights. In the meantime, sunrise, filtering in from the high arched windows of the lobby, signals that it's time for both fiends to rest until nightfall.

—

My name is Madison Cavendish. I'm a detective with the New York City Police Department, and, unknown to me, I'm about to meet the love of my life while simultaneously embarking on a journey into the world of the occult and paranormal.

I'm seated on a wooden bench inside police headquarters at 240 Centre Street, awaiting a meeting with the commissioner. The building is harsh and loud with the sound of typewriter keystrokes, telegraph clicks, and phone conversations. There is a woman seated across from me. We sneak silent glances at one another.

She has a black kinky chignon hairstyle, with a woman's Prussian, blue-banded straw boater balanced atop it. Celestial nose, spiritual eyes, and freckles splashed across her cheeks (no Borax mixed with rose water to bleach them away for her, I guess). She wears a French chalk white summer dress and shoes. I'm lovestruck, yet intimidated, by her beauty, but I feel compelled to break the ice. A copy of the *New York Mirror*, its headline warning of the Great War in Europe, rests near her on the bench.

"Pardon me, miss. Can I have a look at your newspaper?" I ask, stepping over to her bench.

"Read it all you want, sir; it's not my paper."

"Thank you, you know—"

"Cavendish, the commissioner will see you now," interrupts a grumpy sergeant in blue, leaning his bald cranium around the outer office door to my silent perturbation. "Dash it, Woods, did you have to call me in now?" I mumble to myself.

"Take a seat, Detective," Woods says. A gray-templed bullneck of a man, Woods is dressed in a deep gray pinstriped suit too hot for this summer day, a stark contrast to my sky-striped seersucker suit and boater.

"Detective, I assume you've been following the Nelly O'Shea case. It's been a real bugaboo for everyone here at Centre Street."

"The abduction. Yes, sir, I'm familiar with the case."

"The news rags have been hounding us, Cavendish, saying we're not doing enough to solve the case."

O'Shea is to some New Yorkers the second coming of Lotte Gilson, but if you ask me, when O'Shea sings, it sounds like a fussy 2-

year-old. Her shtick of crying in mid-song was as old as a Grand Army of the Republic veteran, but this didn't dismiss the fact that it was our job to find her.

"We're in a real jam, Detective. Your former partner, Layton Hickman, was assigned the case, but by Jehovah, he's vanished too!" Woods explains.

Like me, Hickman is a denizen of the Polo Grounds, catching New York Giant ballgames together when we could.

"That meathead Monk Eastman," Woods continues, "along with his gang, is sweet on O'Shea dating back to her Bowery Theater days and has sent word through some of our officers on the pad that they're going to take matters into their own hands and tear up Lower Manhattan to find her. Cavendish, I'll get to the meat of it—"

"You want me to take over the case, Commissioner. Trust me, I will make it personal, sir."

"Don't strain at the leash, man. As you may know, I've been installing reforms to the department in criminology and sociology. Other cities overseas have incorporated various means of solving crimes by infusing those sciences, which I will start today with you. The other means? The paranormal. It so happens that my wife, Helen, has employed for the last few years a milliner who does custom work on Helen's hats. She also does tarot readings and alleges to come from a family of Shamans. Claims to have had a vision that was ignored: that her former place of employment, the Triangle Shirt company—where she worked as a seamstress—would go up in flames. Be that humbug as it may, her name is Seneca Sue SunMountain. She's been talking for days about how she can help find O'Shea; says she has again had visions.

"Before I continue on, Cavendish, how do you feel about the Negro race?" asked Woods, leaning back in his chair. "Any problems with them?"

"No problems at all, sir." What Woods fails to realize as he stares across his desk at me is the fact that I'm passing, which I first did in order to get a job with the department. I'm the product of a white mother and Negro father, both educators, both murdered down South for the simple post-Reconstruction Amendments that granted Negro children the right to be taught to read, this five years after I was born in 1885.

"What about clairvoyants?"

"Commissioner Woods, seriously?"

"A seer, or whatever you call them."

"No. Do you really need me on this case?" Long ago, the cold hard truth of my parents' murders killed all ruminations in me about things spiritual, or behind the so-called veil.

"I'll answer your question with a question, Cavendish. You ever heard of the Benedetto farm up on 214th Street in Bronx County? Well, those same crooked cops who loved to kiss Monk Eastman's ring and deliver his messages are now kissing Benedetto tomatoes while on the beat up there. Care to join them?"

"No thanks. That part of the city is where law enforcement careers go to die."

"Are you in and playing ball, Detective?"

"I'm had, sir. I'm in."

"Okay, Cavendish. I knew you'd take the case. Get red-assed on it, son. Don't let me down. This will also keep my wife, Helen, from pestering me about using Miss SunMountain. The day you get married, you'll understand the power of a wife's verbal rollin' pin," he said, pressing a buzzer button on the side of his desk. After a few moments the door was opened by the on-duty sergeant.

Hot damn, the woman in the waiting room enters!

"Miss SunMountain, this is Detective Cavendish. We'll be assisting you in, well, whatever it is you do," says Woods to my silent consternation. He has no clue as to how to approach this.

"Hello, Detective Cavendish. Please bear with me, but I feel I can help," says Miss SunMountain, who continues to stare at me as if aware of my secret. She sits next to me.

"My pleasure, ma'am," I say. Gorgeous or not, I figure I'll patronize her for a day or two then be finished.

After receiving a pep talk from Woods, who again hasn't a clue as to how Miss SunMountain and I are going to tackle this strange affair, we leave 240 Centre Street. There's an awkward silence sprinkled by weak small talk. I ask her about the day of the Triangle Shirt Company fire back in 1911.

"I'd rather not talk about it," she says quietly.

Hailing a Hansom cab, a slowly vanishing mode of transportation in the city due to the rise of the automobile, I instruct the driver to drop us off at Debrosses Street Station. We take the Ninth Avenue EL uptown to 50th, then walk to West 52nd in Hell's Kitchen, where SunMountain lives in a rooming house run by a woman who introduces herself as Mrs. Muldoon. She's a kindly Gaelic lady who is progressive of mind and has no qualms renting out rooms by the week to salesmen, women, Negros, actors, and Eastern Europeans. The aroma of chicken fricassee and oyster pie is mouthwatering, coming from Mrs. Muldoon's kitchen on the first floor when we arrive.

Somewhere across the street from the rooming house in a brownstone, someone in a light mood fumbles through a piano rendition of "The Streets of New York" and sings in an off-key voice.

Down at the corner of 52nd and Tenth Avenue, neighborhood guttersnipes find morbid entertainment, poking with sticks the carcass of a dead delivery wagon horse abandoned by its owner, its stench amplified by the summer heat.

"So, you say you're a milliner?" I ask, trailing behind SunMountain, her lilac scent a respite from the nag odor down on the street, as we climb the stairs up to her third-floor room.

"Uh-huh," SunMountain says as she clears off a wooden chair laden with books for me to sit.

The place looks like a secondhand bookstore full of tomes on the occult and paranormal with odd titles like *The Nosferatu Diaries* and *The Hexan Journal*, the latter surrounded by a red ribbon tied tight around its binding cover to restrict its access. A narrow bookcase boasts a small but impressive collection that includes *The King in Yellow*, H. Cordelia Ray's ode poem to President Abraham Lincoln, Herbert Spencer's *Principles of Biology*, and an undetermined political manifesto from K. Marx and F. Engels. All this has me surmise Miss SunMountain to be a well-read woman. On her nightstand sits a deck of well-worn tarot cards next to an empty drinking glass.

"May I ask you a question?" she asks.

"Sure; give it a go."

"Why are you passing?"

This confirms the looking-over she gave me down at 240 Centre Street, but I'm nonetheless left stammering. "That's kind of personal a question, and if I was Negro I wouldn't answer it or like being asked. Can we stick to business?"

"Of course."

"Okay. What do we do now?"

"Here," SunMountain says, "take this pencil and paper pad and you write down what I say as I enter into a vision quest. I know you think this is all bovine balderdash, but please help me, Detective. I've had severe headaches and need for this whole thing to be done with."

Placing her straw boater on a stack of books, SunMountain lays on her bed and closes her eyes before crossing her chest with her arms as if resting in eternal peace. Twenty minutes later, I'm startled out of a light slumber by SunMountain's loud moan.

"One... one... blood... help... blonde women... Nassau... two... fill up... the cup... people... one... one... two... Nassau... O'Shea!"

She repeats the sequence of words five times, then, like a Morse code message, she stops. "Help me up, please, Detective," she asks.

At the touch of her hands, so help me, an image juts into my mind's eye. The look of it, maybe from the deep depths of an ocean, evil with a touch, I flinch. I made a mental note to get something to eat or some coffee to make me right and not delusional. Then I blurt out, "I do it to earn a decent living. You and I both know we can't get a fair shake in this country on account of our race. I hope to one day end this charade. You'll never see me joining a blue vein society!" Blue vein societies are clubs that shun the darker members of our race, and I confess this. She leaves and soon returns from the communal bathroom with a drinking glass full of tepid water.

Pressing the glass to her temple before gulping the water down, she says, "What?" It seems she's forgotten her earlier question.

"You asked why I was passing. I've just told you my reason. What's yours?"

"I'm passing until I'm asked. You'd be amazed at the number of places I've been thrown out of or the many times I've had to prick with force some buckra with my hat pin for trying to make time with me until they find out I'm half Negro." At her confession we both chuckle, and she says, "Please, Detective Cavendish, call me Sue."

"Only if you call me Madison," I counter with pleasure.

She smiles. "Agreed. Now, back to the subject at hand. With what you've written down from my vision quest, what do we do now, Madison?"

"I'm going to try to figure heads or tails of this, but in the meantime, I think you need some rest, Sue," I coax her, which she dislikes. However, given that she's heartbroken and too weak to argue with me, Sue lays back across her bed and waves me off in silence. And in silence I leave her room, passing by a concerned Mrs. Muldoon on the stairs. Down on the street, I crumble the notes I'd taken, then open the lid to a trash can to toss them in. That is until I glance at a discarded *New York Sun* newspaper folded open to a page displaying an advertisement for a pawn shop. The address: 109 Nassau Street.

Repocketing my notes, I rip the page out of the paper, then backtrack into Sue's rooming house to annoy everyone, starting with Mrs. Muldoon, who, returning downstairs, lets me know in no uncertain terms how I've upset Sue. Next, I beg and then order Muldoon, on police business, to interrupt a tenant's phone call so I can contact the pawn shop. Then I vex the pawn shop owner, admitting that the only reason I phoned was to verify the address across from him as 112 Nassau Street.

And finally, to disturb Sue. She nods, yet her feelings change once I tell her the news: "I've found her at 112 Nassau Street."

———

It's as though 112 Nassau Street has a strange hold over people. Strange because no one really takes notice of the architectural design of the obsidian blood-hued brick skyscraper that rises up at a weird angle, a fact Sue and I notice as we gaze at the building from across the street in front of the pawn shop. Mr. Berlin, the pawn shop owner, states that it seemed as if the building had been erected overnight.

"Tsk tsk. We're not open now, pretty boy," a female voice insists. Her skin is like ivory, from the other side of a frosted glass door etched with baroque designs surrounded by an image of a kraken. Green-tinted eyeglasses rest on the bridge of her nose. With a single arm, she blocks our entrance into the building.

"Nelly's here, Detective," says Sue.

"You sure?"

"Pretty sure."

"That's good enough for me." I turn to our aggressor. "Madison Cavendish, NYPD. This is Miss SunMountain, a consultant with the department. I'm going to need you—if you're not the owner—to fetch the building's owner or the manager of this property."

"Here now, listen, cute booley dog, only madra's fetch I—"

"It's okay, Mary. Unlock the doors and let them inside. I'm Vauxhall—Cranston Vauxhall," says the man approaching from behind the woman who, with a shrug, unlocks the side door instead of unlatching the revolving main door. A fair-haired man in a herringbone suit, he too wears tinted glasses, which cast an aura of mystery and foreboding.

We enter into a lobby set in ambient amber light so ornate with its arched ceiling it could double as a church. As I flash my badge I can't help but be in awe by this place. "I'll get to the point, Mr. Vauxhall. I'm sure you've seen the newspapers and tabloids concerning the disappearance of Nelly O'Shea, the honest showgirl."

"No, Detective, can't say that I have. The whole thing sounds a bit trashy muck to me, Mary would know of such things," yawns Vauxhall, while the woman named Mary seems stung by his choice of words. She tries not to show her emotions but fails.

"Be that as it may, sir, you wouldn't mind if we have a look around, would you?"

"The basement," Sue says, nudging me.

Vauxhall briefly seems ill at ease by Sue's comment, but he

replies, "Detective Cavendish, I'm a busy man. But if it'll help speed you on your way, you can have a quick look down in the basement under the condition that your consultant remain here. She seems highly wound up. Are we in accord?"

"Okay, Vauxhall. I agree. Sue, stay here, please."

"Well, thank you very much, Madison Prescott Cavendish!" Sue replies, making no effort to mask her fury.

Never in my life has someone spoken my full name with such disdain. Sue exits the building lobby and steps into the late summer air to wait for me as the mysterious woman suppresses a giggle at Sue's expense.

—

Vauxhall leads me through a pale green door stenciled in black letters: *Basement A and B,* and under the words are strange, etched symbols. With great effort, Vauxhall moves a ceramic urn, reeking of pungent incense, away from the door. Vauxhall then unlatches a door bolt. We descend in dim light down a stairway, and, along the way, rising up, a new scent emerges, one of holy rose water mixed with the rot of something dead. Fear begins to rise in me, which I struggle to subdue. A barely controlled fear not unlike one I had once as a child in a wooden barrel rolling down a hillside, unable to stop. Reaching under my jacket I transfer my 1907 Russian .44 from its holster to my jacket pocket at the ready. Something brushes against my trouser leg, causing me to jump as Vauxhall walks ahead of me. I gaze down to see a midnight-black cat with something dangling out its maw, which it drops at my feet. A piece of fabric. I slip it into my left jacket pocket before Vauxhall can notice. The cat scampers up past me to the lobby.

"Shall we descend to the sub-basement, Detective?"

Vauxhall seems to be challenging me as I look around a dim furnace room absent of heat. "No, Vauxhall, I've seen enough." Prudence and fear get the best of me. We make our way back upstairs to the lobby. "Sorry to bother you, Vauxhall. Seems I've been made a fool by a hoaxer."

"I'll raise a glass to your stupidity, Detective. You will now excuse me. I have business to tend to. "

I want to smack his smug face, sending his green spectacles airborne up toward the Singer Tower, but then again, if I do, I would be twirling a nightstick up in the Bronx. Woods wouldn't tolerate me slugging a businessman—even one who deserves it.

"Um… just one more thing, Vauxhall. Is it me, or has something awful crawled up or down in your basement and died? The odor is dreadful."

"You are always welcome to come back and check out the sub-basement as I offered. Now be gone—by which I mean, goodbye, Cavendish!"

Vauxhall turns on his heels and leaves, while his assistant waits until Vauxhall is several feet away with his back turned, and takes a moment to blow me a kiss before I step back outside.

"How dare—" Before Sue can continue to express her outrage, I politely interlock my arm with hers and march her further along Nassau Street to the corner and down toward Water Street.

"Calm down and look at this," I say, producing Nelly O'Shea's cat-chewed-at-the-edges ribbon that the singer likes to adorn her hair with.

"Are you sure it was one of her ribbons?"

"Without a doubt." I can't believe Miss hoo-doo-now wants facts. "I saw her once with that same ribbon while working to break up a Cee-Lo dice game in the back of a Bowery theater, and as a matter of record, Nelly was one of the dice bowlers. You need to get out more and out from behind those books of yours, and if I had my way, you would."

"Madison, a lot of women in this city put ribbons in their hair. And also, are you asking me out on a date, Detective?" Sue's stare flatly demands an answer to her question.

"A date? Yes, but in due time. Presently, I've got to return to 240 Centre Street and get a squad assembled to raid this building."

"Madison."

"Yes?"

"Do you not sense the evil in that building? This is a building that Mr. Berlin said just appeared out of nowhere and overnight. This is a building enveloped with the scent of death. You really think a flying wedge of cops is going to set things right?"

"You have a better idea, lady?" Simultaneously, we let each other's hands go, unaware that we'd been holding hands as we debated.

"Yes, I do have a better idea, or at least I hope so. We have to go through my books, but before that, we have to catch the EL up to Broome Street. Got any money?"

In my gut, I have a feeling I'm going to be out more than a few bucks.

———

On Broome Street we stop in a little curio shop run by a British expatriate, Miss Elsa Cranberry, who, along with her intimate friend and shop co-owner, Zoltar, of Sikh origin, regard themselves as occult detectives. I find it to be a real hoot. Even Sue, who considers herself a Shaman, finds the two shop owners' self-titles to be presumptuous or, to use Miss Cranberry's word when told of Vauxhall's attitude, "cheeky." With my money, Sue purchases loud-smelling Sulphur, black myrrh, red sadel, putrid apple vinegar, calamus, peony, mint, palm, Hyssopus, and holy water. Back at the rooming house, Sue talks Mrs. Muldoon into letting her use the communal kitchen to boil and mix up the ingredients. Miss Muldoon obliges, adding that Sue and I "make a nice couple." While Sue tends to our liquid solution, I phone Woods.

"Cavendish, where in the Devil's name have you been, man?"

"Working with Miss SunMountain like you—"

"Listen, we've got a new problem to compound things. A settlement house teacher name of Jenny Lee has been abducted off the street while you and Miss SunMountain have been reading tea leaves. It happens that Miss Lee is related to Tom Lee, head of the On Leong Tong on Mott Street. He's letting his street proxy, Charlie Boston, keep an open line with us, but it's been conveyed that if Miss Lee is not safely returned within 72 hours, then Boston's high binders will take matters into their own hands, along with the Eastman's. Do you have any leads? Do you need a squad of men, Cavendish?"

I pause to consider the question and the plan of action Sue and I have in mind. "No, sir. I just need 72 hours like the On and Eastmans." I try to fumble with the phone and hold my nose courtesy of Sue's nose-opener soup.

"You've got it, Cavendish. But remember, most of the tomatoes have been picked up on 214th around this time of year, and walking a beat during winter up there can be brutal."

Woods's pun ends the call before I can respond to the old rectangle-head bastard. We fill up two empty wine bottles with our concoction and a third with gasoline. To avoid further inconveniencing Mrs. Muldoon, we agree to head up to my spartanly furnished apartment on Riverside Drive and 107th Street off the North River to rest. Sue curls up on my bed while I nap on the floor, the three bottles secure in a carpet bag padded with straw.

—

Midnight.

Seeing no signs of life in 112 Nassau Street's lobby, I set to work, pulling out a lock-picking kit I lifted off a master yegg I'd arrested a few years ago, born Lou Matz but known among the criminal element as the Mulberry Street Kid. The kit is handy in situations like this while Sue stands lookout.

"Madison, do you see that?" Sue asks, pointing to the basement door's scratched symbols.

"What is that?"

"Those are bind rune marks. Vauxhall is trying to keep something from coming up out the basement!" After taking a moment and composing herself, Sue continues. "Madison, I must confess, I'm scared yet compelled to find out what's down there."

We both pause, then, after some silent effort, push aside the large urn blocking the basement door. "I'd be lying if I said I wasn't scared myself," I whisper. "I could feel something move under the steps the first time I walked down here with Vauxhall." I hope, in the dim light, she can see my nervous smile.

"Tell you what, Detective, if—I mean *when*—we get out of this, you can take me to a nice little nifty chop suey emporium up on Pitt Street for dinner," she says, returning the smile.

"Or how about Fay's Restaurant up in Harlem?" I counter, to her surprise.

—

As we descend the stairs, screams, mixed with Vauxhall's yelling, rise up the stairway to meet us. At that moment, a magenta glow wraps around us, followed by Sue propelling into my back and causing us to tumble downward with a kick to Sue's back. I land at Vauxhall's feet, who is struggling with a woman I assume to be Jenny Lee. A familiar voice calls out.

"Madison, old chum. How goes it?"

Standing over Sue is my friend and former partner, Hickman, fighting to wrest the carpet bag from Sue's grip. Even in the dim, otherworldly light of the sub-basement, I can see Hickman no longer belongs to this world as evidenced by waxed skin beneath a wrinkled seersucker suit the color of dried blood.

"Madison, embrace Father! Let him show you the cosmos! Think about it. Endless attendance to the polo grounds, chum! You don't need this Negroid mutt sniffing after you either! You can have any woman in the world you want—just ask Vauxhall!"

With a newfound joy, Hickman stretches his arms out as I remove my .44 and put a slug between his red-pupiled eyes. Hickman crumbles to the death-scented floor atop a terrified Sue.

Like that barrel ride of my youth, things began to move too swiftly. Vauxhall, like a cowardly chess master, has Miss Lee by the neck. With his pawn, he backs up against the wall. Just as I stumble off the floor, Mary twists the .44 out of my hand. Backing her way over to Vauxhall, she pulls Miss Lee loose then proceeds to empty my .44 into Vauxhall. The muzzle flashes, momentarily lighting up the sub-basement and providing a glimpse of several giant snakes. To my horror, I soon realize they're not snakes at all. The octopod tentacles emerge from a giant opening. God help me! Like five huge fingers on a deformed hand, the thing envelops Sue, Hickman, and Vauxhall in its clutches, leaving Mary to claw along the wall. Miss Lee makes a fast escape up the stairs. The creature's outer appendages resemble the flexible appendages of a squid, yet the inner three tentacles are clearly not of this world. At the tip of one, a wolf's head growls in harmonic dissonance, its maw chewing on my Sue's throat, lifting her off the floor. The second possesses a pastel-green head, black hair mattes its pupils bloodred. The last contains a strange almond-shaped head with large, oily black and pupilless eyes. The almond shape is indifferent to my screams as the green head drives fangs into my throat.

"Mother, Father!" I cry as the horror head drags me, fighting toward the opening. Gnawing at her neck like an old bone, the wolf's head hasn't had its fill of Sue. Her body lifeless, Sue is no more, to my tears of anger. My only consolation, the brief time that we spent together was kismet.

"Damn you!" My shrill cry is more like a hiss, and with my last ounce of energy, I grab the carpet bag up and heft it into the abyss before Sue's body is pulled along with it.

"No! Noooo!" coughs Vauxhall on his knees.

An explosion erupts across the room and is followed by darkness.

—

My promotion to captain is bittersweet without Sue.

Woods plays the press like a Stradivarius and pegs the mysterious Cranston Vauxhall as a serial killer, making sure to omit the fantastic details. All involved except for Jenny Lee and me are dead or unaccounted for as a result of the explosion and ensuing fire. The Eastman gang finds it more lucrative to transition to other illegal endeavors rather than bloviate any longer over a dead singer. Charlie Boston is joyful about Jenny's return. Rumor has it he sent a reward that was pocketed by Woods. Typical.

After a few days, my pain subsides so I visit 240 Centre Street to search the police archives to try and identify Vauxhall and Mary from memory. To my astonishment, a file on a "One Ear Mary," aka Mary Kerry, turns up. The faded file, with an attached sepia mugshot, lists

Mary Kerry as a member of the Day Light Gang, known for robbing the Vanderbilt railyards on the west side of Manhattan. Problem is, Mary's been dead for more than fifteen years, resting in Potter's Field on Hart's Island.

Vauxhall's file is more confusing. Three different Cranston Vauxhalls were arrested dating back to the 1840s. The most recent Vauxhall arrest was for practicing medicine without a license. I visit his spouse, a confection company heiress named Urraca Chapak-Vauxhall, hoping she might provide insights into this whole affair. Instead, I'm met with a bushel of stubbornness as Mrs. Vauxhall refuses to answer questions.

Then, on a cold September morning, I'm called out to Brooklyn. A body in a morning coat, minus its head and hands, has washed up on a beach in Dead Horse Bay, pockets stuffed with soggy papers identifying it as Vauxhall. I know it's not Vauxhall, but Woods wants a closed case. I can't even get back into 112 Nassau Street; a legal firm, Gaston & Snow, has taken over the building for use.

—

"I have to run more tests, Cavendish, to get to the bottom of this," says my new doctor, Oberlin Pythagoras, a dour, balding, brown-skin man with admittance privileges to Sydenham Hospital in Harlem. My old MD was so unnerved to see the magenta swirls spreading, then ebbing, on my chest he said he could no longer treat me. That, along with sunlight irritating my eyes, the feel of something crawling about the gums under my teeth, a heavy-handedness of crushing doorknobs by applying too much pressure, mixed with Sue's demise, have resulted in an ever-increasing sense of melancholy.

"There's one thing I need for you to do, Madison, between now and our next visit," says Dr. Pythagoras.

I pull on my shirt. "What's that?"

"Let her go, Madison. She's gone. Just be blessed Sue was in your life for those few days."

The doctor, who I've confided in, hands me yet another bottle of Bayer Heroin Powder to accompany the gum water. It does nothing to alleviate the pain inside me. I also make an educated guess the doctor has never known love, although he most likely is right.

My condition worsens to the point that I have to take a leave of absence from the department. Everything comes to a head on a wind-howling, rainy Halloween night, which has curtailed the number of trick-or-treaters "guising" in the neighborhood. So I sit in the darkness of my apartment on Riverside Drive and 107th Street, twisting and turning from this god-awful thing inside me. I can't take it anymore. Staggering from my bedroom to my desk in my living room, I jerk open a desk drawer, pull out my .44, point it at my heart, and shoot myself into nothingness. Mother and Father, forgive me.

———

For some reason, I can see more clearly in the darkness as I revive. What at first I think is a branch tapping at a windowpane, turns out to be some knocking on my door, probably Miss Marcal, my landlady, to investigate the sound of gunfire. No doubt the last straw with me following our last encounter, during which she cheerfully asked what color I would like my door painted, explaining that she'd hired a painter to spruce up the place, and I advised her to paint it black. From then on, she found me to be erratic. I open the door without enthusiasm.

"Sue!" I spit out, along with the .44 slug and a dribble of blood.

"Maddy! My Maddy!" Sue wraps her arms around my neck. She's dressed properly for autumn in a dark wool coat. Rosey red-tinted glasses sit on the bridge of her nose. At her feet: a suitcase and a hatbox, which, for a second, I think quakes.

"Lady, where have you been? Do you know how many times I've been to your residence since that morning, which was, damn it, all a fog to me? Nobody at the scene saw you leave, and Miss Muldoon all of a sudden became a dumb Dora when it came to you. She didn't even clean out your room. What on Earth happened to you? What has happened to us? I'm sick. Do you hear…"

"Well, first, I must say you really look good with your hair slicked back instead of that hayseed part down the middle style. Now you've got a matinee idol look going. I'm a simp for you, Maddy. I must confess, that day in the commissioner's office, I had hoped you would ask for the newspaper." Sue gushed to me. "Uh… Maddy… listen. You're more than sick. The old Madison Prescott Cavendish is dead, just as the old edition of Seneca Sue SunMountain died at 112 Nassau Street. With your detective logic and my Shamanic visions, we are on a new journey, and we can make money along the way." Sue speaks matter of fact in tone as she sits down on my gray Davenport hatbox on the floor beside her. Coat off, she looks exalted in a black hobble dress, her hair now flowing with a magenta streak running through it. "Take a deep breath, Maddy."

At her request, I inhale and let out a cough followed by a loud hiss that comes from deep within me. Fangs extending inside my mouth, I feel a glow of understanding. My enhanced body finds me at peace with the cosmos, yet with a taste for life's flow, by which I mean blood, of course. And I don't mean maybe.

"So, we've become vampires?" I ask.

"Yes and no. I, myself, have lycanthrope propensities. Whoever or whatever Father digested shows that, at some point, all folklore germinates from a seed of fact.

"Lycan, what? Father?" I began pacing around the room.

"Werewolf, Maddy, werewolf. But you have become 'the cats' eyebrows' to me. Speaking of cats, look who's here from 112 Nassau Street." Placing the hat box on her lap, Sue removes the top lid. Pushing the lid up with her head, one, then two, then... three copper-tinted eyes peek out at me, followed by a cautious meow. Moving quickly from behind my desk, I reach into the hatbox and pull it out.

"Hey, kitty. Hey, gal. Hey…!" Poor thing is able to spread her five black, furry tentacles out in fright and attach herself to the ceiling after I fling her up in terror.

"She tells me her name is Sekhmet," Sue chuckles. "As you can see, Maddy, she's been altered too: Poor, poor thing."

After a few seconds, Sekhmet plops down on my shoulders. I shudder as she wraps her tentacles around my neck, but soon feel at ease, even a touch tranquil, as Sekhmet rubs noses with me then licks my face.

—

So, what is the outcome of this story, you ask?

There are several. Woods creates the Office of Special Concerns, which he taps me to run. Sue is made into a full detective, given a shield and firearm, and becomes my partner. I later remind Woods of the alleged Chinatown reward he pocketed. From bogus mediums to ghosts of Confederate spies trying to burn down New York to alligators in the sewers, when City Hall or 240 Centre Street scratch their heads over a case, they call us, the occult detectives, to handle the affair. At the same time, Sue and I try to live with this Gordian knot of a new life from the stars beyond.

THE
SMITH
AFFAIR

1920

It was autumn in Brooklyn. Just before sunrise, NYPD Officer Harold Burnhart grumbled to himself for having opted not to carry his rain slicker. He twirled his nightstick lazily while strolling down Prospect Place in a fleeting drizzle. He was two blocks and less than an hour away from the 60th precinct's shift change, which, to the wiry-burned, umber-haired Burnhart, couldn't arrive soon enough. The beat cop was anxious to switch out of his uniform, referred to by uniformed cops as "the blue monkey suit," and then head home to Hendrix Street and a plate of his wife's waffles and bananas.

Unfortunately for Officer Burnhart, his plans were to be interrupted. The diminutive yet plump woman stood barefoot among wet autumn leaves covering the sidewalk, staring. Her eyes were focused on a nondescript two-story house. Her hands clung tightly to the lapels of a gray overcoat atop a nightshirt to protect herself from the morning's chilly wetness. A mass of black hair, unruly from sleep, tangled down. She stood, continuing to stare at the house and oblivious to the Burnhart's approach.

"A good goody morning minus the rain to you, Miss. As it's my job to keep the neighborhood safe, I… hello? I say, hello?" Burnhart stood close to the woman and waved his free hand in her face. The gesture freed her from a seeming trance.

"Oh… sod it all, Constable, I'm so sorry," the woman pleaded.

"*Officer*, ma'am. Officer Burnhart. Mind telling me why you're eyeballing this place?" Burnhart pointed at the building with his nightstick and took a step back, for the Spanish flu was still in deadly vogue, and it occurred to him that she might have escaped from an area infirmary and could be a carrier. The officer countered this thought by considering that the woman could be experiencing another kind of sickness—the sort related to the recently enacted National Prohibition Act. "Let's start with some basics. Your name?" Edward Meeker's popular song, "Every Day Will be Sunday When the Town Goes Dry," entered Burnhart's mind.

"Smith. I'm an artist. I'm renting this flat as an art studio, and right now, someone or something has invaded it."

"A prowler? Why didn't you go down a few blocks on New York Avenue to the 60th precinct?"

"I'm afraid! Too spooked to go anywhere," Smith said.

"Okay, here is what we are going to do. I'm going to check things out in there. I want you to stand on the top step with this." Burnhart retrieved a handkerchief then laid it on the step. "So your feet don't get waterlogged." Pulling out his flashlight, Burnhart entered the house. "She's probably intoxicated from Scheurebe wine or whatever, I bet."

As he entered the vestibule, a sense of apprehension began to grip the officer. Not the usual feelings that sometimes went with the job but an eeriness that was smoldering in the predawn darkness of the house. To the right, his flashlight shone through an open door, revealing canvases and art supplies. As he passed a hallway connecting to the backyard, Burnhart's apprehensions morphed into fear. A fear he previously experienced twice before. Once, as an apple-cheeked rookie during a gambling-raid-turned-lethal-shootout on Strauss Street in 1913. The other was a member of Brooklyn's old "Red-Legged Devils," the 14th regiment attached to the US Army's Big Red One during World War I. And while his bravery rose on those occasions, presently, it found lacking. Burnhart backed out of the house, struggling with a visceral notion to run from something unseen, something unheard. The only certainty was that he couldn't remain in the dwelling for another moment.

"Well, Const… Officer?"

"No one's in the house," fibbed a grim-faced Burnhart, lifting his cap to enable his perspiring head and face to catch some chilly air. "I don't know what it is… I… Listen carefully to me. Do not stay in that house tonight."

"I thought I understood you to say it was empty."

"Once the sun is up and holy, I'll stay an hour after my shift ends and will come back with you. To gather some clothes. City Hall frowns on it these days, but you can grab some rest on one of the precinct benches. I don't think Captain Nickerson will mind. Maybe even a cup of coffee, too. After that, go across Eastern Parkway. Across from us is a church—Our Sisters of Loreto. Ask for Father Musetti. Tell him Harry the cop sent you. I think he's better suited to help you because, frankly, I can't." *Azazel is in the house,* he thought to himself, remembering the term neighborhood folks of Hebrew origin used. "If you can't stand to walk barefoot, we have a few pairs of discarded shoes at the precinct. I'll find a pair in your size."

"Thank you, Officer. I'm not… I don't fully understand what's happening, but I'm in deep appreciation for your help and will take you up on most of your offers, though I would prefer tea to coffee if possible. As far as help from the church, I think I know of two individuals better suited for my situation.

—

With the venetian blinds and curtains shut tight, I was enjoying the darkness of my combination office/living room when the phone rang. Technically, the office was closed today, but in the occult detective business, you had to be available at all times. Producing a magenta glow in the palm of my left hand—a gift and sometimes curse from a nameless horror from the stars—I retrieved and proceeded to light an Old Gold from my cigarette box and answered the phone.

"Hello? Mr. Cavendish? Oh, this is such a frightfully bad connection!" complained a female voice at the other end.

"Whoever you are, I can hear you okay. Who am I speaking to?"

"Pamela. Pamela Colman Smith." After a brief click, the static dissipated. "I can hear you now. We have a mutual friend in Zoe Churel."

This much was true. Zoe was a conjurer acquaintance of ours. "What can I do for you, Miss Smith?"

"I'm… I'm having a problem that needs to be solved at a flat I recently rented and converted into an art studio in Ocean Hill, Brooklyn." Pamela's accent seemed to waver back and forth between Yank and Brit. "I'm an illustrator by profession."

"I believe I've seen your work recently on a tarot deck."

"It's possible. I've done a few."

"What's the specific problem you're experiencing?" I asked.

"I'd rather not go into details over the phone. Can we meet in the city? It's around one now. How does 4 p.m. sound?"

"Location?"

"The 23rd Street side of Madison Square Park."

"How will I recognize you, Miss Smith?"

"I'm wearing a gray overcoat covering a red dress and a red turban. I'll have on colorful beads, including a rosary. But not to worry. I'll know you. I've seen you and your partner before."

"Is that a fact?"

"Zoe pointed you two out one night at one of her Harlem functions a few years ago, but you and your partner left before I could make my way across the room to introduce myself."

I couldn't recall the night in question, but more than likely, it was one of our soirees connected to our Migonette Society.

"Four this afternoon it is, Miss Smith," I confirmed. "See you then. Goodbye."

I rose from behind my desk, pulled back my window curtains, and raised the blinds to confirm the rawness of the day, but I thought it best to take my green-tinted glasses with me in case the pallor of the afternoon sun became too intense. A phone call to Sue upstairs let her know to prepare for a meeting about a potential affair.

—

A brisk western wind accompanied the briskness of New Yorkers on their way home from a day's work. After parking the avocado-hued 1919 Briscoe along the park, I brought a hot bag of roasted peanuts for us to enjoy while stationed on a bench waiting for Miss Smith's arrival. Sue's a keeper in her cinnamon-red dress, squash blossom, and turquoise necklaces with matching wool coat, heels, and black crusher hat. I was outfitted in a dark suit with my Homburg hat. I skipped the overcoat to enjoy the cool autumn air.

"Hello, Pamela?" Sue inquired, seeing Miss Smith before I did.

"Miss Sue and Mr. Cavendish, hello."

I looked up from my bag of peanuts into the brown mousy eyes of Pamela Smith. Dark hair peeking from under her red satin turban, she was impressive in looks. A thought began to blossom in my mind that Pamela was most likely "passing" like me, although I'm an open secret to our friends up in Harlem. I let the thought die on the vine. I'm not here to judge. Sue, in contrast, let her beautiful statuesque mixed heritage be known.

"A pleasure, Miss Smith." I smiled.

"I feel I've picked too blustery a place for our meeting," Pamela admitted. The Flatiron Building discombobulated the breeze on 23rd Street.

"It's alright. Let's find a more sedate area where we can talk," I said, handing her the bag of nuts as a goodwill gesture and waving off her objections. Crossing 23rd Street in a western direction, the three of us agreed on a cozy working man's diner near Seventh Avenue that served only cackle fruit and bacon around the clock. Once inside, Pamela, who asked that we call her "Pixie," ordered tea and a poached egg while I had sunny-side-up eggs and black java. Sue ordered a plate of bacon, the strips of various degrees from rawness to burned, much to the short-order cook's perplexity. The diner lighting exposed the haggardness on Pixie's face as she relayed her problem to us: a haunting.

"I returned to the States and to my beloved Brooklyn," Pixie explained, "in particular Ocean Hill-Brownsville, in hopes of pepping up my artistic juices. Providence saw me obtaining an apartment just off Eastern Parkway at Prospect Place. I had the okay from the landlord to maintain a studio, provided I kept the place proper and removed any resulting paint stains. It helped my arrangement to reveal that I'm related to Cyrus P. Smith, pre-consolidation Mayor of Brooklyn—though no longer with us—my father's father.

"The summer was uneventful. But as the leaves changed, so did my situation. One morning I awoke to find my bedroom bookcase empty, all of my books scattered about the floor. Downstairs in my makeshift studio, all of my artwork and supplies had been moved to the center of the room and piled high like a Christmas tree, almost touching the ceiling. I felt as if some phantom had crept in during the night while I slept."

"Could it have been a prank by neighborhood rascals, sister?" I challenged.

"No, and before you ask why, the next morning after putting everything back in its place, I found all of my paint brushes had been formed into the shape of a hexagram in my backyard with a... a... mutilated cat in the center. Poor moggy. This wasn't the work of children but of sick-minded adults and dark forces."

"Aren't you a member of the Golden Dawn Society?" my Sue asked.

"I left that rabble years ago. I belong to the Catholic faith now. But I have not gained their trust because the church and I are not in accord when it comes to women's rights. Which is why when a kindly police officer assisted me and suggested I seek out the church for aid, I declined. I'm truly gutted. Please," Pixie pleaded, "I need your help."

"I suggest that due to your state of exhaustion and for your safety that it would be best if you spent the night at Sue's apartment."

"Of course, yes. Thank you, Sue."

"We can discuss a fee at a later date," I added.

We finished our meal and headed uptown to 107th Street off of Riverside Drive. Sue located a sleeping gown for Pixie, who quickly fell into a slumber on the settee and North African harem pillows in Sue's living room. All in all, my doll and Pixie were two bohemian peas in a pod.

The following morning, Sue pulled me away from Pixie's hearing to speak privately.

"Something wrong?" I asked my Sue.

"Not sure. I woke during the night and saw Pixie. She was awake and searching through the living room bookcase."

"Maybe she awoke and needed to read a bit to fall back to sleep."

"Maybe. She's certainly eccentric. Perhaps it's simply that."

We left that issue closed, but I filed it away in my noggin anyway.

—

"I think we should begin with a simple séance," said Sue. It was evening in Ocean Hill. As the night advanced, a number of automobiles, trolleys, and horse-drawn carriages made their way outside Pixie's flat along Eastern Parkway. Inside, we sat around a common circular wooden table. Around us, like a silent audience, leaned paused oil paintings of faeries, Caribbean islanders in agrarian poses in different unfinished phases, and a vacant-eyed self-portrait of Pixie in a sunflower-colored regal robe—a reflection of Pixie's troubles. Oil paint, hash oleoresin, turpentine, and frankincense were the consequent scents in Pixie's studio.

"I feel odd now, not being the conductor of this ghost symphony," joked Pixie, herself a medium. "But I will follow your judgment."

"If this doesn't succeed, we have other methods, including Carnacki's," I explained, although Carnacki's recommended use of garlic only made me nauseous and often launched me into a convulsive sneezing fit at times.

We settled down to a lone burning white candle at the center of the table, surrounded by darkness. We clasped hands and I couldn't help but notice how exquisite Sue looked in her black satin hobble dress, the sleeves in lace, black hair blunt bobbed. Sue's rose-tinted glasses held at bay any unintended pale light from the full moon filtering into the house. For what seemed like an eternity, Sue used a variety of incantations to summon Pixie's gauche, intruding spirit. Pixie, adorned in a purple caftan and scarf, issued frequent impatient sighs until she suddenly slumped forward and into a channeling state before snapping back her head.

"Beware de ocher mon! Beware de ocher man! Beware!" Pixie yelled out in a deep male Caribbean Patwah voice.

"Who are you?" I cried out to the bass-voiced mantra as it faded away. Sue tried to coax the spirit back, but her efforts proved fruitless. "Pull her out," I tell Sue.

"Oh… goodness. What happened?" sighed Pixie, back with us once again and massaging her temples.

"You briefly channeled what we assume to be a spirit with a Patwah dialect warning us about the ocher man. Does that name mean anything to you?" asked Sue.

"I'm afraid, Sue, I've never heard of any 'ocher man,' bloody no!" Pixie said, her tone defensive. "Sorry, it's just tommyrot to me."

"Well, sister," I said, "unless you're channeling your anxiety through a poltergeist, what's the answer?" A poltergeist was my first theory, but like the voice, that theory was fading away. My second theory was that Grandpa Smith had returned to his old "Breuckelen" to visit his granddaughter and, disapproving of her avant-garde lifestyle, chose to hector her from beyond the grave. Sue, using a magenta glow from her right-hand palm, with a stage magician's misdirection skill so as not to place a hint of suspicion in Pixie's mind (we'd hidden a disgruntled Sekhmet when Pixie stayed overnight with us) about our true forms, relit the candle, recasting shadows on Pixie's artwork. At that moment, by 33rd and Third Avenue, a plan hit me. A far reach, like dead center at the polo grounds, but then, as an occult detective, you had to reach beyond the normal.

"I just don't know. What I *do* know is I've had a hat full tonight. I want to retire now, if you don't mind. If you'd like, I could make up the room adjacent to mine for the two of you to rest." Pixie was up and drifting to the staircase, ascending before we could answer and disregarding her own offer.

"We'll be fine down here," I said to her indifference as she closed her bedroom door. "Sue, rest on the couch. I'll rest here," I whispered, moving a stuffed indigo chair out of the artwork room to face the staircase.

"For the love of Signora Laurentini's skeleton, Madison Prescott Cavendish, what are you doing?"

"Waiting, love. Waiting," I said with a wink.

Without a word, Sue blew out the candle.

—

Sensual blood thoughts wormed into my mind as we sat in the darkness. Thoughts of Pixie's exposed neck, nice and plump during the séance, aroused this living vampire. I looked at Sue across the room and saw her toss and turn on the indigo sofa. Evil was making its presence known in this house tonight. My fangs started to extend in my mouth. I blocked the blood thirst from my mind with self-control just as I heard the thud of books on the floor of Pixie's bedroom above. Exactly what I was waiting for.

"Come on," I said to Sue, pulling her by the hands up and off the couch. "Come along, Sue. Apple and pears!"

"Madison. Oh my, Maddy! Your fangs have emerged! Don't let Pixie see them, she... apples and *what*?" said Sue while smoothing out her dress.

"Love, that's Brit for 'up the stairs.'"

"And 'Whatsamatteraferu?' is New York for 'keep the expressions local, dear.' Madison! Your eyes!"

"I know. My blues have exited stage left! Now will you come on?" Sue hated it when my eyes transformed from blue to scarlet red. In stealth, we crept up the staircase to Pixie's bedroom.

"Pixie, it's Madison and Seneca Sue. Please open the door." Behind the door we heard Pixie's frenzied reading as if she must read or die. I backed away from the door a few steps and then launched forward, smacking it open on the first attempt. Sitting crossed-legged on her bed in a cold sweat trance, Pixie was deep into Chambers's *The King in Yellow*, something I wasn't expecting. The damned book finds a sucker every minute with its diabolical verses. It's a causeway for Hastur himself to enter this reality.

"Give... the book... to me!" I demand, to which Pixie replied by socking me in my right eye as if she'd become possessed by boxing champ Benny Leonard. I stumbled back with a newly minted shiner.

"Hold on, Maddy, I'll get her by the..." Before she could complete the declaration, a jaundice slime-covered tentacle grabbed Sue by her ankles, and its pull bounced her back down the staircase. She disappeared into a billowing xanthic mist that caked and cracked the walls. The sound of her rose-tinted glasses breaking wasn't good for any of us involved in this affair.

I tried hard not to make Pixie one of the living dead by biting her to get the tome. A hard yank released *The King in Yellow* from her grasp. Pixie dropped to the bedroom floor in a dead heap, fast asleep. My victory, however, was short-lived, as two tentacles grabbed Pixie and me each by our ankles, dragging us to an unknown fate.

As we were pulled along down a side hallway to the backyard ahead of us, loud growls, snarls, teeth snapping reverberated. It was clear that Sue had made her Lycan transformation into a werewolf berserker and that her beautiful séance attire was now a slime-tattered filigree in shards of fabric strewn along the side hallways, walls, and floor. For every tentacle she bit or clawed off, another appeared, slithering out from under the tattered yellow robe of Hastur himself, who was stationed like a silent humanoid chess piece in the backyard. I attempted to sink my fangs into the tentacles, but the texture was too slimy. Tentacles were vining down on us from the ceiling, and damn it, Pixie was still sound asleep!

I devised one last idea. Still clutching the book, I opened it and emitted a magenta glow, which I pressed onto the pages with my left hand. The book burst into ice-cold flames, according to my hand's touch. Hastur screamed an unearthly scream. The tentacles retreated, and like a bad taste in one's mouth, we were spat out of Hastur's yellow realm, sliding along the floor, back near the staircase.

"Great heavens, oh my…" yawned Pixie, sitting up between a naked Sue and me, both covered in Hastur's mucus, having transformed back to our non-horrifying states. At that same moment there came a rapping on the door; I knew the sound, having heard it often before: a police officer's nightstick.

—

It was Burnhart, the officer who'd helped Pixie earlier on. He did not seem amazed at the site of what had transpired and only asked that we keep the noise level down and Sue get dressed. Declining an explanation from me that would have been Coney Island batter-dipped in lies, Burnhart was blissfully content to remain blissfully content. Hastur was stopped for now in this part of Brooklyn. Sadly, another evil, this time mortal, would be germinated ten years later in old Rosie Gold's candy store at Saratoga and Livonia Avenues. It would be known as Murder Inc., a national crime syndicate composed of Jewish, Irish, and Italian-American gangsters.

With Pixie's help, Sue and I figured out the rest. During the course of Pixie's move to Brooklyn from England, a person or persons unknown placed a copy of *The King in Yellow* within her book collection. It was packed and shipped, among other items, to the States. Procrastination during the summer delayed the debacle due to Pixie's intent to work on her artwork. In hindsight, and no longer in danger, Pixie recalled having finally unpacked. She discovered the item and soon regarded it among her prized books. Flipping through the insane gospel to see what the legendary uproar was about, she abandoned it after becoming unnerved. Yet it seeped into her unconsciousness, reading it in a Hastur-induced trance at night, slowly bridging together the two worlds. Sue, lacking a copy of *The King in Yellow*, explained Pixie's fruitless search the night before. Even our spirit world, sensing the gravity of the situation, quickly sent Sorrel Neville, a purported hoodoo spirit from the Caribbean, to warn her. It was his voice channeling a warning through her during the séance. Alas, the event made.

Pixie's change initiated plans and a return to England. However, the cost of traveling back, combined with the homeowner's demand to be compensated for damages, left Pixie in a financial mudhole.

At that point, Sue and I decided that in lieu of our fee, we would pose for a portrait by Pixie, who fully agreed with the suggestion. Pixie painted an invitation for me and Sue in a variation of the "The Lovers" card found in standard tarot decks. A few weeks later, the painting portrayed a splendidly blasphemous union of vampire and werewolf, which, upon its receipt sometime later, was hung in the study of our duplex apartment just off the Hudson River, where it remained for many years to come.

THE

HURSTON

AFFAIR

1922

Just before dawn on a humid morning, the off-key humming of "Mama Don't Want No Peas and Rice" could be heard along with the clanging of trash cans in the backyard of a row of houses—that were more like shacks—on Fifth Avenue and 140th Street. Mansford Stapleton, recently immigrated from the Caribbean to the black diaspora named Harlem, was going about his morning routine as rowhouse superintendent.

"Why can't they place the rubbish in the proper trash can?" said Stapleton.

He was a broad-shouldered, bald-headed, earth-toned man. Beads of sweat dotted his ban-collared, off-white shirt, its sleeves rolled up to the elbows. He adjusted his dark trousers, which were held up by frayed striped suspenders and well-worn work boots. In the diminishing darkness, a pair of red, gleaming eyes stared at him through a gap in a white-washed wooden fence that separated the tenement properties. The half-human creature, muscles tense, moved silently, anxious to attack before the sky lightened completely.

"What that? Who that lurking about de fence, I say!" Stapleton, who was a grumpy man on a regular day to the row house tenants, grabbed a rake as a weapon and moved to the fence. "Play games, eh?! Watch me rake you damn face, mon!"

Stapleton gazed straight ahead. He should have been looking up. The creature, having leaped over the fence, came down upon him with inhuman speed. A razor-sharp claw tore into Stapleton's left cheek, tearing through flesh and exposing bloodied, fleshy cheekbones. Shocked at the sight of his own blood splattered upon the white-washed wooden fence planks, Stapleton cried out in a howl of pain before he shuffled backward and tumbled to the ground, hands trembling, too afraid to touch his maimed face. The urban predator landed in front of him, a man-sized creature with burnt orange to beige fur speckled with black spots. Except for its upright human movement, it would be zoologically classified as part of the hyena family. It made a bloody mess and meal of Mansford Stapleton before bounding off through backyards in advance of the morning's arrival.

—

"Madison Cavendish. What's the deal?" I said, answering the phone.

I had my feet up on the oak desk and was enjoying a laconic breeze combination from an electric fan and air from the Hudson River. Beige summer suit, a pair of white buck shoes, and tieless, with my straw boater hanging on a hat rack in the corner, I waited for the person on the other end to reply.

"Hello, Madison. It's Dr. Allende. I need your assistance."

Washington Allende was the current head of the Office of Special Concerns. "It's a situation we have that's gaining rumor traction, and we need to put the public at some type of ease. It involves murder!"

"Go on, Allende." I adjusted my green tints. A feeling of intrigue began to wash over me. I wore green by day, Sue wore rose tints by night if the moon was full.

"A hyena in Harlem!" Allende, a man of logic, had to force the words from his own mouth, being the arrogant, anti-imaginative man that he was.

"Doctor, I think you need to phone the Central Park or Bronx Zoo," I half-joked, but in this business, I knew better.

"There are reports of an upright, walking hyena bounding around up there," Allende said. "And now it seems to have committed murder."

Just then, Sekhmet, our familiar and part-time student of human speech, slithered up onto my desk and, with forepaws, pulled up to be coddled.

I could feel the doctor's smug smile on the other end of the connection, for the doctor knew he had me interested. "Okay, Allende, where do we meet for this affair?" I asked.

Allende provided the details, and we ended the call. I pulled a page from a yellow legal pad and was in the process of writing a note to Sue with directions to the crime scene when I was interrupted by the unlocking of my apartment door. No doubt it was Sue back from brunch. Hushing Sekhmet, I hustled her into one of my desk's lower drawers. Then, with a finger-to-lips gesture, I closed the drawer, for Sue had a guest in tow.

"Noon to you, love. We're back from brunch," said Sue, entering and followed by Zora, one of her new acquaintances. Both attractive women, they could not have been more of a contrast to each other. My Sue, statuesque, sand complexioned or "passing" as folks around Harlem called her. Her psychic sensibilities are in conflict with the Lycan gift (or curse, depending on the situation) she inherited back in 1914. Zora, a mocha-complexioned doll with high cheekbones, her hair in dark waves, dealt in the here and now, not the afterlife I sensed from our brief, prior conversations. Spiritual dogma had no part in Zora's life, although she did have a love for Southern folklore, which is how the two of them met during a lecture one day at Columbia University.

Both Sue and Zora were dressed, respectively, in pastel aqua and yellow summer dress outfits. They offered appreciative smiles as I turned the electric desk fan in their direction.

"Hello, Zora. I take it you and my Sue had a fantastic brunch. I never could understand why folks like to eat in between breakfast and lunch," I joked while crumpling up the unfinished note and pitching it into a metal wastebasket stationed next to my desk. "Uh…Sue, we got a call from Dr. Allende. Wants us to meet him uptown, Fifth Avenue and 140th Street. We've got an affair, my darling." I hesitated because I should have known better, then added, "It involves murder."

"Yowza! Well, then the three of us could head up there and investigate," said Sue, joyfully anxious to show Zora Hurston a sample of our line of work (minus any issue paranormal in nature that might disclose our true selves).

"So, y'all are really into this private eye jazz. Interesting." Zora's Floridian accent seeped into her syntax.

"Uh… Zora, my dear, this line of work, I think, may be a little harsh for you. This is murder we are talking about," I said, at the same time issuing Sue a sideways glance.

"What happened?" the soon-to-be author asked.

"A man was attacked by some unknown animal, maybe sicked on him by its owner." I walked around from behind my desk, tapping my foot on the drawer as Sekhmet, with her three copper eyes, peeked out.

"Mahey!" lisped Sekhmet.

"Huh?" questioned both ladies, although I took Sue's *huh* to be a signal for Sekhmet to keep quiet based on the look on her face.

"What I mean is, I don't think you'll like our work, Zora. It's really mundane stuff."

But Hurston, who was a student of anthropology at Columbia, wanted to tag along. "Please, Mr. Cavendish. I love a good murder mystery. What do you say?"

"Come on, Maddy, my Maddy, just this once." Sue nudged me with her elbow, then planted a wet kiss bribe on my living vampire cheek, like that was going to change things. Okay, so it did change things.

"Okay then. Let's get going. But pray hear me out, Zora. You may not like what you're about to see," I said, while grabbing my straw boater and securing my tints. While sunlight didn't cause me to burn up like earthbound living vampires, it nonetheless sapped my energy to a normal human degree without eye protection.

"Youu phooey damn twoo!" Sekhmet lisped, seething, hopping out of the desk drawer as I locked the door.

Once outside, Zora, Sue, and I walked to my 1919 avocado-green Briscoe. Had she known she was accompanying a man who was prone to a vampire blood thirst at times and a woman she-wolf with a taste for human and warm animal flesh, Zora might have reconsidered her choice of friends.

—

"Doctor Allende!" I shouted as we arrived at a backyard grisly crime scene. The stench of chewed-up fleshly death mixed with overturned trash cans gripped one's nose. A swarm of black flies enveloped the body.

"Over here, please, you two," said Dr. Allende. The doctor was trying his best to examine the crime scene without kneeling and dirtying his off-white summer suit. A Panama hat and white buck shoes completed the outfit. A vivid red band wrapped around the hat blended in with the blood splattered on the fence and surrounding the backyard. Thick-faced, which, if you asked us, went along with his skeptical thick headiness when it came to matters of the paranormal, the doctor was a big-framed man totally devoid of gregariousness or positive disposition. Black mustached with his slick hair combed back, the doctor was Iberian in family roots.

"What do you two make of this? Hello? Who's this you've brought along?" Dr. Allende was full of questions as he continued to point to what I discovered later via the preliminary report to be Mansford Stapleton's ripped-up remains, a few feet from the fence. A few colleagues from the OSC were going over the crime scene while a number of tenants whose windows faced the backyard peeked from behind drawn curtains. Typically, the windows would be open and curtains pulled back to try luring a summer breeze regardless of how rancid the aroma of trash might taint it.

"This is Miss Zora Hurston. She's a student of anthropology. We feel her academic insight will help us on this affair," Sue said, vouching for Zora at Dr. Allende's skeptical glare.

"Wouldn't a zoologist be better suited?" challenged the doctor, ignoring Zora, who was now transfixed on Stapleton's remains and, for reasons unknown, massaging her right arm.

"Dr. Allende, are you familiar with the legends of hyena man or woman?" asked Sue. The blood of a werewolf in her veins made her knowledgeable about the scent of other half-human, half-animal monstrosities like herself.

"This sight is mighty horrific," said Zora, who, like some people and certain law enforcement officers, found it difficult to remain composed when it came to witnessing their first murder crime scene. Allende finally gave the okay, and a member of the OSC covered Stapleton with a white sheet. Blood quickly soaked through to form an abstract design on the cotton material.

"Listen, based on the descriptions I received from the tenants, I'll have to hold back on this hyena stuff. Personally, I think it was a dog, thank you very much," said the doctor. While he and I debated the matter, Sue went over to check out something wedged in a knot hole in the fence. Meanwhile, Zora began to sway.

"Maybe you should wait in the car, Zora." I offered, holding on to her elbow and interrupting the doctor's bloviating.

"I'm just peachy…" said Zora, but a breath later, her sarcasm lost out to nausea. "Oh, yeah. I think I'll take your advice, Madison." I helped Zora back to the Briscoe.

"So, what do you two intend to do about this?" Allende asked, shaking his head at my return. "City hall wants this mayhem settled quickly."

Sometimes I regret the decision Sue and I made to step down as heads of the OSC back in 1919 when dealing with Allende, who had taken our place after R. E. Enright was appointed police commissioner. Allende spent too much time trying to debunk and end cases or affairs too much on the fly.

"We will do what we have to do on our end, Doctor," I said.

"We'll get back to you." Sue smiled the type of smile an adult might offer an annoying child.

Sue and I walked to the car and found an unsteady Hurston seated on the passenger side with the door open. She tried to compose herself as Sue and I sidestepped Zora's Sunday brunch, which was now splattered on the sidewalk. Sue and I glanced at each other, and I hailed a taxi for our guest.

—

Early Sunday morning around midnight, approximately eight hours before Stapleton's demise, Lucas Penrose jerked up in bed in cold perspiration. "I've got to do something about this!" he vowed while fumbling for his glasses on a wooden stool serving as a makeshift nightstand in a communal Harlem art studio. "Am I possessed by a demon animal?" the thought tumbled over again and again in Penrose's mind. In sweat-damp pajamas, the up-and-coming artist rose from his bed and walked across the hardwood floor and into the bathroom. He switched on the light and opened the faucet to the water basin. Penrose pulled up his left pajama sleeve and looked at the scar that was the cause of his unhealthy thoughts, nightmares, and, perhaps, actions. Massaging his arm with cold water to ease the throbbing pain, Penrose debated the worth of the half-truth he told his lover and fellow artist, Edward Vesper, that he needed the solitude of the collective studio to create for a few weeks. In fact, Penrose needed solitude to solve this problem. The nightmares had started a few months ago, after a cultural trip he'd taken along with his fellow creative circle of writers, artists, poets, and musicians, each of whom now constituted part of the Harlem Renaissance to Africa. The junket to Tanganyika was to charge their creative spirits and to channel that creativity upon returning to the States. But the colonial racism they encountered in Tanganyika made them bitter, as they thought they'd find a respite from the racism seen on a daily basis back home. The group was comprised of Zora Neale Hurston, Anita Coleman, Octavius Walker, Langston Hughes, Nancy Prophet, William Grant Still, Aaron Douglas, and Penrose. During the last two weeks of the journey, a horrendous incident occurred. While taking a tour of the Town of Tunduru in the Lindi/Mtwara southern region of the country, a hyena attack or, as villagers whispered, a *bultungin* ("I change myself into a hyena" when translated from old Bornu Empire folklore) happened in the dead of night. To the layperson, hyenas are known to be equal parts hunter and scavenger, with a howl that's mistaken for a laugh, but on that full moon luminous night, it was no laughing matter.

The creature, unseen until the last moment, leaped onto the front porch of the European-style villa in which Penrose and his companions were residing. It belonged to a forward-thinking German businessman named Dieter. The hyena ripped at, scratched, clawed, and bit every member of the party, travel guide Hadzabe, and the businessman. In the midst of upended tables, shattered drink glasses, and screams of chaos, the businessman and guide managed to fire two rounds each from their revolvers into the upright-standing monstrosity before it loped off toward the Tanganyika savanna. Throughout the night, while waiting for sunrise, the victims bandaged themselves and barricaded the villa. Penrose and Dieter stood guard at windows with rifles while the guide, Hadzabe, had left to obtain a doctor. Later that Sunday morning, the naked body of a man unknown to villagers in those parts was found dead beneath a tree. He'd been shot four times.

The next few weeks were filled with anguish. Healing hindered the group's return to the States. Once a medical okay was given, the jazz-age Harlemites booked a steerage steamer to Europe, then passage on another steamer home to the United States. During the voyage, Penrose felt as if a change had come over him due to the bite wound on his arm. Now, at this hour, Penrose lay back down on his cot. Unable to sleep, the artist hoped to drift off, then wake up to a serene Harlem Sunday morning dawn.

—

"I don't see any validity whatsoever in this were-hyena jazz you're pushing," Zora said, pausing from sipping a glass of iced tea. Across from her, Sue and I shared a plate of fried dumplings. Two glasses, one containing iced tea for Sue and the other filled with iced lemonade for me, were both spiked with hyssop oil. Sweets adorned either side of the plate. We were dining in the light of red Kongming lanterns at Floyd and Jimmy's Fish Fry and Chop Suey Emporium on Lenox and 129th Street. Floyd, a South Carolina native, handled the fish fry part of the business, and Jimmy, from Chinatown, oversaw the chop suey side. The restaurant also doubles as a second contact place for Sue and me if we weren't available by phone at Riverside Drive. On such occasions, Jimmy's wife, Jenny, a part-time settlement house teacher, took down the affair information by phone, feeling eternally indebted to us for having saved her life, as recounted in "The Cavendish Affair."

"You saw for yourself, Zora. Whatever that thing is and what it's capable of," said Sue, spearing a dumpling with a single chopstick.

"I saw my daddy kill a pig for supper down South once. Got sick at the sight of it, too. But that didn't make it a paranormal event. Look, maybe your doctor is right, and maybe someone unleashed their dog on the poor man." Zora playfully plucked a dumpling from our plate with a fork. "Well, kids, I got some writing to do. Is there any way the two of you can drive me home?" Zora finished her iced tea.

"We can do that," I said, as I eyed Zora's preoccupation with her arm.

After we dropped her off, Zora hurried up to her CCNY off-campus apartment near Morningside Park. Once inside her apartment, not bothering to unbutton the yellow summer blouse sleeve, Zora doused and dampened her arm with cold water to cool off the hyena bite mark while trying to erase the events of the last few hours from her mind.

—

Monday Evening

"I hope that you, my friend, do not genuinely believe that you're a werewolf or some sort of jumping-around hyena-man because of these sensational rumors," said Octavius Walker, whose claim to fame was being the lone member of color in the Ash Can collective of New York artists. Light-complexioned, clean-shaven, but with a mane of unruly black hair, Walker, outfitted in a brown suit, sat in a simple wooden chair, tapping out a tempo with his cane. He watched as Penrose stared at a blank canvas. "Nightmares is all. You're having them, like the rest of us. Only nightmares. An unfortunate upshot from our Tanganyika experience."

"Please give Lucas the benefit of the doubt," said Vesper, sitting at the other end of the bed, wishing Walker would stop with the irritating cane tapping.

"How do you know this to be true, Octie?" asked Nancy Prophet, who stood on the opposite side of the bare canvas perched on a wood easel. She gazed down at the street scene four stories below. Nancy, brown-skinned with dark hair pomaded back and lanky of body, over which hung a striking royal-blue dress, was considered eccentric by her colleagues and was phenomenal in her medium, which was sculpture. The Tanganyika incident had left her with a scar that ran partly down her spine. "We live in a strange world. A world of large, gray, mysterious areas. Nothing is merely black and white, Octie."

"We are creative people, Nancy. But not prone to let our imaginations run too wild. Yes, we encountered some type of strange aberration in Africa. And while I admit I, too, have had unstable sleep, like Zora, I believe, in essence, it's a lot of manure," Octavius said, glancing over to Zora, who stood with her back to him in the kitchenette washing dishes. She hated the way Penrose kept the studio in such a messy state whenever it was his turn to utilize the place. Besides which, turning the water to cold helped soothe the discomfort in her arm.

"From what I saw on Sunday, I don't know what to believe," Zora confessed.

"What do you mean?" Penrose snapped out of his daze and

joined the debate. He and Vesper's eyes met with concern and worry.

"I was at the crime scene with Sue. Some of you have met her. She's the red-boned flapper who's been to the soirees at my apartment." The majority of the group nodded, recalling memories of Sue in a flapper outfit. Nancy, a bit of a loner, admitted that she'd not met Sue before.

"She occasionally does private detective work with her faux Negro of a boyfriend, Madison Cavendish, on hire to the NYPD. They're investigating the murder."

"Really?" This was a new turn of events for Penrose, which, for him, brought on new options to ponder. Nancy also wondered about this development. A summer breeze blew in from the open window, momentarily soothing the pain she felt from the scar on her back.

"I can't take it!" Penrose snapped. "I know I had something to do with Sunday's murder! I know it!" He stretched across the studio cot, head in hands. Vesper stepped out of the room and returned momentarily with a packet of BC Powder and a glass of water.

"Calm down, Lucas," Vesper pleaded, helping Penrose to a sitting position to take the BC.

"Facts, man! Facts, damn it!" Octavius yelled, his cane taping more incessantly.

"Facts? Okay then. Fact: When I woke up later in the morning, I was naked. Fact: The window in the room was open. These are two habits I do not subscribe to when I sleep," said Penrose. "There are your facts."

"I sleep in a natural state, but does that qualify me as this creature we are discussing?" Nancy interjected, her back now to her friends, making it difficult to gauge her emotions.

"Then how do you explain this?" Penrose asked. He walked over to a wooden Gold Medal milk crate covered by an oil paint-stained smock. Penrose pulled out a blood-stained strip of what once was a striped shirt, the sort of shirt someone like Mansford Stapleton would fancy. Penrose tossed it so that it folded across the blank canvas. Sickly-smelling dried blood flaked onto the canvas. His creative friends fell silent.

"I'm merely suggesting that we each view this objectively," Octavius quietly said, sounding like a defense attorney who's been subdued by overwhelming evidence against his client. His cane tapping slowed its tempo. "It could have been blown in through your window." All present groaned at his theory.

"Lucas, maybe you need a break. Perhaps you need to go away. I have friends who can get you to an artist retreat upstate in Woodstock, New York. It'll be conducive to your health," said Vesper. "I could take care of you. I still have funds from the Edna May Oliver portrait commission."

"I have a better idea," Zora said. "Since we each have keys to the studio to work on our craft, we could stay with you on a rotating basis while you complete the project."

"That may work. Next week, I'm to do commission work on a portrait for Miss Bella de Costa Greene, head of the Morgan Library collection, and she's paying me a nice fee to get a portrait done. Sorry to turn the offer down, Vesper, my belle, but Zora's idea may make me secure and focused. But you and Octavius will pitch in and help, won't you?" The notion of a support network made Penrose's anxiety lessen. "I'll see about an extra cot and a typewriter for you, Zora. Just one condition, Nancy. When you visit, you can sleep with the window open but not in a natural state so as to not have any carnal implications between us. " Penrose and the others laughed, but deep down, each knew the situation was taking a macabre turn if it hadn't already.

—

Tuesday Evening

The humidity had subsided and a breeze brushed around for Harlemites to get a comfortable night's sleep. Folks on the front stoop of a brownstone on 134th Street were catching some of the breeze while, in the back, Willie John Parker was finishing up assisting the building's superintendent, Emit Newson, around the building for extra money. Thin-framed, mocha-hued with curly hair in brown corduroy knicker pants, white T-shirt, and rubber-soled shoes, young Willie had two dreams: one of playing first base for the New York Yankees, but that dream was out of reach considering the current racial climate of the country and Major League Baseball; the second, teaching in the New York City public school system. Because of role models like educator William Lewis Bulkley, Willie thought he might one day achieve this goal.

The morning silence was shattered by mocking laughter in the distance.

"Hello?" Willie asked, suddenly aware of the red, gleaming eyes in a dark, small fence opening that neighborhood kids, cats, and rats used to move from one back way of a building to the other. Inching closer to the fence opening, Willie smelled a husky canine odor. A transformed half-human's furry paw swiped at Willie, narrowly missing his face. Fortunately for Willie, the creature was too large to slip through the fence opening. A terrified Willie knocked over trash cans while scrambling back on the ground. "Glory be!" he cried. "What the hell!"

Rising to his feet, the child retreated back enough to pick up a trash can and hurtle it at the fence opening. The creature responded with a queer laugh and a growl as Willie sprinted from the backyard along the building basement alleyway and out onto the street where, in his panic, he knocked down Emit Newson, who was enjoying an ice-cold Moxie soda and chatting with his wife, Olivia. The collision sent the bottle crashing onto the sidewalk, but Willie escaped alive.

I parked the Briscoe on 134th. Sue and I walked the block to the scene of a hyena-man sighting. We made our way through the crowd milling about and stepped down into a basement alleyway and then into the super's basement apartment. Following introductions, we tried to get some straight answers.

"It tried to grab you from the fence opening? What were you doing back there at this hour anyway, boy?" Dr. Allende, who stood alongside OSC Sergeant G. F. Peterson, asked.

Willie's dad, who stood next to his son, tried to contain his anger at the way Allende was conducting the interview. Emit Newson, a rail-thin, dark-skinned, former Harlem Hell Fighter veteran of the Great War, stood outside the room along with his wife, waiting for the questioning to end.

"I was helping Mr. Newson straighten up the backyard, sir. It's best to do it at night when it's cooler," explained Willie.

"Is that so?" Allende said with an air of skepticism.

"The boy is telling the truth. He never was one to lie," interrupted Newson.

"Easy, Doctor," I said.

"Matter of fact," Allende said, turning to Newsom, "where were you? How do I know you weren't back there playing a hitchy-koo prank on the boy? Talk to me, shine. I'm getting mighty tired of running uptown every time you people—"

Before he could say anything else, Newson was toe to toe with the doctor, Newson's forehead bending the brim of Allende's Panama hat. I placed a restraining hand on Newson's arm as Sue rested a comforting hand on Willie's shoulder.

Emit Newsom was livid. "One: I am not your shine! Two: If Willie said he saw what he saw, then he did. He's a good kid! Three: Sir, I'm a veteran of two wars—the Great War and the Red Summer of 1919—and I will be god damned if I'm going to let someone like you enter *my home* and act like some lord of the manor! You'll get a busted nose first!"

Peterson stepped in between the two men.

"Hey, Peterson, how's it going these days?" I asked, greeting the sergeant in a summer suit as I hustled the doctor out of the basement apartment.

"You know him, tight ass as usual," Peterson said in a low voice in reference to Dr. Allende.

"I've got a good mind to…" the doctor said, stammering.

"You've got a good mind to stay outside with Sue while I talk with Emmit and the young man!" I demanded.

With pen and notebook in hand, I took down Willie's information. The child was more than happy to relay it. Soon after, I closed the notebook and joined Allende and Sue at street level. Peterson followed shortly behind me.

"I was going to break him, you know!" barked Dr. Allende.

"The only thing on the verge of being broken was your nose by Mr. Newson," giggled Sue.

"Listen, City Hall picked you to head OSC not to debunk first but to gather information and then act on it in a discreet manner. Not to mention that Dr. Pythagoras, Sue, and I recommended you." My feelings for Dr. Allende were building past a foundation of dislike veering toward hate. "That's how I ran the office, Doc."

"But you don't run this office anymore, Cavendish. I do, and I'll run it my way. Don't ever interrupt me while I'm questioning a witness. You and your partner's strangeness doesn't faze me, and one day I'll find an explanation to you two. Presently this hysteria has to be contained to Harlem and not spread across the entire city. Understand?"

"Sue, Madison!" Zora called to us from the slowly dissipating crowd in a blue-green floral-patterned dress and dark shoes. Dr. Allende eyed Zora yet again with annoyance. He headed toward his police-issue Ford but did a sudden about-face and walked toward the up-and-coming author.

"How did you find us here?" Sue asked.

"Word travels mighty fast in Harlem, you know," said Zora. "Can I speak to you two back at my flat?"

"What's this all about?" interrupted Dr. Allende.

"As I said before," I began, "Miss Hurston is providing us with research. One more thing, Doctor. Your case or not, don't lean on the Parker kid—or *any* kid—like that again." I glared at him and saw his expression morph from righteousness to logic to fear. He hastily retreated to the Ford without further comment while Sue and I accompanied Zora to her apartment.

"You're saying you had something to do with this hyena running around Harlem?" Sue asked, searching Zora's face to determine if her friend might be withholding information.

"Hot damn, no!" Zora sat behind her writer's desk, an unfinished page in her typewriter among stacks of open books waiting for her to continue her research and studies. We had to find open space among still more books to sit on Zora's couch.

"Then why wait until now to tell us about the incident in Africa?" I wanted to light up an Old Gold but couldn't locate an ashtray.

"I had to prove to myself that I wasn't the cause of this madness. I can't wrap myself around a person being able to transform into such a creature," said Zora, to which Sue gave her a sideways glance that could have been read as *If she only knew*. Sue had by now gotten a scent from the fur chuck she'd shown me in her purse. The hyena-man (or woman) had been in Zora's living room.

"How did you prove to yourself that it's not you?" I asked to Zora's back. She was up and crossing to her little kitchen cove to fetch an ashtray, having tired of my head bending and twisting in search of one. She mentioned that the ashtray, an odd little pink ceramic heart, had been molded as a gift from Nancy Prophet.

"I know it isn't me. I mean, I'm here with the two of you, right? Right here in front of you two." Zora rubbed her arm.

"That really doesn't equate to an alibi, and it certainly wouldn't hold up in a court of law," I explained. Zora shot me a look of annoyance. "It's curious," I added, "how you found your way down to where the Parker kid was stalked."

Zora walked over and stood adjacent to me with arms folded. She kicked aside another stack of books onto the carpeted floor.

"Listen, Madison, it's like I said: Word travels fast in Harlem," she said, following up the comment with a dig at my biracial roots: "Maybe your other ofay cracker half don't know this!"

An uncomfortable silence filled the room for several long moments.

"Sorry, Madison. I shouldn't have said that. Please forgive me."

"It's okay, Zora. I get that jab at times," I said. Sue fumed but kept silent.

"I think I know who's responsible," Zora said. "Nothing supernatural, more psychotic in nature. My friend needs help." Sue and I heard the sound of a muffled phone ringing nearby. Following the phone cord to behind the couch, Zora picked up the black candlestick phone and answered. The conversation soon became intense, her tone back to how it had been a moment ago with me. "I'm on my way!" She clicked the earpiece back on the hook and turned to the both of us. I sprung up from the couch and snuffed out my Old Gold.

"The friend I was talking about is at the communal studio we share and is threatening to take his life. Hurry, please, we have to go!"

—

Penrose straddled the windowsill, his body half in and half out of the studio. He kept his fellow artists at bay with a pistol clutched tightly in his right hand. Outside, neighborhood residents glanced up and waved, unaware of the drama unfolding above them. Those aware of the studio assumed Penrose was being creatively eccentric, aware that creativity and eccentricity went hand and hand, a recent example of which had been Nancy Prophet's habit of walking through Harlem with a clucking hen under her cloak on cold days. Now, however, Nancy was terrified, phone still in hand from her recent call to Zora and trying to stall Penrose. Octavius stood rigid and also tried to talk to Penrose, while devising a plan to disarm him. Vesper, strangely enough, was nowhere to be found. After what seemed like an eternity, there was a pounding at the gray studio door. The upper half of the door's frosted glass revealed three individuals awaiting entrance.

"Answer the door! No, don't answer it!" yelled Penrose, trying to wipe perspiration from his face and support the window with his shoulder as it wouldn't stay up on its own. All this while keeping a gun leveled on his friends.

"Be a swell dear and let me answer the door. It's most likely Zora, dear. Let's be a sport," pleaded Nancy.

"Yes, good fellow. Let Nancy answer the door." Octavius took a step closer, tapping his cane.

"Penrose!" I yelled, as the door was finally opened. Penrose stood awkwardly in the studio window. No longer waving the gun, his eyes were locked on the moonlight.

It was the scent that gave him away.

Sue removed her rose-tinted glasses and locked eyes with Octavius, who issued a shrill hyena laugh and growled. Eyes bulging, saliva spitting, he began a grotesque, inhuman transformation as shirt, pants, and jacket were ripped apart at the seams. Quickly using the butt of my gun, I shattered the lightbulb nearest the door. Trying to summon as much self-control as possible, Sue backed out of the studio while Zora, oblivious to Sue's departure, surged forward. At the same time, Octavius bolted across the room and after Sue. In the hallway, Lycan transformation destroyed Sue's favorite maroon outfit and shoes.

Grappling huntress after deadly prey, she and Octavius tumbled down the stairs and outside onto the sidewalk. Penrose attempted to step back into the studio but fumbled back out the window. Had the window not slammed down and pinned his knees to the windowsill, the manic artist would have fallen to the street below. I took hold of his legs as Nancy and Zora lifted the window. Together, we wrested him back inside the room. Penrose sank to the floor, quivering. I disarmed him and stashed his firearm in my suit jacket pocket, noticing it was little more than a weathered starter pistol.

"Where's Sue!" Zora asked as she and Nancy helped Penrose onto the communal studio cot.

"She followed Octavius out to the street," I said, taking an educated guess. "You two stay with Penrose. I'll find Sue." As I'd hoped, it appeared that by busting the lightbulb, Sue's transformation had gone unseen by Zora and Nancy.

"I'm coming with you," demanded Zora.

"I trust Sue and Madison can handle this," Nancy said to Zora. "Stay here with Lucas and me. Please, Madison, if Octavius is behind this chaos, don't hurt him." Nancy cradled Penrose's head. I learned later that Nancy had, in fact, witnessed Sue's transformation in the semi-darkness and sought to spare Zora the carnage that she sensed was about to unfold. To her credit, Nancy guarded Sue's secret until her death.

"Nancy's right," I said. "Please stay with your friends, Zora. Phone Dr. Allende and explain what's happened. Tell him I said not to make any moves until he's heard from me." I flung Allende's business card in Zora's direction and was off. As I raced down the stairs to join the chase, I unintentionally bowled over a man I later learned was Penrose's lover, Vesper, who was returning from a nearby grocery store.

With Sue's ripped clothing and twisted shoes in tow, I jumped into the Briscoe and peeled off in the direction of nearby screams of Harlemites. Several hundred yards ahead and beneath the glow of streetlights, two rapidly moving shapes came into view, a pair of horrid souls dodging cars and pedestrians as they bounded up and down railroad flat stoops. Sue's silvery gray-coated, magenta-streaked growl and Octavius's taunting hyena laugh echoed in the breeze across 125th Street. I continued my pursuit as, at 110th Street, they entered Central Park North.

I parked the Briscoe and quickly fished from the trunk a bag containing a full-length blue wool coat, pink rose-printed slippers, and an extra pair of rose-tinted glasses. A backup wardrobe for Sue was essential during these occasions. I entered the park in the direction of the sound of the unearthly battle. "Geoffrey Daniels!" I cleanly cursed as I fell to one knee on blood-slicked grass that sloped up to a thick wooded area. "Should have smelled it before I saw it," I quipped, fighting the start of cravings.

"Sue? Sue, love?" I whispered. Lost among the summer foliage, the blood scent became more pronounced. The sound of wet flesh being chewed upon intermingled with growling, drawing me forward to a thick entanglement of bushes. Prone on the ground was Octavius Walker, rapidly transforming back to human form. Sue, crouched over Octavius on hands and knees, ripped at his neck to the point of separating the poor soul's head from the rest of his body. Soon, Sue's wolfcoat gave way to her nakedness. Jerking her head up, blood dripping down her chin, Sue lurched at me but pulled back to seek shelter by a patch of shrubbery when I issued a vampire hiss warning.

"This is going to take some time," I said, and found a tree to lean up against a few feet away. I lit up an Old Gold and waited with the fresh clothes bundle at my side.

"Maddy, I'm cold," Sue mumbled, spitting specks of Octavius's flesh from her mouth as she staggered from the bushes. I jumped to Sue and helped her dress.

"Got to get you cleaned up and then find a phone booth to call Allende. I think I saw a Rexell's Drug Store over on Fifth. They're open late. I'll get you an egg cream if you want." The offer, intended to soothe Sue, instead caused her to vomit some of Octavius's remains on my white bucks.

—

Saturday

"It was the luck of the draw for Octavius, Maddy," said Sue as she picked at a plate of fried pork and chow mien. We were dining at our usual table at Floyd and Jimmy's, discussing the recent incident, later to be filed as "The Hurston Affair."

"Luck of the draw?" I asked, distracted by a bowl of Mai fun noodles with strips of rare liver. I looked into Sue's rose-tinted glasses for her reply and noticed that the slight magenta scar under her left eye was still in the process of regenerating. She wore a cheongsam outfit, all black, as if in mourning for Octavius Walker.

"He was the only member of the group involved in that incident in Africa to have a blacksmith in his family tree. Once you receive the bite of a bultungin with that ancestry, you're doomed. Walker had a relative who was a slave apprentice to a blacksmith in Antebellum, Mississippi."

"No need going over it again, Sue love. You had to do what you had to do. No telling what additional havoc Octavius would have created if not checked. He killed Stapleton dead, he almost got the Parker kid. Between the bloody shirt strip and cane-tapping mesmerism, he was setting up Lucas Penrose and driving the entire group out of their minds." I looked past Sue to see a white-jacketed waiter usher Zora to our table. We fell silent and braced ourselves for a litany of questions.

"Sue, I was worried, having not seen you since poor Octavius's sad end. Madison said you had twisted your ankle when Octavius knocked you down. How'd you make it to the street?" Zora helped herself to tea and. Having no appetite, Sue pushed her plate to Zora.

"Curiously, it didn't hurt initially. But once we got in the car, it was all downhill, Zora honey. I fell apart. My ankle, some type of stomach flu. Just awful." My Sue adjusted her glasses. They made her feel secure telling lies in this world of mortals.

"Dr. Allende says Octavius owned wild dogs and was terrorizing Harlem until the dogs turned on him, killing him in Central Park!" Zora continued with the questions.

"That's what he told us too," I said, drawing chopsticks loaded with Mai fun to my mouth.

"It's bullshit!" Zora said. "Octavius never owned dogs." Sue seemed to be growing uncomfortable with the direction the conversation was taking. Her shoulders tensed.

"I'll give it to you straight, Zora," I said. "The truth is, I'm an occult detective who also happens to be a living vampire."

Sue relaxed and chimed in. "As long as we're being truthful, I'm an occult detective with werewolf tendencies."

After a nerve-pulling moment of silence, Zora responded to our confessions with a hearty chuckle. "Yeah. Okay, sure. Honestly, the dog story made more sense. As the saying goes, 'Ask no questions, and you won't get any lies.'"

Our combined laughter was followed by a quick change of subject and an order of Mongolian beef—rare, naturally.

THE
CONSUMER PARK
AFFAIR

1923

The distant wailing of a fire engine on a run enhanced the nervousness of BRT train conductor Louis Wertz as he, abreast with trackman Dan Boreli and police officer Glen Crabtree, walked (and sometimes stumbled) along the southbound tracks of the Brighton Beach line. Flashlights in hand, the men were on a special assignment at a chilly 1 a.m. with the line shut down. The trio had volunteered to get to the bottom of sightings of the alleged Malbone Street ghost train, which had intensified following its annual fall appearance, throwing Brooklynites along the line into a panic.

Operations manager Waldo Fenner had ordered Wertz, Boreli, and Crabtree to patrol the length of the line tracks north to south and back, then report their findings in the morning. Mr. Fenner did not believe in ghosts or the supernatural and was anxious to debunk what he called "nonsensical malarkey."

"I don't like this," moaned Wertz. "I shouldn't have volunteered." Wertz was a diminutive man. He wore his blue conductor's cap pulled down tightly on his head to avoid injury from future falls onto the track bed, having already suffered several.

"Look, you're one of the saps that reported this jazz. So now you're stuck with us!" Boreli barked. He spat a glob of tobacco juice that arched into the cold night air and landed a few feet in front of the men. Dressed in his work denims and a black fedora, Boreli feared nothing or no one except his wife, Anna. "Good thing you're on the side of the tracks near the platform, or you would have kissed the third rail and your ass goodbye a long time ago the way you waddle like a wigeon, Wertz!"

"Listen, you. I've had enough of your—" Wertz started to yip.

"Come on, you two, take it easy," said officer Glen Crabtree, dark-haired and sharp-looking in his NYPD uniform. "We're getting overtime for this. Let's make the best of it without making each other sore." Crabtree hoisted himself up on a three-rung metal ladder and helped the two men onto a grimy, soot-covered concrete outcrop that led them to the Consumer Park Station platform that made up the tunnel section of the line. "Listen, you guys," Crabtree continued, "Fenner has the line closed for the night. All we have to do is go plant ourselves on those benches over there and wait until sunrise. Nobody will know." Crabtree tried to sweeten the plan, literally, and create a truce by reaching inside the pocket of his policeman's great coat, pulling out three Abba Zabba candy bars, and handing one to each of the two men. Wertz took a bar, but Boreli spat more tobacco juice onto the ground, which Crabtree took as a hard pass.

The three men sat down.

"So Wertz," Crabtree said, "what was it again you saw? Hello? Wertz?"

Wertz's eyes widened, though not in response to Crabtree's question. They were locked on five pale, green orbs slowly zigzagging toward them along the track. The orbs twisted together before flowing out into a billowing beryl-green cloud.

"That's it! That's it! Mother help me! It's the ghost train! I told yous so!" shrieked Wertz, panic-stricken. He jumped up off the bench, only to spiral downward, still clinging to his unopened Abba Zabba bar. He hit the platform in a faint, skinning his forehead.

"Abbastanza! Enough of this silliness! Looks like Will-O-Wisp gas to me. Compost from the botanical garden up on street level. I'll bet my last piece of chaw that's what it is," said Boreli, ignoring Wertz and moving to the edge of the platform, then scrambling down to the track bed.

"Boreli! Come back here! Don't go down there, you horse's ass!"

Instinctively, Crabtree reached for his service revolver from under his greatcoat, unease flowing up inside him, the air seeming to get colder as three wooden EL cars, out of service since 1918, roared out of the mist. Police procedure had Crabtree fire three warning shots into the station ceiling, loosening concrete. He then fired directly at the phantom train as Boreli's scream echoed into the night, mixing with high- and low-octave moans from within the cars. The impact coated Crabtree, who stumbled to the platform floor, joining an unconscious Wertz enveloped in a crimson and pink mist of what had once been the BRT trackman. Eyes shut tight in fear, Crabtree thought of his wife, Maggie. Finally, the patrolman moved unsteadily to the edge of the platform to peek down. He vomited immediately upon seeing the bloody remains of Boreli as the orbs twisted apart, southbound. Leaping over Wertz, Crabtree bolted upstairs and out of the station.

He found no callbox in sight and resorted to locating a manhole cover to tap out a call for assistance using his nightstick along with toots from his whistle. Minutes later, Crabtree's brothers in blue arrived to assist their now hyperventilating colleague.

—

"As with every meeting, we're going to close it out with Miss Seneca Sue SunMountain singing our anthem, Scott Joplin's "Slow Drag/Marching Onward," announced Dr. Oberlin Pythagoras, sliding behind a piano to accompany my Sue as she strutted her way past white linen-covered dining tables in a carnation, pink-tiered evening gown with a matching silk turban and hand fan. Sue's my gal; my name's Madison Cavendish; we're in the occult detective grind, and this is our story.

The Mignonette Society was established by people of various occupations and colors who were students and masters of the occult and paranormal. We met monthly to discuss or debate research and/or investigations over oysters dashed in mignonette sauce. Magicians Black Herman and Elle Armstrong, voodoo priest Shango Jack, occultist Rollo Ahmed, hoodoo leader Scat Johnny, conjurers Zoe Churel and Mamon Dragonne, and alchemist Dr. Oberlin Pythagoras were among our dues-paying members. In white tie and tails for the men and ladies sparkling in gowns and pearls, we raised our glasses, singing along when a waitress approached me.

"Mr. Cavendish, there's a phone call for you at the coat check counter," she whispered. We were on the second floor of the Chrispus Attucks catering hall in Harlem.

Thanking the young lady, I slipped out to the lobby. "Cavendish here; it's your nickel, so don't waste it."

"Cavendish! Doctor Allende here. I've called your Riverside Drive apartment, Sue's apartment upstairs, that chop suey joint on 135th where you two hold court. They gave me this number. Don't you two ever stay put? Where the hell are you, Carnegie Hall? I hear singing in the background." Dr. Washington Allende, head of New York City's Office of Special Concerns, was a brisk, sour man.

"That, my moody doctor, is my Sue singing at our club meeting. Now what is it?"

"Listen Cavendish, Brooklyn Rapid Transit is having a problem with one of its lines out in Brooklyn. You remember the Malbone Street accident back in 1918?" asked Allende, awakening my interest.

"I do. It happened right before I got stateside from the Great War. As I recall, the train tried to take a curve too fast, heading into a tunnel with a barely trained clerk in the motorman's booth."

"It's been bad PR for them ever since. A new company is taking over the BRT, and they're doing away with some of the EL lines. The city has done its part by changing Malbone Street to Empire Boulevard. But the sighting hokum of a ghost train continues. The hysteria has claimed the life of a track worker and has sent a conductor named Wertz to the assorted nut ward in Bellevue. I have a backlog of cases here at OSC. Do you want it or not? You and Sue will receive your usual fee from us, the rest from the now BMT," said Allende, which translated into "This case had too much paranormal applesauce for OSC." Allende liked to cherry-pick cases, taking on the easy ones like fake mediums he could debunk quickly.

"Okay, Doc, we'll take it," I said, getting a silent irk from Allende, who hated to be called Doc. I removed a pad and pencil from inside my tuxedo jacket and took down the information, which had us contacting operations manager Waldo Fenner of the Brooklyn-Manhattan Transit Company, located on Front Street in downtown Brooklyn, tomorrow morning at ten.

"Madison Prescott Cavendish. What gives with you walking out on me while I'm singing ?!" Sue demanded as she playfully used one of her string of pearls to lasso me around the neck as I ended the call. A beige beauty with what I called happy freckles splashed across her face. She was a head-turner.

"Sorry, love, but we've got an affair. We head out to Brooklyn tomorrow, so let's get our coats," I said as our friends and fellow members filed out of the hall, shaking hands or pecking our faces with kisses to the cheek.

"What's the affair, Maddy?"

"Ghost train," I said as I helped Sue with her coat.

"You're joshing."

"Wish I was. We'll get the dope from a guy named Fenner tomorrow. In the meantime, love, slip your tints on. Can't have accidents before we start the affair."

Sue donned her rose-tinted glasses. We stepped out onto 125th Street. Overhead, a bright moon glowed down on Harlem, romantic in its fullness, but it had the paradoxical power to erupt the Lycan propensities in my Sue, hence the need for tinted glasses.

The next morning we took the Ninth Avenue EL downtown and caught the Fulton Street ferry from Manhattan across the East River to

Brooklyn's Fulton Street and were soon sitting in Fenner's thick-leathered Front Street office.

"Mr. Cavendish and Miss SunMountain, I presume the two of you will keep this assignment quiet. No talking to the newspapers. Dr. Allende assured me your discretion."

From his gray, three-piece suit to his head topped with silvery white hair over a narrow, ruddy, weather-beaten face, Waldo Fenner had the look of a man who had worked his way up through the transit ranks. He also wore the look of a man trying to control something that was beyond him in a normal, everyday scope.

"We tend to work in the shadows, Mr. Fenner. So you can count on us to keep quiet. When did these sightings start?" I asked.

Sue, sitting next to me, was in burgundy from cloche hat down to high heels, while I wore a dark suit, a Homburg hat, and, so as not to prevent any accidents, green-tinted glasses mellowing out the sun's rays.

"It started in November back in 1919 on the anniversary of the accident," Fenner recounted. "I was a BRT trackman back then. We managed to keep it all under wraps, let the public play with it as folklore. But now it's become a nightly event. The front two cars that didn't wreck up from that day are laid up in a railyard in Queens. We at the new BMT want to start fresh and get this old BRT crap behind us."

"What's the name of the trackman who died?" Sue asked.

"Daniel Boreli. We made up a story that he fell in front of a train. Hushed up his wife with a payout of money. There was a police officer there that morning—Glen Crabtree. Lives over in Brooklyn Heights." Fenner handed me a slip of paper containing Crabtree's Pineapple Street address. "He's taken a leave of absence from the force. I have a lot riding on you two solving this problem. The board of directors is holding my feet to the fire. I need this shit to end once and for all." Fenner reached into a desk drawer, pulled out a checkbook, and scribbled out a fat sum on a check.

After taking half of our fee, the remainder of which we'd receive after correcting the problem, we headed over to see Crabtree, who lived on the second floor of a boarding house with a view of the Brooklyn Bridge. His door was ajar, and the window shades were pulled down. The room's darkness made me, a living vampire, feel at home. We found Crabtree in a fitful fetal position on his bed, white shirt damp with sweat, dark pants rumpled, his service revolver, and a bottle of bootleg popskull (three-quarters empty) on an adjacent nightstand. It was a suicidal combination. Crabtree twisted upright when I tapped his pants leg.

"Who the hell are you two?!" he demanded, jerking his head

toward his firearm.

"My name's Cavendish, and my associate here is Miss SunMountain. We're from the municipal government on behalf of Brooklyn-Manhattan Transit. We're here to—"

"Go away; I'm resting. Go away." Crabtree sank back down on the bed.

I didn't have to tell Sue anything, as she grabbed an empty drinking glass off a round wooden table covered with newspapers, Abba Zabba bar wrappers, and household bric-a-brac. She headed to the communal bathroom to fill it with a cold wake-up call for Crabtree. After a splash and a scream, the officer was on the same page as us.

"What do you two want?" Crabtree asked, water dripping onto his bed from Sue's gentle ministrations.

"Listen, old man, we need for you to tell us about the other night so we can bring conditions back to normal on that line. How about cleaning up and joining us for a bite to eat?" I offered.

Sue rose to fetch another glass of cold water at which point Crabtree accepted our offer.

We soon were seated on benches near Brooklyn borough hall. As we munched on hotdogs, Crabtree divulged the real reason he'd volunteered that night.

"Just like that, she was taken from me. Her name was Maggie; she was my wife. That wasn't even her regular train, lord help me. She was late trying to get home. We lived in Kensington on Albemarle Road. All because of a stalemate of a transit strike, management placed an idiot in the motorman's booth that damn evening. I was in the Army, stationed at Fort Riley, Kansas, at the time, awaiting orders to be shipped to Europe. The orders never arrived because of the armistice. Maggie's love letters are what kept me sane from the boredom of camp life and the fear of going to Europe." Crabtree paused in reflection and continued his tale. "Once I received the news of Maggie's death, I had more of a time fighting US Army red tape, tied together with being sick with the Spanish flu, trying to get to her funeral than ever fighting, much less seeing a Hun." Crabtree stared off at Cadman church across the street as if he recognized someone or something staring back at him. "So what do you two intend to do?" asked Crabtree, shaking himself out of a daze.

"It's early afternoon. Sue and I will head back to Manhattan and come up with a plan of action, then come back to Brooklyn around 11 p.m. to put the plan in effect."

"Listen, Mack, I don't think there's a plan on Earth that will stop that train, or whatever it is, having seen what I've seen. That's why I'm quitting the force," said Crabtree, looking perplexed as to why Sue ate her two hotdogs without the buns and condiments while mine overflowed with "Liberty Cabbage."

"Look, Crabtree, I could be wrong, but I think you're not an apple-stealing cop," I said. "Too good to quit the force."

"How about helping us? Please, Crabtree, Maggie would want you to," said Sue.

Crabtree molded the end of a hotdog bun into a ball and flicked it to a gang of pigeons that were pecking around us but avoiding Sue, sensing the wolf inside her.

"Okay, I'm with you," said Crabtree, again distracted by someone or something in front of the church.

—

We decided to pick up Crabtree at the boarding house around 11 p.m. Back at Riverside Drive, Sue told me that while we were sitting on the borough hall benches, she'd felt a presence across the street from us. We spent the rest of the evening searching through our collection of books on the occult for a proper remedy for the subject at hand. We checked *The Necronomicon, Tobin's Spirit Guide,* an autographed *Black Herman Covers the World, Major Milford Fulbright's Use of Applications Concerning Spirits,* and others, but we finally settled on a recipe from *C.J.S. Thompson's Blue Book of Magic.* The same recipe that, back in 1914, exterminated a creature—patricide, you could say—from beyond the stars, in Lower Manhattan, even as it damned Sue and me in perpetuity to our present mutual conditions.

We downed cups of hyssop tea to control our cravings and were soon off to Brooklyn.

"It was right here. We were sitting on these benches killing time until sunrise, then we were to call Fenner with our report," said Crabtree, eyeing my leather bag while simultaneously wondering why my Sue was walking up and down the length of the platform as if measuring out something. Fenner had closed down the line again while our 1919 Briscoe was parked on street level along Parkside Avenue.

"Okay, old man, I'll need for you to put this around your neck," I said, handing him a small earth-toned leather gris-gris bag necklace filled with sage. "And in these bottles, in case you're wondering," I explained, pulling two dark green-corked wine bottles out of the larger bag, "contain sulfur, black myrrh, red sandal, apple vinegar—a little putrid, I must say—red wine, and arsenic. The second is a mixture of calamus, peony, mint, holy water, and a little gasoline for a kick."

After sizing up the gris-gris necklace and our bottled solutions,

Crabtree shouted, "What a load of raspberries!" His right hand tightened into a fist as if to take a jab at me (which, incidentally, would not have been wise, as I would have caught it midflight, breaking every bone in his hand). "You mean to tell me I came along with you two so you can pour dirty wine on that green devil subway train? Cavendish, you're looney! I've got to be mad to go along with this!"

"It's worked for us in the past, Crabtree. You're not a mad old man. Sue sensed Maggie in front of the church just as you did," I said quietly. The deadly seriousness that passed over and stayed on my face convinced the police officer I meant business.

"Do you think I can see Maggie one last time? Will it put those people, including Maggie, to rest? Please, I've got to know," Crabtree pleaded as he placed the talisman around his neck.

"I make no promises, Crabtree—" I began, but our conversation was interrupted by the rustling of newspaper.

Sue had spread out a copy of the *Herald Tribune* on the platform floor. She removed a midnight-black wool coat to reveal an equally dark hobble dress that flashed violet in the dim station light. She hiked up the dress a little, kicked off her shoes, and sat cross-legged on the papers. Cloche hat pulled off, my gal's black/magenta hair cascaded down around her shoulders.

Crabtree and I retreated to a platform bench and waited. And waited. Nearly thirty minutes passed before any of us spoke.

"Maddy, get ready, dear," Sue finally whispered, her eyes closed. A magenta glow began to radiate from her open palms. I slipped the wine bottles into my jacket pockets.

"Good god!" yelled Crabtree.

Five beryl-green orbs streaked towards us, then bounced onto the track into a cloud mass. Three wooden EL cars emerged from the smoky mass, rushing at us. The expanding of Sue's rippling field of magenta mixing with the phantoms' green billow produced a dark gray mist. The train halted with an inhuman shudder.

"Maddy, love, I can only hold it but for so long. So if you're going to get on, do it now!"

"Stay here, Crabtree!" I ordered.

"I'm coming too!" Crabtree demanded, jumping up from the bench to stand alongside me.

The phantom train idled with violent rocking as its doors slid open, permitting Crabtree and me to step aboard. "My Maddy, I love you," Sue, distant, said, her voice growing faint. She cried out with a nervous Lycan yelp.

I hissed, "I love you too," hopeful she heard me.

Inside the ectoplasmic subway car, the nimbus before us were strap-hangers in horrific forms of mangled and contorted death. Some had been maimed by glass shards, some impaled by wood splinters, and still others decapitated, their screams repeating as the train pulled out with a roar.

"Crabtree, I have to move to the front of the car so I can—" A shrill scream erupted, followed by an ectoplasmic fist to my face with enough force to knock me to the car floor.

"Boreli!" screamed Crabtree with fear in his voice as the specter of the trackman thrust his hands around my neck.

This time, my vampire hiss was one of rage. I grabbed the second bottle from my right coat pocket, uncorked it, and splashed a fair amount onto Boreli's ghostly green face. The paranormal aftershave had the acid effect of sizzling the lower half of Boreli's face off, which brought on another shrill scream by Boreli's specter as it crashed through a car window down to the track bed.

Righting myself, I yelled, "Crabtree, don't!"

Crabtree was indifferent to my plea as he embraced an apparition of a petit woman, her neck lolling to a right angle as if broken.

Crabtree had found Maggie. But I couldn't wait for him.

Into the front car I sprinted, pulling a cross of silver studded with purple gems on a choker from inside my shirt. On occasion, this talisman had given Sue and me a mixed signal, and a tingle when in use. On some days, the cross, known throughout history as the St. Issacs cross, is copacetic. On other days, it wants to burn a hole in your hands. I grabbed the two bottles out of my jacket pockets and made my vocal pitch before smashing the bottles together: "ECCE CRUIS SIGNUM FUGIANT PHANTASMATA CUNCTA!"

The ghost train and its passengers turned to a bright emerald, green mist, disappearing as I was thrown, and then bounced down along the train tracks in forward momentum until finally I stopped bouncing and sat up, covered in soot and transit dust. *Yet another ruined suit.* I mentally frowned as I rose to walk back to the Consumer Park Station platform.

"Oh, Maddy, he didn't," Sue sighed as I showed her the gris-gris talisman, its string looking as if it was snatched off.

"Glen and Maggie Crabtree are together again." As to which one of them snatched the talisman off, that will remain a mystery.

Glen Crabtree was considered and marked as having resigned and left the state, and that was the official story for all not in the know. I had Fenner destroy the undamaged two cars in Queens, which were the catalysts for the ghost train's routine returns. This impetus to return from the restless spirits was relayed to Sue when she connected with the ghost train in the station. Consumer Park Station is no more; it's now Prospect Park Station and the Brighton Beach line is now the Franklin Avenue Shuttle. Some say on summer days, when people ride through the station, they can smell the loud spectral odor of tobacco juice before they get to Ebbets Field to root for their beloved Robins, aka the Dodgers.

———

This affair was a pyrrhic victory for Sue and me in that we'd never lost someone on the paranormal/occult grind working with us. Sometimes love can be powerful in that it can reach beyond death. Glen Crabtree not only embraced Maggie one last time, but he also left this mortal plane to be with her. Whether to heaven or damnation, I don't know. Even with the strange skills Sue and I possess, we don't have a monopoly on what goes on, on the other side of the ethereal yashmak.

THE
PILGRIM HOTEL
AFFAIR

1925

"And this card shall be what is to come to you in time," I declared as I held the Three of Wands, raising the card over my head for dramatic effect. I was working my trade reading tarots for Elizabeth Kingfield, a high society matron by day, dabbler in the occult and paranormal by night. This evening, Mrs. Kingfield seemed distracted during our session. I soon discovered why.

"Dearest Susan, can I ask you a question and maybe seek some advice?" she asked, in the subdued candlelight of her library *wguke* sitting across from me at a small writing table. Mrs. Kingfield was thick of body. Her snow-white hair sat in a bob above her oval face. She could be gruff at times but now, like her plum evening gown, portrayed a motherly quality.

I placed the card revealing her future on the table. "Sure, Mrs. Kingfield. What can I help you with? Herbert hasn't been acting up again, has he?" Herbert was Miss Kingfield's deceased husband whose spirit, from time to time, belittled her from beyond the grave whenever he felt that the financial empire they'd created together was moving in a direction his spirit did not approve of. Mrs. Kingfield was one of the last of the "400" New York high-society families.

"Oh no, dearest. Herbert has been quiet lately," she said. As if knocking on wood for good luck, we both looked across the room at his portrait oil painting. It was a classic pose capturing Herbert standing against an ornate curtain, his right hand in his charcoal three-piece suit vest pocket. The artist had expertly rendered both his dark hair, which was parted down the middle, and his bulbous nose. Herbert was as silent as the day his body had been shipped back from Scotland. In 1920, Herbert Kingfield, a tycoon adventurer with verve, had led an expedition in search of the "Gray Man" of Ben Mac Dhui. It proved to be Herbert's last quest, for after he failed to return as scheduled, a search party had gone looking for him. His body was soon found on a fog-misted plateau. The cause of death was a broken neck.

As she leaned forward to light a Nat Sherman cigarette snug in an ivory cigarette holder of a lonely white candle-wicked flame between us, Mrs. Kingfield confessed, "I've never told you, but one of my holdings is the Pilgrim Hotel down on Fifth Avenue and 15th Street, the old 'Ladies Mile' part of Manhattan. Mercy me, I don't know what you young people call that part of town these days." Mrs. Kingfield spoke with a rare smile as she gazed at my satin blue, black boa flapper outfit. It was a getup she often requested I wear to her mansion so as to rub her stuffed shirt neighbors the wrong way up on Carnegie Hill, just off Central Park, when I made my monthly visits.

Before I could respond, she continued. "The Pilgrim Hotel was once, and to a lesser extent remains, a respite for New Englanders to stay here in comfort away from the rudeness of New Yorkers while shopping in the city.

"Recently, my night manager, Thomas Griffin, informed me of paranormal activities. He confessed that there were minor incidents in the past, but now they have increased."

"Have there been any recent deaths at the hotel ?" I asked.

"No. The house detective, Gordon Cohee, who is also my nephew, says he can't find any facts to the incidents. He's of the mind that the night staff should be fired if they are found to be spreading around ghost stories. I'll get to the point, Susan, since you and your partner deal with the paranormal. I would like to retain you and Madison to get to the bottom of what's going on at the Pilgrim."

"I'm afraid I would be short-handed, Mrs. Kingfield. The reason being Madison is, as we speak, in Detroit working on 'an affair' as we like to call our cases." My partner and love of my life, Madison Cavendish, had been hired by the city government of Detroit to cut a deal with a pesky "Imp" known as "Nain Rouge" to get him to leave the city.

"Oh, dearest, I'm confident you can handle the Pilgrim haunting on your own. Now let's talk turkey, as my Hebert would say." Mrs. Kingfield rose from the writing desk and, slow but steady of step, headed to a larger desk where she kept her pen and checkbook. First, however, she drew back the library curtains, and autumn's full moon beams filtered into the room. With quick deceit, I pulled from my clutch bag my rose-tinted cheaters, slipping them over my eyes while her back was turned. Not only would a moonlight Lycan transformation be an embarrassment to me, but it could abruptly result in a horrific end to Mrs. Kingfield's life. After writing out and handing me a check, Mrs. Kingfield turned the library lamps up.

"I promise, Mrs. Kingfield, I will get to the bottom of this."

"Thank you. I'll make arrangements for you to stay in one of the suites."

"That's okay. I have a better plan of action. I'll..."

—

"Carlotta Hollander, since you're the new girl, I'm matching you up with Bellaluna. She'll show you the ropes. Please don't mind her mumbling," said Tom Griffin, the night manager. Griffin was a rotund man built like Oliver Hardy, yet he managed to look dapper in his dark suit. I was among two rows of five colored women of various shades in gray-green double-breasted pin cord housekeeping uniforms with lacy maid caps. The Pilgrim's bell boys had already received a start-of-shift pep talk from Griffin and were off to tend to their duties in a gray-jacketed rush.

The lone woman not laughing at the other end of my line was, I assumed, Bellaluna Grace, a sallow brown yet "riny" gal with a dap of "Sweet Georgia Brown" scented pomade slick onto her hair.

Dismissed to attend to the floors we were assigned (Bellaluna and I had floors six and ten), my path was suddenly blocked before I could get to Bellaluna. We were in a hallway from the staff area to the lobby. The man stood there, an imposing stranger clearly up to no good.

"Bet you didn't know you would be working with so many Negros, did you," said Gordon Cohee, a dark-haired boulevardier in a tortilla-brown Brooks Brothers suit, the hint of illicit hooch on his breath. A house detective who I sensed needed a house detective to check on him. "I call this the darkie shift. Your name's Carlotta, right?"

"Are you inquiring if I have a problem with the shift's racial composition? I do not, being that I'm part Negro myself." My response seemed to set Cohee aback, but only for a moment. Lecherous fool that he was, little that he knew his wolfish-woman-harassing ways could have him encountering a real-deal she-wolf.

Cohee stared at my face as if trying to see where one race ended and the other began. "Well, now, you could have fooled me. With my help, you might get put on the day shift. Naturally, I'd expect something in return, if you know what I'm getting at."

I knew what he was getting at. Cohee was the type of man who felt his manifest destiny was to tomcat with as many women as possible on the job.

"No thank you, Cohee," I said, momentarily wishing moonlight would hit my eyes. I also had a quick vision in which, instead of ripping out Cohee's throat, my Maddy comes down to the Pilgrim and pummels Cohee. I've witnessed my Maddy's fisticuffs. It's top shelf, laying aside his vampire propensities.

"Carlotta! We got work to do, child!" yelled Bellaluna, giving Cohee a weird look, as if one minute she despised him but pined for him the next. Cohee wasn't stepping aside.

"Cohee, do you or do you not have floors to check?" Griffin asked, making sure no one was lingering.

"Ah, go tell it to Sweeny! I'll start when—" the smug house detective started to protest.

"No. You start now! Your aunt may own this place, but I rule the overnight hospitality here!"

After stepping to the side so I could pass, Cohee slinked away at Griffin's pronouncement.

"Hi, Bellaluna. You can call me Lotte. I've done some housekeeping here and there. But what's with that house shamus? I see he likes to work fast with the ladies. Bellaluna?" Bellaluna, her back to me, whispered to… someone. I had to find out who, for maybe it was the key to what was transpiring in the Pilgrim.

Bellaluna turned to face me. "Stay as far away as possible from him. Thinks he's a real cake eater. Ain't nothing but an ofay alley cat looking to make time with any woman that moves on this here night shift. Savvy?"

"I hear you, sister. You'll have no beef with me," I reassured her. In silence, we went about our tasks, fixing up rooms for any new guests checking in, removing room service trays and carts left in front of occupied rooms. During this time, Bellaluna held a low, clandestine conversation with an invisible entity. I couldn't take it anymore.

"What?" I asked.

"Not you," she said.

"Then who?"

"No one. I just think my thoughts out loud. No law against that, is there?" Bellaluna spoke defensively.

"I'm not here to ridicule you. In fact, I may be able to help. I deal in things from behind the veil."

Bellaluna perked up. "Can I trust you ?" All the pain in the world seemed collected on her face when she spoke. Just then the ping of the elevator found Cohee and a mocha wisp of a housekeeper named Nicey stepping off onto our sixth-floor assignment.

"I see you and Mumbles are getting along good," chuckled Cohee, his arm around the young lady. He dangled a room key tag from his fingers.

"And I see you stills be using room 602, canoodling and..." started Bellaluna, anger rising in her to mix with her present agitation.

"You need to mind yo' damn business, Mumbles!" Nicey chimed in before Cohee could answer.

In that instant, every hallway light fixture exploded, bulbs bursting into blue flames and white sparks. I assumed it was Nicey's work, a little paranormal presentation. She screamed and got to the stairway exit with Cohee ahead of the rest of us.

"Lawd, Lisette, stop! Stop!" yelled Bellaluna in the darkness.

Grasping Bellaluna by the hand, we followed behind the two workplace lust birds down to the lobby. We stood at the concierge's desk after summoning the bellboy captain, Andy, to go wake up Filmore, an old navy machinist-mate-turned-hotel-handyman, to replace the bulbs. Griffin ordered us to go back upstairs and clean up the broken glass.

"Okay, Bellaluna, who is Lisette?" I held the dustpan while Bellaluna swept up on a ladder, with Andy's flashlight as a guide. Filmore's sentences were down to half-curses as he was midway finished rebulbing the floor.

"Hush up. I'll tell you the rest on our break. But I'll let you chew on this: Had it not been for what Cohee did to Lisette, we'd have no ghost problem and I wouldn't have the nickname Mumbles."

"And what did Cohee do to Lisette, Bellaluna?"

"He murdered Carlotta. He done killed that woman, and I'm cursed with her spirit."

———

Her name was Lisette Haley. She was an Alabama girl who came to New York from the South for a better life. Like some of us, she started in the Bronx, getting day labor work at Simpson Street, or as we colored folks called it, the "Slave Market." Then she got to the Pilgrim. "Lisette just wanted a good job and finally got it until she met Cohee," said Bellaluna.

We were on our break, and an empty Borden's milk crate held a side door of the Pilgrim open for us. The illuminated view revealed the ever-growing skyscraper lights shining uptown. The night air was cool, and I wished my Maddy were here to drive me up to Westchester County so I could transform and frolic in bliss in a wooded area out of sight.

"So where does the murder part factor in, sister?"

"One night, I see them go into 602. I hear an argument about a baby coming. Then I don't see her no more. Nobody don't see her no more, then that popinjay Cohee soon starts lies saying she left town. Telling us that like we a bunch of dumb Doras.

"A week later, I get visions of her in my dreams. I'm telling you, the bastard did it." Bellaluna began to sob.

"Tell you what: In a few days, we will, during our meal break, we'll have a séance in room 602. That is, if the room's vacant," I offered.

"You a conjurer woman? Can you work some roots on Cohee's ass?"

"I want to speak to Lisette first, Bellaluna. But, uh, yeah. I do have some trickin' bags."

———

In talking with other staff, I soon learned of indecisive loyalty. Mrs. Kingfield kept Griffin, Cohee, and Bellaluna Grace on and never considered firing them for any reason. I guess Miss Kingfield never considered termination due to murder.

A week later, on a fresh Wednesday morning around 2 a.m., instead of taking our break in the Pilgrim's delivery driveway, we slipped up to room 602 to conduct the séance of Lisette Haley to bring justice and closure to her spirit. I took out a wedge of alabaster-colored chalk I had hidden in my apron pocket and drew a pentagram on the paisley-carpeted floor. In the middle of the pentagram, I placed a white embossed dinner plate with a maroon Pilgrim Hotel "P" in the center. I placed a white candle on the plate.

"Okay, Bellaluna, park yourself on the floor inside the pentagram while I turn off the lights, then we'll join hands."

After pulling the curtains and switching off the lights, I sat across from Bellaluna using what mortal magicians call misdirection. I lit the candlewick with a magenta glow off my right hand without her seeing.

Holding Bellaluna's hands in silence, I waited for the infinity pull to surge along with Lisette up in me. After a few moments, as I was about to call out to Lisette's spirit, a shaft of light from the hallway entered the room, brought on by the opening of 602's door. A moment later, the wall light was switched back on.

"Ah! This explains why you were so cold with me, Miss Lotte mongrel," Cohee said, standing in the doorway with Nicey giggling behind him. "You got the sweets for Bellaluna, I see! Wait until I tell Griffin and my aunt. You won't be able to keep your job this time, Bellaluna. You and your sister are as good as gone! Now scram!"

We both rose to our feet, yet Bellaluna kept rising until she was levitating a foot off the floor. This is when all proverbial hell opened up.

Lisette's spirit pushed Cohee inside 602 and Nicey out into the hallway. The room mirror shattered. A table by the bed began spinning, then sought to entertain us by doing a jig on its legs. A bloodred mist spiraled from the hands of Bellaluna, forming murky red fingers that wrapped around a gasping Cohee's neck, pushing him to the floor in a death grip.

"Bellaluna, let him go!" I yelled, the air in the room tight with pressure.

"I can't. It's Lisette doing this! She wants Cohee to die!"

"It's not Lisette! It's you!" I insisted, trying to get the mist from around Cohee's neck, an action that got me pushed to the floor, the smell of burning flesh and little tell-tale strands of fur from the top of my left hand. "Lisette is alive and living in Portland, Maine, with her daughter! Please, a phone call, just one phone call, will prove me right! Please, he's not worth it!" I moved toward Bellaluna just as she collapsed to the floor in a faint.

—

Yes, Lisette was alive.

No, there was no ghost.

Poltergeist, yes; ghost, no. The reason I had delayed the séance a few days was to enable me to make a trip up to Simpson Street so as to find anyone that knew Lisette. Not only did I find a close friend of hers named Edith Waddy, but Waddy disclosed that she had talks with Lisette by phone and letters. In a phone conversation I had with her, Lisette stated that once she confronted Cohee with news that she was with child, Cohee took an oath that he wanted nothing to do with her and the baby. Hence, the argument Bellaluna heard that night.

The following morning Lisette said she was giving up on New York totally. She left for Maine to stay with relatives who had found work in Portland. Lisette also stated that whatever problems Bellaluna was going through (I kept the paranormal part of this affair away from our conversation) stemmed from the fact that Bellaluna and Cohee were lovers at one point, or at least Bellaluna thought so.

"The bastard did a number on that gal's mind! Someday he'll get his!" said Lisette over the phone.

—

I felt that Bellaluna, with her telekinetic powers, needed a new start, so I made arrangements for her to go to the Caribbean island of Dominica for some rest, staying at the vacation home of Elsa Cranberry. After some time, I received a telegram from Bellaluna stating that she had decided to enter a convent to become a nun, which soon turned out to be a plus—she became a paranormal investigator in her own right. Over the decades, Madison and I would refer cases to her.

That poor child Nicey… well, that night, she ran off into the darkness. It wasn't until a few years later that I ran into her on 125th Street during the Christmas season. Unnerved at the sight of me, she crossed the street. As for Lisette, who longed for Cohee, he had returned to his tomcat ways to "get his." I made another visit to Mrs. Kingfield to set another plan in motion.

"Listen, honey, all is forgiven. Bellaluna was such a stick in the mud. So, are you going to help me get my job back? Maybe even work the dayshift like you promised?"

Cohee had given me the key, which I used to unlock 602, shrouded in darkness.

"We'll see how you rate with me first, toots," said Cohee, one hand on my backside and the other clutching a brown bottle of something bootleg. "Hit the lights, toots…. toots?" asked Cohee.

I had circled around him and fled out the door. After locking the door I stepped back as a pale white glow began to emit from under the door.

"You snot-nosed, lantern-fuel-drinking little shit! You're a black eye to this family! You wondered why, when I was alive, I hated for you to be in my infernal line of vision, you sickening welp! I have a good vaporing consciousness to slap you over to the other side with me!" bellowed the portrait of Herbert Kingfield to the screams of soon-to-be-ex-house detective Gordon Cohee.

Standing outside of 602, Griffin, Andy, and I shared a hearty laugh as Cohee's screams shrunk down to whimpers.

THE M.B.L. AFFAIR

1926

A Civil War-era house sits outside the town of Falmouth, just north of the Marine Biological Laboratories at Woods Hole, Massachusetts. As the black-capped chickadee flies, it's late spring evening on a Friday.

Professor E.E. Just, a fairly tall, light-complexioned man in a white shirt, bow tie, and dark three-piece suit, lays his coat on the back of a sheet-shrouded sofa. He's about to stretch out to get some much-needed rest. Though he has no irrational fear of the dark, he leaves his brown wingtip shoes on and lights a single candle on the dining table, just in case. The dark room renders it almost mockingly futile. Left on the table along with the candle are an empty tin of Gold Dollar sardines, a plate of rye breadcrumbs, and half a mug of now-cold Chase & Sanborn coffee, remnants of a dinner that fell far below his culinary tastes. A dinner that made him miss his wife, Ethel.

"Ethel and the children will love this house; they won't see it as a bunch of huckleberries," mumbles the professor to himself, ignoring the house's strange reputation. The thought of venturing upstairs to fetch a blanket—since there seemed to be a drop in temperature—is interrupted by the formation of a milky blue mist at the foot of the sofa, numbing the man's feet. Pulsating between a human form and a remnant of a micro-marine organism he had once studied under a microscope at Woods Hole, Professor Just lets out a high-pitched yelp and bolts upright on the sofa.

—

A cheerful Sunday morning washes Riverside Drive in sweet spring sunlight. The professor, having made a hasty retreat from Woods Hole and arriving in Manhattan, makes his way from door to door, trying to match an address to one written on a folded piece of paper in his hand. Just, a rising star biologist, is determined to meet with the two individuals who can solve his problem. A car pulls up as Just reaches the residence of Madison Cavendish and Seneca Sue SunMountain, renowned occult detectives. Three individuals exit the vehicle, happy and disheveled from a night of fun in Harlem, far from the stuffy ruminations of Riverside Drive.

"Hey, Professor!" I yell, approaching our front door while searching for my damn keys and recognizing Professor Just. Meanwhile, Zoe, a gorgeous mahogany-skinned woman dressed in a turban and brown fur coat, is in the midst of telling Sue another off-color joke, prompting Sue's honking goose laugh as she parks our black Caddy, a successor to our beloved 1919 Briscoe, which has long since passed on to automotive heaven.

Zoe Churel, a Mississippi Delta conjurer with magical skills who resides in Harlem, walks arm in arm with Sue, who wears a maroon cloche hat covering her jet-black hair pulled back into a long ponytail, a maroon dress, a string of white pearls around her neck, black silk stockings, and a flapper's garter belt hidden higher up on her left thigh (awaiting the day of our wedding when I'm to slip it off), all wrapped in a mink coat.

Zoe has joined us for an after-party brunch of slowly warming prohibition champagne hot off the back of a truck and cardboard containers of chop suey, aka "Tsap Seui," following a night of celebration for Sue and me after successfully resolving a case that will become known in our files as "The Enchantress Affair." The celebration started at Madame Walker's mansion on 136th Street and now ends in front of a perturbed E.E. Just, who seems just as upset about missing the shindig.

"Cavendish, the Western Union telegram stated that we are to meet at noon today to discuss retaining you for a problem I have. I know I'm early, but I had no choice but to catch an early train to New York. It seems perhaps providence that I'm seeing you in such an unprofessional manner," Just quakes in a high-pitched voice. "Hello, Zoe," he adds, his demeanor softening at the sight of her.

"Hello, E.E. It's been a while. I could head up the hill and catch a taxi so as not to interfere," Zoe says with a smile.

"No, no, Zoe. Please stay. Please," Just pleads, in a voice that implies he's likely to melt before Zoe's captivating eyes.

"Relax, Professor. Relax. We'll be alright." I note his protest and fumble for the keys to the front door. "We be fine. Just, just fine." Sue approaches from behind me and snatches the keys from my hand.

"My Maddy, you're my niftiest sheik, but you're taking too long."

Sue unlocks the door, sprints for my apartment that doubles as our office, and disappears into the bathroom, her garter belt having slipped off (a detail she divulged a while later).

"I apologize for you seeing us like this," I say to Just. "Truth of the matter is that Sue, Zoe, and I were out celebrating last night and held the tiger by the tail a little too long, if you know what I mean." Once inside the apartment, I usher Zoe and the professor to my desk. They each take a seat. Zoe removes her coat to expose a creamy white flapper dress, an ebullient contrast to her skin tone that leaves Just at a loss for words. These two have a history. My mind flashes back to a dinner party given by our mutual friend, Alain Locke, and how one minute Just and Zoe were in a corner in a quiet debate about science versus mysticism and, in the next moment, had snuck out of the dinner party.

I walk toward the kitchen to brew a pot and place the bag with the champagne and chop suey in the ice box while E.E. Just, having picked up Sue's garter belt, unthinkingly deposits it in his suit jacket pocket. "Coffee?" I ask our guests.

"Yes," Just says. "Cream and two sugars, please. Maybe I was too hasty with you, Cavendish. I mean, I *am* early." He is clearly trying to backpedal on his early criticisms. Returning to the desk, I switch on the lamp to help the daylight peeking in through closed shades and curtains, yet keep my tints on.

"I'm a man of science…" Just pauses as Sue returns, shoes and stockings in her hands. She stretches out on my green Davenport behind Just and Zoe, her coat doubling as a comforter. "I don't deal in hocus-pocus nonsense," Just continues. "But you see, Cavendish, my newly-rented house is haunted, I hate to say." Just pulls at his starched shirt collar.

"How so, old man?" As I retrieve a yellow legal pad and a pencil from a desk drawer to take notes, I can't help but smirk.

"I work under a grant at Woods Hole Marine Biological Laboratories, a research center in Massachusetts. I'm given a stipend for living arrangements, which I put toward renting a house with an option to buy, located a few miles west from the center."

The aroma of the brewing coffee slowly enters the living room. I retreat to the kitchen to get our cups o' Joe.

"Why not reside at the research center itself?" Sue asks between yawns. "Don't they have on-site living quarters?"

"Certain researchers don't approve of mingling with the Negro race, be it in work or social settings, so it's best to live off-site. When my work requires me to stay overnight, I sleep in the laboratory—or at least that's the compromise my colleagues and I reached. However, I soon found and easily rented a house for my family and me; maybe it happened too easily.

"The split-level, furnished in Federal style, belongs to a New England whaling captain named Ordway. At first, I attributed the aloofness of the residents in the nearby town of Falmouth—where I stop to buy household items—to the difference in our races. That is, until a gas station attendant let the cat out of the bag."

Just takes a gulp of coffee and continues. "Well, I decided to see for myself what was going on before spending money and later trying to get out of a deal with the realtor. You see, I'm a frugal person, and there has to be some logical explanation for what's occurring. I feasted on a simple supper that night and then drifted off to sleep on the living room sofa. Around one in the morning, something grasped me by the ankles, yanking me off the couch and onto the floor. Jumping up in dim-lighted panic, I shook off my stupor and saw the image of a milky blue, not-quite-human form pulsating in the darkness, like a micro-marine lifeform I've encountered in my research. The faint glow it emitted showed it was stationed between me and the front door. Composing myself, I tried to circumvent it, but it blocked my advance. Horrid moans that I cannot decipher rumbled from the mist. Seizing my fear by the reins, I feigned left, then turned right and ascended the stairs to the second level. Jerking open the bedroom window, I lowered myself out and to the ground, jumped into our family Ford four-door, and sped off nonstop to Woods Hole. Later that day, I wired you the telegram."

"What do you want us to accomplish?" I light up an Old Gold cigarette and lift a silver ashtray from a desk drawer to Sue's cosmic Lycan frown of annoyance at anything silver.

"Want accomplished?! I want you to get rid of the damn thing! That's what I want you to do!" The professor's voice is animated, but he calms himself once Zoe reaches over and places a hand atop his.

"It's not that simple," Sue explains. "We have to find out if it's a spirit, poltergeist, apparition, demon, or djinn—although a djinn would be rare in this part of the world. You may not like what I'm going to say, but the phenomena could be vexed that you and your family have invaded its home. Didn't you say a sea captain owned the residence?"

"If that's true, it'll be hard to egress the old sea captain from his home," Zoe warns.

"We'll help you, E.E.," I say to the biologist's relief.

"I don't know how much of a fee you charge, but here's what I can afford. May I borrow a sheet of legal paper and a pen, please?"

Writing quickly, as if that will solve the problem right here and now, Just jots down his budget, pushing the paper across the desk to me and holding his breath. I glance at the potential first half of a retainer fee and hand the paper to Sue, who is now standing behind me. She shrugs her shoulders and makes a chopping motion with her hands before returning the paper to me.

"Doc, we are going to charge you half. We don't want to put you in debt, but we have one stipulation: Zoe must accompany us on this affair. We'll give her part of our fee," I say, winking at Zoe and downing a sip of coffee.

"Thanks. You don't know how stressful these last few weeks have been. Between work, trying to gain at least mutual respect from my colleagues, and now this incident shaking my belief system, I'm only looking for peace of mind so I can conduct my research," Just exhales, casting a longing look at Zoe. "I wish I could join the three of you, but I have to be at the Howard University campus to make arrangements for Ethel and the kids to travel once I receive word from you that the place is safe to occupy."

"When do you want us to start, Professor?" Sue asks, nursing her coffee with one lump of sugar and a dash of cinnamon.

"Here are the extra keys to the house; it's just outside of Falmouth, a few miles north of Woods Hole." Just digs around in his inner coat pocket and produces the keys, a road atlas, and an envelope with our retainer fee, handing it all to me. "I've marked off the route in red pencil. Maybe a fresh start for you in the morning would suffice."

"We'll start out just before noon tomorrow and should arrive by evening. Give us a phone number down at Howard so that we can contact you."

Just jots down the number on the pad, rips off the lower half of the page, and hands it to me. He looks at Zoe and starts to scratch the same number on the upper half of the page but then has a change of heart and scribbles it out.

"Splendid!" Just shouts abruptly. "I shall now begin my journey to make Penn Station and catch the first train to DC."

Although having to bend to the paranormal world for a solution, Professor Just's academic cockiness seems to have returned now that he's paid to handle the problem. I suspect that later his cockiness will disappear, particularly if his Ethel finds Sue's garter belt in his jacket pocket. I consider mentioning this to Just and reclaiming Sue's garter, but instead opt to let fate play out as it will.

"I'll drive you to Penn Station," I offer.

"Good day, Miss Sue and Miss Zoe." Just nods and then tips his hat to Zoe in particular as he and I head out the door, to which Sue gives a sly grin to a joke to which only she and I know the outcome.

—

Back from 34th Street, I find no trace of Sue or Zoe in my apartment. I head upstairs to Sue's dwelling and find them there. Sue stands at the kitchen counter opening a can of tuna while Zoe is in the living room nervously petting Sekhmet, who's nestled in her lap, forepaws clinging to a ball of pink yarn, while her tentacles playfully tap Zoe's knees. The place is covered almost wall to wall with large folklore-themed pillows and cushions of Asian, African, Celtic, Native American, and Persian, all in a kaleidoscope of color. The only chairs to be found are in the kitchen. Sue now wears a black silk robe, her hair wrapped in a hand-painted scarf that Isadora Duncan would love to own.

"What do you ladies think of the professor and his problem?" I ask, while searching for and fishing out champagne coupes from Sue's kitchen cabinet. I intend to go back downstairs and retrieve the champagne and chop suey.

"He's a bit cocky," says Sue.

"But humble enough to seek us out. I'll give him points for that," says Zoe. "I also sense that E.E. knows better than to give me the number to his Howard University household with Ethel there," Zoe adds. It's clear she's too good a soul to get into a deep peccadillo with Just.

—

The drive up into New England starts out fun and refreshing for us but soon becomes tedious after so many hours on the road. The thruways of New York and New England soon give way to rutted backroads. Falmouth has a subdued Main Street, a fish industry town that might easily inspire several designs by lithographers Nathaniel Currier and James Merritt Ives. I keep our Cadillac moving through the town and adjust the sleeves of my St. James tweed coat. About two miles out of town, a much-needed stop at a Sinclair gas station is in order.

"Fill 'er up, buddy, and if you have any coffee, it'll help too. Say, are we in the right direction to the Ennis Ordway house?" I step out of the Caddy while Sue and Zoe stay in the auto and dig their faces deep into their coats for warmth. On either side of the rutted road, naked trees scratch against a gray evening sky. It may be spring but New England winter refuses to relent.

"A Negro teacher is renting dat place, case you don't know," the attendant says in a voice that sounds more like a warning than a casual exchange of information. "Don't know why they purchase the place if'n you ask me." He eyes Zoe as if he's never encountered a colored person before.

"I'm not inquiring about the occupants, brother. I'm asking for directions and coffee," I say.

"You're in the right direction. No offense intended, and no coffee, friend."

The lanky gas jockey fumbles around, spilling regular until he finally fills the tank. "Keep on this road and look on your left."

"Okay, brother. Now that the tank's set, I'm well aware who's renting the place. Name's Cavendish. I'm a property appraiser, and these are my assistants, Miss Susan SunMountain and Miss Churel," I lie and nod in Sue's direction, to which she giggles. The lanky man's eyes narrow as if he's being mocked. "They're thinking about buying."

"Darkies or not, they need to be careful. It's not a good place. Ever since Captain Ennis Ordway built dat place in 1857 and him dying in '97, it's been rocking like an old horse and buggy with queer ghost stuff." The attendant looks around as if afraid to get caught talking to strangers.

"Excuse me?" Sue says. She steps out of the car to stretch her legs. Underneath the gray wool coat, she wears dark jodhpur pants, a lambswool sweater, jodhpur boots, dark cloche, and a wool scarf. In this business, your clothes have to be functional, as my Sue would say, horse to ride or not. A Browning .32 revolver occupies her clutch bag. Zoe is dressed in a pink-trimmed black sequin dress, seal-skin boots, and a mink coat. Zoe, too, sports a dark felt cloche hat.

"As the story goes, some apparition is wandering around there. God forgive us," the attendant says while wiping the car's windshield. He continues looking over his shoulder while I step back in the auto.

"Buck and a quarter, please." He pushes a palm open into the auto in front of my face as his eyes narrow in malice on Sue.

"Here is two and a quarter. Keep the other buck for giving up information." I wake the Cadillac back up while Sue and Zoe, now both inside again, bundle up.

"You three ain't staying long, are ya?" The lanky man's question mists into the auto, along with the smell of halitosis and gasoline.

"Don't know. Why you ask, brother?" In addition to a number of warm layers, I've got a .44 under my tweed coat and am ready for whatever comes next.

"Cause."

"Because of what?" I ask. "Okay, brother, I'll go along with the gag."

"Cause." and with that, the long-limbed stranger goes around the back of the Sinclair station, leaving us perplexed. We drive on.

—

The house, from the look on the outside, if free of the situation it was apparently in, could be a tranquil place: split level, rustic design, carved into a spot of land with white pine woods in the background and a white picket fence signifying the property area. A pinch away from the road back to Falmouth.

Our Cadillac's headlights illuminate the front of the house, the only light for miles. An overcast night vetoes the moonbeams, bringing jubilation to Sue, given her Lycanthrope tendencies. For the briefest moment, a blue mist floats past a bedroom window above.

"You two see that?" Zoe asks as I weigh and bounce the professor's keys in my hand, walking up to unlock the front door.

"Yes, I sure do! I think we're in for a wingding! The old captain doesn't want to leave his home!" Sue exclaims as I enter, scraping a matchstick against one of my boot heels. We quickly secure candlesticks to light our way.

"A séance is in order, but before we do that, let me check upstairs," I say.

"Okay, but I need time to connect when we start," Zoe replies, sounding like a paranormal long-distance operator.

"Take all the time—" Before I can finish, something grabs me by the ankles and drags me hard and viciously up the stairs to the bedroom, ensuring the back of my skull hits every step.

"Zoe, run!" yells Sue. As she rushes to my aid, her hair and sweater catch fire from contact with the blue entity—this is the last thing I see.

—

With the candles burning serenely on the dining room table, we let the regeneration process take effect from within the safety of our car.

"We'll go back inside soon," I tell Zoe and Sue. "Once the captain sees he can't get rid of us, maybe then he'll communicate."

I hold a bloodied, magenta-oozing handkerchief to the back of my head while Sue pulls a black-and-red floral scarf from her clutch to cover her regrowing hair. A burnt wool smell from her sweater permeates the car.

From the back seat, Zoe looks at us in stupefaction. "I wish I had your powers," she whispers.

—

"Madison, Sue, hold on to my hands and do not let go unless I tell you to," Zoe orders in the dim candlelight. Seated at the dining room table, we wait in silence until Zoe speaks again. The wait isn't long.

"THOU SPIRIT, THOU KNOWEST THAT GOD DOTH AND IN EARTH, IN AIR, IN YE WATER, AND IN ALL PLACES, BY YE TRUTH OF GOD, I CONJURE YOU." Using an incantation universally known through the ages, the sound of an empty tin of sardines hitting the floor cuts through my head like a knife as I'm still woozy.

In the candlelight, we see Sue's head jerk back; her shallow breathing is audible. Behind my chair, a hovering presence scribbles on a notepad, the sound of pencil on paper echoing from an oak writing desk across the room.

"EEEEEEE AAAH AHHH! HE… HE AAAH MADDY… DON'T… FOLLOW!" Kicking over her chair, Sue jerks away from our hands, jumps up, and sprints like her occult life depends on it, bursting through the kitchen door and, with the agility of an Olympic athlete, hurtles over a white picket fence in a hysterical, howling run into the woods beyond.

"Let her go, Madison," Zoe says, pulling me back down into my chair. Knowing it's best to listen to Zoe in these situations, I quietly get up, find an unlit candle in its holder, and light it for a better view. As I walk over to the desk, I see the pencil and notepad I heard being used in the darkness. Picking up the pad, I read the message:

I NoT CapsttaN Odwey helP mE!

—

Three hours before sunrise, the sound of Sue's voice in lighthearted conversation comes toward us in the darkness as I stand at the kitchen door, waiting for her return.

"Oh my!" Zoe exclaims, joining me at the kitchen door.

Helping Sue over the picket fence is a now more solid and defined young man, still glowing in a milky blue. Dressed in what I surmise are Native American accouterments, he's about the same height as Sue, with high cheekbones, eyes that glimmer in a soft blue tint, and dark silky hair accented with seed beads around his neck.

"Zoe, Madison, meet… uh… we'll just call him Misty for now, of the Nauset Tribe. Let's all go inside so I can tell you Misty's story and find a way to correct his situation. Also… I'm freezing!"

"Captain Ordway was never the apparition," Sue begins as I set a cup of steaming coffee in front of her, apologizing for no milk, only sugar and a pinch of cinnamon. I also pour a cup for Zoe.

"I know. When you bolted out of here like Morgan Taylor at the '24 Olympics, Misty also left a message for us." I show Sue the notepad. Sue smiles across the table at Misty, whom I've placed a cup of coffee in front, hoping to make him feel at ease, even if he can't sip it. To my amazement, the hot liquid slowly drains out of the mug. I then sit down to enjoy my own cup and listen as Zoe takes over, explaining Misty's tragic history.

"It seems he's been here in real chronological time since the 1600s. Misty became separated from his family in a snowstorm during 'the Great Dying.' Trying to find shelter, he says he fell asleep when, in truth, he froze to death. After wandering the hills for centuries, he befriended Captain Ordway when he built the house in 1857. Ordway treated Misty like a son, even checking up on him during his naval service in the Civil War. When he died in 1897, Misty says they never connected on the other side. Not really bound to this place, Misty nevertheless stayed," Zoe explains.

Sue searches my face for an answer.

"Why doesn't she just let go and walk into the light?" I start to feel the pressure from Zoe and Sue, their faces reflecting concern.

"Madison, he wants one more chance at life. I have an idea that may be ethically debated. Sue, can you look in the kitchen and grab the lantern from under the sink? Then clean it out and ask Misty if he could fit into it," Zoe instructs.

We bid the old house, now barren of ghosts, goodbye, with Misty in the lantern, which has been carefully placed between Zoe and Sue in the back seat. I drive toward Falmouth, where long-distance phone calls need to be placed.

The first call I make is to Professor Just at Howard, giving him the good news that the house is ghost-free and that he, Ethel, and the children can move in. The second call is to Dr. Oberlin Pythagoras, a prominent Black doctor at Sydenham Hospital in Harlem by day, an alchemist and researcher of the paranormal world by night. Along with Zoe Churel, Dr. Pythagoras has helped us with past affairs.

A 1924 Studebaker Big Six, tan in color, parks in front of Riverside Drive and 107th Street. A brown man with receding salt-and-pepper hair exits the vehicle. He's nattily dressed in a dark suit and walks toward me as I stand at the front door to greet him.

"Good lord, amazing! In the name of God, amazing!" Dr. Pythagoras loudly proclaims, spellbound by the blue mist in front of him, the room dark since Sue has pulled down the window shades and drawn the curtains.

"Doctor, how many children die in your hospital from various ailments?" Zoe asks.

"Too many, even if it's just one." Pythagoras reaches out to touch Misty, whose image ripples like a stone dropped in a pond. I ask, "What if we could merge a restless spirit who left this world too soon with the body and spirit of a terminally ill child? Wouldn't that give the loved ones a second chance and the child a life?" I can't gauge the doctor's immediate reaction; he's engrossed in examining Misty.

"You three are playing God now?" Pythagoras asks in a gruff voice to match his attitude.

"No, just trying to set things right," Zoe replies.

"But what about the infant's consciousness?" The doctor seems tempted to retrieve his black bag from the Big Six. Misty sits down in one of the black armchairs, rightfully now a client of Sue and me. "Would that be ethical?" the doctor asks.

"It would be a merger, not a replacement. Sue has done it already with no ill repercussions," Zoe says, standing and trying to stroke Misty's hair, which only produces more ripples.

"Why don't you rent him space in your freckled head, Sue?" The doctor cackles at his little pun.

"I would, but I have too much going on inside my skull as it is," Sue retorts with a laugh that sounds like a combination of a goose honk and a wolf's maw snicker.

"Alright, Doc, aren't you a defender of Carl A. Wickland and his book *Thirty Years Among the Dead*? This would be a great case study for you to submit anonymously as an author," I bribe. The doctor's eyebrows arch. The debate goes on for another minute or so, at which point Pythagoras turns to Misty once more.

"Can he hear me? Misty, we are going to try to start things anew for you." Turning to Zoe, Sue, and me, Pythagoras advises, "You three will have to be on call until a situation arises; only the four of us will know about this."

As a gift, the doctor is allowed to go retrieve his black medical bag so he can take a sample of ectoplasm. The rest of the day is spent making Misty comfortable, dropping Professor E.E. Just's keys in the mail, and settling down to wait for Pythagoras to call.

—

On a gray Harlem morning, chilly spring rain turns the streets and sidewalks to ice. The cold cuts to the bone, a depressing time to be in the hospital awaiting the death of your newborn child. Sadie Lovett, wife of bricklayer and general laborer William Lovett, a former sharecropper from Georgia, hoped things would work out better with the birth of their son, Titus. Unfortunately, the lad is born prematurely. He is now fighting pneumonia, and the situation looks grim. It's likely only a matter of time before the final word comes from the maternity ward below Sadie's room on the fourth floor. Exhausted from praying, tears race down Sadie's honey-toned cheeks, keeping pace with the raindrops on the hospital windowpanes.

—

Decades later, Harlem old-timers still reminisce in whispers about Dr. Pythagoras, accompanied by three nurses—two women and one man—faces hidden behind surgical masks. Details of the story have been passed on from person to person and it has come to be known as "the Phantom Ghosts of Sydenham Hospital." The most recent iteration tells of a doctor carrying a lantern with a strange milky blue glow inside. The doctor orders the staff of the maternity ward to leave for several minutes, an action he never attempted to explain for the rest of his life.

"Who's baby be hollering like that?" Sadie Lovett asks. She sits up in bed, depressed and angry, but these emotions quickly fade as a nurse enters the room with a crying infant wrapped in a blue blanket— the cries of a healthy child. The nurse hands Sadie her son, Titus M. Lovett, to hold and cuddle.

"But… lord, I thought the doctor said he was pretty much done for?" Sadie, joyful and crying, looks down at her baby, who looks like his father except for the blue irises of his eyes.

"He'll be alright, honey," Zoe says through the surgical mask with a wink. "He's a fighter. Just make sure y'all show him love, sister. Love is all he needs."

THE
AHMED
AFFAIR

1927

The spring sunshine glistened off the outer hull and deck of the *S.S. Grandview* ocean liner as tugboats nudged her into her berth at Pier 23 on the Hudson River. The hustle and bustle of Pier 23 seemed not to disturb Nigel Dunmore in his cabin as he raised a glass of premium scotch and soda to his dapper mirror image. Dressed sharply in a three-piece tweed suit with a matching fedora, overcoat, and oxblood-colored leather shoes polished to military standards, Nigel had brown hair and mustache, dull blue eyes, and the face of an upper-class British gentleman. He smugly saluted himself again in the mirror.

"To the top! The very tip-top, you old rajah!" Nigel drained his glass of scotch. "Oh, and to you, old chap! It will be with your aid too!" He winked in the direction of a chained wood and metal box, about the size of a shoeshine box, resting upon a nightstand in his cabin quarters. The box shook in reply. Looking around the cabin, Nigel made sure everything was in order. The ship's service would pick up his luggage, but he would hold on to the box as he disembarked. The main objective was to keep the box safe, find a phone, and make the stateside connections he had established. Adjusting his suit one last time, he said, "We're off!" to the box, tucking it under his arm, and left the cabin in search of the gangplank, mixing in with the rest of the passengers.

Evening found me in the middle of a blood sausage dinner at my desk. Sue, my partner in the art of occult detection and the love of my life, was at the moment visiting with Daisy Felton, esteemed "vampire finder," over in Queens. We had recently wrapped up a mortal insurance fraud case and had some time off to ourselves. I was enjoying the quiet solitude that accompanies dining alone when the buzz of the intercom from the vestibule interrupted my meal.

"Cavendish here, who is it?" I said moodily into the intercom.

Didn't people know it was dinnertime?

"It is me, Rollo Ahmed. I need to talk to you on a matter most urgent," came the voice from the other end in a crisp British accent.

"Rollo?"

"Rollo Ahmed! Rollo Ahmed!"

"Well, shit!" I said, buzzing him in. Now, you had occult detectives, and then you had Rollo Ahmed. He was right up there with Carnacki in legend. I rose from behind my desk to greet him.

"Madison? So glad you're here, my good man."

"Hello, Madison," echoed a silky voice from behind Rollo.

"Zoe! Zoe Churel!" I replied and, upon seeing her shapely body and sweet mahogany-hued face, ushered the duo into my apartment. "Have a seat, you two," I offered, tapping the door closed behind them with one of my wing tips.

Seated in front of me was Rollo Ahmed, noted authority on the occult, in a dark three-piece suit, red fez, high-collared white shirt, and spat-covered dark shoes. The product of an Egyptian father and Caribbean mother, Rollo wore his dark beard pointed at his chin. The dark beauty seated next to him was Zoe Churel, dressed from head to toe in regal purple. She wore a tight-fitting dress wrapped in a wool sweater with a gold Egyptian scarab brooch pinned to it. Zoe, a tarot card reader and magic stick conjurer from Harlem, had helped Sue and me in "The E.E. Just Affair."

"Okay, Rollo, what gives?" I asked. Rollo adjusted himself in his chair. I lit an Old Gold cigarette. I took a puff and leaned back in my desk chair to get the scoop from these two. "I didn't know you were stateside, Rollo."

"I need your help in a matter most evil," Rollo said.

"Rollo, old pal, old buddy, are you fit as a fiddle?" He knew why I asked.

"Madison, please. I was possessed by the Lux gem at the time, but now I'm proper. What we have now is a new danger—a demon box, if you will—and the confused soul who possesses it must be stopped by all means." Rollo had had a bad go of it during "The Lux Gem Affair" back in '24.

"A demon box?" This was getting interesting.

"Yes, the Demon Box of Ebril!"

"Never heard of it. But I'm sure Sue has some info on what you're saying." I found myself wishing Sue would walk through the door now with the ice cream she promised.

"Enlighten me anyway," I prodded.

"From the ancient city-state of Ebril in Persia came the tale of a demon of antiquity that was captured by mystics and locked away in a box—actually a small chest—for safekeeping. If anyone should come into contact with the entity, they would begin a false quest for power, enticed by the demon," Rollo explained.

"But," Zoe interjected, "if controlled and held under the most optimum conditions, the demon can be of service." A look of worry crossed Zoe's face as she crossed her legs and leaned back in the black leather club chair.

"Now, a Mr. Nigel Dunmore, formerly a British Expeditionary Force Captain of our late War to End All Wars, has come into possession of the box. All we know is that the artifact hunter who had it locked away was found dead, decapitated."

Zoe let Rollo continue. "Yes. Dunmore first dabbled in the occult during the war. One night during the Battle of Ypres, he and a few fellow officers necromanced a deceased British soldier," Rollo said, concern etched on his face. "Ghastly, I say!" Rollo exclaimed. "Dunmore was purged from the Golden Dawn Society."

"And where do Sue and I fit into this stew?" I asked.

"Nigel is headed for the United States. If he's not here already. I was lecturing in Cuba when I was contacted by my friends in the occult community, who are concerned about Dunmore's recklessness," Rollo explained.

"Or are they mad because he has the toy and they don't?" I countered.

"Cavendish, please believe me when I say the occult community does have ethics. He must be stopped." Rollo paused. "We want the box destroyed!"

—

Seneca Sue SunMountain, dressed in an ankle-length crimson dress, coffee-colored stockings, semi-heeled red shoes, and topped off with a Bycocket hat featuring a ring-necked pheasant tail planted at an angle, made a statuesque fashion statement. She unlocked the door and entered with one hand while holding a paper bag containing two pints of ice cream: vanilla for her and strawberry for me.

"Rollo!" Sue yelled, having not seen our dear friend Rollo in years. "Zoe! What's shaking, sister?!" Sue and Zoe hung out in Harlem clubs so much that they earned the nickname "the Salt & Pepper Girls."

"Sue darling, you're here right on time." Zoe smiled.

"Come in, love, and let Rollo and Zoe fill you in on a new affair,"

I said as Sue parked herself, as usual, on my desk. Not before she scooted into the kitchen and returned with four ice cream sundae bowls and four spoons for all of us to partake in some ice cream and more details.

"You sure Rollo didn't drop glass on us?" Sue teased me, still seated on top of my desk.

The glass she was talking about were precious gems and diamonds of various colors and sizes; their value was fantastic when sold. I had been rolling them around on the desk blotter despite my partner's sensual curves obstructing my view.

"Oh, they are the real McCoy, all right," I said, carrying the empty bowls to the kitchen.

"Madison, I have to tell you, while Rollo has always been a good chap, as the English say, I sensed he wasn't forthcoming about this affair. Didn't you sense it too?" Sue asked.

"You tell me," I countered. "You're the psychic part of our business." Although I did sense something, I didn't want to admit it.

"I know Zoe; she's like a sister to me. She's as right as rain. As for Rollo, something is not right, and I do sense fear in his case," Sue said as I washed and she dried the bowls, standing side by side at the kitchen sink.

An hour had passed since Rollo and Zoe left Madison and Sue's Riverside Drive place of business. The nightlife of Harlem flowed up and down Lenox Avenue as they made their way to Zoe's brownstone on 131st Street.

"Zoe, can we stop for a moment?"

Rollo halted in front of her brownstone, where he was to stay while in New York. Drawing Zoe close to him, Rollo attempted to kiss her, the apex of long-hidden feelings for her that he could no longer hide. Zoe pulled away. "No, Rollo," she rebuffed him.

"I'm sorry for being forward, but I thought we were in accord about my feelings for you," said a crestfallen Rollo.

"I'm sorry if I led you on without intending to, but maybe we can discuss our feelings, or lack thereof, after we have located the item." Zoe moved up the front steps to the brownstone door. Rollo let her go first to prove he was still the gentleman. Just as Zoe began to use her key, her servant Saipan opened the front door.

"You are home, ma'am, with your guest." Saipan beckoned the two inside. A well-built young man of Asian and African descent, dressed in a white Jodpuri jacketed suit and sandals, made Rollo wonder if this young man was his rival for Zoe's affections, given how she brightened up as soon as she saw his handsome face.

"Mr. Ahmed, this is Saipan, my servant," Zoe said, introducing him.

"How do you do, sir?" Saipan and Rollo sized each other up, looking for some invisible weakness in one another.

"How do you do, Saipan? A pleasure to meet the hired help," Rollo remarked, delivering a subtle verbal jab at Saipan's position in Zoe's life.

Zoe sensed where this might lead and changed the subject. "Did Mr. Ahmed's luggage arrive?" she asked while ushering everyone into the vestibule adjacent to a Victorian-era decorated sitting room, although New York was in the midst of the Roaring Twenties, and Art Deco was beginning to rule the aesthetic.

"I took the liberty of taking Mr. Ahmed's luggage up to the guest room," Saipan replied.

"Well done, Saipan," Zoe said, rubbing the young man's shoulder. "Rollo, would you like a late supper, or was Seneca's ice cream enough to hold you until morning?" she offered. "I could have Saipan fix you a late-night plate of cheese, bread, and some condiments from the icebox. Maybe a glass of chardonnay and a few kumquats." Zoe was trying to make amends for the hurt look on Rollo's face.

"No, save the snack for the morning, please. Right now, I need to get some rest. I would also like to gain access to your occult book collection for research, if I may," Rollo instructed.

"I will have Saipan show you the library room, as I call it, tomorrow when you're ready. I myself will be gone most of the day doing psychic readings and fortune-telling house calls. High society beckons; their love for tarot readings is a never-ending thirst." Zoe smiled. "Do you think Madison and Sue can locate Nigel?"

"I do not know, but to be properly prepared, I will need to get to your books to find a solid counter-spell. I could meet with you if you want or call you from Madison's office if you like. I intend to rendezvous with them in the evening."

"That would be nice, Rollo, and sorry about the mixed signals. Saipan, will you show Mr. Ahmed to his room?" With that, Zoe, the delta conjurer, made her way into the kitchen from the foyer to start a pot of water boiling for tea.

Morning found Sue and me on the case. I put in a call to Lt. Stuart Kirkland, head of the New York City Police Department's secret Office of Special Concerns. Created to investigate paranormal incidents and high strangeness in the greater New York area, Sue and I had helped the OSC out on more than a few cases, and so Kirkland returned the favor whenever we needed help. It was a bit ironic that I had been the first head of the OSC back in 1914.

"Well, Madison, we did get an information bulletin from US Customs about an Englishman claiming to be a diplomat with Britain's foreign office. He had false documents and slipped a box past them among his luggage. He disappeared into Manhattan, but we have a description," Kirkland advised from the other end of the phone connection. "I'll call you, brother, if we get anything," Kirkland promised.

Meanwhile, Sue made her way down Sixth Avenue by the EL train to the diamond district to appraise the diamonds and gems Rollo had submitted as a fee for our services, taking one emerald gem with her. Offers ranged from $500 to $5,000, but Sue just said she would get back to them. One jeweler even tried to bluff and say the gem was stolen and that he would call the police if she didn't hand it over. Sue, with a Lycan growl, called him on it, and sensing terror, the man backed down.

"Maddy, it's the real McCoy, love. We got good offers for it," my Sue said over the phone.

"But why is Rollo overpaying us for this affair?" I asked.

"That's for us to find out," she replied. "Well, I got through to Kirkland, and he said OSC and US Customs are interested in old Nigel Dunmore, too." Kirkland was a little too Ivy League for a cop for Sue's taste, but she liked him. "Do you remember Edith Blaine?"

"Sure do; she's that snotty heiress, patron of the arts, and fool who thinks she knows about the black arts," Sue huffed. "Don't tell me…"

"Catch the EL and meet me in the West Village at 50 Thompson Street. If anyone knows of Nigel's whereabouts, it should be her," I figured.

"You talked with Rollo?" Sue asked.

"Yes, he's holed up in Zoe's library doing research. At least, that's what the house servant Saipan said when I called, and Zoe is out and about plying her trade as a tarot reader."

"Okay, Maddy." Ending the call, Sue left the phone booth and dashed up the stairs to catch the EL southward past 14th Street to the West Village as it pulled into the station.

—

Fifty Thompson Street was part and parcel of almost a whole city block of apartments owned by coal, bauxite, and lumber heiress Edith Blaine of the Blaines of Montana, no relation to the political Blaines of Maine. Edith, a high-society patron, belonged to an underground network of covens that studied the black arts. She was attractive but pouty-faced, alabaster complexioned, with light brown hair done in a pageboy style. Her inverted triangle-shaped body was tight in a black furisode kimono, and she was in her spacious kitchen, fixing an afternoon meal of bacon pulled from the pan just before it burned, along with scrambled eggs—partly out of hunger, the other part just to show the hired help that she could cook when in the mood.

"Miss Blaine, the front desk states that you have visitors, ma'am," half-whispered Edith's butler, Emerson, dark-suited, white-haired, and hawk-nosed, as he stood at the kitchen door, taking in the aroma of the late breakfast while waiting for a reply.

"Well, did ya find out who it is, Emmy? Did ya?" Edith commanded in a loud, nasal voice. Many a stockholder or board member hated when Miss Blaine opened her mouth to speak. She had transferred the food from pan to plate but was just standing near the kitchen counter, picking at her creation with her fork.

"Yes, ma'am. A Mr. Cavendish and a Miss Seneca Sue," Emerson announced.

"Well, tell him and his gal to come on up, Emmy," she ordered. "Let them in, and after you do, help yourself to these bacon and eggs on the counter; they're really grand, Emmy. Really grand, I say."

"Yes, ma'am." Emerson did as he was told before the eggs became cold—not that it made much difference; hot or cold, he would eat them anyway. Miss Blaine, oh so rich, paid Emerson oh so poorly in wages.

"Your butler sure moves fast for his age, Edith," I joked as Sue and I sat down on a plush biscuit-brown couch, part of a high-end living room set; the style of Mission artwork was all over the apartment. Meanwhile, Emerson disappeared into the kitchen.

"How, Sue!" Edith said as a way of greeting, trying to be cute but really being insensitive to Sue's Native American ancestry.

"Hello, Edith," my Sue said, showing no emotion but trying really hard not to slap Edith; I sensed it.

"So what brings you here, Madison, with your friend?" Edith asked, seated on the other end of the couch, showing just enough of a gap under her black kimono to confirm she had no underwear on.

"Do you know Nigel Dunmore, Edith?" I continued. "He was a former member of the Golden Dawn society."

"I heard of him by way of letters from my overseas associates, but I don't know him personally. Why do ya ask?" I sensed Edith knew more than she was letting on.

"He is in possession of an item most dangerous, and he is here in the States," I warned.

"I wouldn't know if he's here in New York or anywhere else in the States."

"And what about Rollo Ahmed?" Sue asked.

"Oh, that uppity sand Negro! I don't care for him or his writings on the occult. He does not respect me or my coven. Uppity, I tell ya, doesn't know his place. Better watch him," Edith warned.

"Then again, you should know a thing or two about being uppity solidly right hey now, Sue?" At that comment, Sue's pupils were slowly shifting from grayish black to hazel.

"He's an authority on the occult to which you can't deny." I gave respect when it was due.

"Stick his authority in a Montana cow pie and maybe it will mean something to me." Edith's temper was starting to boil over. "And why you keep staring at me like that red Negro woman!"

"It important that we contact Nigel, Edith," my Sue said, while not breaking her glare at Edith, which I saw was starting to make the tycooness uneasy.

"Well, guess what! I do not care about this fool fellow Nigel, and he better not come to my door creating problems. And you, Sue, Madison, and Rollo can take a long walk off a short pier into the goddamn Hudson! Now Emerson will see ya out! Emmy!" And with that, Edith jumped up off the other end of the couch and disappeared into her bedroom.

—

Sue wanted to go to a jeweler on Mott Street to see about another offer for the gem. After we had debated Edith Blaine's involvement in this affair, we decided to go back to Riverside Drive. Entering my office just in time, I saw Sekhmet, who handed me the phone with one of her tentacles.

"Madison?"

"Kirkland?"

"We found your buddy, Dunmore," Lt. Kirkland said.

"Where is he? You picked him up?"

"At the President Rutherford B. Hayes Hotel over on West 38th Street, on the edge of the tenderloin."

"You holding him for customs?" I asked.

"No, I'm holding him for you. He's not going anywhere anyway; he's as dead as a flounder on ice down at the Fulton Street fish market."

"Murder?!"

"That's right, my friend. Murder! The inventory firm of Rigor & Mortis has already started work on him, so you better get down here!" Kirkland ended the call.

—

Nigel Dunmore's naked body lay face down on his hotel room bed, hog-tied with life-ending bruises on both temples. Dunmore's room was in quiet disarray, with clothes and luggage thrown about—as in a robbery.

Lt. Stuart Kirkland, young for his position, took off his gray felt hat and ran a ruddy-complexioned hand through his defiantly unruly brown hair. In a dark blue suit and tortoise shell-framed glasses, Kirkland looked more like a studious young college professor than a detective.

Waiting outside the crime scene in the hallway was a thin Mr. McEwing, who worked the front desk in a double-breasted liosliath suit and red tie. He wiped sweat off his pink bald head.

"Hey, Lt. Kirkland, how much longer do we have to wait for that private eye friend of yours?" Kirkland's assistant, Muckenstern, queried as he stood among his crime scene kits.

"As long as I say so," Kirkland replied.

"Madison, Sue, over here," Kirkland beckoned us from the other end of the hallway.

Escorting us into the deceased Nigel's room, Kirkland also called to the weak-kneed McEwing to follow us inside.

"And you say room service found the body around 6 p.m.?" I asked McEwing.

"Yes, the door was ajar, and my waiter Aaron came down to the lobby and told me. I entered the room, saw the body, came back to the lobby, and called the police." McEwing wiped his brow. "What is all this about? First, the regular police came, then left, and now you other detectives show up. I have guests who are starting to ask questions." McEwing was getting pushy, repeatedly folding and unfolding his now-damp handkerchief.

"Did you notice a small box with the deceased's luggage?" I asked, ignoring McEwing's concerns while Sue waited for a sign from me.

"Yes, sir. When he checked in, he had a box with him at the front desk, but he declined to put it in the hotel safe for safekeeping. We offer that option to all guests with anything they deem valuable. Please, again, may I ask what is all this about?"

"Mr. McEwing, I cannot speak for the police; I'm just here to advise..."

"Maddy?" The way Sue said my name softly meant it was time for her to do an infinity pull. I had Kirkland usher everyone out of the room and leaned against the wall, puffing an Old Gold while Sue went to work, cupping her hands around Captain Dunmore's bludgeoned temples. After a few moments, Sue finished. The look on her face told me that conversing with Dunmore in death hadn't been cordial. During Sue's work, something on the floor caught my eye.

"Okay, Kirkland, you and Muckenstein can go back in; we're done," I said.

"You mean that's it, Madison? Okay, what gives? You mind letting me in on the deal?" Sometimes, Kirkland felt like the bass drummer in our marching band, but city hall and police headquarters liked paranormal crime cases closed quickly, and that's all that counted. He knew this, so he kept the tempo.

"In due time, Kirkland, in due time. Right now, we have to locate that box," Sue said, and with that, we headed to the elevator, my arm around Sue's waist, the infinity pull sapping her strength.

———

The evening was balmy and clear as we parked our car in front of Zoe's Harlem brownstone, hoping we might find Rollo. After endless knocks on the front door, I picked the lock open with a magenta mist and entered the dark vestibule, followed closely by Sue. I pulled out my .44 from my holster while Sue did the same, producing a .32 from her clutch bag.

"Madison, you have to stop Rollo!" Zoe called out as she made her way up the stairs from the basement, stumbling at my feet. We put our weapons away.

"Where is he?" I asked, helping an unsteady Zoe to her feet.

"Down in the basement. He tried to get me to conjure the box open, and when I refused, we struggled, but I managed to overpower him!" Evidence of the struggle showed in the bloodstains on the white and purple satin robe she wore, and her turban wrap was missing, revealing long black hair.

Following Zoe down the stairs, we entered a room filled with ambient light, exposing a shrine to the occult world. Warm ruby and black drapes lined the walls, contrasting with the cold concrete floor. A long oak table with candles at either end illuminated the outstretched naked body of Edith Blaine, with a dagger sticking between her breasts. Blood drenched her torso, trailing down her sides onto the table and beneath her armpits. The dagger was a gift for allowing herself to be lured to the brownstone. Beyond the table, on a lectern, quaked the unchained chest containing the Demon of Ebril. Off to the right side of the table lay Rollo Ahmed, spread-eagle on the floor and dazed, with some type of chalk writing next to him. I checked him for a pulse.

"Why did you murder Nigel, Zoe?" Sue asked grimly. Zoe's back was to her.

"What on Earth do you mean?" Zoe said, turning to face Sue, her expression poker-faced.

"Sister, you know what I mean," Sue said, stepping toward her. I restrained Sue and took over. "You see, we were almost at a dead end when Lt. Kirkland called us to the Hayes Hotel—Nigel's room—after he was found murdered. We were also starting to think Rollo was using us until Sue did an infinity pull on Nigel's remains, and I found this on the floor in his room," I said, producing Zoe's gold scarab pin.

"That limey bastard. He said he loved me and that when he got stateside, he and I would have the box to help us do as we pleased. But before he arrived, that poor, educated fool Rollo had cabled me that he was on his way to stop Nigel, not knowing I was with Nigel since day one.

"I was to secretly meet Nigel at the Hayes. I slipped in dressed as a maid—ain't nobody going to pay attention to a colored woman dressed as a maid. During the course of sex, which was submissive on his end, he told me he really loved Edith and not a Hottentot like me. The bastard should have waited until he was untied to say that to me. The heat of the moment can kill you; it sure as hell killed him! I bashed his head in with the demon box itself, wrapped up the box in my wool, and left downstairs by the back delivery exit door like they always want folks like me to do—the same way I entered.

"Ha! Hmmm?" Zoe was losing her sanity—that is, if she still had any after what she did to Nigel.

"And Edith?" I asked, trying to figure out an end to this situation while keeping her talking.

"Oh, I iced that high-society bitch before you two came!"

"And Rollo?"

"The poor lovesick man. It's the box I love, not him. The box! And to think he wanted to destroy it. He's such a good egg. Fool Negro, he makes me sick! Ha! Hmmm?"

Saipan emerged from behind a curtain located behind the lectern. An emanation of ram-like horns had pushed its way up through Saipan's scalp, his eyes bloodred, his body naked, and his skin now sapphire blue with black fingernails that appeared clawlike. The demon of Ebril was now in residence in Saipan. We moved back from the demon in apocalyptic apprehension while Rollo still lay on the basement floor, waving me away from him.

"Zoe is your name, child?" the demon asked in Farsi, French, and finally in English, in a voice so sweet, syrupy, and peaceful, totally counter to its appearance.

"Yes, my lord, I have given you an offering!" Zoe replied, answering in the same order of languages as the demon and pointing to the lifeless Edith Blaine. "And I have also given you my servant and lover as a vessel to house your strength and wisdom. In return, I ask—"

"In return, you ask nothing of me! You beg nothing of me! It was foolish of you to free me from that shaholahi box!" The situation was changing fast. I looked at Sue, and after she returned my gaze, we both slowly moved to either side of the demon, reaching for our weapons.

The demon beckoned Zoe with a grayish-blue hand, and in the blink of an eye, Zoe was in his embrace and caress. The lips that were once Saipan's now covered her mouth, sucking all the conjurer power and life out of Zoe. Instead of screaming, bitter tears of lost love rolled down her cheeks. Grabbing Zoe by the neck, the demon flung her like an empty wine bottle up to the ceiling, cracking her skull. Landing on the floor, Zoe now joined Nigel and Edith in death.

"And what do we have here, more souls to drink?!" the demon laughed, looking from me to Sue. "This should be sporting! To the top, the very tip-top!" the demon laughed in a voice that morphed from Nigel's to Edith's to Saipan's and finally to Zoe's.

I took a chance, pulled out my .44, and emptied it into the entity's gray/blue body, filling the basement with the haze and copper/rotten egg smell of gunpowder. Sue did the same with her .32. By all that is cosmic and terrible, it would take more than bullets to rectify this situation.

"I will rule this dimension!" proclaimed the demon of Ebril in a sweet voice full of joy.

"Khodeto Bokun!" I retorted, to Sue's surprised side glance at me, not knowing I knew a little Farsi.

"Stop!" yelled Rollo Ahmed, now standing—unsteady but standing—with a blood-trickling gash on the right side of his head. "You are a FAKE! A mere djinn of no importance! Madison, you and Sue step inside this circle! Now!"

Drawn on the basement floor with chalk was a double circle, and within the double circle, a five-point pentacle with the hastily written words: IN NOMINA + ALPHA + OMEGA + ELELOHYM +

SOTHER + AGIA + TETRAGRAM + AGIOS + OTEOS + ISCHIROS. While Zoe interacted with the demon, Rollo had managed to scribble the rest of the incantation that Zoe had interrupted with a blow to his head earlier. Turning to Sue, the low-level demon blocked her path to the circle and grabbed her by the throat.

"Sue!" Rollo and I both shouted.

The hands of what would later be renamed the Saipan demon were squeezing my Sue by the neck, trying to reach her mouth to suck the life out of her. Just then, a magenta glow of energy flowed from her right hand onto the demon's hands, causing the demon to howl out in a high-octave pain. At that moment, Sue wished for a flick of a moonbeam in her eyes to bring on her Lycan condition.

"Rollo!" Sue yelled, her voice strained while struggling. "Whatever you're doing to this thing, finish it! I can only hold it for so long!"

"Madison, get the box!" Rollo ordered, just as I stepped outside the circles to come to Sue's aid. I grabbed the box off the lectern, then the ancient lock and chains placed on the table next to Edith.

"I renounce you, pretender! Back to your limbo state and eternal prison!" Rollo commanded.

"Do you not want your Zoe, your love, reanimated?" purred the demon in Zoe's voice.

"Rollo, don't fall for it!" I ordered.

"Rollo, you mug! Don't you dare!" Sue coughed as the demon lifted her off her feet.

Pulling a small beanbag-like object from his pocket, Rollo aimed and threw it at the demon as it continued to struggle with Sue. The harmless-looking bag contained asafoetida and fresh garlic. When it hit the demon's neck, it formed a mist-like necklace. Releasing Sue, its human form began to break down. The demon, like a smoke bomb thrown in reverse, trailed smoke back into the box, howling in the voices of its victims as it retreated. Once inside, I locked and chained the box. Rollo followed, wrapping two garlands of asafoetida and garlic around it.

"Now what?" Sue asked as she and Rollo sat on the floor, Rollo staring at a bedsheet covering Zoe's body, part of the sheet torn off by Sue to bandage Rollo's head. I had gone upstairs to get another sheet from one of the house beds to cover Edith's body out of respect. I then went looking for a phone to call Lt. Kirkland and his people to help close out this case and, to his dismay, clean up the mess. Zoe, Nigel, and Edith would end up in the newspapers and scandal sheets as a love triangle gone wrong as a cover story. And Saipan just disappeared, which, in essence, he did within the djinn.

"We have to dispose of whatever it is, somewhere no one will be able to find it."

"Why do you keep saying 'whatever it is'?" Sue asked as she looked at Rollo, who stared at Zoe's body with tears in his eyes.

"I say 'whatever' because if it was the real demon of Ebril, this flat—or as you Americans say, brownstone—would have been blown off its foundations. At most, it was a roguish djinn. You know, evil spirits can be cheap knockoffs, too."

"You really loved her." Sue could not hold it in any longer.

"Yes, I would have crossed over to evil," Rollo said, wiping his tears away with his chalk-covered coat sleeve. "For her."

The box shook, as if kibitzing in on their conversation.

"Really?!" Sue now felt like she should have held it in.

"Candidly… yes, I would have," Rollo confessed.

The box's shaking grew a little more intense. Rollo and Sue looked at the box and then at each other.

"Maddy… Madison… Madison Prescott Cavendish! Get down here now, please!" Sue yelled.

———

An hour later, officers were loading the demon box into what looked like a cross between a paddy wagon and an armored car. Sent by Lt. Kirkland to take charge of the operation was Sgt. Samuel Battle, a large brown man known for not putting up with any nonsense.

"Is that box chained down tight in the back of the wagon?" I asked.

"Done! It's chained to the wagon floor, Madison," said Sgt. Battle. The wagon doors shut and locked, and they were ready to pull out with a police motorcycle escort.

"I hope this idea of yours works, Cavendish," Sgt. Battle challenged. "This isn't us trick-taking at the card table, you know."

"I hope so too, Samuel," I answered. On some weekends, Battle and his wife would partner with Sue and me for Bridge at our Riverside Drive home when Paul and Eslanda Robeson were unavailable. A game of Bridge was good for me when I couldn't rest in peace during the day sometimes.

"Maddy, are you sure you don't need me with you?" Sue asked, with a head-bandaged Rollo trailing behind her as they walked up to the wagon before we pulled off for Idlewild Field.

"No, Sue, I'll be alright. Plus, you've been through enough.

Hubert's meeting us at the field. Take Rollo home and wait. Trust me, I'll be home." I sensed unease in Miss SunMountain's voice. Although immortal, there's always the thought of something other than the full voltage of the Consolidated Edison substation looming over on 110th Street that might finally get you.

Sue and I embraced and kissed. I took my Scala felt hat off to hide the private moment from the officers, Sgt. Battle, and Rollo Ahmed.

"Okay, enough of this 'Sue and Madison sitting in a tree, K.I.S.S.I.N.G.' bunk. Let's roll out!" Sgt. Battle barked with a smile.

"Oh, Maddy, I totally forgot to ask during all this rush, dear. What did you yell at the demon box? Kho...Khodeto Bokun?!" asked Sue.

"My dear, your Mr. Cavendish told the demon to 'Go fuck itself' in Farsi," chuckled Rollo before I could answer.

"Good luck, my friend," Rollo blessed me as the Ford A paddy wagon and the motorcycle escort roared out of Harlem, the escorts forming a flying inverted V with the wagon within it.

Hubert Julian, aka the Black Eagle of Harlem—pilot, arms dealer, globe-trotter, and scoundrel, as some people would judge—would also be there if you needed his help, of course, at a price. He was at Idlewild Field, waiting for our group after a call from me.

"So, you want me to take you up, fly over Long Island Sound, so you can drop a box in the sound, and that's all?" Hubert was in a mustard-yellow flight suit, leather flight cap, goggles, and brown boots, leaning against the wing of his World War I Sopwith Camel, painted yellow with black stripes and a black eagle in a striking pose on the fuselage. Dapper, with a pencil-thin black mustache, slight dental overbite, and light brown complexion, Hubert thought himself the ladies' man. "What gives, Cavendish?"

"Don't worry, and don't ask questions, Hubert," I said, as Sgt. Battle and his officers waited for the okay to take the box out of the wagon.

"Idlewild has the go-ahead, and they have a flight plan. Lt. Kirkland and City Hall saw to that."

"And payment?" I needed help, but the Black Eagle of Harlem needed compensation.

"Here, take this gem as payment." I dug into my suit pants pocket and came up with the bauble in payment for Hubert's services. "It's been appraised at $500."

"But how do I know—" Hubert protested.

"Is there a problem, you guys? If not, let's get this show on the road," a towering Sgt. Battle interrupted. "I'm no flying ace, but I do know from what I see that the wind socks are in your favor, Julian."

"All right, all right," Hubert agreed, tucking the ruby into his breast pocket and zipping it closed. Up among the clouds, Julian tried to hold the controls steady, calming his nerves upon seeing the box shake on its own as I held on to it in the front cockpit seat.

"Just a little bit more, and you can drop that box overboard, old boy!" Hubert Julian yelled over the roar of the plane's engines.

"Good!" I yelled back. Just then, wind turbulence made the box bounce up in the air, and I grabbed it, much to our sigh of relief.

"Shit, man! Sue's going to have my head on a plate if something happens to you!" a horrified Hubert Julian yelled out, suddenly remembering he'd forgotten to give me a parachute.

"Khudahafaz, Demon Box of Ebril!" I bid farewell to it, which, in return, came with a shower of multi-voiced curses as the box nosedived, crashing into the water, then sinking to the bottom of Long Island Sound, its new home.

THE
WENDEL
AFFAIR
[BEING A TALE OF ST. VALENTINE'S DAY]

1928

A late winter morning had me in bed debating whether to get up or remain stationary until nightfall. Work was slow. This business is a topography of peaks and valleys. My inner contemplations were settled by a sudden and persistent rapping on my apartment door. I threw on my smoking jacket atop my pajamas and snatched the green-tinted glasses from my nightstand. As I approached the door, I felt there was a possibility I might slug the knock-happy stranger.

"Who's there?" I shouted.

"Telegram for Madison Cavendish," a young voice announced.

I snatched the door open, revealing a baby-faced kid in an over-brassy buttoned gray messenger uniform. I made a mental note to check the building's main entryway since he should have had to buzz me for entry. After stumbling around for loose change to feed his awaiting palm, I closed the door and ripped the envelope open.

WESTERN UNION

Received at 34DV A 10
NEW YORK 547A FEB 13 1928
MR. CAVENDISH

    I REPRESENT A CLIENT WHO AT THIS TIME WOULD LIKE TO REMAIN ANONYMOUS DUE TO A STRANGE AND CONFIDENTIAL MATTER. AFTER AN INTERVIEW YOU MAY BE RETAINED AND PAYED. SINCE THE CLIENT AND I DO NOT USE TELEPHONES, WE MADE USE OF THIS TELEGRAM. WE WILL GIVE YOU TIME TO REPLY BY SHOWING UP AT 442 5TH AVENUE TOMORROW BETWEEN 1 AND 130 PM. IF

YOU DO NOT SHOW, I WILL ASSUME YOU ARE NOT
INTERESTED.

SAMUEL BARTLOW

The address sounded familiar, but I couldn't recall why. At that moment, Sue entered. An easy feat given that we both have keys to each other's flat.

"Morning, Maddy," said my Sue, rubbing a kiss on my cheek.

"Morning, love. You've come at the right time. Look at this." I handed the telegram to Sue. She was already dressed for the day, donned in a purple cloche hat, a purple wool sweater with matching dress, coffee-colored stockings, and black heels. Sue took her usual spot and sat atop my desk.

"Well, I'll be," I said. I was on my way to the kitchen to retrieve two bottles of Moxie soda for us since I was out of coffee and tea, and the only edible items in the ice box were leftover fried cauliflower and a jar each of caramel mustard and piccalilli. Sue's hectoring that I visit a market was surely forthcoming.

"You'll be *what*?" Sue asked.

"This address—442 Fifth Avenue—is the House of Mystery, a mansion owned by the Wendel family, old New York real estate money. Mucky mucks on the same level as the Astors."

"What's the mystery part?" Sue asked.

"The head of the family, John Wendel, died in 1912, and no one has seen the surviving sisters since. Only the servants have been seen going in and out of the mansion as servants do. A tour bus even rolls by on Fifth Avenue with out-of-towners gawking at the place." I sipped my Moxie while Sue sat on my desk staring at her soda, which she thought tasted vile.

"Who do you suppose referred them to us?"

"I guess we'll have to wait until tomorrow afternoon to find out."

The rest of the day was spent filing old affairs into our file cabinet, then it was off to Bohack's Market to forage for supplies. Once back at my apartment, Sue decided to guest with me for the night. We slept until late morning the next day.

—

Afternoon found us at Wendel's address.

Wrought iron gates separated our 1920s Jazz Age modernity from the Wendel's nineteenth-century Gilded Age comfort, yet Sue and I, having both been born in 1885, could sympathize with the Wendels living in this mansion anchored on the corner of Fifth Avenue and East 38th Street. The golden lion's head knocker was loud against the door but produced no activity from within the place. I took an impatient turn to leave.

"Wait a minute, Maddy. Someone's coming." Sue had picked up the faint sound of shoe heels on the floor. The door opened without fanfare—no haunted house creaking schtick. There was, however, a rush of stale air combined with an assaultive, putrid mixed scent of mothballs. It was also apparent that one or more cats had free reign to piss within the mansion. Our noses crinkled. The aged decay of a once-important New York family was the secret of the House of Mystery.

"Good afternoon. I'm Samuel Bartlow. Your presence tells me that you received my telegram. I handle most of the Wendel family affairs along with Martha Edmonds, the family attorney, and Paulson, who manages all Wendel property both upstate and here in the city. Follow me, please."

Bartlow was white-haired with a walrus-style mustache. His dark suit, replete with stray hair, confirmed the presence of a feline.

"I need to ask you a few questions. If I'm satisfied, I'll retain you two. I'll introduce you to Miss Ella at the end of the interview. Is this agreeable to you?"

We nodded, and Bartlow guided us by candlelight as it appeared the house had not been wired for electricity. We entered a large room with floor-to-ceiling bookcases on each wall. The massive library housed several thousand ancient tomes. We were directed to a pair of stuffed velvet purple chairs on either side of a doily-covered table. Bartlow sat in a nondescript wooden chair and faced us. The Baroque-style candleholder on an oak desk next to us stretched our shadows along the bookshelves.

"I assume you both have experience in the paranormal?" asked Bartlow, producing a wedge of letters from a suit pocket. The cache of papers was tied by a red ribbon.

"Mr. Bartlow, what is the specific problem that needs to be solved?" my Sue asked.

"I would ask that you answer my question first, my dear," said Bartlow, playing with the now untied collection of letters like a deck of cards. I was intrigued as to their content.

"Madison and I have more than thirty years combined experience in matters of the paranormal," Sue answered.

"You can communicate with the dead?"

"It's among our specialties. We sometimes engage in séances or use other methods to connect with the other side," explained Sue.

"I trust our resumés are satisfactory. Now tell us what this is all about," I said, my patience waning. "Get to the heart of the matter, man."

"Of course. Simply stated, one of the Wendel properties is haunted." Bartlow shifted in his chair as if he struggled to believe his own admission.

"Continue," I prodded.

"Miss Ella Wendel is the last of the Wendel family. There are no other heirs. Miss Wendel, along with her late sisters—Augusta, Georgiana, Corina, and Rebecca—and their brother, John, have vast real estate holdings in greater New York and upstate. Miss Ella believes her time on this mortal plain is short. She wishes to donate most of the property in an expedited manner. As the head of the family after John's death in 1912, she feels Rebecca and Corina's property should go first. Rebecca had revolted against John's wish that the sisters never marry by wedding Luther Swope in 1903 and relocating to Central Park West. The following year, Corina fell in love with and became engaged to a man named Ethan Collins. The couple had contracted with local builders to have a mansion built upstate near the village of Apple Tree, New York as their newlywed home. They took residence in a nearby cottage in 1904."

"I assume things didn't work out for Corina," Sue said.

"I felt so bad for Corina. It seems Ethan got cold feet weeks into their marriage. He was last seen with a carpet bag, leaving his flat and disappearing. Some say he hightailed it to Alaska in search of gold, though the precious metal was largely played out up there by then. Others whispered that John Wendel had him done away with. The ordeal proved too much for Corina. She lost the zest for life, stopped eating, and died an emaciated shell of herself in 1905. Construction was halted on the mansion that year, and it has been in a structural purgatory until recently," explained Bartlow.

"And now?" I asked.

"It's to be converted into a rest home for old and disabled railroad workers formerly employed by the New York Central Railroad." Bartlow seemed to develop a cramp in his leg and stood up to stretch, walking over to a bookshelf and pulling out a book he most likely had no intention of ever reading. He seemed fidgety.

"And so?" I ask.

"As I said, the mansion is supposedly haunted. Workers refuse to stay. The sound of a woman crying on the second floor is often heard at night. Shrill screaming from the basement is a regular occurrence. Windows installed are found broken the following day. The glazers replace them only for the glass to be broken yet again. The loss of time and money has made the situation most urgent, bordering on untenable. Paulson had resorted to patrolling the grounds at night with a shotgun, but fear has now got the best of him, for he admits most likely a shotgun won't 'stop the enigma.'"

"Have you witnessed any phenomena yourself?" asked Sue.

"I don't believe in such rubbish," scoffed Bartlow. "I've been in employment to the Wendel family most of my adult life, mainly with Corina until she left us. Never witnessed anything strange. This is Miss Ella's doing, not mine. Now, if you two want an item that may help you. The original property had an old ghost story—or tall tale, if you will—about a Torie loyalist family that had a farm on the property. The story goes that the family was massacred and the farm burned down by colonials during the revolution. Do you perform exorcisms?" Bartlow abruptly asked. I found it peculiar that Bartlow derided the paranormal in one breath but asked about exorcisms in the next.

"We do what it takes. Besides séances, we use Carnacki methods, Shamanic rituals, Infinity pulls, *Blue Book* incantations, Rollo Ahmed's *Black Arts Guide* book recipes, and/or prayer." Sue stated. "We'll even try the scientific Flaxman Low route if necessary."

"References?" Bartlow handed me the letters. I recognized the name and address on the top letter.

"You can cable E.E. Just, a biologist at Woods Hole Laboratory in Massachusetts; Waldo Fenner, an operations manager for the BMT subway; Stuart Kirkland, head of the Office of Special Concerns; Mrs. Kingfield's, owner of the Pilgrim Hotel in Manhattan. I could go on. But tell me, Bartlow, how did you find us?" I asked simply for confirmation of the address on the letters.

"The late Dr. Washington Allende. We were mutual friends by way of the Murray Hill Correspondence By Mail Chess Club. When not trying to checkmate me, he sometimes wrote letters confiding in me about the strange 'Affairs' all of you handled for the city Office of Special Concerns. At the time, I thought better than to believe them. Now, however, time, money, and Miss Ella's wishes are paramount. Although I remain skeptical, I'll do anything to get this project finished." said Bartlow. "You may retain the letters, Mr. Cavendish."

It was odd, considering Allende was a solid debunker at constant odds with Sue and me. He'd met his end four years earlier during the "East River Affair" of 1924.

"Although Allende believed in your work behind closed doors, the good doctor couldn't admit this publicly. He envied your strangeness. His word was good enough for me, so I will not be contacting your former clients," said Bartlow with a smile.

I have no idea if Allende wrote in depth about my background, but if Bartlow peeled back the onion skin, he would have certainly found out about my mother, Miss Isabella Denton, a white woman, who not only jumped the fence with my father, Edward Cavendish, a Negro educator, but had also jumped the broom by giving birth to me. Sue, of course, was descended from Negro and Native Americans from Seneca Village in what became known as Central Park. If Bartlow knew of our backgrounds, he never voiced it.

"Please," he continued, "I need the spirits gone if they are behind the trouble. For Ella's, New York Central's indigent workers, and for my sake," pleaded Bartlow, retreating behind the desk to sit and pull out a checkbook from a drawer. "Write in the amount to you and your partner's satisfaction, within reason," Bartlow said in a tight-fisted warning.

"Has anyone considered that Corina might be the unsettled apparition?" asked Sue.

"As sad as her mental and physical condition was self-inflicted, I believe she's with the good Lord now in His glory and in a better place. Now let's go see if Miss Ella is awake so she can meet with you two. She likes to nap before supper," explained Bartlow, ushering us out of the library. Down a hallway begging to be dusted, Bartlow stopped at the entrance to a sitting room and cracked the doors open, barely enough for Sue and me to peek over his shoulder at Miss Ella, nestled asleep in a brick-colored, stuffed leather chair. Hair sliver, Miss Ella was dressed in all black, as if in mourning for the 19th century and repudiating the more up-tempo 20th century. We departed the dusty House of Mystery and retreated back to Riverside Drive to prepare ourselves for the affair ahead tomorrow.

—

Just outside Apple Tree, Upstate New York, Paulson opened the front gate for our metal cherry-red '27 Pierce Arrow 80 to drive up to the front of Corina Wendel's star-crossed mansion, surrounded by pastoral rolling hills. The grand lavishness of the Queen Ann-style mansion gave silent testimony to the late Corina's rebellion to the taste of her family's Federalist Fifth Avenue household. An unfinished ode to her pigeon-hearted, town-skipping fiancé, Ethan Collins, a heavy heart had made her reclusive and, in turn, waste away. An editor friend of ours at the *New York Herald Tribune*, Stanley Walker, had done a quick news item search on Collins for us. It seems that an unconfirmed story about Collins circulated that he may have blown himself up in Alaska in 1909 during a drunken attempt to thaw out a few sticks of dynamite.

I parked behind a black Studebaker Dictator and discretely checked the item I had earlier placed in my tweed winter coat and met up with Sun. Meanwhile, the driver-side door of the Dictator opened, revealing a tall woman sporting a dark cloche hat with curly blond hair peeking from under it in a dark wool coat hopped out of the Dictator and walked toward us. Her eyes, intense blue like mine, gazed at us with scrutiny.

"I'm Martha Edmonds, Esquire. A hearty hello to you two. I'm the Wendels' lawyer," Edmonds said. "Bartlow asked if I could drop off this extra set of keys for you since I live not too far in the village of Apple Tree near the Teutonic Parkway. Paulson will help you with your needs, at least until sundown. After that, he takes a powder." Edmonds smirked as a gray, receding-haired Paulson limped up to us in a three-piece dark corduroy suit. Chilled, sour look on his face, similar to Bartlow's, I suspect that he, too, must have sacrificed the best years of his life to the Wendel family.

"Madison Cavendish and Sue SunMountain," I said by way of introduction.

"Good evening," Paulson said, without a smile. "Nice to meet you." Paulson wasn't wearing an overcoat, which, for this time of year, signaled to me that he was a tough old bird or a fool.

"With all due respect, I think this entire matter is a waste of time and resources." It was clear that Edmonds had a robust candidness.

"How so?" Sue asked.

"Most paranormal incidents, if given time and deduction, can be explained. These incidents have occurred recently, which makes me think someone very much alive is behind them," Edmonds said, staring at Paulson, who gazed back with venom.

Edmonds jingled the keys into my hand. "Be forewarned: If I get the slightest notion that you two plan to nickel and dime Miss Wendel for expenses, you'll be hearing from me," Edmonds, the occult no-nothing-novice, glared at the three of us as if Sue and I were in cahoots with Paulson.

"Miss Edmonds, we take our work seriously, as I'm sure you do," retorted Sue. "We're not running a racket."

Edmonds ignored Sue's remarks. "I would take you two on a tour of the place, but my husband and I have tickets for a play, *The Butter and*

Egg Man. It's running at the Longacre Theater, and we don't want to be late. Besides which, haunted or not, I don't exactly care for this dreadful place. Knock it down is what they need to do!"

Edmonds folded into the front seat of her auto and wheeled the Dictator off the property. Paulson limped with us on a tour of the picked-bare apple orchard near the regal mansion like a dour museum guide, that is, until he noticed the changing tint of the sky, signaling a winter dusk sunset.

"I've made you two a bed in a bedroom on the second floor. Go to the top of the stairs and turn left. You'll see the door open. The electricity is out of service. I've left wood and a bucket by the fireplace so you can heat some water from a pump outside. Cans of goose paté, Armour dressed beef, beans, utensils, and dishware are in the pantry. Understand that construction stopped on this white elephant in 1905 and didn't resume until recently, so whatever you two are attempting to do, sorry for you having to rough it. But if it's what Miss Ella wants…" Paulson trailed off. He handed us some mothball-scented linens he'd retrieved from his auto.

"Paulson?" I asked, trying to squeeze some answers out of him as he hurried to get into his overcoat and cap.

He stopped in a limped rush. "Yes? What is it?"

"Is it Corina ?" I asked.

"I don't know. But I am certain Miss Edmond is wrong. These incidents have been transpiring for years. If it is Miss Corina, she's happy if you can call it that when she's upstairs. But down in the basement, she's melancholy and angry. That's where we found her when she snapped her sanity in two—in a corner mumbling nonsense. I guess the moment of clarity finally hit her, realizing Ethan was gone, no letter, no telegram… nothing. Only a report of the bum skipping out of his flat and out of town, carpetbag in hand. Well, the sun has gone, and now I'm gone, too. Good luck and, for God's sake, be careful." We watched from the sidewalk as Paulson hopped into a Buick Master parked off to the side and carefully drove off along the snow-slushed road as the evening advanced. I opened the stately front door. We switched on our flashlights as we stepped inside.

"Let's make ourselves at home, dear." Sue smiled. I removed my overcoat and homburg hat revealing a tweet suit. My bewitching beauty, Sue, from beret to heels in a raspberry outfit, pulled off a dark overcoat. With the evening darkness closing in, Sue slipped on her rose-tinted glasses while I placed my flashlight in my mouth and braced it by my fangs, which, with Paulson and Edwards now gone, I let extend. I pulled closed the thick, dusty curtains to prevent any moonlight from seeping in on my gal. We hadn't checked the newspapers for the cycle of the moon and certainly didn't need Hecate's help right now.

"Sue, since… after midnight we'll be working, I… just want to say…" I fumbled to get the words out like a kid on his first day at school.

"What are you trying to say, Madison Prescott Cavendish?" Sue asked in a tone that gave me pause.

"Happy Valentine's Day!" My sweetheart and I chuckled in unison.

Fumbling the gift box out of my overcoat, I handed her a necklace and a magenta/onyx cosmic stone pendant. Moments later, she pulled out her coat and handed me a black pearl ring, which I must say was a good match for my black fingernails. I could tell we were equally in love. By our flashlight beams, we stepped up to each other, embraced, and kissed.

"Okay. Let's focus," I said as we came up for mutual werewolf and vampire air. Rest assured, there was nothing provincial about our exchange.

"*Carnacki methods?*" I asked Sue, looking over the set of suitcases and a trunk containing the tools of our trade I had brought inside from the trunk of our Pierce Arrow.

"No, love, let's keep it simple, with a combination *Blue Book*/infinity pull," Sue suggested, referencing a method she had perfected herself. I was relieved because Carnacki's methods involved the use of garlic, which, frankly, nauseated me. We set up our occult basecamp in the grand living room.

—

By the crackling amber glow of a fire I lit in the fireplace, Sue drew an infinity symbol on an uncarpeted parquet floor using a wedge of sky-blue chalk two thumbs in length after having scouted the room for a reception point. We sat on the floor, facing one another, the infinity symbol between us. She had scrawled ANAXIMANDER on the floor in honor of the Greek philosopher who, according to legend, originated the design. Next, Sue placed the *Blue Book of Magic* by C.J.S. Thompson on top of the symbol. Lastly, she place an already-lit white candle in its purity, secured by a gold holder, atop the book. All of this was a causeway to the other side since we didn't have an actual body or grave to use as a conduit.

"Grasp on to my wrists while I grasp yours," Sue said, closing her eyes.

"And then what? Doze off while you chant?" I teased.

"Hush up! You know the routine, you mug!" My Sue geese laughed and whispered, to which I made matters worse with a hiss laugh retort.

We quickly composed ourselves for the task at hand, and Sue began her incantations. Soon the air above us began to feel tight as if some type of pressure, laced with sadness, was bearing down on us, as if a milk-white mist was secreted within the ceiling. Suddenly the candle exploded between us, spraying hot wax on anything in its vicinity, including our faces. Despite the sting of the wax, we held on to each other until, one by one, phantom fingers latched on to my throat as if a hand was reaching up from the floor. I knew I was thrown on my back by an invisible force, phantom hands throttling me. The grip made it hard for my fangs to contract themselves in my mouth. I was being dragged across the floor with Sue now holding on to my legs for dear life.

"Let go of him!" yelled Sue, hugging my legs as she was dragged along to the room's entrance. Then, as if the pressure of sadness above our heads and the choking menace below canceled each other out, the attack stopped and the grip on my throat released.

"You okay, Maddy?" Sue asked. We were still on the floor but leaning up against each other's backs for support.

Gaining my voice again while chipping wax off my face, I asked, "So where do we go from here?"

"We seek them out," Sue said, rolling up on her knees to stand.

"Them?" No ghosts or sinister razzmatazz was going to get the better of this living vampire. Not whatever family who picked the wrong side during the Revolutionary War.

"Yes, it's more than one spirit. What I think should be done is I'll go upstairs and open myself up, and you stay downstairs and do the same," said Sue. While I understood channeling, I didn't like the idea of sharing my body with whomever.

After collecting ourselves, we grabbed our flashlights and exited the grand living room.

"I'll see you later, kiddo," I said, kissing Sue.

"Ah, you swell. It'll be okay," Sue replied, sensing my inner unease. I headed down into the basement.

My senses were open; something was trying to control them.

Consternation, anger, hate, and confusion flooded my mind in the vast dampness of the basement. I dropped my flashlight. I hear the faint screams and moans of Sue from upstairs. I emit a vampire hiss because I can't help her. Violent bitterness possesses me. But then the channel breaks. I pace back and forth among workmen's tools, hissing. In a far corner of the room, a scarlet red glow begins to form. It advances toward me, attempting to make an otherworldly connection with me again.

"Your play!" I yelled. Grabbing a sledgehammer from among the workmen's tools, with rage and a vampire roar, I swung through the red phantom, cracking the concrete floor again and again until part of the basement floor was decimated. Having freed Ethan, his essence merged with mine until we became one. I rushed upstairs and searched for Sue, who had, similarly, found and merged with Corina. Our bodies were now merely vessels for their temporary use. We were led to the bedroom with the nimbus stipulation that once we exposed Ethan's murderer, they would go into the beyond. Now reconciled, we gifted the lovers with the use of our physical bodies for an evening of pleasure that lasted until dawn. At the appointed time, Sue and I bade them a melancholy goodbye.

———

That afternoon, I wired a cryptic telegram to Bartlow at the Wendel Real Estate company on 175 Broadway in Manhattan.

THE CAT'S IN THE BAG AND THE BAG'S IN THE RIVER. HAVE LOCATED THE TORIE FAMILY REMAINS IN THE WOODS. PLEASE BE AVAILABLE THURSDAY EVENING TO HEAD UP TO APPLE TREE 9PM.

———

We met as scheduled, though there was a slight change in plans.

"I thought you said we were going into the woods!" Bartlow said, obviously anxious as we descended into the basement, moonlight peeking in from a small, frosted window.

Sue, flashlight in hand, and I were dressed for a soiree later that night in Harlem—white tie and tails for me.

"Why, Samuel?" I said softly, tapping an Old Gold cigarette firm on the back of my right hand, then lighting it with a magenta glow from the palm of my left hand to Bartlow's nervous amazement. His eyes were moist as if he might burst into tears. Sue beamed her flashlight down on my morbid demolition work from two days ago. The remains of Ethan Collins were laid out in a shallow, makeshift grave. A dusting of calcium oxide had advanced his decomposition but less than would have been expected.

"I loved Corina," Bartlow said. "We were both the same age. I put my life in service of this family from a young man, but when everything is totaled up, I was to most of them a Pitt Street, Lower East Side slum lowlife. John Wendel used to say I was lucky to have the job." Bartlow whined and kicked concrete dust and pebbles back on Collins's remains as if that would change his situation. "But Corina wasn't of that view. We were in love until that stuffed shirt, high-horse muck, Ethan Collins, came along with his refined gentleman horse manure. I made it my business to stop their purposed union!"

I saw tears trail down Bartlow's cheeks. Bartlow went on to confess how he had managed to lure Collins up to the work-in-progress mansion on a chilly Saturday afternoon in February 1904 on one of the construction crew's rare nonwork days. His pistol drawn, he marched Collins out to the woods, exchanged suits with the poor man (being they were of similar physique), and fired two shots into his temple. Buried in a temporary grave in the basement that sufficed, Bartlow, disguised as Collins with the aid of hair dye, a felt hat pulled down, and a carpetbag stuffed with paper, made sure to be seen leaving Collins's Manhattan Third Avenue flat from a distance so as to add eyewitness credibility that Collins had jilted Corina. As for the real Ethan Collins, his body was reinterred in the basement as workmen unknowingly cemented over his burial site.

"I guess the two of you should be able to fit down alongside Collins, right?" Bartlow asked as he quickly slid back and produced a Colt Woodsman .22 pistol from his jacket pocket.

"Now, now, Bartlow. You're not seriously thinking of shooting your way out of this mess, are you?" I asked. I glanced in Sue's direction, but it was too late.

Sue had already snatched off her tinted glasses, absorbing enough full moonlight through a nearby frosted window. Her Lycan transformation ruined her sensual, violet-hued flapper outfit. Pouncing on a screaming Bartlow, Sue knocked him down on top of Collins, but not before Bartlow fired a shot that grazed Sue's arm, singing her silvery-gray fur. Sue's half-human/half-Lycan-clawed hand smacked the .22 from Bartlow's hand. The weapon bounced and slid with a metallic sound into a dark basement corner.

"Sue, ease up," I said, pulling aside my she-wolf. She stood and straddled the scorned lover. Her maw examined Bartlow's throat with hungry eyes.

Because of his grimy actions, I gave Bartlow two choices. Option one: He would return home and put his affairs in order, then turn himself in at 3 p.m. the following day at the 240 Centre Street police headquarters. Option two: He would be given the .22, empty it of all but one bullet, and ask for mercy before ending it all right here right now. Getting his deeds off his chest, Bartlow confessed that Ella Wendel, in recluse isolation on Fifth Avenue, had no knowledge of what Bartlow was up to with Corina's mansion. Having worked for the family all these years and knowing their simple penmanship, Bartlow had become proficient at forging documents and checks right under the nose of Miss Martha Edmonds, Esquire.

On rubbery legs, Bartlow walked into the dark corner of the room. We heard the sound of Bartlow scrambling to his knees. This was followed by dull pings of metal hitting the floor as he emptied the magazine of all but one round of ammo. After a few seconds of silence, he sighed. A flash and deafening pop of the .22 sealed Bartlow's fate.

A visit to his apartment near Isham Park in the Inwood section of Manhattan found a journal detailing Corina and Ethan's haunting of his jealous mind and entries basically damning the Wendel family to Hell. Had Bartlow not taken a shot at my Sue, I would have not offered him such a stark choice to end this affair. But if you mess with my occult soulmate, all bets are off. Happy Valentine's Day.

Eventually, we would have to return after being retained by Miss Edmonds to egress Bartlow's spirit, but that's a tale for another time.

THE
STUMPVILLE
AFFAIR

1930

PROLOGUE

The new cycle of a full autumn moon cast a cold, icy glow over August Mason's farm. Mason woke at 3 a.m. to the sound of his livestock. While the old farmer hated to venture out at this hour, he needed to find out why the hens were riled. Stepping out into the darkness, thoughts of Deacon Talbert—the local priest who had been recently murdered in the early morning hours—sent a chill through Mason's body as Wellington boots crunched atop the frosted grass as he walked to the barn.

"Something's got these hens worked up," said Mason, buttoning a denim peacoat. Brown earth mixed with manure caked his work boots as he rushed to the henhouse. Hatless Mason cupped his eyes, avoiding the moonlight's glare, as its brightness made him nauseous.

Stumbling up to the henhouse, Mason blindly felt around the inside wall, eventually locating a pair of dark-tinted welders goggles, a memento from his days in the Navy during the Great War. He slipped them over his cowlicked auburn hair.

"Now, what are you ladies cackling about? Where's Mugsy?" Mason wondered aloud, inquiring about his king rooster. He suddenly felt a presence behind him. The hens fell silent in an almost humanlike terror. Stepping out of the henhouse, Mason, a loner with no wife or children, turned around to face what was going to end his life.

The creature snatched at him as razor-sharp fangs bit into Mason's right arm, snapping it off at the elbow. Blood, bone, and muscle mass splattered about in the moonlight. Mason's lower arm sailed end over end into the air, finally landing atop the weathered house roof. As shock set in, August Mason howled in pain, body quivering involuntarily. His cries reverberated into the village of Stumpville before trauma carried him into eternal darkness.

Just before dawn, the day laborers Mason had hired approached in a dirty pickup. As the headlights grew nearer, the creature, which had been feasting upon Mason's crimson and pink flesh, vanished into a nearby tree line. The hens, which had remained silent, resumed their frenzied cackle as Mugsy the rooster emerged from the crawlspace beneath the henhouse.

1

Times were tough, even for occult detectives. Our clientele, those high society moneybags who hired Sue and I to chase ghosts or perform tarot readings, had dried up as a reliable source of income. Contract work from the city's paranormal Office of Special Concerns had slowed because of budget cuts.

It was Tuesday, 12:35 a.m. Dressed in stripped azure PJs and my red smoking jacket, I was in for the night. I sat behind my desk, rolling around a nice-sized emerald from our stash on a desk blotter, wondering how much it might fetch. Off in the distance, a tugboat horn mewed deep on the Hudson River. At least the tug captain had work, unlike the occupants of Riverside Drive and 107th Street. A mug of hyssop tea on my desk curtailed my cravings as the silence of the room was suddenly interrupted.

I answered the phone on the first ring.

"Hello Kirkland," I said, aware that only Stuart Kirkland—the young "boy wonder" and head of the OSC—was the only person who would call me at this hour. "How goes it with you?"

"Hey, Madison, old pal. I'm peachy. Listen, I know that times are rough all over with this depression crud going on, so I figured you and Sue might be available for a job."

"Much appreciated," I said.

"Besides, this one's out of our jurisdiction."

"What's the affair?" I asked, intrigued.

"Upstate New York, Sullivan County. Village of Stumpville. The local sheriff, Kilroy Bertrand, has two unsolved murders which he believes were committed by… well… a werewolf."

"The sheriff's a real forward-thinking fellow," I chuckled. "How did he decide to reach out to you?"

"You remember *The Life of a Lycan*?"

"The monograph you coauthored with Sue."

"That's right. She'd used the nom de plume *Anonymous*. Bertrand read it. He thinks *Anonymous* can solve their problem up there because *Anonymous* 'must be a werewolf to know so much,'" said Kirkland.

To me, that monograph was nothing but trouble. "So what's bub looking for, a Lycan to catch a Lycan?"

"I guess so, Madison. He sounds desperate."

"Yeah, but I'm also desperate for people *not* to know of Sue's propensities," I warned. "Okay, Kirkland, I'll ask Sue. She was under the weather last night and retired to bed a few hours ago. It's her call."

"Fair enough," Kirkland said.

"One question: the village of Stumpville. This a sundown town?"

Persons of mixed heritage like Sue (half Native American and half Negro) and I (half Negro and half white) knew better than to work where we weren't wanted, money tight or no money tight.

"I'm ahead of you, Madison. Bertrand says it's an all-American, progressive town. They even have a few farms in the surrounding areas run by people of color," said Kirkland, beaming.

With that, I pulled a yellow legal pad and pencil out of my desk drawer and took down the sheriff's information.

"I'll phone you later in the morning after I speak with Sue. Good morning, Kirkland."

"Good morning, Madison."

I pulled an Old Gold from my cigarette case, lit it with a magenta glow from my left palm, and took a few quick puffs before snuffing it out in my tea mug. I left the smoky room and headed upstairs to Sue's apartment on the second floor, unlocking the door with her spare key.

"Sekhmet, sweetie. What you doing, gal?"

Hanging upside down from the ceiling, Sue's pet cat, Sekhmet, meowed. Jet-black fur tapered up to five silky black tentacles which held her in place while her forepaws played with a pink ball of yarn that trailed down to the floor among Sue's kaleidoscopic-colored harem pillows. Three innocent, copper-tinted feline eyes blinked at me.

"Come on, gal," I ordered, to which she plopped down on my shoulder, paws and tentacles secure in a piggyback ride to Sue's bedroom with me.

Sue lay sprawled out, face down in a black nightgown, throat rasping, and sniffled a sign of a cold in motion.

"Sue. Sue? Wake up, love. I think I've got a paying affair for us if you're interested." I knelt by her bed and tapped her arm as Sekhmet hopped on my love's back, doing her best cat shimmy to break Sue's slumber.

"Madison Prescott Cavendish, do we have to talk now?" Sue asked, voice syrupy thanks to her cold.

On more than one occasion, my Sue had been mistaken for Harlem starlet Fredi Washington, even being a stand-in for the actress during a film shoot. But at this hour, rolling over to see me kneeling beside her and feeling Sekhmet resting atop her stomach, glamor was not on my beloved's mind.

"Job? Wha… what is it? Where? I don't… feel so good. How much does it pay?"

"It's upstate. Stumpville. I have to phone the local sheriff in the morning if we take it," I said.

"What's he want, a séance?" She sniffed.

"He… um… wants us to catch a werewolf."

Sue sat bolt upright.

"Come again?"

"A werewolf," I repeated.

Sue's pupils turned from black to hazel. Even her happy freckles, as I liked to call them, on her beautiful face were becoming inflammatory with anger.

"Seriously?" she asked.

"I kid you not. According to the lawman, this werewolf has already munched two people to death during a full moon. As I'm sure you know, the full moon is in cycle this week. I figure we go up there, catch the creature, detain it until morning, then give it a one-way ticket out of town, no sore feelings. I know you were looking to celebrate Halloween, but we need the dough."

Sue frowned. "What if this werewolf is like me?"

My mind flashed back to 1914 and a nameless cosmic horror whose encounter in a Lower Manhattan basement had changed our lives in ways we wouldn't have imagined possible.

"I guess we'll see what happens when we get to that bridge, my love. So, how about it?"

"Let me sleep on it, Maddy." Looking around but finding nothing upon which to wipe her runny nose, my Sue playfully ran it across my pajama sleeve as Sekhmet's tentacle tapped displeasure on Sue's arm.

"Goodnight or good morning, dear," said Sue, rolling over to return to dreamland with Sekhmet snuggled in her arms. I quietly retreated back downstairs to await her answer.

2

At eight o'clock sharp, Sue stepped into my apartment while I rested in peace. Rousing me awake, she looked fabulous in Halloween-colored attire. An orange bycoket with a black quill pointing out the top adorned her head, while her body was clothed in a black-belted orange sweater dress, black stockings, and semi-heels, all cloaked beneath a black trench coat. The overnight bag in her left hand meant I could phone the sheriff.

I dressed quickly: a gray tweed suit and white shirt matched by a gray fedora with black bowtie and wing tips.

Our first stop was across town to leave Sekhmet in the care of our friends, Zoltar the Magician and Elsa Cranberry, occult detective, both of whom were on idle time. Next, we were off to Stumpville.

The concrete and asphalt of New York City in the midst of a depression faded into rural Upstate New York, also in economic blues, as we cruised up the Hudson Valley in a dark cherry red 1929 Packard 640 Roadster. After a few hours I swung the Packard onto Stumpville's Lincoln Avenue, the town's main thoroughfare, where Halloween jack-o'-lanterns sat as festive sentinels at the base of lampposts. Along the avenue, villagers went about their business, looking as if they had recently stepped out of a Norman Rockwell canvas. A few individuals of color confirmed what Kirkland had told me.

While Sue's nose continued its defiance, I parked the Packard in front of Sheriff Bertrand's office. The building was sandwiched between the Stumpville Post Office and an American Legion post that doubled as the mayor's office. I made an educated guess that Stumpville's population hovered around 400.

"Hey there, you must be Madison Cavendish and Seneca Sue. If not, I'll have to write you a ticket for parking in front of the sheriff's office in a spot reserved for official business," chuckled Sheriff Kilroy Bertrand, puffing on a pipe, hand outstretched to greet us as we stepped out of our automobile. He was a hearty soul, the kind you'd expect was born to work in law enforcement. Average height, rust-colored wavy hair under a dark felt hat, rosy cheeks, defiant light brown eyes that would rather squint than wear glasses, Bertrand wore a black suit covering a tieless plaid shirt. A badge on his lapel and a Smith and Wesson .38 holstered in a gun belt hanging at an angle below his pants belt were the only indications of Bertrand's occupation.

"Please, come inside. Glad you came," he said, as we entered into a drab pastel green atop Kelly green office with wooden courtroom-like barriers, benches on one side, front desk on the other. Bertrand ushered us into his office, past two deputies in khaki uniforms, each wearing surplus New York City police caps and engrossed in a game of chess. Dimly lit holding cells loomed in the back of the building.

"A few introductions are in order," Bertrand said, pointing to the three individuals seated at a table before us. "This is Mayor Douglas, Miss Katherine Livotti, and Doctor Neilson Zellner. They sort of make up the village council. We had a fourth council member, August Mason, but he was killed during the last cycle of the moon."

Sue, Bertrand, and I found empty seats. Mayor Douglas, a rotund man in an expensive navy pinstripe suit, had that old Roman Warren G. Harding look about him. Miss Livotti, a lanky woman with midnight dark hair saturated with pomade, looked tired in her royal-blue dress. My impression was that she just wanted this problem to be over with. From the dagger-cold stare he issued, I suspected that the salt-and-pepper bearded Dr. Zellner, decked out in a blueish-gray double-breasted suit, didn't want us here. He wasted no time confirming my suspicion.

"I just want to," Zellner began, "for the record, voice my objection to this whole affair. It's a waste of village time and funds. Meaning no disrespect, what precisely do we know about these two hokum artists anyway?"

"Calm down, Neil," said Mayor Douglas. It was becoming obvious that this council wasn't exactly pleased with our presence. "We've already voted in favor of hiring Mr. Cavendish and his associate to help our village, and by Saxon, that's what is going to be done!" The mayor's voice rose to a bellow.

"Please, everyone, let's relax. We are most certainly *not* hokum artists," said Sue as she sniffed, to which the council lightly smiled (though I continued to receive icy looks). After giving them a redacted oral resumé, Sue asked, "How about letting us and the sheriff work out details and a plan in private?"

The council nodded in agreement. Filing out of the sheriff's office, the good doctor seemed to be preoccupied in thought.

"Thank you," whispered Miss Livotti, finally perking up.

Bertrand retrieved a desk map of the village and surrounding area. Two red pencil-marked Xs denoted the recent killings and the time the bodies were found.

"Deacon Talbert died here," said Bertrand, pointing to a church in the south end of the village. "August Mason died here." An X marked his farm just outside the east end of the village. "I feel the next attack will come in the north end," surmised Bertrand. I made a mental note that the sheriff's prediction seemed odd.

"Okay, Sheriff," I said. "We'll need a pair of handcuffs, your map, and some type of anesthesia like diethyl ether."

"That's no problem, Mr. Cavendish. I'll have one of my men catch up to Dr. Zellner for the ether."

"We'll set to work around 11 tonight."

"I've set you up with accommodations. Drive further down Lincoln Avenue and you'll see the Doyle Hotel. Old Paddy Mullins will be behind the front desk, most likely napping. He'll have two rooms ready for you. I didn't know if you two were married or not, and we don't do hot sheets up here," chuckled Bertrand. "Across the street is Carmella's Chop House. Put anything you order on Mayor Douglas's tab." Again, Bertrand chuckled.

"We'll be sure to do that." Sue sniffed.

We soon headed down Lincoln Avenue. While stopped at a red light, I watched as a woman in a pea-green coat and tam with matching clutch bag chatted with a merchant in front of a sundry storefront. Next to her, a cherubic little girl dressed as a smaller version of her mother munched on a shiny scarlet apple. Me and the cornsilk ponytailed child made eye contact. I smiled and turned my green-tinted sunglasses that protected my eyes and caught the light as it turned green. The little darling launched the apple into the car like she was on the mound at my beloved Polo Grounds, knocking my fedora off. Sue sat, too into her cold and her eyes closed to notice. I felt an unexplained, strange vibe about this place, but couldn't understand why.

3

At Doyle's Hotel, we settled into our rooms to freshen up before crossing over to Carmella's Chop House.

"You're having steak. The iron will help with the cold," I explained.

"I'm really not hungry," Sue said.

"A rare steak for the lady. Hot water for me," I told the waitress, as she stood over our table.

"You only want water?" she asked.

"Yes. Hot water. For hyssop tea."

"We don't serve hyssop tea." The indignation was palpable.

"Then I suppose it's a good thing I brought my own."

The raven-haired waitress jotted down the order with Hellenic disdain and stepped away.

At the appointed hour, we got to work. This consisted of driving around the north side of the village, car windows rolled down so that Sue, despite her cold, might pick up the werewolf's scent.

Dawn finally arrived. Low on gas and with nothing to show from our nightlong patrol but a shivering Sue, we returned to the Doyle Hotel, where I made Sue a hot cup of hyssop tea with lemon.

"Get some rest, love. I'll be back to your room around 11 p.m.," I said, but the tea had already sent Seneca Sue SunMountain to Morpheus. Before turning in, I gassed up the Packard at a Sinclair station. The attendant seemed roiled when I asked him to fill the tank. We were a long way from New York City.

4

"I'm feeling better, sweetie." Sue smiled as we started our second night of werewolf hunting, just one hour prior to Halloween Day. Similar to the night before, Sue wore only her trench coat, a pair of maroon house slippers, and rose-tinted glasses. This after so many ruined dresses resulting from spontaneous transformations. A change of clothes was in the back seat of the car. Cold gone, Sue enjoyed the night air for a few mundane hours.

"Ooh… woo!" Sue grabbed my right arm suddenly. "Maddy!"

"What's wrong? You pick up a scent?" I braked the Packard to a stop.

"Yowzah! This village! I can smell so clearly now! This is… Maddy, we're in a village of werewolves! I can detect their scents all around me. Feel their blood pumping. One of their pack is sick."

"Well, hot damn, this is a problem!" I exclaimed.

Indeed it was a problem, particularly for me, a living vampire. Historically, werewolves and vampires did not coexist well. This explained the vibe I felt earlier, not to mention the apple to my fedora.

"Quick, continue down the road a bit more until I say stop!" ordered Sue.

I drove along until her cue, stopping in front of a pleasant, whitewashed, two-story house. A well-picked pumpkin patch appeared to be the source of the jack-o'-lanterns lining Lincoln Avenue. Beyond a tree line nearly naked of leaves, a large shadowy figure emerged and trudged toward the house. A little girl screamed from inside the house, its lights off and curtains drawn. The minty glow of the moon provided a spotlight for the final act of this affair.

A large, puss-dripping pink mass pushed its way out of one of the dark fur shoulders of the former Lycan. No longer a werewolf, it was in the process of sprouting a second head. The maw of the first head sagged as if having suffered a stroke. One leg, devoid of fur, was rubbery black skin. Presently, the thing turned in our direction. Sue handed me her eyeglasses before leaving the Packard. She then slipped out of her trench coat, kicked off her slippers, and flicked her head to the moonlight. Knocked to the ground, on hands and knees screaming, her eyes bled as they turned from blackish red to bestial hazel. A grayish-magenta fur rose to cover my love. I issued a vampiric hiss, but before leaving the Packard, checked my Colt .45. Though loaded with silver bullets, I felt it would be lacking, so I removed my suit jacket. If I had to jump in, a vampire versus werewolf encounter would not be pretty. Doubtless, it would be more deadly and chaotic than a Pier Six longshoreman's brawl along the Hudson.

A horrid, grappling struggle ensued as Sue and the creature slammed into each other. Claws swiped, dirt flew, and pumpkins were crushed beneath the moon's stoic beam. I glanced quickly back at the house. The curtains, now pulled back, revealed the same apple-throwing little girl, mouth open in horror. A moment later, an unseen person snatched her away. Sue's claws were wrapped tightly around the creature's throat as she struggled to avoid its bite. A deadly tug o' war, which seemed to last forever, played out before my eyes. Sue gained the upper hand by lifting the creature off the ground before eviscerating it with a clawed swipe that dropped the were-thing to its knees. Steaming innards spilled out onto the frosty dark ground. Another swipe from Sue decapitated the beast. Its head spiraled like a football in search of a goalpost, blood misting into the night air. It landed beyond the tree line and rolled into the woods.

———

"Put that shotgun away, man!" I minced oath to the shadowy figure pointing the weapon at me from the second-floor window of the house. "I need to use your phone to call Sheriff Bertrand. I also need a sheet to cover the body and water for my gal to wash up. We're working for the sheriff and the village council."

I clutched the were-thing's head, which I'd retrieved from the woods. Sue was bent over the back of the Packard, vomiting. Whoever held the gun likely didn't know that a full side of buckshot wouldn't kill me. After a quiescent few minutes, the door opened. A plump man wearing a nightshirt stood in the doorway.

"Name's Culver," he said, handing me a sheet. "I already phoned the Sheriff's Office. Deputies Trusdale and Issacs are on their way. Your lady friend is welcome to come in and wash up."

In the distance, Sue began transforming back to her sparkling human form. I yanked the sheet from Culver, placed the were-thing's head in the pumpkin patch next to its torso, and covered the remains. I then helped a dazed Sue to the house before waiting inside the Packard for the deputy sheriffs to arrive and for the sunrise to reveal who rested under the sheet. *Where*, I wondered, *is the good sheriff?*

5

"Help me understand something," I insisted, stepping up to Sheriff Bertrand's desk as he sat behind it with folded hands. "Since Stumpville is a village of werewolves, why didn't you take care of Miss Livotti's situation yourselves?"

Sue stood behind me, dressed from cloche hat to heels in black as if in mourning for Miss Livotti, whose vacant chair was next to Mayor Douglas and Dr. Zellner.

"Mr. Cavendish, I'm sorry," Bertrand said. "The people of this village have, for decades and from around the world, immigrated to Stumpville for a safe haven away from being butchered over lies and folklore. It's no accident that our village is named after Peter Stump of Germany and I myself am a descendant of the Bertrand family of France, so-called infamous names in Lycan history. Our ancestors settled in peace and harmony but with two rules: One, do not harm humans. Two, Lycan shall not kill Lycan."

"So, you made me, an outsider, her catspaw executioner?" Sue asked, trying to keep her anger in check.

"She made *you* her own executioner, Sue," said Dr. Zellner, choking back emotion. "I loved Kathy with all my heart. Earlier this year, she made the fatal mistake of picking and cooking wild mushrooms. The variety she picked, while nonpoisonous and delicious to humans, were poisonous to Lycans from Southern Italy. She developed rabies. After farmer Mason's death, by her own volition, Kathy decided something had to be done. Sheriff Bertrand stayed with me all night so I wouldn't interfere. How I loved that woman."

Now shaking, Zellner eased into his lover's vacant chair, head in hands, sobbing.

"You loved her? Yet now, Sue, the love of my life, has become infected with that mushroom-triggered rabid illness!" I couldn't help but be tempted to make the doctor his own patient. "You could have told us!"

"Maddy, calm down, you lug. Whatever toxins were in me are long gone, or have you already forgotten the heaving incident behind the Packard? I'm as good as gold, and you're still my man," said Sue, planting a kiss on my immortal cheek to the mayor and sheriff's blasphemous gawks. A vampire and a werewolf canoodling, indeed!

"On behalf of the Village of Stumpville, I apologize for any duress. Katherine Livotti, rest her soul, is now at peace," said Mayor Douglas, speaking in an official tone as he handed us an envelope containing our wages.

"Madison and Sue," said Bertrand, as he escorted us out of his office to our Packard, a gray leather-bound book under his arm, "don't think what I'm going to give you is quid pro quo. It's from the heart. Tomorrow is All Saints' Day."

Sue and I stared curiously at Bertrand, unsure where he was headed.

"I'll be sending down to the city a truckload of venison meat on ice and apples. Seeing how times are hard down in 'Olde New York,' we in the village figured we could help out."

We nodded appreciatively.

"And look," the sheriff continued, "some nefarious person has placed two bottles of deer blood and a jug of fine applejack in your vehicle. We're still in prohibition, you know, so I hereby order you to drive the applejack out of city limits and enjoy it. Lastly, for you, Sue, a tome on Lycan heritage."

"*Histoire le Famille Bertrand*," Sue said, reading the title.

"I wish vampires had a village like this," I lamented.

"Corcosa," said Bertrand.

"What's that?" I asked.

"Corcosa, New York, up west near Buffalo. Them boys and gals up there like to work the midnight shift on the grain silos and elevators. We reached out to them, even challenged them to a game of baseball once, but they have yet to reply. Maybe they don't know the difference between a winged bat and a baseball bat," chuckled Bertrand.

Sue and I winced at the sheriff's attempt at humor.

After saying our goodbyes, Sue and I headed out of Stumpville. Halloween evening festively encroached. Children in costumes and others as natural walking-upright wolf cubs were already trick-or-treating. We were invited to stay for the grown-up activities, which included a Mardi Gras—style bash around midnight, a Lycan run in the surrounding woods, and an oration for Miss Livotti, but we were both missing Sekhmet and wondered what sort of feline mischief she'd been up to.

I stopped for a red light and saw Mrs. Culver with her apple-throwing daughter, Emma, dressed as a pirate and approaching us from Lincoln Avenue. The little darling released her mother's hand and ran up to the Packard. But instead of throwing another apple, she nervously handed me the candied variety before running back to mommy.

"Happy Halloween, Stumpville," I said, as we motored off back down to the Big Apple.

EPILOGUE

The sheriff was good to his word. We donated bags of apples and boxes of venison to folks in Harlem, the Bowery, and Hell's Kitchen. They needed it a lot more than we did.

In the years that followed, Sue and I made an annual October trek to Stumpville, each year growing more appreciative of its small-town charm and the glow of jack-o'-lanterns lined up along Lincoln Avenue.

THE
URRACA
AFFAIR

1931

A bank teller's scream rises above an exchange of gunshots from within the Eastern Bank at Fortieth and Third on a spring afternoon. Three masked men in identical gray flannel suits, brown fedoras, and black scarves concealing the lower halves of their faces, wave gats, daring customers to move. A fourth urban desperado is sprawled out on the floor, a bullet hole ventilating his forehead courtesy of the bank's gray-uniformed guard, now on his knees with a bullet wound to his arm. Eastern Bank's penny-pinching refusal to upgrade in design and security makes it an easy mark in 1931.

Mr. A bellows instructions to his crew, voice deep with a metallic edge. "Mister C, grab up the money bags and hustle them to the cars! Mister D, grab the bank dick! He might come in handy if things go south! Mister B is useless now—leave him!" He turns to face the unfortunate bank customers bearing witness to the burglary. "Down on the floor, boys and girls—now! If you're smart, you'll stay there for the next five minutes! Don't any of youse be a wisenheimer!"

"Please, I've—" Before hoary-mustached guard Wilbert Scanlon can finish pleading for his freedom, Mr. D raps him across the chin with the butt of a .38. "Shaddup, youse!" Mr. D, often sadistic, likes working folks over.

Mr. C and Mr. A walk briskly out the bank doors and hop into a black 1930 Ford sedan. A rubbery-legged Wilbert is pushed by Mr. D into an identically colored Ford van that sports a spinning radar dish on its roof. A fifth criminal, Mr. E, sits behind the wheel as a mysterious figure in the back turns knobs on a radio console. Under the shadow and roar of the Third Avenue El, the getaway cars peel off from the curb with an exquisite haul.

—

My name is Urraca Vauxhall, an occult detective, and this is my tale.

Evening finds me at my desk typing out a new etiquette column for tomorrow's *New York Evening Journal.* When not conveying social dos and don'ts, my other status of employment is subcontract work for my dear friends Madison Cavendish and Seneca Sue, private investigators of the occult, paranormal, and mundane.

"Miss Uvee, you ready for your supper?" It's more a timid demand than a question from my maid, Audrey Standhope, a plump strawberry-blonde-haired woman. She's holding a silver tray with my food and a folded copy of this evening's *Journal.* Draped over one of her arms is my bloodred silk kimono, which, par for the course, matches almost every item in my apartment, which has been done up in various shades of red. I adore the color.

Audrey interrupts my cerebral flow. "Wait until you see your employer's headline. Boy howdy, the city's in a crime conniption!"

"What's that you say, Audie?" Advising readers on the proper way to eat raw oysters will have to wait. Unfolding the newspaper next to my plate of sweetbreads, eggs Portuguese-style, raw carrots, and lemon tea, the *Journal's* headline shouts of another bank robbery earlier today over in the Turtle Bay neighborhood of Midtown Manhattan.

Abruptly, the telephone's bell comes to life across the room; before I can look at Audie, she's flicking the phone cord out so I'll be able to answer from my writing desk.

"Hello, Urraca? How ya doin', love?" asks Madison Cavendish in his 33rd-and-Third-Avenue-with-a-dab-of-Harlem-spice accent.

"Evening, dearest. I get the feeling the pace of my evening is going to pick up."

"What's the affair?" Pointing to the kimono, I shoo it and Audie away, sticking with my crème-red blouse, black slacks, midnight pearls, and pumps. This call is going to interrupt my viola-playing regimen after dinner, I figure.

"I need your assistance. Have you perused the front page of your paper yet?"

"I see a bank robbery. But what's that got to do with the occult?" I poke a little sweetbread up with my fork to answer the hunger pull of my stomach.

"More like what's it gotta do with *you*," Madison chuckles, which I don't find amusing. Money is tight, but a female John Dillinger I am not. "The Eastern Bank was knocked over by a gang of zombies!" Madison stops chuckling, and I drop my fork. "Part of a string of robberies."

"How do you know this?" I am skeptical; it is just too ludicrous.

"One of the robbers was shot in the head. When detectives arrived at the crime scene, the body had accelerated in decomposition, accordin' to witnesses. The bank guard, Bert Scanlon, was winged and taken hostage. Later he was found in an alley near Leroy Street in the West Village, the top of his head cracked open, and his brain scooped out as if it was a three-minute egg. As usual, when the city's Office of Special Concerns feels a case has too much weird mustard for them, they farm it out to Sue and me, but for this, we would value your help," explains Madison. Sue is Madison's partner/gal/shaman by day, werewolf by night, depending on the moon's nocturnal mood.

"And what do you need me to do, Madison?" If all this is true, it will make for an uncanny affair—the type I crave.

"I need your connections. I need for you to get the skinny on who's behind this," says my quasi-boss. You see, I'm the Elsa Maxwell of the occult world and paranormal underground. Creepy gossip mixed with blind items are what I deal in, along with solving enigmatic affairs.

"You know you can count on me. I can't turn you down, dear." I am sincere about that, given our history. I am grateful to them. Had Madison and Sue not come across me—a quivering mess cooped up in a cage due to my diabolical ex-husband Dr. Cranston Voaxhall's alchemist experiments—I would have languished away in Cranston's lab forever and a day, on Welfare Island, back in 1921. To this day, I get antsy at the sight of cages or jail cells.

"Fifty percent of the reward is yours. Plus, the Stonenan family has kicked in some money, bein' that Eastern Bank handles the Giants' vendor accounts. It's not a far reach to say, Urraca, that Harry M. Stevens is hot like one of his wieners about this," Madison cracks wise about the Polo Grounds concessionaire. I like his offer.

"Bayonne Benny." His name pops into my head. "Who?" Madison doesn't know of my connection.

"He's a ghoul that skulks about in Woodlawn Cemetery up in the Bronx. Used to be muscle for Kid Dropper out in Coney Island. Made the mistake of shacking up with a strumpet from the Bronx named Molly, who poisoned him in a fit of green-eyed envy. She got the chair, and he got a huzzah of a funeral. I'll take the job." Due to the sorrowful economic times we're in, the fortune I made as owner of the Peerless candy and confection company was shaved in half, hence my current employment.

"Okay, Miss Voaxhall. Do what ya do best and get back to me," Madison says, ending the call. Not that I need to, but by doing my best, he means my femme fatale charm. I call Audie out of the kitchen. We've got work to do.

"Oh, for corn's sake, Miss Uvee. You know I hate—and I do mean *hate*—going up to Woodlawn at night!" When not fussing over me and being a total round bundle of nerves, Audie is a first-class folk medicine woman and conjurer adept in powwow from Hex County, Pennsylvania.

"Oh, come on, Audie. You know you'll be splendidly safe," I assure her.

"Well, just in case, I'm going to smudge my body with sage and Saint John's root before we leave, and I'll sit with Melbern at the front gate guardhouse when we get there. Don't want to be around that man."

"Be that as it may, Audie dear, get things ready. We visit Benny after midnight," I say, nibbling on my dinner before it gets too frigid.

—

After dinner, Audie helps me apply flesh-colored theatrical makeup to my face and other exposed areas of my skin. The special makeup that covers up my gray pallor, concocted by an associate of Madison's, Dr. Obelin Pythagoras, makes it possible for me to be out in public for long periods of time, except in arctic cold or desert heat. A transfusion of vampire blood of the cosmic horror variety from Madison back in 1921 christened me a vampire/cognizant zombie hybrid—and, if I may say, laced with a touch of Park Avenue elegance and panache.

"Please be careful, Miss Uvee," whispers Audie while securing our imperial-blue Studebaker near the front gates of Woodlawn. The second-to-last-gates legions of souls inside pass through before going up to the pearly ones or down to the gates of Hades.

"Benny's never been a problem before. Sometimes a bit too touchy-feely, but I can handle him." In a fire-engine-red cheongsam dress wrapped in a mink coat, I look delectable, but I have something more delightful for Benny in a pink hatbox secured by a pink bow.

"Well, I'll be Mississippi goddamned! How ya'll be doing? It's been some time, Miss Voaxhall and Miss Audrey." A portly Black man dressed in a horizon-blue guard uniform lumbers to the gate and greets us. Melbern St. Henry has a touch of voodoo knowledge and was behind Benny's resurrection to help get Melbern through the lonely graveyard shift hours.

"Hello, Melbern dear, has Benny been around?" I slip a crisp Lincoln fin into his hand. Melbern retreats into the guard office to examine the bill's authenticity under a lone desk lamp.

After a minute, Melbern returns and opens the gate for us. "Miss Voaxhall, he be at his usual spot, but ornery since I beat the lightning out of him in a few checker games. Benny don't like to lose."

"Well, I've got to see him, dear. Audie's going to keep you company while I go over to his mausoleum. Audie can give you a quick game of checkers while I'm gone." And with that, I leave the two of them to walk into the darkness of Woodlawn, Audie's voice making a game wager in the distance.

The path to Benny's not-so-final resting place bisects damp grass and headstones, the moisture receiving a burst of a spring breeze that rustles elms and sycamore tree leaves in the witching hour. Every now and then, I feel an infinity pull, as Seneca Sue likes to call it, when the worlds of the living and dead cross from graves of poor souls wanting to gush or moan about their former life and why they haven't entered the final gates. Sorry, I just don't have the time to chitchat.

"Benny?" I whisper into the darkness of his mausoleum. "Oh, Bennyyyy?" I say a little louder in a singsong voice.

"Well, well, well! I'll shave a cat if it hasn't been a month of Sundays since you and those gams of yours have been here to visit. I was just about to hop in my box, sweetie!" says Benny. Even though Benny is half dead, he still looks a little dapper in a tattered black suit, its style cut from a decade ago. Icy dead-as-a-halibut blue eyes and hay-golden hair mottled with mossy bald patches of gaunt gray skin shows how much of a step down Benny—a former thug, pimp, gunman, and police informant—has taken in the underworld. Benny has a Jersey accent that could rival Madison's.

I take a seat on top of his casket next to him. "Benny, I'll get straight to the point. I need some dope on a bank robbery."

"You gotta be kiddin', right? Bank jobs are for the livin'." In the light of the moon filtering into his resting place, I see his bony hand moving towards my silk stocking-wrapped thigh and shimmy away.

"Benny, it was knocked off by a gang of zombies. Come on, handsome. You've got to know something." I shouldn't have made that handsome quip.

"Who wants to know?" His bony hand is at it again. I place the hatbox between us; it is a good bulwark.

"I do. The last bank robbed does business with the Giants' front office."

"I'm a Dodgers fan, so good for them." Benny's bones crack as he shrugs.

"Listen, Benny. The powers-that-be are going to treat me lovely if I help them out on this affair. Any dope you have on the crime will go a long way with me. Here is an incentive…"

I untie the bow and take the lid off the hatbox; Benny stares down at the human brain that resides within.

"Looks yummy, doesn't it?" I bribe. "It's yours if you give me a tip on who's behind these robberies."

"Whose is it?" Although his pallor is gray, Benny's face makes a noncommittal, almost fleshy grimace as though he is looking over the brain in an Essex Street butcher shop. Benny is picky.

"Shark McCoy, a Tenth Avenue thug. I managed to get it through my coroner's connections after the cops riddled him with bullets down on Pitt Street when they walked up on him sticking up a swell. Had it in my fridge for special occasions." I let Benny sample it with a bite.

"Uh… okay, okay. There's a doctor I see named Belmont Langora. Ten years ago, he was big muck in the world of medical research on the brain's five waves after death—not the voodoo stuff our buddy Melbern does nor the alchemist necromancy bunk of your ex-husband. But Langora got caught doin' unauthorized surgery on primates in Brooklyn, so's the AMA sanctioned him but let him keep his shingle, see."

"And what's the connection to the bank jobs?" The cool night air vapors my words, but not Benny's; his are of rot and compost.

"Langora's been makin' the rounds of cemeteries seekin' out zombies or ghouls like me, givin' us a song and dance about electropulse rejuvenation. But he charges a fee, and whoever is short on funds knocks over banks to make the amount to get it," Benny says between squishy bites.

"And his location?" I push the hatbox closer for him to enjoy his thawed-out snack.

"Long Island City, near the railroad tracks behind Bloomingdale's warehouse. Can't miss the house cuz it sticks out in the neighborhood. The front of the joint he uses is an electrical massage parlor caterin' to high-society biddies on the hunt to look young again. Just a money-makin' ruse. Did I ever tell ya I love ya, Urraca?"

Wow. His *I love you* came from left field.

"Let's talk about that some other time. Thanks, Benny." I'm grateful.

"You're welcome, toots!" says Benny, sulking as I leave him to enjoy his after-midnight snack.

Back at the gates, Audie is minus three bucks via Melbern.

—

A phone call and a few starry nights later finds me in front of a sinister-looking house that could have been designed by Franklin Lloyd Wright if I didn't know any better by its modern yet temple-like structure.

"Just park up the block, Audie, and give me a solid hour to snoop and ask questions." I step out of the Imperial in a sunrise-red beret securing flowing midnight hair, wearing a red dress with a silver lizard brooch pinned to it. My gams, as Benny likes to call them, are covered with man-catching black fishnets, and I'm wearing shiny black high heels. A .38 is in my clutch bag at the ready. According to the appointment I made with Dr. Langora, electropulse electrodes attached to my temples will produce a soothing pulse that would give me vitality.

"Hello, Miss Vouxhall. Welcome," says Dr. Langora, ushering me into an azure and gold Egyptian-looking sitting room with plush couches in stalls past it. The doctor, an imposing man in a lab coat with a noticeable black widow's peak, gives off an air of European regalness. "I'm glad you kept your appointment. So sorry to have you come in after hours," says the doctor.

"Oh, doctor, I do hope this helps slow down Father Time for me per our phone conversation," I say in rich dowager character while signing "don't litigate me" release forms, freeing the doctor from negligence.

"Now that the paperwork is signed, my dear, shall we go for a treatment?" Instead of going to a stall, Langora beckons me behind a glass counter stocked with beauty items. One button clicked by Langora locks the shop door, and another click slides a wooden wall panel open. Mysteriously beyond it, primary-colored lights blink, fighting the room's darkness. "Come in, my dear. You're not afraid, are you?"

"Me? No. But it would be divine to see where I'm going." I feel around in my clutch bag to locate the .38. Suddenly, a light switch is flicked on, illuminating the room.

"Benny!" I yell.

Langora wrenches my clutch bag out of my hands.

This is *not* good.

"Benny, you double-crossing heel!" An arrogant shove by Langora has me bumping up against Benny, who plants a foul-breathed kiss on my cheek. Ew!

Sharply dressed in a gaudy tangerine and lime-green pinstripe suit better fit for a sideshow barker, a small, metal pentagram-shaped device is stamped behind Benny's right ear, blinking my favorite color.

"Listen, you! You shouldn't have come by Woodlawn askin' me questions, see!" Benny's voice is now a metallic basso profundo. His grip on my wrists is cold and tight—so tight I can feel the stitches that keep my right hand attached to my body loosen. "A dame like you likes to play with a ghoul's feelings. Well, I'll settle your hash!" thunders Benny.

"Benny, you're hurting me!"

"Shaddup or I'll blacken those pretty blue eyes of yours! Stop strugglin'! So help me, I'll—"

"Now now, Benjamin. She's needed alive…if that's what she is," chuckles Langora, hefting up my dress sleeve past the theatrical makeup exposing my gray skin. "Compose yourself, my friend. I promise after I'm finished with her, she's all yours." Again with the chuckles. A funny man he is.

"Some of that vampire blood in your veins, I'm told, could work in tandem with my electropulse console. Could be an asset to me," says Langora.

"You mean *us!*" snarls Benny.

I see a double-cross in their future. But right now, I have a bigger problem. Looking around, what I now see is a laboratory, and I get frantic. In a corner is a holding cell…

"So I guess you're going to create a zombie army and take over the world. Am I right?" Gotta be sassy to hide my growing terror.

"Please, I'm in it only for monetary gain," says a smiling Langora.

"If you play ball with me, maybe you can take Mister B's place, aka Lenox Lenny, in the gang or be my gun moll. Whaddya say?" Benny's got feelings, I guess, but …

"I'd rather hang, Benny!" I can't help it. A whack across my mouth draws a trickle of my glowing magenta blood the doctor is so interested in. I feel sorry for Benny because now he's taking it to another level. "You're going to pay for that slap, Benny."

"Lock her in the holding cell! We've got to go over the plans for the Yonkers bank job. We will tend to her later!" commands Langora, to which Benny, with a metal laugh, waltzes me over to the holding cell against my panicking struggles. With a palmed mush to my face, I'm shoved and locked in.

"See ya later, toots!" crows Benny in that sickening voice.

Langora brings the console to life before they head down to the basement. With the door left open, I hear the moans of the living dead morph into lively thug bravado. I scream as the encroaching feel of the steel cell bars starts to affect me.

"Poise, Urraca, poise. You can't go back …" I whisper to calm myself. But my screams turn to zombie moans. Looking down at my right hand, the stitches are loosening to a dangle. I start to mindlessly grab about my body.

"Got…to…be…a…way…out…Urraca."

Then I feel the brooch.

—

Leaning up against the cell bars, I take a deep breath and grapple with the lock using my brooch pin. The voice of Langora rises like a muffled college lecturer from the basement mixed with metallic-edged questions being asked. "Got … it!" I rasp. Slipping out of the cell, I feel my strength flowing back, but my right hand's almost detached.

Standing in front of the console, I have no time to figure out Langora's oscillating monstrosity's control over the gang. Summoning up all that's in me, I lift up a wooden chair with my left hand. I make like Benny's parched leathery face is the console and come down hard on it. The blow throws me, along with a plume of colored sparks, across the room. My right hand rolls around on the floor. The console's eruption is filling the room with choking smoke. Like a cerebral light switched off down in the basement, the gangs revert to their walking-dead selves.

"Back! Back! Stop! I made you! Go no further, I order!" shouts Langora, backing up the basement stairs with the sounds of a horrific struggle. I am frantic to locate my hand so I can get out. Langora's shrill screams cut throughout the lab. Fighting like the devil that he is to avoid the grasp of his former gang is to no avail. Pulled down to the gray lab floor, his former partners in crime commence their feast. Flaying the doctor's hair and skin off, his skull is cracked open to a succulent cerebral cortex. I must say that for a second, I want to join my zombie brethren, but coughing from the acrid black smoke brings me back to the job of getting out. I throw my right hand into my now-singed red clutch bag and start crawling away.

"Hey, toots, where ya goin'?" Benny asks with a shrill other-worldly laugh, yanking me up off the floor.

"You and I will rot in hades, Benny! I … I …" It's the last thing I remember yelling before the smoke overtakes me.

—

The magenta liquid life force coursing through my veins brings me out of the dark void I know all too well.

"You'll be ready to go back to your column and bass fiddle in a few days, love," whispers a pencil-thin mustache to me. Focusing my eyes, I realize the pencil mustache belongs to my quasi boss, Madison Cavendish. He's lying next to me with his sleeve rolled up, a transfusion of his blood into me courtesy of Dr. Pythagoras, who's standing at the edge of the bed I'm in, his brown face a dour mask.

I feel a nudge to my right wrist and look over to see Seneca Sue seated next to the bed, finishing work to reattach my right hand with surgical stitching.

"Yowza, honey! Glad you're back among the living, for what it's worth," says Sue, a mystical sepia beauty.

"Boy howdy to that!" Audie stands is at the foot of the bed, nervously wringing her hands. After a minute of zombie moans, my voice and syntax return.

"What happened?" Groggy or not, I have to hear this.

"Well, Miss Uvee, I didn't like you inside that place, so I shaved a few minutes off the wait time you had told me, and good thing I did. I pulled up to that evil place, smoke billowing out. I sent a few .38 slugs into the door to open it up. The panel door was a bit harder, so I hexed it open in time to see that Bayou … Bay … whatever, Benny dragging you to where only the spirits know, while the rest of those undead hoodlums were gnawing on that … that … doctor! But I fixed Benny but good, emptied the rest of my slugs in Benny's head, I did. He won't bother you no more, Miss Uvee!" At hearing this from her, I am surprised at Miss Standhope's grit.

"For Audrey to be a nervous Nellie, she sure has in her some elan," says Sue.

"Thank you, Audie." I mean it. "Now, where am I, and how long have I been here?"

"You're at Madison's apartment on Riverside Drive, and it's been a few days. Audrey felt it was best to bring you here. Everything was touch and go. That's when Madison decided to give you another transfusion," says Dr. Pythagoras, placing some of the tools of his trade back into his black house-call bag. "Audrey's a gem. She's been ghostwriting your column. I submit that you give her a salary increase." I wish the good doctor hadn't said it, but he is right, and I will.

"And?" Everyone is aware of what I want to know.

Sitting up, Madison rolls down his shirt sleeve. "The Office of Special Concerns sent a forensic squad out to Langora's place once the fire department gave the okay. Mostly ashes there. Langora was a piece of chewed-up barbecue.

That mysterious machine is blackened rubble, which makes it hard for us to figure out its function. But we do know that the gang consisted of Leadfoot Fritz, a getaway driver from Yonkers; Lenox Lenny, a gambler from Harlem; Nick the Greek, a yegg from the Lower East Side; and Roy Lamont, a sadistic stickup man from Maryland. All recently deceased. Sorry, youse two…no Bayonne Benny. The graveyard-shift guard up at Woodlawn was found murdered, and Benny's body has vanished."

"Boy howdy," says Audie. Her nervousness is returning. Me, I am more upbeat. If Benny comes back next time, I'll be the one to deal with him, not Audie. I say a silent prayer for Melbern St. Henry.

"Viola," I say.

"What?" Madison looks at me, waiting for the gag line.

"It's a viola, not a bass fiddle," I say. Everyone chuckles, even Dr. Pythagoras.

I know you'll be back, Benny. And I'll be waiting.

THE
WAR MEMORIAL
AFFAIR

1937

My sweetheart sits behind my desk, lounging feet-up. She wears flesh-colored knee-highs, a black pleated dress, and an onyx cotton sweater torn at one shoulder—to be mended once we get some dough. Sekhmet is napping atop Sue's lap, tail lazily flicking side to side as Sue strokes the feline's nape and back. I had just entered our apartment which also doubles as our place of business.

"How did the meeting go with the *little flower*?" Sue asks. "Will OSC get the ax?"

"I suppose it went okay, love of my life," I reply. "Kirkland took me to Mayor LaGuardia's private residence on Fifth and 109th, away from City Hall, to help plead the Office of Special Concerns case discreetly and explain why we should not be on the fiscal chopping block and are still a necessity. Police Commissioner Valentine, grumpy as usual, was in attendance for support, but he kept mostly silent while the mayor droned on, asking ridiculous questions like, 'What good is OSC if we're not going after the rackets, mob bums, and tinhorns?' His Pudgy Honor even cracked a fat-mouthed joke, eyeing my all-black attire and asking if I was an undertaker or a racketeer. At that point our buddy, Kirkland, handed the mayor a copy of 'The Empire Affair.'"

"He didn't," Sue remarks.

"He did. You should have seen the color drain out the little flower's face as he read the tale."

"The Empire Affair" took place back in '31 to make peace with—or make the walk through the veil in the Empire State Building—the ghost of five workers who perished during construction of the famed skyscraper. Kirkland, Mohawk Shaman Raharakwasere, Sister Bellaluna of the Holy Rosery Convent, Sue, and yours truly were tasked with exorcizing the spirits. For skeptic even-handedness, the labor powers-that-be asked to have Harlem Socialist Grace P. Campbell present as an observer at the affair. It didn't matter to us. It was an ugly job, but we'd gotten it done and escaped unscathed.

I hang my well-worn homburg and overcoat on the hat rack, then walk behind the desk to relieve Sue of cat duty.

"So?" asks Sue as she pulls the room curtains close. I begin to feel more comfortable in the darkness and remove my green cheaters. Sue takes her usual seat atop my desk.

"Sew pants," I quip. "But seriously, after looking over the file and with a little… influence… from me, OSC stays."

"What do you mean 'a little influence,' Maddy?" asks Sue. She stares at me as if she's a teacher and I'm a student who's just plagiarized a report.

"Okay," I admit, "I may have exerted a hint of mind control on the mayor. But look at it this way: everyone still gets paid and—"

My justifications are cut short by the ringing of the phone. Sue answers the call on the second ring, which, in truth, is supposed to be the job we've been training Sekhmet to handle.

"Cavendish and SunMountain, investigators of the strange and mundane."

Sekhmet raises her head and gives Sue a quizzical look with her triangular trio of copper eyes before drifting back to sleep.

"Oh… you're a lieutenant now? Congratulations. Yes. Uh-huh. Uh-huh."

The *uh-huhs* continue on for a few minutes as Sue pulls one of my top desk drawers open and retrieves a pad and pencil. She quickly jots down the caller's information. I glance at the address, perplexed, and wonder why we're needed there again. Sue hangs up the candlestick earpiece.

"Was that Major Fulbright's kid on the line?"

"Yup."

"So?"

"So *you* sew pants now," Sue answers. "The Fulbright kid wants to meet with us at the Golden Rod Bar and Grill on Trinity Place near Thames Street at 7 p.m. tomorrow," Sue giggles.

"Is this about his dad? Did the major come back?" I ask.

"He said he'd fill us in on the details tomorrow night, but in short, something strange has arisen in the major's mansion. For now, my Maddy, since our coins are too low for the Claremont Inn, let's go crosstown to Clover's Delicatessen. I'm hungry."

Sue hops off my desk and scurries upstairs to change clothes as I stroke Sekhmet and wonder what the heck is going on now with the Fulbright estate.

Flaxen-haired Lieutenant Russell Fulbright looks anything but sharp in his Navy-issue dress uniform. He resembles his mother, Lucy, more than his vanished father, Major Milford Fulbright, an old US Army mule calvary man. Father and son are a study in contrast and have been at odds since Russell's childhood. Hence Russell's decision to join the US Navy out of spite and against his old man's wishes.

He sits across from us and nurses a sweating glass of Ruppert's beer as Sue and I sip mugs of Piels-made tincture with an eyedropper of hyssop oil to chill our blood-and-flesh cravings. For reasons unknown, we need the oil or tea as a crutch more than in the past. I fear it is becoming somewhat of an addiction. We sit in a booth in the back of the Golden Rod as, outside, the lazy roar of the soon-to-be-extinct Sixth Avenue EL erupts overhead.

"I guess what I'm saying," Russell begins, "is that something is spooking around in my parents' mansion, unrelated to my dad's *ghost mirror* experiments. I don't know if it's a waggery or an evil spirit, but it needs to be gone."

"Odd," I reply matter of factly. "We smashed all of the mirrors in your father's guesthouse-turned-laboratory back in '35 after being contacted by your mother, Lucy, rest her soul, to try to dissuade your father."

Russell's father had, by then, entered into insanity with his experiments—or rather, captures of ghosts. He'd funded his projects by marrying into old money, Lucy Devens, whose ancestors founded Deven's Corners, Connecticut, in 1735. The town is noteworthy for being a hotbed of paranormal activity.

"Cavendish," Russell snaps, "this isn't a subject trapped in a mirror. It's roaming the house at night. Last month, two neighborhood kids broke into the place. Today they're sporting gray hair from having been scared shitless. Listen, I just want the house up to speed so it can be put on the market, along with the property. But that can't happen while that… *thing* is running fucking amok!"

Russell finishes his Ruppert's, then motions the waitress to bring another round. She complies, eyeing the empty beer nut bowl and then us with suspicion. The beer nuts are tucked in a napkin in Sue's clutch bag.

"What does the entity look like?" asks Sue, feeling safe enough to surreptitiously munch on the concealed crunchy snack.

"Listen, I'm a North Atlantic Fleet man married to the *USS Helena*. Most things, including my father's bullshit, don't phase me. But this does. The best I can say is that it sounds like someone or something is walking around at night wearing wooden clogs. Here's the deal: The Navy is routing the fleet to the North Atlantic for maneuvers, and I have to catch a taxi to the Brooklyn Yard, where my lady is in berth, having recently undergone maintenance. We're shoving off to meet with the NAF, seeing as Uncle Sam is cognizant of world events. I'm placing my parents' housekeys on the table. If you touch them, it means you're accepting the job. At that point, I'll retrieve an envelope with your fee from my breast pocket. Fair enough?"

Given our economic circumstances, Sue and I waste not an instant and are in a dead heat reaching for the keys. We summarily abscond with a jar of piccalilli adjacent to the empty beer nut bowl. Although, as a vampire, I can barely taste food, I adore piccalilli.

—

As a ghost finder, Major Milford Fulbright wasn't content to merely encounter ghosts. He wanted to control them. The box and burial method, along with the white candle process, were unscientific and beneath him. Milford developed a technic he dubbed "mirror transfer and containment" or MTC. He would travel to various locations across the globe upon receiving a lead.

Through various channels, he learned, for example, of the Aoi Maru mirror. The object was aboard a fishing trawler, and it purportedly held the spirit of a Japanese deep-sea diver who saw his own death by shark attack reflected back to him in 1912.

After purchasing the haunted looking glass and transporting it stateside, the major placed it in a position facing a specially crafted mirror of his own design, its bottom layered with materials identical to those used in occultist P. B. Randolph's "magic mirror" theories. It was backed by an electro-ecto suction field, which would pull the apparition into a captive new home more foolproof than a Tesla Spirit Radio. The major gained success to the point of disappearing back on that horrific night in '35.

There is little moonlight, which is good providence for Sue. The Connecticut Valley is serene at night. Red maples and black birch, their leaves long gone in keeping with the fall season, slope up across Putnam Lane before continuing on to the mansion's cul-de-sac and property beyond. We enter inside the Fulbright/Deven residence with our Pierce parked in the sprawling driveway outside.

"It would have been nice if Russell had left the electricity on," I grumble, flicking light switches in hopes that the large overhead crystal chandelier will cut on and illuminate the spacious hall. Despite possessing night vision, I remain human enough to bump into a footstool every now and then.

"Knock on wood, dear," says Sue, handing me a flashlight.

"Yeah, I do think we'll need some luck."

"No, Maddy. That isn't what I mean. Listen. You don't hear that wood sound?"

We sweep our flashlight beams across white, sheet-shrouded furniture in what I remember from '35 to be the mansion's spacious living room.

"There, Maddy! Look!" Sue shouts. Something darts behind the covered form of a loveseat.

"Hot damn. I see it!" I hiss. At one end of the loveseat, I can make out the wagging of a black tail. I motion Sue to the opposite end as I creep up on my end. Just as we crank our heads for a better look, it springs over the loveseat to face us.

"Do you see it, Maddy? Oh my goodness!"

Sue's tone signals she's feeling antsy.

"I see it, Sue. Boy, do I see it!"

It appears to be about three feet in length. A hand-carved painted image of a beige horse. Its mane and tail appear to consist of authentic black horsehair. The body is pockmarked with about ten small red holes, its eyes two chips of black coal. Strips of leather, fashioned as a rein, hang from its neck.

I ask Sue, "Do you think you can grab it by the rein?"

"Really, Love, you know how horses feel about me," she whispers.

Historically, Sue's lilac perfume and her Lycan scent tend to agitate equines. We're not sure why.

"It's a *wooden* horse, Sue."

"A wooden horse that's alive, you clodpate!"

"*Clodpate*, dear? I see we've been reading." I take the lead, changing positions with her slowly.

"Come on… uh… Knockwood. Come, boy."

I move forward. Knockwood snorts and steps back.

"*Knockwood?* Really, Maddy? Knockwood? How in the name of Aleister Crowley do you figure it's a stallion and not a mare?"

"You got a better moniker?"

I remove my tweed overcoat and suit jacket and crouch down, trying to coax Knockwood near me so as to swipe the reins.

"Got it!" I exclaim, though my victory is short-lived.

In a dash, Knockwood drags me from living room to foyer, up the grand staircase, and then back down again. Its wooden gallop echoes through the house like a radio show sound effects man playing with two coconut half shells. The reins slip from my hands, and I tumble across the floor, plowing face-first into a living room wall.

Out in the grand hallway, unable to bear the strain foisted upon it by our paranormal steeplechase, the chandelier crashes onto the floor in a thunderclap.

"Oh, Maddy," Sue says. She softly hugs me as I lean, dazed, against the wall, suddenly aware that I'm minus one fang. Knockwood, meanwhile, has retreated back behind the loveseat in a nervous idle.

"Let me try, sweetie." Trepidation fills Sue's voice. "If I can hold on to the reins long enough, I can get an infinity pull going."

"No… don't try it. Too dangerous."

My warning comes out in whistle hisses, thanks to my missing fang. Sue rises and approaches the loveseat.

"Come here, honey. It's okay, Knockwood."

In the beam of Sue's flashlight, I see her reach behind the loveseat. This time, instead of a wooden horse, an eerie, powder blue, semi-transparent roan warhorse rises up. The creature is outfitted in full Native American battle regalia, its body pockmarked with bullet holes.

Bucking the loveseat to pieces, Knockwood uses its head to violently back Sue into a corner, knocking her cloche hat to the floor. Like a *payaso* at a bullfight, I try to distract Knockwood. Sue turns to escape as bucking hooves rain down on her back. She screams just as Knockwood blinks out.

"Sue, my freckled baby doll, speak to me! Sue!" I embrace my beloved.

"Maddy… say no more," Sue giggles through grimaces of pain, "cause with that whistle you got going… you're making me laugh. One… one more thing…"

"What's that, my precious?"

"*I can't feel my legs!*"

"Maddy, you okay?" Sue asks, rousing me out of resting in peace while sliding behind our auto's steering wheel. Sue places a container of coffee, an old-fashioned doughnut, and a bottle of hot water for tea between us.

I press my tongue against my newly incoming fang before answering, "I'm top shelf. It's you I'm concerned about."

After our disappointing encounter with Knockwood, we

retreated. I carried Sue to our auto so we could undergo regeneration. Then, with sunrise taunting me, we drove to a diner on the edge of Deven's Corner to regroup. For her effort, Sue had been unable to establish an infinity pull.

"I'm all sunshine, Maddy. But, oh my goodness, this coffee is putrid!" I lean away from Sue, declining to taste the java and confirm her critique.

"I have a new plan of action. Don't know if you'll go along with it."

"What's the plan?" Sue's frown from the coffee doesn't help with the idea I'm about to pitch.

"Nellie de Carlo." I brace for impact. As if on cue, the morning sky slides into cloudy overcast.

"Madison Prescott Cavendish, I guess you're serious because it's morning. If this was a full moonlit night, I'd swear you're pulling my tail. You're serious?"

"Yes. I am."

"Let me grasp this. Besides a little wooden devil horse knocking the bejesus out of me, I'll now have to deal with Nellie's 'Old Cuss'?"

I look at Sue, aware that the 417 freckles on her face are not actually glowing with intensity, aware that this phenomenon does not really occur when she's mad (like she is right now) and that it's simply my imagination. And yes, one year ago, after I'd consumed an overabundance of gin and tonics and Sue had gotten drunk on Elderberry wine, I counted them. All 417.

"If it will end this affair? Yes."

"You're lucky I love you." Sue's frown breaks for a second with a brief smile as she fires up our 1935 metal cherry Pierce-Arrow Eight.

"I love you too, my pretty…"

"Hush up, hush up, and please, sweetie, hush up," Sue cuts me off and rolls down the driver's-side window.

Once we've driven beyond Deven's Corners town limits, Sue's face tightens with frustration. She swerves our auto and chucks the offending coffee out into the woods beyond. With a wolfish grin, she plops her twice-bitten doughnut into my tea. I hush up. We speed back to Manhattan with me resting in peace.

The following morning, Sue and I are standing outside Nellie de Carlo's residence, a basement apartment in a tenement on West 60th Street, just inside Hell's Kitchen. Of course, colored folks—or half-colored folks like us, along with newly arrived Puertorriquenos, mixed begrudgingly with Erin and Sicilian families—call it San Juan Hill.

After a few knocks turn into pounding, I apply a left-hand magenta glow, opening Nellie's front door. Street-level sunlight barely seeps into her abode. The living room is a temple to the simple life—an unfinished knitting project on her couch and a saddlebag in one corner. Nellie's Western garb hangs in a doorless closet. Candy wrappers crunch beneath our shoes.

"She's in here, Maddy," Sue announces, as she creaks open a bedroom door ahead of me.

On the closet door, held up by two sawhorses, rests Miss Nellie de Carlo.

Motionless, her eyelids half open to expose pale green pupils, Nellie's arms cross her breasts. Her coffee and milk-toned skin is covered by a grandmotherly calico nightshirt. Nellie's auburn hair flows along her sides, ending at her waist. Suede, forest-green cowgirl boots with *Calochortus* and *Rumex* flower designs adorn her feet. The door shows signs of spur scuffing.

On the floor in an empty pie tin, enmeshed with bits of custard pie crust, lay a flattened rat drained of its blood. I assume Nellie had indulged in a nightcap before retiring at dawn.

"I'll wake her," I announce, bending down to lace a soft, whispered hiss into Nellie's ear.

Nellie blinks open her eyes and yawns.

"Who's there?" she asks. "Crepusculo? Ocaso? Well, hot damn and howdy! Hail, hail, the gang's all here, ya'll!"

Nellie levitates off her roost doing a slow-floating somersault, holding secure her nightshirt so as to not expose flesh (being the proper cowgirl vampire from Nebraska that she is). Slightly bowlegged, Nellie lands in front of Sue and me. She hugs us and kisses our cheeks.

On a winter's night in 1879, six years before Sue and I were born, Nellie, the daughter of an ex-slave-turned-hard-scrabble-rancher, had encountered a cyanobacteria-colored monstrosity (a variation of the magenta cosmic horror that infected Sue and me) encased in a meteor on her father's property. The only difference between us was that her entity withered and died, whereas Sue and I had committed patricide on ours.

"Sorry to wake you this morning, Nellie, but we need your assistance with an affair," I explain.

"Ah, pshaw. Don't fret about waking me up. Ya'll are like kin to me. Get it." Nellie wraps herself in a pink morning robe and ushers us into the living room.

"Now, ya'll go on and tell me what's what while I go into the kitchen a rustle up some coffee for us. Just yell out what's busted and needs my help. I know you city kin like Chock Full o' Nuts, but I have a stash of Arbuckle's Coffee from out west that should suffice."

Nellie, a fish out of water or, in her case, a New York underworlder in light, emotionally latches on to our visit. Sue and I, being of the same condition as Nellie—although Sue is Lycan—can understand the loneliness and Nellie's joy in having our company.

"Nellie, how is Tenth Avenue these days?" Sue asks.

"Job's fine. During the overnight shift, I just make sure to keep drunks and the like from stumbling or passing out on the tracks. Stop traffic from trying to beat the freight trains at crossings. Again, thank ye for the job."

Nellie is what's referred to as a "Tenth Avenue Cowboy." Her job is to guide New York Central freight trains along the dangerous street-level tracks headed further uptown to warehouses. Some years back, Sue and I called a favor in to Waldo Fenner, the former BMT honcho (now in retirement). Waldo had connections in New York Central. He pulled a few strings to get Nellie the job after her stint as a trick rider with Colonel Cornpone's Dynamic Wild West Show went belly-up, one of the many victims of the Crash of '29. The demise of the Wild West Show had left Nellie stranded in New York. Ironically, during our first encounter, Nellie was our deadly nemesis.

"Other than work, I keep to myself, except for, I reckon, Holly Weeny. That's when I make the neighborhood little ones stand and deliver a nickel or candy in trade for a ride on Old Cuss," Nellie says with a smile.

Instead of the couch, the three of us sit cross-legged on the floor as if around a campfire. Nellie resumes a knitting project as Sue and I recap the affair. For a moment I have a feeling that Nellie isn't listening, but then she abruptly stops knitting.

"Ya'll got a war memorial on yo hands," Nellie says quietly.

"A *what?*" I exclaim.

"Enlighten us, dear?" Sue asks.

"A war memorial. It's a wood carving made by Native American warriors in honor of their prized horses that died in battle against the US Calvary during the Plains Wars. I reckon you couldn't get an infinity push."

"Pull. Infinity *pull*, Nellie," Sue replies.

"You couldn't grab on 'cause horses be sour on you, Sue, sorry to say," says Nellie, smirking.

"Can you help us?" asks my Sue.

"We'll split the payment three ways," I add.

"That's Jim Dandy, you two. I appreciate it. But I… uh… surely do need for you two to sweeten the deal." Nellie issues a sly, fanged smile before taking a sip of coffee. Her posterior teeth are in constant regeneration due to a persistent weakness for Barratt Sherbet Fountain candy.

"Uh-oh, Maddy. Here it comes!" Sue warns, but I'm way ahead of her.

"The doctor?" I smile.

"Yip-yip yeah, Madison. I love that brown, egg-domed cutie pie, but he's scared to visit me. I done promised him, 'I ain't gonna bite you.' Fix me and him on a date and we got a deal savvy."

Nellie was smitten and mud-bug for Dr. Oberlin Pythagoras, our mortal friend, would-be alchemist, and ad hoc assistant on affairs.

"I'll do my best, Nellie. So, are you in?"

"Deal me in. And Sue, I'll do the best I can to get Old Cuss to mind his manners.'"

Sue rolls her eyes at the frail pledge.

"I see something in the woods," Sue says, as I drive to the mansion along Putnam Lane. Sloping up to the lane from the trees, we see by moonlight a pastel-green glowing rider atop a galloping horse. The rider yells, "Huzzah!" interspersed with, "Ha-cha!" and slows to a trot, dodging around maples and birches. The horse's whinny echoes in the night air.

The waft of Northern coyote howls and whimpers push through the night at the glowing hooved movement. Rider and horse lope over the lane's low stone wall to reveal themselves.

"And a hello howdy to you two," says Nellie, reining up to our auto. A squadron of little brown bats native to the region circle over Nellie's head and then flap away, their escort service complete. Sue shudders, and Old Cuss gives a flinty underworld snort as they make eye contact, his horsehide a sleek, dark jade green.

"Whoa, whoa, Old Cuss," coaxes Nellie, trying to calm her four-legged nightmare companion.

"He's okay, Sue," says Nellie, to which Old Cuss retorts by turning his rear end in our direction, letting loose a pungent, flatulent toot.

"Okay, Nellie. Time to put Old Cuss away and get to work," I announce, crinkling my nose.

Nellie wears a dark fringe ghost shirt, black wheel skirt, gauntlets, and her ever-present cowgirl boots. A black silk scarf with a stitched green pentagram covers her hair. She dismounts with two lariats in hand.

"Come on, Old Cuss, *et relinquim. Relinquim,*" she says.

Nellie points a pulsating, Eden emerald ring at Old Cuss. To Sue's relief, the phantom horse dissolves into a mist that is quickly absorbed into the ring. My Sue looks more relaxed, no doubt happier to hear the incantation for Old Cuss to vanish rather than appear. Nellie removes the ring from her finger, placing it in her saddlebag.

"I reckon Old Cuss may not like another horse promenading with me," Nellie warns, as she hands me the saddlebag. I place it in the back seat of the Pierce.

"That's the noise ya'll spoke of?" Nellie asks.

Sue nods.

We make our way from the foyer through the entry hall to the living room.

"Okay, as we discussed, Nellie and I will take the lariats. Sue, you get Knockwood's attention. We'll be on either side of him when he chases you out of the living room. We'll collar him so Nellie can calm him down." Like cathode-ray tubes, the lariats came to life in a beryl-green glow.

"This had better work. Regeneration process or not, I don't like hooves to the back," sighs Sue, kicking off her semi-heels. She adjusts her secured rose-colored tints, modified with an elastic band, as Hecate is in full bloom tonight. A Lycan transformation is the last thing we need.

Knockwood bobs up and down behind the loveseat.

"Here, Knockwood. Come on, honey. Come on, gal," Sue beckons.

Faster than a head nod, Knockwood transforms to its roan blue state. The chase is on. Hefting up her black séance dress so as to run faster, Sue heads for the door with Knockwood close behind.

"Now!" I yell to Nellie. Sue is already outside of the mansion. She runs to a window for a safe peek inside.

The lassos sizzle around Knockwood's neck. Pushing and pulling, Nellie and I are, despite our exertions, losing this battle. Knockwood's spectral power is immense. Nellie attempts levitation to gain an advantage in the struggle but is knocked to the ground.

"We can't let go, Madison!" Nellie shouts.

Knockwood drags us toward the stairs. In the heat of the confrontation, we become entangled. The air within the house gusts up, knocking objects over. The crystals of the fallen chandelier violently tinkle. Like a storm at sea, Knockwood, in lieu of a helm, lashes us to the marble banisters and balusters of the staircase in a death pinion.

"Sue!" I hiss out with rope tight around my chest. No answer.

Nellie's rope is wrapped around her neck, strangling her speechless. From outside, I hear Sue yell at the top of her voice.

"Old Cuss out and play! Out and play! *Ingressus! Ingressus!*"

In an explosion of multi-shades of green light, Old Cuss vapors solid through the open mansion door behind Sue, who quickly jukes out the way. Old Cuss now focuses on Knockwood. The lariats loosen. Both phantom horses pull even with each other and begin to converse in snorts and whinnies they alone can understand. The Fulbright/Deven home becomes suddenly tranquil.

"I reckon they both needed companionship. Thanks a heap, Sue," Nellie says.

The rope burns on Nellie's neck, as well as those on my chest, are already in regeneration.

"Don't mention it, Nellie," Sue says. "I told you Knockwood's a gal, Maddy,"

Sue hands Nellie the riding ring before sitting atop the marble stairs. She begins massaging the balls of her feet.

"I stand corrected, Sue. But right now," Madison says, "there are still a few hours remaining before sunrise. How about we take them into the front area of the mansion? It's large enough so we can ride them around."

With that, Nellie leads them out for a stretch. Old Cuss sticks out his tongue to lick the side of Sue's face as he passes by.

"Ew! Old Cuss!" yells my Sue, mortified.

Nellie decides it's only fair and just to take Knockwood to the Dakotas for a reunion with its owner or a family member. They depart on their journey to the Wakan Tanka. We learn later, via telegram, that following the conclusion of her westward quest, Nellie had run across her former employer, Colonel Cornpone. The colonel explained to Nellie that he'd received WPA funding and was relaunching his Wild West Show. She was happy to leave her New York Central position and is presently performing with the troupe across Minnesota.

The mystery of how the major came into possession of the war memorial remains a mystery. Sue and I find no related entries within Major Milford Fulbright's notes back in '35. His son, Lieutenant Russell Fulbright, upon his return from the North Atlantic, shrugs his shoulders and says he hadn't a clue.

—

We meet up with Nellie again two months later when the Wild West Show pulls into town. It provides Sue and me an opportunity to take Nellie out for a bit of Harlem nightlife and fulfill a promise.

We arrange for Nellie and her crush, Dr. Oberlin Pyhtagoras, to meet us at 125th Street. As planned, Doc, completely in the dark, arrives first.

"Thanks for joining us, Doc," I say.

He tugs on the lapels of his tuxedo. "You mentioned earlier this was a black-tie affair. I trust my attire is up to snuff."

"The annual Mignonette Society Ball has always been a formal event," I reply. "I suspect it always will be."

"I know it's a formal event. I'm a member," Doc replies.

"I need to level with you, Doc. You're not the only guest we've invited tonight."

"Who else? Anyone I know?"

"You know her, Doc; Nellie is joining us," Sue answers.

What follows is a series of backpedaling protests so profound that I resort to using a lariat I'd borrowed earlier in the day from Nellie in anticipation of the doctor's protests.

"Obie, relax," I say, securing him within the lasso. "We've got a full card tonight. Madam Dragonne has gone through the trouble of securing Memphis Minnie and her husband to open the evening's affairs. They'll be followed by society member Ellie Armstrong, the Mistress of Modern Magic and Math Tricks. Then, direct from Los Angeles, female impersonator Fredrick Kovert will be shimmying out of his Phantom Trunk. Lastly, Jimmy Lunceford and his Chickasaw Syncopators will have everyone shaking on the dance floor."

"Release me at once!" Doc commands. He struggles against the lasso to no avail.

"We passed around a mighty big hat to fund this ball, Doc!"

"Doc, you don't really want to miss all the fun by being a grumpy Gus, do you?" Sue chimes in. She holds a thank-you gift for Nellie—a paper bag filled with Barratt's Candy.

"I've no hesitation to miss all of it!" Obie says. "Let me go!"

"Come on, be a pal," I plead. I consider a touch mind control to end his incessant protests.

"You, sir, could be a pal and—" The doctor stops in mid-sentence.

"Howdy, Doc."

Our heads turn in unison, lured by the sultry greeting.

Walking toward us from the direction of Lenox Avenue, Nellie de Carlo, dressed in a metal green, silky, draped duchess high-low evening gown, is mesmerizing. Her hair, waves galore in style, is courtesy of an assist from Sue earlier. Around her neck are necklaces of sleeping beauty and Carrico Lake turquoise, and an Esmeralda-green pendant depicting Old Cuss and Knockwood playing horse tag in a mist. Cowgirl boots and spurs complete the ensemble.

With Doc still restrained we adjourn inside and walk the short distance to Christus Attuck Hall and soon arrive at a table.

"And I thought I could trust you two against any high jinks like this!" Doc protests.

"A promise is a promise," Sue says.

"Turn me loose!" Doc insists.

"Come on, Doc. I done says I ain't gonna bite you. Let's curl up in a pod like two peas for this here function. I warn you, though, when we get on the dance floor, I'm expecting you to skin that smoke wagon. I hear you a regular brown Fred Astaire." Nellie smiles while mentioning her fellow Nebraskan. She retrieves Sherbet Fountain Candy from her purse as a date night peace offering to the doctor.

"Come on, Obie. For you, tonight. Like Memphis Minnie sings."

"You're selling your pork chops?" Doc asks.

"That's right, and giving away all the gravy you can handle. Ha-cha!"

For Nellie, there are no bushes to beat around.

Doc turns toward me. "Cavendish, why are you standing there like I'm Josh Gibson and you're afraid to throw one down the middle of the plate to me while Sue's in the stands idling about, selling flat beer and burnt peanuts? Untie me so I can escort Miss de Carlo in all of her Western beauty to the ball!"

I undo the lariat and Doc shakes his hands to relieve the numbness from having been restrained.

"Nellie, my dear," he says, "I hope you know how to do the ball and chain."

To Sue and my surprise, he's gone from stormy to sunshine so fast he should get a speeding ticket. Doc takes one of Nellie's gauntlet-gloved hands.

"You look aces tonight, my dear," he tells Nellie.

It's a rare sight to see Nellie blush, being that our kind are not prone to such emotional triggers.

THE
EAST 55TH STREET
AFFAIR

1938

A wind-blown, empty tin can bounces down East 55th Street, past a nondescript house on a cold November morning. Its sound stirs visceral suspicion in a large-framed man, a lock of blond hair interfering with his tortoiseshell eyeglasses as he strides down a dimly lit hallway to a section of the house facing Broadway Avenue. The man is large. So large, in fact, that he carries another man over a dark-flannel-suited shoulder as if he was little more than an extra sweater.

To the distant observer, it would appear that the man is being carried to safety. Closer inspection, however, would reveal a recent strangulation. A pencil-thin mustache above blue lips matches the iced-blue death stare of his eyes. The poor soul, a lake sailor, is about to have his head detached from his body with sharp-knifed precision. Back in the far end of the house, the laker's dipsomaniac companion lay face down, resting on a kitchen table in a post-18th-Amendment repeal blackout, and will soon meet the same fate.

"Now hold still, sir, and lie here. Not that you could move." The large man chortles as he dumps the victim atop a steel mortician's table, a tool of the business that makes up the Broadway Avenue side of the house. Crossing the room, then back to the table, the large man wields a huge, glimmering knife, the type suited for bloody work in a Chicago slaughterhouse.

"Time to join the club, sir," the large man says. He tugs down the victim's navy-blue turtleneck and places the knife on the man's neck, intent on slicing into the space between the first and second vertebrae.

—

Cleveland is in the midst of a powdered sugar doughnut dusting of snowfall, with flakes dancing around our New York Central's Cleveland Limited as the passenger train slows on approach to the station. I step down from our steel-green Pullman car at Cleveland's Union Terminal and immediately peg a quartet of men in fedora hats and trench coats who are quickly approaching. Detectives, without a doubt.

"Gentlemen, are you looking for us?" I ask, savoring the last puff of an Old Gold before dropping it to the platform and crushing the tip beneath my Oxfords.

"Depends on whether you're Madison Cavendish and Seneca Sue SunMountain, the PIs from New York," the eldest-looking of the quartet says.

"That's us, honey," Sue confesses. She tips the redcap and takes our luggage from him before handing it to the youngest of our new acquaintances. Judging from the newness of his pithy trench coat, I figure he's only recently joined the squad. He issues a puzzled look but nonetheless takes our bags by their handles.

"Our boss is waiting for you on the 12th floor of the Hotel Cleveland; follow us, please," the oldest of the troupe says. The men form a circle around us as we leave the misting steam of the train platform for a corridor connecting the terminal to the hotel.

The swank lobby of the hotel is replete with plush chairs, Persian rugs, potted plants, and flowers no doubt glad to be inside, away from the cold. The place is anything but a flop house, the décor a matching display of greens, reds, and goldfinch. From behind the front desk, a live broadcast of ballroom music plays on a radio, the volume set to low. A three-fingered brush across the nose from one of our escorts alerts the concierge that we're headed up to the 12th floor and are not to be disturbed.

Off the elevator and onto twelve, we enter the suite following two raps on the white- and gold-leaf-trimmed door. The baby-faced man, light brown hair parted down the middle, wears a dark-brown suit. His hands outstretch to greet us, but he flinches at our touch. Blue eyes visually size us up. We recognize him, of course, as Eliot Ness, the former Chicago Prohibition-era gangbuster who now serves as Cleveland's public safety director.

"Okay, you guys go down to the lobby and grab coffee or something. I want to speak with Mr. Cavendish and Miss SunMountain alone," Ness says. His team of "Unknowns," as he calls them (the "Untouchables" tag was Chicago's and Chicago's alone) retreats while Ness leads us to the sitting area of a suite decorated in Art Deco blacks, teals, and ivories. The style is fading from fashion slowly and unsteadily, like the 1930s itself. Helping my Sue out of her black, g-winged-collar fur chinchilla coat reveals that she's wearing what she describes as her "séance dress," laced satin black-magic onyx and violet. She removes a dark beret, and black hair streaked with magenta flows down onto her shoulders. If her image doesn't stun Mr. Ness into viewing us as a mystery, Sue's rose-tinted glasses may do the trick. A three-piece black suit, Homburg hat, bow tie, and St. James tweed overcoat is my "meet Elliot Ness" attire. We take our seats on two club chairs offered to us and Ness gets down to business.

"I want to first off thank you for making the trip to Cleveland, and also please pass my thanks on to Stuart Kirkland at the Office of Special Concerns in New York for directing me to you. I only hope you can deliver. Permit me to rehash our recent phone conversation. For the past few years, a sadistic madman has terrorized Cleveland. Some refer to him as the Mad Butcher of Kingsbury Run; others call him the Torso Killer. Whatever the vile name, the public nightmare he created must end!" Ness is seated on the suite's sofa, leaning forward and rubbing his tense hands; it's apparent that the case has gotten to him in spades. Next to Ness on the sofa is a flat manilla envelope, along with a white envelope, its contents bulging. A cardboard box rests on the coffee table. A strong smell of ink emanates from the box as though its contents had only been recently printed.

"You'll find mimeographed summaries of twelve cases we feel he's behind; look them over."

"When did he last strike?" Sue asks.

"This August past. Excuse my French, ma'am, but the piece of shit dumped his eleventh and twelfth victims in view of my office in the Central Standard Building. The bastard thought he was being cute." Ness's blue eyes glare, full of vengeful anger.

"And his methods?" I ask.

Ness exhales slowly. "He likes to decapitate and then emasculate the victims while they're alive or right after he's strangled them. He sometimes dismembers his female victims straight, no chaser." Ness moves to the window, looking down on the neon lights of the mostly blue-collar city as if the snow will make this case—or affair, as we call them—melt away.

He walks back to the sofa. "Speaking of methods, Kirkland was a bit closed mouth about yours. He did give me a list of people who could vouch for you. Professor E.E. is in Europe and couldn't be reached. Mr. Robeson is in England on a singing recital tour. Is that *the*

Paul Robeson? Anyway, I spoke with Sheriff Kilroy Bertrand from Upstate New York. He was as vague as Kirkland, although he affirms you two get the job done 'like a sip of apple jack,' whatever the hell that means." Sue and I smile at our former client (and now friend's) endorsement, remembering an earlier case, "The Stumpville Affair."

"I don't like to go into details about our ways and means either," I said, "but be assured we will find your degenerate assassin, whoever he may be. And yes, that is *the* Paul Robeson; he was a client back in '36."

"We already know who the suspect is," Ness admits.

"Come again?" my Sue asks. "You know who he is?"

"Name's Francis Sweeny. He was a prominent surgeon until a taste for strong drink slowed down his career. We hauled him into this very suite for questioning for a full week; had to dry him out a few days first. He failed a polygraph test not once, but twice." Ness leans forward and rubs his hands again in agitation.

"And?" Sue and I ask in unison.

"We haven't a direct tie in evidence for Sweeny, whom we, confidentially, refer to as Gaylord Sunheim. He's well-connected in Democratic politics. As a member of the Republican Party, I'd have been vilified by the press for going on a witch hunt," Ness admits, as we shake our heads in bewilderment. Regardless of our political affiliations—Sue is a New Deal Democrat while I'm a Progressive LaGuardia Republican—we would never allow our allegiances to bend our judgment in an affair.

"My hands are tied. But yours, Mr. Cavendish and Miss SunMountain, are not. In a way, I'm glad that you're confidential about your methods. I've exhausted my options. I want Sweeny behind bars. We need to nab him in the act." Ness reaches for the envelopes, then pushes them across the coffee table to us. Inside the white envelope is the first half of our hefty fee.

"You have a unique problem, Mr. Ness, and we provide unique solutions," I say, sounding like a smooth-voiced radio pitchman. Without fanfare, Sue places the white envelope in her black leather clutch bag.

"The county sheriff and his boys tried to get ahead of us with an arrest," Ness explains, "but the only result was the man they nabbed on dubious evidence ended up dying in their custody."

Ness retrieves the cardboard box from the coffee table and rises from the sofa. "I should let you two get anchored in. You're registered downstairs as Mr. Carl La Fong and Miss Tessie Garfield. Order anything you two want from room service. Around 9 a.m. tomorrow, Detective Merylo will pick you up for a tour of the crime scenes. Inside this box is a letter I've written to Cleveland's chief coroner, Dr. Gerber, asking his permission for you to view the assorted remains of the victims he still has preserved."

"Why a letter?" my Sue asks.

"Let's just say the doctor and I are not exactly cordial."

After handshakes, which again cause Ness to flinch, most likely due to the coldness of my hands in contrast to the overabundance of pulsing warmth from Sue's, Ness heads for the door with overcoat draped over an arm and with hat in hand.

"I'll phone your room at 6 p.m. tomorrow for a progress report. Sorry I didn't think to reserve two separate rooms. Are you okay with the setup?"

"Maddy will sleep on the sofa," Sue lies with a quiet snicker.

We make ourselves at home. Unpacking, I change into a red smoking jacket and ochre PJ bottoms while Sue wears my ochre PJ top, which I long ago concluded I'll never get back. I recline on the suite sofa, enthralled by the viciousness of the killer's work as I read the case summaries. The reports contrast with Sweeny's kindly neighborhood doctor image and the black-and-white photograph I remove from the manilla envelope. Movement on the teal carpeted floor of a long black telephone cord snaking from the sitting area into the suite's bedroom indicates my Sue is still checking in with New York. A knock on our door denotes the arrival of room service.

"You've been behaving yourself? Purr the truth now," I overhear Sue ask to the meowed maundering reply of our housecat/familiar, Sekhmet, whose meowing every now and then is mixed with a lisped human-sounding, "Yes, ma'am," which she learned to say a while ago. In my mind's eye, I picture the black-on-black image of Sekhmet, her furry tentacles wrapped around the candlestick phone of our friend and fellow occult detective, Elsa Cranberry, while Elsa, with British calm, waits to get on the phone to report to us the devilment Sekhmet has gotten into.

"Sue, tell Sekhmet I send my love. And tell Elsa I'll pay for whatever Sekhmet has already broken or will break, but right now, our food is getting cold, sweet stuff," I explain. For Sue, a few hotdogs minus buns and condiments. My meal consists of hot water for a pot of hyssop tea and a plate of liver and onions with undercooked liver. It was the only palatable option since blood pudding wasn't on the menu. Off the phone now, Sue is cozy and entangled with me on the sofa, noshing and reading. She sits up and issues an enquiring look.

"Maddy, do you think this Dr. Sweeny is human?" Sue asks, staring at the doctor's photo.

"Don't know, love. He could be possessed by the demons in his own mind, or he could be possessed by some entity like the one Rollo Ahmed helped us track down in '27—the Demon Box of Ebril. For all we know, contrary to Ness's opinion, Sweeny may not be the killer at all. But if he is some type of demon, my dear, you, me, Ness, and the city of Cleveland are in for more murders."

—

Cleveland's weather refuses to be up-tempo during our stay. A gray, moody, overcast sky, along with the coldness of Cleveland's modest (by New York standards) skyline, is punctuated by airborne soot from the area's various industrial complexes. I'm quite sure this city's melancholy ambiance, mixed with our search for the Torso Killer, could rival London in 1888 when Jack the Ripper prowled that city's gray streets and alleys.

"Careful making ya way down now; there's patches of ice on the ground," Detective Pete Merylo cautions. A pudgy and graying man, Merylo has worked on the case the longest. We take the advice and carefully step our way down Jackass Hill into the barren Kingsbury Run, a watershed area replete with freight and commuter train tracks. Trees and bushes robbed of their leaves by autumn winds add a gloomy touch. Once a haven for hobos and the downtrodden, and before that, a picnic site for the Gilded Age well-to-dos, today, all that remains are ghostlike memories and trash. I wouldn't be surprised to learn that if we stood in this area long enough, we'd hear the faint, haunted crooning of Trixie Smith's "Freight Train Blues" vaporing through the Run.

"The victims were dumped here?" Sue asks Merylo. She peeks into a clump of bushes before Merylo can show us. I can tell by her expression that Sue senses what she often describes as an infinity pull of death, still active after so many years, in the chill air. "How'd ya know, young lady?" asks an amazed Merylo. "Victims two and three were found here."

"Just a hunch, Merylo," says my Sue, winking, minus the rose tints. At times I worry for my love. The infinity pull is a nexus to the underworld. It could manifest itself into multiple raging voices and screams reaching out to her with ghastly tales. Failing to block them out could be very bad.

Merylo points a thick finger to the left. "Down that way is where Ness had the shanty town burned down. Had the bums rounded up and marched outta there."

He can tell right away by the looks on our faces that Ness hadn't mentioned that desperate act to us. I figure it was the reason the city newspapers soured on Ness, too. The rest of the crime scene tour, alas, produces nothing.

Merylo chauffeurs us to the coroner's office on Cedar Avenue, a two-story building that also houses the Cleveland Department of Health.

"I'll be out here waiting for ya," he says to Sue and me. "That doctor rubs me the wrong way, and we've had too many clashes through the years over this case. Sammy Gerber listens to too many junior G-man radio shows. Wants to solve cases from his office chair!"

Merylo steps out of the sedan and opens our door. He's nothing if not polite. "Come pick us up in an hour, Merylo," I say, to which he yells something about lunch before returning to the driver's seat and speeding away.

We're soon inside the reception area of a very clean and antiseptic powder-blue first floor. Sue and I are growing irritated as Dr. Samuel Gerber stands before us in a white lab coat. He's already read Ness's letter twice and begins reading it a third time, just for spite, as we stand in silence. Gerber adjusts his thick glasses and runs a hand through his receding black hair.

"Ness had no right to send you two here to me," he says. "I told him before, I answer to the citizens of Cleveland, not him. He can contact the mayor with this request. That's the protocol. Anyway, who are you? Doesn't matter. Have Ness contact the mayor and then come back tomorrow."

"Dr. Gerber, we're kind of pressed for time," Sue explains.

"It can wait until tomorrow," Gerber replies, handing back the letter. He turns to walk away, but I jump in front of him and block his path.

"Young man, what in Sam Hill are you doing? Get... get away from me, I say!"

"Dr. Gerber, look at me," I order. I remove my green-tinted glasses and make eye contact, immediately gaining control of his mind. Soothing him at first with a mental flashback to his childhood self, dressed in knicker pants and reading *Tom Swift and the Visitor from Planet X* on his parents' front porch, I then project an image of what will befall him should he refuse to accommodate us. The doctor quietly gasps in terror.

"I apologize. What can I... do for you?" Gerber stammers.

"Show us the bodily remains from the Torso Killer case, Doctor," I insist, retaining eye contact.

He walks slowly to the receptionist's desk. "Miss Herrington, call down to the basement. Tell Vernon… I'm sending two people down… to examine the physical remains related to the Kingsbury Run case. They're not to be… interrupted… in any way. Also, tell Vernon he can take lunch now."

Lula Mae Herrington, a mahogany-complexioned plump woman in a flowery print dress covered by a rust-colored sweater, barely glances up from her desk. She looks uneasy as she picks up the receiver but simply nods and replies, "Yes, Dr. Gerber."

We step away from Herrington. I turn to Gerber and whisper, "Doctor, you will go upstairs to your office, sit calmly behind your desk, take the phone off its hook, and wait for me."

Gerber quietly ascends the stairs while Sue and I begin our trek into the basement morgue.

—

"Right this way," Morgue Assistant Vernon Quincy, a tall, lean man of fair hair and gray temples, says. Vernon opens a dark wood cabin then gingerly removes a large glass jar. The smell of tissue-fixative and embalming formaldehyde sweeps across the morgue room to engage. It's equally as bad as Vernon's lunch, a wax paper-wrapped egg salad sandwich resting on a nearby stone slab sink counter. He retrieves a wooden box and places it on the same counter. "I guess you can start with victims four and eight. I'll be back after lunch if you need to look at more. If not, just leave the evidence on the counter. But be careful; I don't want Doc Gerber to be sore with me if something happens." Vernon removes his lab coat and hangs it on a hook near the doorway. He then opens a body locker and pulls out a cold bottle of milk, grabs his sandwich, and heads out.

We get to work.

The jar before Sue contains a male human head. A tag affixed to the lid reads Tattoo Man No. 4, E. 55th St. The victim appears to have been in his late twenties. My Sue unscrews the lid and immerses her hands into the jar. She tilts the victim's head at an angle so that their eyes meet. The dead man's eyelids flutter open. Whispering, Sue begins to converse with him.

I open the top of the wooden box labeled *Rose W., No. 8 Lorain-Carnegie Bridge*. To one side is a dried blood-encrusted burlap bag; the other side contains a collection of bones: ribs, humeri, ulnas, radii, and femurs. I bite my fingertips, drawing magenta-speckled blood. I touch the haversack and several bones, and a tortured voice enters my mind:

"I'm Rose. It's a sweltering, liquored-up blues song

warbling summer night. I leave a roaring Third Ward Bar with a large ofay man who says he's got the hots for a little brown gal like me. He wants to take me to his home and love me for a price. I don't believe the love spiel, but what the hell? It's the good time that counts. He places a hand around my waist as we walk toward East 55th Street. He points to his house in the distance. The closer we get, the tighter his grip becomes. 'Ease up, love,' I say, 'ease up.' He leads me inside the house and locks the door. His hands surround my neck like a vise. I try to wrest free but... Jesus... I can't breathe! My body grows more limp by the second. Oh Lord... I..."

I pull my fingertips away. Rose's life, no matter how hard a road she'd traveled, was important and didn't deserve the fate handed her. She mattered. And although we don't look it, Sue and I are of mixed race. (It's an open secret in Harlem.) The kinship of ethnicity we share with Rose fills me with an added incentive. We must stop the maniacal doctor.

Back in the here and now, I look over at Sue, who's ended her conversation with tattoo man, tears streaming down her freckled cheeks. We embrace each other to steady and compose ourselves. Sue tells me that even in death, tattoo man wouldn't reveal his identity as he wished to spare his family from the emotional turmoil he believed they'd suffer should they learn about his life's actions.

—

As promised, Merylo returns to pick us up.

"So, ladies and gentlemen, how'd ya make out?" he asks, looking down at the bandages (given to me by Lula Mae) on my fingertips.

"Swell, Merylo. Just swell," I answer, more than a little fatigued.

"How about a few Polish boys?" he offers.

"What?" I ask.

"Excuse me?" demands Sue.

"Ha ha! The best of Cleveland." Merylo explains that a "Polish boy" is a hotdog with everything, including fried potatoes. Having been through our latest ordeal, I welcome an activity as benign as eating a hotdog.

"Sounds exquisite," I say. "But first, a short detour at the nearest thrift shop if you don't mind."

"Maddy!" Sue screams, as the three of us set into the flivver as Merylo prepares to pull onto the road. "You forgot about Dr. Gerber!"

"Shit!" I exclaim, darting from the auto and running back into the building to restore the doctor's free will.

—

Two days later, around 1 a.m., my blood, along with whatever the lifeforce of a horror from beyond the stars lurks within me, rushes to my head. Sweeny is carrying me, my body folded over his left shoulder, down a dim hallway. Destination unknown. Sue is in the kitchen, face down on the table, feigning unconsciousness from excessive alcohol consumption.

The good doctor believes he's strangled the piss out of me. We enter another room. The same scent from the Department of Health enters my nostrils. I'm dropped onto a cool steel table. Motionless, I look up at Sweeny and issue a blue-eyed, dead carp stare.

"Now hold still, sir, and lie here. Not that you could move." Big man laughs at his own tired pun. "So nice of you and your female friend to have accompanied me to my home. But now it's time for you to join the club, sir." Sweeny places a knife, just the right size to gut a steer, to my neck. At that moment I hear Sue scream from the kitchen as she begins to rise in willing surrender to the full moon's glow from a nearby window. The start of her Lycan transformation begins. I also rise.

Sweeny turns, distracted by Sue's scream. I use the opportunity to grab the knife from him and swing my legs off the table. The doctor backs away but then advances, his face blushing with rage. The sound of dress fabric being torn apart can be heard in the kitchen.

"Listen, old man, you're not in a good position," I explain. Then, to prove my point, I tighten the grip on the knife with my right hand and thrust its blade into the palm of my left. After a moment's pause, I withdraw the knife, snap the blade in two, and toss it to Sweeny. He backs into a corner of the room, knocking over a metal stand and a tray containing shiny surgical tools of the undertaker trade.

"Nasty people," Sweeny says, voice cool as frost. "Have to understand I'm not well. Family, fellow doctors, they all have tried to help. But not enough help to get me away from these nasty people around me. Nasty people. I was the only one to do good among my brothers, but nobody cared. Look at you, you Great Lakes bum. You're one of those nasty people, too. You and that drunken mutt you brought along. What do you think you're going to do? Take me in? Nasty people. Schoolboy Ness couldn't prove crap. I'll plead insanity. And that little knife trick won't stop me from ripping your nasty head off."

Sweeny babbles on, and it's clear he'll keep babbling on, so I step to him and issue a good old-fashioned left hook to the face. His glasses fly across the room. I lift him off his feet and hold him up by his murderous neck. Sweeny manages to bellow out a baritone scream as I bare my fangs.

Claws scratch at the door Sweeny had closed to perform his sick work. "Excuse me, old man," I say.

With Sweeny dangling and struggling in midair, I unlock the door. My sempiternal love growls, lumbered in wolfish silver-gray fur with a magenta streak running down her back. Sue, now twice her body size, surprises me. Typically, she would have bashed the door into pieces. My Sue and I gaze into each other's eyes, knowing we can't let Sweeny go on. I drop him and then jump down beside him as he lies whimpering on the floor.

"I'll see you nasty people in Hell!" snivels Sweeny.

"I wouldn't be surprised if you do, old man," I reply. "You see, in the course of our business, we do travel to that sordid part of town from time to time to drop mugs like you off in person. Either way, the commissions are good."

Sue growls a giggle and I bite into Sweeny's neck. His warm, alcohol-laced blood flows down my throat like a recently uncorked bottle of vintage Moët. I make room at his bloody trough for Sue to gnaw on his throat. She wastes little time in chewing up pieces of flesh, flipping the choice bloody bits in the air, and then snapping them into her maw. The man who had terrorized Cleveland for over five years is finished at last.

After our repast of the doctor, we clean up and discard our thrift store wardrobe. Suitcases with a change of clothes, which Sweeny thought to be the sad belongings of two vagabonds, await us in the kitchen. There are also two bottles of Schenley's Golden Wedding Rye— one full, one empty—bait Sweeny used in his effort to lure us in.

Now we face the dilemma of getting rid of Sweeny's body since we've gone against Ness's arrest order. Or have we? I gaze at the doctor's instruments and formulate an idea.

—

The following afternoon is sunny as we pack our bags in anticipation of the evening Limited back to the Big Apple. Ness meets us at our hotel, and we bring him up to speed on recent events.

"Sweeny was able to get away with his crimes by renting out his house of horrors from an absentee undertaker landlord strapped for money," I explain. "When he wasn't luring victims from taverns to his home, Sweeny made money 'no questions asked' by working as a mob fix-up doctor, treating gunshot wounds and the like for the underworld."

"Maddy and I figured Sweeny would venture onto new hunting grounds," Sue continued, charming as always. "His old pick-up place, the Buckeye Inn, had become too hot. Too many of the victims had a common roost there. We decided to lure him to us by masquerading as the type of victims he coveted. Enter Carl La Fong, an unemployed Great Lakes merchant marine, aka Madison, and his hard-drinking shrewish girlfriend, Tessie Garfield, aka yours truly. We settled on a bar on East Ninth Street named Nap's Tap Room. It was Sweeny's type of watering hole, and we provided the silage to satisfy his lust for bloodshed."

Ness sits uneasily on the sofa. The white envelope next to him contains the second half of our fee. In the corner of the room, a white linen-covered serving cart holds the remains of our breakfast—plates of meat pies, well-spiced in a rich sanguine gravy, along with the blood pudding I so often crave. I had slipped the kitchen staff a Ben Franklin for use of the space so that I might perform some predawn culinary magic.

"But, what about Sweeny? What happened to him? Where's the body?" Ness asks, leaning forward impatiently.

"Forgive me, old man, but you really didn't want us to bring Sweeny in alive, did you?" I ask.

Ness pauses a long while before answering, "For the greater good, the doctor had to be finished." He pauses again, and I suspect he finds it ironic that he sounds as if he's confessing. "We just couldn't have him on the streets. You know that. But again, what did you do with him? I can't have any loose ends."

"It's all been handled," I explain. "Let me give you some veridical advice, Ness: let it go, old man."

Sue and I issue a stoic glimpse in the location of the room service cart of heavily spiced leftovers. Ness, being the sharp-as-nails lawman that he is, follows our glimpse to the cart and begins walking to it. He soon, however, catches the scent of an unusual aroma. A look of horror and nauseousness crashes onto his face as he takes a closer look at the contents of the cart and spies a radius bone partially covered in tissue and a partial thoracic spine unmistakably of human origin.

"Excuse me," Ness manages, and flees to the bathroom to retch.

Later, before leaving Cleveland, we settle accounts with a peaked-looking Ness who, still visibly shaken, maintains a slight distance from us.

"I hope you shall not be needing our services again," I say, "but if you do, you know how to reach us."

Ness nods with an expression that seems to ponder if the cure wasn't worse than the disease.

"Do you think we'll ever see him again?" my Sue asks as we hail a taxi.

"Hard to say," I reply. "He's a good man with a long history of dealing with the underworld. What he didn't realize until today is there's more than one type of underworld."

THE
BLUE DEVIL DOG
AFFAIR

1941

Beginning in 1897, West Virginia had been plagued by a "blue devil dog," a name coined by local farmers and hunters in Randolph County who ventured again and again into the hills and forests to put a stop to the creature feasting on sheep and other livestock. What follows is a detailed narrative of our involvement in bringing the hound to heel.

"Okay, sweetie, when I say 'Lift!' you lift the back of the car. And I should remind you not to lift it by the bumper guards," I said, reminding Sue of how her Lycan strength had pulled the guards off our Pierce Arrow, the result being our new car going into the shop yet again.

"Oh, like how you crush doorknobs when trying to open doors, my Maddy dear?"

"Touché dear. Now come on, ready? Lift," and with that, Sue lifted it in the blink of an eye.

I had changed the flat tire on the left rear wheel. We had made sure no one came motoring by in either direction so as not to witness our Bia and Hermes shtick. Now, with that chore finished and me too mortified to let Sue know she has a line of road mud across her maroon diem plaid overcoat from the lift, we continued on our way to find a hunter's cabin owned by Joshua Portefaix. "Did you check the moon's position tonight?" I asked after taking a last bite of a rare hamburger smeared with piccalilli while Sue picked pepperoni out of what locals call a pepperoni roll. We had stopped at a diner a few miles back on this road "Old Scratch" would be proud of.

"It will be a quarter moon after sundown at 6:48, so I won't need its pushy help tonight," Sue answered me while chewing. "At the most, a quarter moon is like a tailwind glow. Now let me ask you this, dear. When are you going to admit we're lost? Admit it; we're lost. Well?"

"Listen, as crappy as this road is, we're headed in the right direction, Sue."

"Says who?"

"Says the next shack or cabin we get to, to ask directions."

"And if you're wrong?"

"Well, Seneca Susan Alberta SunMountain, breakfast for you, minus cackle fruit and pancakes, at Pete's twenty-four-hour pancake joint on Times Square, or a movie at the Apollo on 125th Street, and if I'm right regarding our direction? What do I get?" I love to see Sue cringe when I use her middle name, Alberta.

"How about a little libation from my neck when we get back to New York?" Sue gave me a coquettish smile, knowing I couldn't pass up that wager.

"It's a bet, love." In truth, it wasn't a bet 'cause at the end of the day—or in our case, the dead of night—Sue would get her bacon and OJ, and I would get my nibble puncture treat anyway, and what my doll doesn't know is when I do, I plan to gift her a loop of Akora black pearls that I had hidden back home. I tell you, brother, we smother each other.

Stopping in front of a rundown house set back from the road, we saw on a porch a gentleman with a weather-beaten face in bib overalls and flannel shirt, and next to him a stern-faced woman in a plumberry country dress, and they were in their chairs slowly rocking away time, while a gaggle of dowdy rowdy children stopped playing after-supper tag and stared at us, as we exited our auto.

"Hey friend, my name's Carl La Fong, and this fabulous young lady next to me is Tess Garfield. We manage the Tammany Hall Rod and Hunt Club in Queens, New York, and we're looking for a Joshua Portefaix. I hear he's good at training blue tic coon hounds." Back in '38, Eliot Ness had christened Sue and I with those aliases during an affair in Cleveland, and we liked them so much we kept using them.

"You can say that, though he sold his dogs. My name's Larkin." Larkin's wife gave him a "You're giving out too much information" look.

"Which way can I find him? Looking past Larkin, I give the wife a mind control "calm down, ma'am" gape, which gave her a jolt and then made her return a confused smile.

"You would have found Frenchy by now if you hadn't stopped to ask directions. His cabin is just a holler up the road, a crick and woods, to your right, his cabin to your left."

"Thanks much, pal." Sue sucked the air between her teeth at my "I told you so" smile. "But y'all best be careful; we got that blue devil dog roams round these woods at night. Don't want to be caught on foot!"

"I'm sure we'll be fine," I said, giving the husband the same look I had given the wife, and we drove on.

It was during the Great War that I met Joshua Portefaix. The federal government had got wind of Sue and my exploits with the Office of Special Concerns in New York and invited me to join the US Army Corp's secret "Hoo Doo" bureau led by Major Milford Fulbright, an old calvary man and occultist. Sue would stay stateside and handle affairs in old New York. We were an odd bunch, from Astro "the seer" Kerby and his N rays to Joshua the hunter, to yours truly; we would go behind enemy lines at night and work our trades. At first we didn't gel, to the point of Joshua and I engaging in city versus rural fisticuffs, but once he tasted my knuckle game, he calmed down. It also helped that I saved his tail from a Kaiser patrol one night. "You think Joshua's okay?" Sue asks with concern in her voice.

"I hope so. These woods on the other side look ominous, and perfect if looking for a folklore legend. There, that should be it." I pulled in—or should I say I bumped along—for all of the odds and ends of junk that littered the front yard, parking next to the carcass of an old model T Ford, to see, among all of this mess, Joshua's cabin. Sundown finished, the glow from Sue's quarter moon plus stars are more in abundance than what we city folk can view back in New York, and they are helpful. After a few yells for Joshua go unanswered, I gave Sue an "I know what I'm doing" look before applying a soft magenta glow to turn and unlock the cabin's front door.

Once inside, after a brief look around, scanning for electrical help, a ceiling fan light sparked on, displaying a cabin that had either been lived in too much or was the scene of a horrific struggle. Empty tin cans of Armour-dressed beef were strewn on a rickety, bloodstained dining room table. In a corner is a toppled-over RCA Victor phonograph, and scattered around on the floor were 78s, the making of a Mildred Bailey record collection that was now worthless chips of shellac.

"Maddy, take a gander at this," Sue ordered, standing in the doorway of the cabin bedroom. Inside, a bloody, slashed, ripped-up mattress and box spring had been upended.

"This is not good Sue."

"You don't think the blue..." Sue started.

"I think we have to find Joshua pronto is what I think."

—

Sue clears the dining room table while I retreat to the Pierce to get our suitcases.

Returning to the cabin, I found Sue, with one hand on her hip, waiting for me. Oh, boy, was she waiting for me. In the other outstretched hand was her now-earth-toned overcoat.

"You mean to tell me, Madison Prescott Cavendish, you didn't notice the mud on my coat?" When Sue's irises and pupils did that hazel back and forth, brother, she was mad.

"I didn't notice, dear," I lied.

"I bet you did!" said Sue, violently bushing her coat. The heart of the matter was the coat was a match to her dress and veiled pillbox hat, or it would have been if she'd smeared mud on said dress and hat, which I, for one, had no plans to suggest she do.

"I tell you what. When we get back to Manhattan, we'll have it cleaned, and I'll even throw in a surprise." I flashed my cute fangs, which got her all the time and got me out of trouble.

Placing her coat on the back of one of Joshua's wooden chairs, Sue stepped to me, wrapping her arms around the back of my neck. With her optical rant subsiding, Sue whispered into my ear, "You mean that string of black pearls you thought you hid from me in that hollowed-out copy of Zanly Norwood's *Alchemist Recipes*, which Sekhmet showed me," Sue cooed.

Zanly's book was not good, I saw, as a hiding place, just as it was not a good alchemy book in general. I also made a mental note to talk to that nosy, tentacled feline when we got back. We smooched, which may turn into a mongoose versus cobra amore entanglement if we didn't cease.

"Okay, let's get to work, love," I told Sue after we came up for air. Outside, a night mist had arrived, and both our ears picked up a ghostly howl among the sycamores. The only way we figured to meet up with the blue devil was to go after it. With that thought in mind, Sue undressed.

Out of dress, unmentionables, stockings, square-toed block heel shoes, and before we headed out the door, I pointed to Sue's pillbox still on top of her head, which she handed to me with a smirk.

Once outside, with the aid of a Tilley lamp, Sue got down on her hands and knees, gripping grass and soil while I stood to the side with a house coat and slippers. Eyes closed, Sue was silent until she cried out, "Oh, Maddy, please. I can't!" Sue's plea turned into growls and baying a grayish fur with a magenta streak bristles up through her skin, legs, and arms stretching into her fore and hind legs. Back in 1914, after we were infected, over dinner at Shanley's one night, I asked her how the transition felt, and with tears in her eyes, my Sue said it was like being torn apart while having the sensation of her brain being on fire.

Rising up, Sue jerked her head in my direction but recognized me, and she bounded off across the road into the misty woods toward that howl that had come closer. I retrieved from the holster under my tweed jacket and overcoat my .44 to check the bullets resting in its chambers. I waited like Joe Louis's corner man, Jack Blackburn, parking myself down on a rocking chair on Joshua's front porch. We were going to meet this devil dog and find out what had happened to Joshua.

—

After an hour or so, frenzied barking and howling jangled and jarred me to a standing position on the porch. Through the mist, Sue returned in a slow lope switching to an upright hind foot toe walk, and behind her strutted a bipedal canine, its coat a slate blue. Stopping suddenly, it dasheed behind a tree. The sinister snarling from behind the tree ebbed into a human cough as Sue entered Joshua's cabin to calm down and change.

"That you, Cavendish?" came a nasal voice from behind the tree. "Greetings, Josh. I see old habits die hard," I teased.

"I reckon so, buddy, but before I fill you in, could you kindly go into my cabin and fetch my work boots and a red Union suit from out my middle dresser drawer? Darn chilly it is tonight."

"Sure thing, Josh." I guessed Sue must have overheard us, for before I could knock, the door opened just a bit, and my sweetie thrusted out what Josh requested, being as she was in the midst of dressing herself.

"Cavendish, what brings you here, and who or what in the Sam Hill is it that chased me out the woods?" Josh, now dressed somewhat and in front of the tree, was a long-faced man. His brown hair was in a bowl cut, and he was buttoning up his union suit.

"That, old man, is my love afflatus, Miss SunMountain." In the few letters we mailed each other over the years, I never went into detail about Sue to Josh. "Sue, you decent?"

"Yes. Come in, sorry to put you out of your own place, Joshua."

"Aw shucks, don't mention it, ma'am." Inside, as a politeness to us, Josh refrained from sniffing Sue's backside as he was prone to when encountering other cryptids.

"What happened, Josh?" I asked, looking about the disarrayed cabin.

"Bad business, Cavendish. Last year, I had bamboozled folks into thinking the blue devil dog bought the farm, used a wolf carcass dyed blue, then placed it on a farmer named Cooley's land. Let him take credit, which the old sod shifter gladly did, sorry Sue."

Sitting across the table from Josh, Sue silently nodded. But I knew, in truth, she didn't like to hear of a distant kin of hers being destroyed.

"I figured willpower would win out, I reckoned. I reckoned wrong. Tonight I was listening to music, but I started pining for the feel of fur on my body and the hotness of blood in my maw. I fought it and won first prize—first prize for wrecking my place, that is." Josh picked up an empty dressed beef can off the table, examined it, then pitched it violently across the room. "Say, what y'all doing here anyways?" Josh's expression changed from anguish to suspicion.

"Well, old man, as you know from the state of the world, this country is going to be pulled into war whether we like it or not. The war department has whispered to the US Army Signal Corps to resurrect the 'Hoo Doo Bureau.'"

"Are you shitting me?" Josh jumped up out of his chair at attention as if a commanding officer had burst through the cabin door to verify his unevenness, even in human form. Sue's freckled face was a mask of stoicism, hiding a silent guffaw at Josh's histrionics. "But didn't you write me one time saying that Major Fulbright had died?" asked Josh, sitting back down.

"Sure did; he passed in '35. Stuart Kirkland from New York will take over the bureau with oak leaves on his shoulders, and he's a good egg, Josh. Uncle Sam needs you."

Josh pondered the idea a bit. "I'm in. I'm sorry-assed tired of these here and yonder hills. Gonna sell this cabin and land, but I gotta find somewhere to hang my hat."

"Maddy, how about Stumpville?" A lightbulb clicked on over Sue's head before mine. "Stumpville?" Josh's question was laced with the hope of a new start.

"A nice little village of Lycans and other cryptids living in Upstate New York; you can get settled down there before your induction at Fort Meade," I said. "I think you'll fit in."

Sue sweetened the deal. "I'll even help you replace your Mildred Bailey collection."

"Well, I'll be a galvanized Yankee in mint condition. I'm really in now!" and with that, Josh preceded to attack our ears with his rendition of Mildred Bailey's "Darn That Dream." Fuck.

—

Joshua Portefaix did fit in. He was the ancestor of Jacques Portefaix, a survivor of an attack by the Beast of Gevaudan that had unleashed a reign of terror in France during 1764. The curse was handed down from generation to generation and crossed over into the new world. Settling in Stumpville, Josh jumped into the social mix and began dating Regina Kupman, the village's librarian. They were wed in the brief period of time between Japan's attack on the US naval base on Oahu Island, Hawaii, on December 7, 1941, and the influx of American males enlisting in the armed forces at Fort Meade. While we attended Camp Franklin Signal Corps School at Fort Meade, Regina soon found herself carrying their first child, Reggie. Once the war got rolling, we were assigned to Patton's third army.

Our cover story, like in the Great War, was as radio operators by day. By night, we went behind enemy lines, killing on sight any of Adolf and Benito's boys. To assist us, we had on loan spring-heeled Jack from the Brits MI-6 and from the French resistance, Fantômas, both working to earn their clemency-pardon deals from Sicily to EL Guettar to Metz to the Bulge.

By the time of the Bulge, Sue was also in Europe as a lieutenant in the 6668th, and we worked at our bloody trade. In Sicily, among the tombs of Necropolis of Pantalica, I met and befriended an Ethiopian vampiress, Gonda, who was more than happy to join us in our traveling blood banquets. After the war, the Portefaix family grew with the addition of Darlene and the baby of the family, Connie, her hair blue like her dad's fur.

During the 1950s, the bell rang again for us, but this time it was for Korea. Now, with the 8th Army, we were at the Chosin Reservoir, helping the 1st Marine Division bug out from the Red Army. At that ice-cold debacle of blood, Joshua went MIA.

In 1968, while puttering around at MACV Pentagon East in Saigon one night, waiting, along with my handler, Lt. Hulan Brown, for my next kill orders, I came across a classified intelligence teletype item. A man or "Gwai lo" was sighted in a village near the North Korea-China border in the midst of a hand-to-hand, pickax-to-pickax violent schism between scarlet and red guards. The man was reported to be an American. The teletype also mentioned that the troops on both sides were reporting having many of their number culled by a tremendous and terrible dog, a devil hound, they called it, that troops reported glowed blue in the moonlight.

Once again, I knew my friend was alive and told Sue I would use my next leave to find him and help him return from a life of killing to a life with his family in Stumpville.

THE
DICKERSON
AFFAIR

1946

It was a mild Thursday evening in an ornate study of a tenth-floor apartment building facing the East River along York Avenue. Bookcases filled with obscure volumes pertaining to the occult world and speculative fiction lined the walls of the study. Through an open window, the sounds of a tugboat passing on its way downriver, a foghorn blaring, and the slight odor of midtown stockyards—soon to be replaced by the nearly completed United Nations Secretariat Building—wafted through the air. The sounds of typewriter keys being tapped mixed with the ambient noise and smells. The typist was E. Abbott Logan, a bombastic bestselling pulp author and self-proclaimed expert on all things paranormal. His horrific tales had allowed him to live a comfortable life, but they had also earned him a few enemies within the pulp fiction business.

With pompadour hair the color of ginger, a narrow face, pale complexion, and slight build, Logan preferred a scarlet smoking jacket over a well-pressed white shirt at this time of the evening. A scarlet string tie, black corduroy pants, and black slippers completed his comfortable, creative ensemble. A slow-burning Pall Mall cigarette in a green glass ashtray next to a half-empty glass of Petre port quivered with the tapping on the desk. In the living room, Nancy Ward, Logan's housekeeper, did some final dusting before leaving for the evening, her job for the day done. Mrs. Ward, a former Hotsy Totsy girl whom some remembered from her days as a showgirl on Broadway, had mousy brown hair that was now gray. Over the years, her slim, curvy figure had expanded considerably. In a blue day dress, she looked haggard from past showgirl adventures and birthing four children, the oldest of who had been killed in action at Anzio.

"Mr. Logan, I'm headed out now. Your supper of Lord Woolton

pie is in the oven, and hotdogs and potato salad are in the icebox!" she yelled from the living room. "Try not to burn up the pie like last time if you're going to heat it up!" Nancy could get away with ordering him around because they both knew he needed her to keep order to the residence. A heavy thumping at the apartment door stopped Nancy midway into her coat. "Whoever's calling on Logan in the middle of his writing time is going to catch hell!" she exclaimed.

"Mrs. Ward!" Logan called out. "Two things: first, what did you yell about the oven? Second, what the hell are you doing with the front door?" Logan was at his Smith-Corona, typing like a squirrel gnawing at an acorn in Gracie Mansion Park.

Ignoring her employer, Nancy slid back the peephole for a look. "I should have known it would be Mr. Dickerson," she grumbled to herself. "Oh, Mr. Dickerson, hold on while I open the door, please." Unlocking the door, she continued, "Evening, Mr. Dickerson. The doorman didn't tell me you were on your way up. I'm afraid Mr. Logan is—"

Dickerson pushed the door into Nancy with such force that it knocked her back against the wall and into a potted yucca plant, leaving her dazed and with a fractured right wrist as she tried to break her fall. A.Q. Dickerson, author of pulp horror stories and rival and critic of E. Abbott Logan, shuffled past the prone Nancy and headed toward Logan's desk, his heavy shoes shuffling and raising a nap on the gray carpet. The horror author was tall and awkward but solidly built, with a pockmarked face and neatly combed sandy hair. Dickerson wore a dark pinstriped suit, a dark bow tie, and a mindless expression, as Nancy would later tell detectives. He had a white scarf around his neck. Oblivious to his surroundings, Logan continued to hack away at the first draft of a nonfiction manuscript titled *The Demon Box of Ebril: Fact or Hoax?*

"What in Hell are you doing here unannounced, Dickerson?" Logan called out to his housekeeper but received no response. "Still upset because I designated your latest 'literary' work a bowl of fur-balled mishmash?" chuckled Logan, who excelled at getting under the skins of his rivals, friendly or otherwise. As president of the American Horror Story Craftsmen Congress, he felt he had divine literary edict. In silence and with unnatural speed, Dickerson advanced to the edge of Logan's front desk, unraveled and lassoed his white scarf around Logan's neck, and yanked the arrogant author over the typewriter and desk, knocking the Pall Mall, Petre port, and ashtray to the floor. He pulled the scarf at the ends taut and didn't stop pulling until all signs of life were extinguished from the bulging eyes of Logan, whose slippery struggle from side to side mimicked that of a drunken sailor.

Dickerson loosened the scarf and let it and the body of his literary nemesis fall to the floor. As Dickerson exited out the door, Nancy Ward was recovering from her daze. She let out a howl of pain and fear as the murderer, like a sluggard, passed the lightheaded cleaning lady. Nancy staggered her way to Logan's writing area and let out screams that sent doors on the tenth-floor opening as she looked down into the eyes of her now-deceased employer.

Down on the street, Dickerson, ignoring the doorman and his regular cabbie, slid into the back of a green delivery truck and rode off into the night, while back upstairs in the apartment, the Pall Mall burned a hole in Logan's carpet.

—

I sometimes couldn't sleep during the day, like normal vampires do. When I could sleep, of course, my mind produced images of that bastard, Cranston Voaxhall, a partial catalyst of who I am today. The ringing of the phone woke me from my cosmic horror would-be rest. Reaching out from under my bed comforter, which shrouded my body, I answered a black Crosley phone stationed near my bed.

"Madison Cavendish here; it's your dime."

"Madison, it's Upton Edwards, defense lawyer," the energetic, crisp voice at the other end heralded me.

"Hey, Edwards, what's up?" I hadn't heard from Edwards since the beginning of the war. I had gone off to do dirty work for the United States Army Signal Corps paranormal section in Europe while Edwards ended up in the Pacific Theater, most notably, the Battle for Okinawa.

"I need to meet with you as soon as possible. I take it you've seen the morning papers?"

"No. In my business, I wake late, you know. I'm an evening paper fuddy-duddy."

"Well, E. Abbott Logan is dead—murdered. A rival writer, A.Q. Dickerson, has been charged, allegedly, with the crime. His wife, Roberta, and a gentleman named Cydell Amaro have retained me as defense, and I want to look into retaining you to snoop for us. How soon can you get out to my office at 16 Court Street in downtown Brooklyn, Cavendish?"

"Give me an afternoon time." I needed a while to let any regeneration occur, drink a hot and hard cup of hyssop tea—hold the sugar—and, as we used to say during the war, shit, shower, and Parmley fang floss.

"Three p.m. I'm on the twelfth floor, across the hall as you exit the elevator. Thanks, Cavendish." Edwards exited the call. Just as I placed the receiver back on the base, the kettle phone jumped, ringing again.

"Hi, Maddy. Just checking in." The sugary voice on the other end was my soulmate and business partner, Seneca Sue SunMountain.

"Hey, love. How's it going up there?" Sue was doing some pro bono work in Maine, helping to rid a town of a Were-Moose that was terrorizing the townspeople, the original tribal people of the area, and lumberjacks. We would later file it as "The Twillhook Affair." I had asked her to keep me posted.

"Tomorrow, Professor Twillhook and a few others and I will head into the forest and set up camp."

"Hmm. Well, not to cut you off, but we've got a paying affair down here. Upton Edwards, Esquire, wants us to help him defend A.Q. Dickerson, the horror writer. He's in jail for allegedly murdering E. Abbott Logan."

"Did I hear you correctly? You said Dickerson is the alleged murderer of Logan?"

"That's right. Old smartass Logan must have quipped too much, and now a grave has to be dug for him." Logan had snapped our caps with his investigative prying about Rollo Ahmed and "The Demon Box of Ebril Affair," a year after the 1928 incident.

"Wow. Well, they're a bunch of fools who consider themselves experts on our world anyway."

"So, how fast can you get back to Manhattan?"

"I can't, Maddy," said Sue.

"But I need you down here." We had worked on separate cases before, but it was more fun working together. Like the proverbial ham and cheese sandwich—we worked well together.

"Madison, I promised the people up here I would help them."

"So what do I do?" I grumbled.

"Find another partner. Maybe whoever is left from the Mignonette Society or the Crime Stoppers. Oh, wait! Go to the file cabinet; you'll see a file on a Cordelia Lovemilk. I told you about her. We met while serving in the 6888th Mail Battalion in France during the war while you were in Italy. She's a quintessence conjurer witch and has had the gift—or curse—longer than us. You know I'd be there with you, love."

I knew she would. "Well, I guess I'll seek her out." I just could not bring myself to call, but money was involved.

"Trust me, love, she's a doll. You two should work well together, maybe too well." Sue was half-joking, half-serious.

"But I trust you. I'll be back to you as soon as I'm finished. Gotta go now. When the day comes that we're burned at the stake, we'll be together. I love you. Bye," Sue joked as our long-distance connection ended.

I walked over to the file cabinet and flipped through files until I came across one labeled *Cordelia Lovemilk*. I was stunned. How in the world could Sue hint at being jealously concerned about me and this woman working too well together? The black-and-white photo staring back at me was of a stern-looking female with an unsmiling face, prudent black hair waved and pulled back in a ponytail, and large but quiet eyes behind horn-rimmed glasses nestled on top of an aquiline nose. An ankle-length dark dress with a matching jacket over a white blouse opened at the collar was the only element remotely approaching risqué, and only if going by nineteenth-century standards. Rounding out the attire were black high-laced brogan ladies shoes and, in one hand, a wooden staff, which I hoped she used for casting spells rather than hitting. I recognized the background of the photo as Morningside Park in Harlem. Under the photo, paper-clipped was a sheet of paper onto which Sue had typed the following information:

DOB: 1838 (?)
Place of Origin: Florida
Heritage: Negro/Native American
Arrival in New York: 1911
Current Occupation:
>Part-time art teacher, New York Public School District and the Harvest School of Art

Prior Occupations:
>1915-1918: Belly dancer (Little Singapore), Hagenbeck-Wallace Circus
>1911-1918: Fortune teller, sideshow performer, and aerialist, Starlight Park, Bronx, NY
>1911-1918: Stage assistant to the Hugo Bataille, magician (now deceased)

Known Family: Septima (daughter), also a witch and conjurer
Leanings: Sorceress, Conjurer, and Witch in the light
Last Known Address:
>898 Wyatt Street (177th Street adjacent)
>Bronx, NY

Phone: TY3-666-5555

By "Sorceress in the light," Sue meant that Cordelia wasn't out to harm anyone. I figured it couldn't hurt to reach out, so I dialed her number. After a few electrical clicks and someone's unearthly whispering in reverse English, I was connected.

"Miss Lovemilk? I'm Madison Cavendish. I work with and walk on the same journey as Seneca Sue."

"Oh my, how are you, Mr. Cavendish? Sue's told me so much about you. How is she?" Based on her cheerful tone, I assumed Cordelia to be very straight-laced and doubted if she even swore.

"Sue's peachy. She's up in Maine handling an affair. That's why I'm calling this morning. You're familiar with the type of work we do, and Sue suggested you might fill in for her during her absence."

"I would love to if I can work it around my schedule. As you probably know, I teach art part time."

"I'm meeting with the client's lawyer later today. He's accused of murder."

"Oh my!"

"You'll receive fifty percent of any earnings if we're hired following the meeting."

"Does this case also involve our underworld?" Cordelia asked.

"Possibly. Those involved think they know of our world, but they're largely mortal jackanapes."

"The money would certainly help me to supplement my income. What time should I meet you?"

"It's nearly eleven now. How about in two hours under the Third Avenue EL at 14th Street?"

"No can do, Madison, my dear. I'm teaching an art class at P.S.77 up here in the Bronx this afternoon, and then after that in the evening, I model at the Harvest School of Art on Second Street and Avenue A." Looking at the clock on my bookshelf was clear we weren't in sync.

"How about I meet you at the art school?" I asked.

"That's perfect. I start modeling at 6 p.m. and finish at seven. You can fill me in on the details at that time, Madison." Something about the naive and innocence of her voice aroused me.

"Thank you. See you then."

I hung up. Now that both meetings were set, I pulled my comforter off, then located my green shades. Grabbing a towel and a new tube of Brylcreem from my dresser drawer, I showered and dressed, braced by a cup of hyssop tea for daylight's burn.

—

An hour later, I stepped out of my apartment and onto Riverside Drive in a double-breasted maroon suit, gray fedora, crisp white shirt, hand-painted gray-maroon tie, gray shoes, and under my suit jacket, a holstered Luger P08. The gun was a war trophy I'd smuggled home from Italy to add to my collection.

—

Roberta Dickerson, a wholesome, fidgety homemaker with sable-black hair, sat in front of Upton Edwards's law office desk, trying to remain still. She kept flashing me questioning looks as we waited. Edwards, at his window, was deep in thought after listening to Roberta recounting her actions and those of her husband, A.Q., on the night of Logan's murder. Edwards ran his fingers up and down the brown window curtains, part of his office's auburn decor contrasted by a red law book. I felt restless myself, waiting for him to give me my private eye marching orders. Suntanned from his years in the Pacific Theater during the war as a Seabee, Edwards was stocky and raven-haired. He considered himself the people's lawyer, despite having a taste for the Stork Club and Brooks Brothers suits, like the ash-colored one he wore now, complemented by a black bow tie, white shirt, and a pair of spit-shined black shoes polished to USN standards. Finally, he came around and sat on the edge of the desk in front of Roberta and me, carefully choosing his words before speaking them.

"Your husband owns a white scarf similar to the one the police recovered at the crime scene, right?"

"Yes, but he lost that scarf! He misplaced it a month ago after a dinner!" Roberta's face flushed. I looked at Edwards, and we silently agreed that it was best to let her vent by yelling.

"It was lost in the IND subway after a dinner for Saul Pressman, *Two-Fisted* magazine's publisher," said Roberta, regaining her composure. "Mr. Edwards, I swear to you again, A.Q. and I spent a quiet evening playing Parcheesi the night Logan was murdered. A.Q. may write horror stories, but when it comes to violence, he's soft as butter!" Roberta's head fell into her hands as if it might roll off her shoulders, and she was holding on for dear life. This affair didn't look good to me. I pulled out an Old Gold cigarette and glanced at Edwards. He nodded in approval and I lit up, exhaling smoke toward the half-open window and beyond to Brooklyn Borough Hall.

"Well, Roberta, we will fight this to the last, especially since we need to thank author Cydell Amaro for his monetary help. Truth will win out." Edwards took Roberta by the hand and helped her out of a black leather armchair. I tried to make her feel better by showing an assertive smile, but I didn't think it won her over.

"Thank you, Mr. Edwards and Mr. Cavendish." Roberta straightened her dress and pulled on a matching overcoat. "Please see

Miss Owens out front, and she will phone a taxi service to take you back to Queens."

"I will tend to A.Q.'s bail hearing tomorrow morning. In the meantime, Mr. Cavendish and I have to discuss strategy, so you must excuse us." Edwards ushered Roberta Dickerson out to Miss Owens, the receptionist.

"What do you think?" Edwards asked. He was now seated behind his desk, enjoying an Old Gold he had bummed off me.

"The doorman recognized him," I said. "Nancy recognized him. A cabbie recognized him getting into a green delivery truck. The scarf might be pinned to him. His word against three witnesses. He and Logan were barely on speaking terms. We have a tall order here, Edwards." I flicked an ash, and we both shared a coffee mug quarter-filled with water as an ashtray.

"You and Seneca Sue can start by interviewing Mrs. Ward."

"Sue isn't on this case, Edwards; she's up in Maine working another case. But I have someone equally qualified for the job—her name is Cordelia Lovemilk." Edwards frowned at the unexpected change in the batting order.

"Fine. Just remember, Cavendish, A.Q.'s fate hinges on whether or not he sits on 'Old Sparky' up in Sing Sing, depending on what we produce."

I arrived at the Harvest School of Art studio located at 520 Second Street a few minutes before six. It was a collective created before the war to salute the regionalism style of Thomas Hart Benton. Composed of old longhairs and would-be artists waiting for the Pollock/Rothko revolution to start, they gathered every Wednesday to sketch classical nudes, as the brochure stated. For the life of me, I just couldn't put Cordelia and nude sketching in the same sentence.

"This way, please. She told us you were expected," said a pleasant-looking woman resembling Margret Hamilton, minus the *Wizard of Oz* emerald-green makeup. She wore a black sweater one size too large and a dark dress. A number-two pencil was nestled behind her ear, which she had been using to sketch on a sheet of paper at the front desk when I entered. She led me down a dimly lit corridor to a larger room that served as a classroom. The room was brighter than the corridor and opened to a circular arrangement of two rows of chairs, occupied here and there by students, each sketching in a frenzy, focused on the subject reclining on a pea-green velvet chaise lounge placed on a dais.

In a reclining pose on the lounge was Cordelia in the nude,

looking nothing like her file photo. She was tantalizing to the eyes—skin like soft caramel candy, jet-black hair coiled like earmuffs on the sides of her head. With a voluptuous body, her hands were folded behind her neck, her right knee arched up, and a pink silk veil was placed between her legs, I guessed, to keep things from being too risqué. A hint of makeup graced her face, and as her head tilted in my direction, she winked at me as I stood in the back of the classroom, firmly transfixed.

At 7 p.m., black sweater lady returned and banged a gong with a mallet, signaling the end of the sketching session and the start of an hour of peer-to-peer critiques, which, as the school legend went, might end in fisted altercations. I navigated to the dais, sidestepping easels and departing students alike.

"This way, Madison," Cordelia beckoned as she pulled on a white bathrobe. We navigated through salutes and dreamy-eyed looks of passion from both male and female artists and made our way to a roomy supply closet. Cordelia switched on a lightbulb that exposed more easels, stacks of old paint cans, and a mound of dried clay on a mud mat board. Marionettes, ancient in appearance, hung from the closet's walls, staring at us in silence.

"So glad to meet you, Madison, in person. I sense vitality from you!" Cordelia threw off the robe and began dressing, facing me. Not skipping a beat, I recounted A.Q.'s predicament.

"Where is he now?" Cordelia asked while adjusting a beige halo hat between her hair muffs. The color of the hat matched her figure-hugging turtleneck wool sweater dress, stockings, high heels, and a leather clutch bag. Only a brown shawl and a wide brown leather belt, which gave her an hourglass shape, countered her outfit's color.

"He's in the Tombs down near Centre Street. His attorney, Upton Edwards, will try to spring him out on bail tomorrow morning. You know, you look nothing like the photo Sue has of you!" I blurted out. At my comment, she smiled a coy smile. Damn, if Cordelia wasn't the perfect blend of regal mixed with sex appeal.

"Question, Madison: Does Edwards suspect you're a vampire? And what am I to do in relation to A.Q.?" Cordelia had picked up her check from the black sweater lady, and we were now on Avenue A, walking uptown, absentmindedly interlocking our arms as if we were a couple on a date. I didn't know if she was conjuring me or if this was a real attraction we had. You were right, Sue.

"I think he sees me as eccentric at most. I worked with him before the war, so he knows I get results. I don't think he's aware of Sue, either. Edwards is the hard-boiled type; he deals in what he sees as fact.

What I need from you is to sense A.Q.'s guilt or innocence if we can meet with him." If anything, Cordelia was empathetic like Sue. "After that, we'll track down Nancy Ward, the doorman, and a cab driver. Are you familiar with the writings of E. Abbott Logan or A.Q. Dickerson?" I asked as we continued to stroll up to 14th Street on a crisp fall evening.

"I never bothered to read their work, but one of our kind, Cydell Amaro, poses as a pulp horror writer and travels in their circle." A frown glided over her face.

"You know of him? According to Edwards, Amaro is footing the legal bills." I had lost track of the New York occult scene. Other than periodic nasty dealings back here with occult/super-science groups like the Vril Society, the Dark Ocean Society, and the Silver Shirts, I was on the battlefield during the war years. The blue neon sign of a delicatessen caught my eye as we turned onto 14th Street. "By the way, are you hungry?" I asked.

"Not so much. But Cydell's been around less than I have. I met him in 1918. At first, we had a dalliance until an incident in Indiana that year, which I would rather not discuss. The last time I saw him was at a mortal witches' coven party on Hester Street in the Village four years ago. I didn't like his carnal forwardness that night, so I left. He's a fairly weak alchemist who keeps himself on this earth through Saint-Germain alchemical poisons. He could still cause trouble, but since he's paying for Dickerson's defense, I guess Amaro has found convictions and turned over a new pentacle."

"He sounds interesting. Not hungry, then? Not even a turkey club sandwich and an egg cream?" I bribed, knowing I really couldn't taste food, but it was the thought that counted.

"That actually does sound fabulous! Vitality, Madison!"

We headed to a nearby deli for clubs and U-Bets. While dining, Cordelia revealed a bit of her history. She lived in the former town of West Farms, now part of Bronx County, located on the east bank of the Bronx River that snakes through the borough. She had worked at Starlight Park, a long-defunct amusement park on the west bank of the Bronx River that closed down in 1932.

"How have you managed to conceal your powers over the decades? Sue and I could use some pointers right about now." We were approaching Union Square. I had left our Lincoln Continental, aka "Black Betty," parked on 107th Street, as Sue had driven "Old Cherry," our old Pierce Arrow 80, up to Maine. We had to catch the IRT to get uptown, and for Cordelia, throw in a trolley ride or two once we reached the Bronx.

"You learn to go in and out of the shadows and try not to be too popular. Where are we to meet with Edwards for Dickerson's bail hearing?" Cordelia asked.

"It's set for 10 a.m. at the downtown Manhattan Court. I'll write down the information on where you and I are to meet." I pulled out a small notepad and my pencil, but as I started to write, I noticed a frown emerge on Cordelia's face. Figuring she wanted her half of the retainer fee, I reached into my coat pocket, retrieved an envelope, opened it, and counted off her share of bills. "Sorry, here you go." But she still wore a frown, though not enough to stop her from depositing the money in her clutch bag.

"Truth be told, Madison, I really wanted you to accompany me up to West Farms. Sue has told me so much about you. It's not often that our kind get together and interact. Maybe we can compare notes on this curse that has put us in this condition." Cordelia moved a step closer and looked up at me with subdued eyes.

"Fair enough, but we have to make our way to the Bronx by the EL." We continued along 14th Street to Third Avenue to catch the EL up to the great Northside, as the old-timers called it.

—

A mansion of Victorian-era design sat among residential houses, with the Bronx Zoo looming to the northwest. We exited the late evening "B" trolley, which continued to click-clack along 177th Street toward Morris Park. We stepped onto Wyatt Street. New York autumn leaves had gathered in Cordelia's front yard after New England's seasonal lead. She unlocked a chipped, horizon blue iron gate and then an intimidating old front door, leading me into a foyer where the scent of strawberry incense filled the entire house, which seemed larger once inside.

We stepped down into her living room, more like a love museum full of curiosities from Cordelia's paramours and two late husbands. As I toured the room, I noticed the pine wood staff I had seen in her photo, the top stained maroon with the scent of blood. The name *Maldade Lovemilk* was carved into it. On one table, a silver lavaliere lay atop a calico quilt from Mother Bickerdyke, next to a stuffed two-headed wolf, which she claimed was a gift from Nyarlathotep, the "Outer God."

There were multicolored silk veils from "Xelma the Mayan," a gold locket containing a strand of hair from Annie "Flat Boat" Christmas, and a yellow tulip that bloomed, grew, withered, and died in a nonstop cycle—a romantic keepsake from Zoltar the Great. This surprised me since he was supposed to be betrothed to our occult detective associate, Elsa Cranberry, who had not yet returned Stateside from the British Isles where she had been aiding Alistair Crowley and MI-6 in fighting Nazi spies.

Finally, there were pleading love letters from Paschal B. Randolph, master of sensual "Magia Sexualis," all her tributes encased in glass. *Cordelia really shares a lot,* I mused to myself.

Hanging on a red damask-papered wall was an oil portrait of what I assumed was a bald-headed, intense, umber-eyed Hugo Bataille in white tie and tails, fanning a deck of cards in one hand. Across the room hung a silent movie poster depicting Cordelia and Hugo in histrionic struggle poses in a film entitled, *Hugo the Mysterious versus The Temptress!*

"I see you're very popular with the gentlemen and ladies," I remarked, to which Cordelia issued a sly smile. "How did you get away from old Nyarlathotep?"

"Most of my relationships end on bad terms," she sighed, her smile evaporating. "Nyarlathotep is still sore about our breakup—unable to deal with my sexual freedom."

Changing the subject, I asked, "So when did your journey begin?"

We were seated on a plum-colored loveseat among her artifacts. Instead of answering, Cordelia placed her hand on top of mine, and images flooded into my mind's eye. Swamps and everglades somewhere in Florida, a creature similar to the one Sue and I encountered down in Lower Manhattan (but with a lifeforce color of leather yellow instead of magenta). A slave master's sacrifice of slaves to this creature included Cordelia's parents, a slave revolt, the creature slashing Cordelia across the back, and the plantation owner being killed by her, an act that resulted in Cordelia's lynching. An overseer had hung Cordelia on three occasions, but she never stayed dead for more than a few hours. Finally the overseer acknowledged Cordelia's immortality. A yellow mist had then appeared in her left hand, a powerful enigmatic energy, and she had used the mysterious power to cut herself down, stealing away deeper into the swamp.

Cordelia released my hand, and I fell back, my head now dizzy.

"What year?!" I panted, trying to regain myself.

"It was 1857," she recollected. "I was twenty years old. See?"

With her back to me, Cordelia rose just enough off the loveseat to pull her sweater dress up and expose her back to me. What I hadn't noticed before in the supply room was a thin, hardened, translucent yellow scar running from her upper left shoulder down across her back to her lower right buttocks.

"I was born in 1838. I migrated to New York in 1911," Cordelia said, confirming the date on her file as she let her dress drop back into place.

"So I guess what has been a mystery to Sue and me is just as much a mystery to you," I said as she pulled her sweater more snugly over herself, and I pushed up on my elbows to sit up. Cowgirl Nellie de Carlo and her similar encounter in Nebraska popped into my mind.

"I spent the better part of decades in research, and the only theory I can come up with is that these things landed from beyond the stars in other parts of the world with indifference to life on this planet. They adapt to the climate they're in, take on the characteristics of the life they feed on, and pass it back to any poor soul who survives an encounter." Cordelia removed one of her shoes and massaged her foot.

"Sister, you're lucky you don't have to deal with Sue's Lycanthropy or my vampirism."

"Praise the sky that you don't suffer from the 'spells' I have. I am damned with proclivities of an alligator, but right now it's getting late, and we need to get a little rest. We still have human needs and desires." Taking me by the hand, Cordelia led me upstairs to the guest bedroom, one of many, while hers was at the other end of the hallway. Outside, a late-night B trolley, perhaps on the last run of the night, click-clacked toward West Farms Square, stopping in front of the Coliseum, a former show venue now a bus depot. To the north, a Dyre Avenue EL train pulled into the old New York, Westchester & Boston Railway at the 180th Street Station, taking late-night straphangers further into Bronx County, then into Manhattan and beyond to Brooklyn.

"It's really fabulous to have you here for company. Hope you're comfortable, Madison." Watching her head down the hall, I pondered what would happen if we went through with what seemed like a mutual lust. I blocked it from my mind and flopped down on the guest bed, drifting off in an attempt to rest in peace, which was challenging since it was nighttime.

After forty minutes, I was up, carnal thoughts pushing me out of the room and across the hall to hers. I wanted to make love to this woman. I could see she was awake too. Was she waiting for me? The room door was slightly ajar. Pushing the door wider, I found Cordelia sitting on the edge of her bed, rolling down silk stockings off her caramel legs, while her hair muffs uncoiled themselves as if by an invisible chambermaid, then braided into two long black braids. Downstairs, a grandfather clock chimed a subdued 1 a.m.

"I'm fighting it too, Madison," she said, her quiet eyes searching mine. I didn't know if she was looking for me to surrender or for me to be loyal to Sue.

"Sue's a friend, and this would not be an ideal situation to get into."

Oh brother, she was right, but Cordelia didn't help the situation by continuing to undress while standing at her bedroom door. Once naked, Cordelia slipped into an aqua see-through negligee any femme fatale would envy.

"Well said and so true, sister. I just can't." With that, I retreated back to the guest room, flopped back down, my fedora covering my face, and waited for dawn's arrival.

Professionalism kicked in that morning along with the green tints on the bridge of my nose. We went after the business at hand: finding out who really murdered E. Abbott Logan. Small talk made for a more relaxed trip down to the court in Lower Manhattan.

Later that morning, Edwards was unable to get Dickerson out on bail, as Judge James C. Matthews Jr. denied it, remanding Dickerson back to the Tombs lockup on Centre Street. Cordelia could not get close enough to sense anything from Dickerson.

We stood outside the front of the criminal court, Edwards preparing to return to his Brooklyn office, Cordelia and I about to start our investigative legwork.

"You two ever meet Cydell Amaro?" Edwards asked.

"I have, but Madison hasn't," Cordelia said, sounding ashamed to know Cydell Amaro.

"What's the deal, Edwards?" This was going somewhere.

"Amaro wants you to join him for lunch at the Potluck Diner on Waverly Place, across from Washington Square Park's west side, at 2 p.m." Edwards held out a hand, signaling he wanted one of my Old Golds and a light.

"He's not meeting with us to advise us on how to conduct the investigation, right?" The last thing I needed was a client telling me how to do my job. Edwards took a drag off the cigarette, releasing the smoke by way of his nostrils.

"Nothing like that. He just wants to see the other defense team players. And at the end of the day, he's paid us nice fat retainers, so you guys and gals be good." Edwards sucked in another drag.

"I'll be as good as you say as long as he doesn't step on our investigative toes." I felt this was more about Cordelia than Dickerson. Probably not intentionally, but Edwards must have let Amaro know about my partner.

We arrived at the diner a few minutes before 2 p.m. The Potluck Diner seemed to offer little in the way of luck. It appeared to be, at best, a rundown greasy spoon. That the place served any food at all surprised me. Red vinyl-cushioned seat booths with white Formica tables filled the interior. In the back, hunched over coffee cups, I made eye contact with Amaro and what I guessed was a hired flunky.

"That's Amaro," Cordelia whispered just off the back of my left shoulder. Sharply dressed in a green double-breasted suit, shoes, and tie, he had well-maintained auburn hair, a goatee, and a pencil-thin mustache like mine. His face, albeit handsome, was devious, and I could see why Cordelia fell for him back in '18.

"You'll have to wait to be seated!" a thin waitress in a full pink uniform with a blond perm yelled, cutting into my stream of thought, even though the joint was empty but for one other customer.

From a distance, Amaro waved a hand behind the waitress. "You lovebirds can double up with Mr. Amaro," the perm waitress said, switching up on us. Amaro's mind control had clearly changed her demeanor with that wave of his hand.

"Ah, Cordelia, it's been a while, my love, and greetings and salutations to you, Mr. Cavendish." Amaro rose, shook my hand, and planted an unwanted kiss on Cordelia's cheek while sliding his hand down her back toward her backside before she swatted it away.

"Ah, Mr. Amaro, let's throttle back on the touchy-feely, shall we?" I couldn't let him get away with that; I had to let him know my battleships were in his harbor. But I bet the house Cordelia could handle his crudeness on her own.

"Forgive me. I should not act in such a way, but then again, Mr. Cavendish, I don't think Cordelia has told you how she brings erotic fluster and, pray tell, murder out in mortals and immortals alike, or has it already happened with you two? Can't be since you're alive. She's such a siren, you know." Amaro chuckled.

"Can we get down to business, Mr. Amaro?" Cordelia fumed. An ominous yellow mist started to form around her hands.

"Who's your friend?" I tried to deflect and focus while grasping Cordelia's right hand, silently signaling her to stay cool.

"This is my assistant, Diego Bosch," Amaro said, keeping his eyes on Cordelia. Bosch looked like he was a few days removed from the Bowery—bloated but sober, with gray hair in a three-piece dark suit and brown shoes. The man smelled of port wine and urine. Bosch offered us his seat, but his aroma made us decline and remain standing.

"So, Amaro, how goes it with you?" I asked. "You must be tight with A.Q. to foot the bill for his defense. I figured there had to be more to it."

"He's a stalwart member of our writing group."

"Well, what's the dope on who you think did it? Maybe he didn't like the way Logan ran things."

"The dope's over there, friend." Amaro's eyes directed me to a scrawny man in a charcoal wool suit, black tie, dingy white shirt, and black gym shoes. "He's been nursing that teacup and watercress sandwiches for hours."

"Who's he?" Things were getting juicy.

"Howard Eggmont. Scientist, pulp science fiction writer, and President of the Astonishing Fiction Writers Association, or AFWA," Amaro whispered. "They look upon us, the AHSCC, as hack writers of myths and wives' tales. The Atomic Age has given them the audacity to stomp around. But they're just a bunch of comic book- and pulp magazine-reading eggheads." Amaro took a sip of coffee. "To them, we are outdated speculative fiction in a world where super science is the gateway to the future. But we know better. Just by the three of us here now, as underworlders talking," Amaro said.

I looked at Cordelia; her eyes were strained, anger still bubbling from within. As soon as we could leave this dive I intended to refocus her on the affair. "You mean to tell me Logan's murder is the start of a pulp genre war? You're joking."

At that moment, Eggmont stood up from his booth, threw two dollars on the table, and quickly exited the unappetizing place.

"Bosch, follow him!" Amaro ordered. Bosch sprung up and strode out.

"It's your job to get A.Q. off, right?" Amaro demanded.

I was just about to tell him we had to look at all angles when a sudden loud buzzing erupted from outside, followed by an explosion and screams that thundered into the Potluck. Amaro sat rock still while Cordelia and I ran outside to see what the commotion was. The smells of burnt flesh, ozone, and electrical parts mingled in the black smoke flowing from East Eighth Street to the diner.

"Horrendous!" Cordelia exclaimed, while I looked, mouth agape, at the charred remains—two pairs of legs intact below the knees, one in dark trousers and the other in charcoal, next to a 1939 Dodge Woody station wagon parked with its back open. "Stay here, Cordelia! I'd better get the Office of Special Concerns involved in this!" I ran back into the Potluck to use the pay phone. I looked around for Amaro and the blonde waitress, but both had vanished!

—

"Heat ray gun! Definitely a heat ray gun. A struggle over it, and it sizzles both Joes," proclaimed Skip Basil, senior forensic scientist and intern head of the Office of Special Concerns. Basil, in a white lab coat and black horn-rimmed glasses, constantly stroked his black hair away from his forehead as he stood with us. Absently, I knelt down and lit a cigarette off one of the smoldering pant legs for my Old Gold.

Basil frowned. "Cavendish, heck, is that how you go about things? Could you and your partner walk with me, please?" We strode into Washington Square Park while the OSC crew continued its investigation amidst a crowd of gawking NYU students and faculty.

"Heck, so this is what Kirkland meant when he said OSC are the last to be called and the first to clean up when it comes to you, Cavendish." Basil seemed upset. Kirkland was a former head of OSC.

"Trust me, Skip, it's not like that at all. We walked into this. It didn't start out as a paranormal or super-science case."

"Well, it's become one, and OSC is involved. What do you have for me?" Basil was trying to sound like a detective, but it just wasn't working given that he was originally a chemist from Akron.

"Nothing yet. But the two ash heaps are Howard Eggmont, a science fiction writer, and a guy named Bosch, a Bowery bum."

"Madison is correct, Dr. Basil," Cordelia vouched. Basil looked at me and then at Cordelia, knowing that no other shoe was dropping at the moment.

"Okay, okay. Keep me in the loop. I want to speak with whoever is responsible for this BBQ."

"I will, Skip," I lied. I intended to do things my way.

—

After placing a call to Edwards to advise him of what had transpired at the meeting with Amaro, Edwards said the show still must go on to get Dickerson off. We got a ride from one of Basil's people up to 107th Street to pick up Black Betty. From there, we headed down to 53rd Street and Ninth Avenue, Hell's Kitchen, to see Nancy Ward.

"What did Amaro mean when he said you bring out 'erotic fluster'—those were the words he used—in mortals and immortals? Also, what about the murder comment, Cordelia?"

"Madison, that's why I stay to myself and in the shadows. I tend to unintentionally place men and women into spells of want and desire. That's why, at one point during my days at Starlight Park, I had to stop belly dancing and become a fortune teller." We stopped for a red light, crossing Manhattan and then down the west side. "Had to cover my face back then too, you know. As for murder, yes, I did kill my first husband, Maldade Lovemilk, because he was abusive, but you can't tell that to his six daughters who, to this day, after they chased me out of Alabama, put a curse over my head. With Hugo, it was self-defense—the cause and effect of a love triangle between Hugo, Amaro, and me. Hugo is buried behind the mansion in the backyard, and the mementos you saw in my living room—the givers all at one point became perturbed with me because they couldn't control me. I'm my own being!"

"So that's a spell I feel for you now?" The feeling of being suckered by a black widow washed over me.

"No, no, Madison. What you and I have is real and mutual, but it's best to leave it alone because of Sue. Amaro wants to poison everything. He's a heel and a first-rate bastard!"

—

"You can ask me over and over again. It was Mr. Dickerson I tell you. I know his face."

We were sitting in Nancy's once-crowded apartment. With her husband and oldest son both deceased, one son still in the service, the youngest son attending CCNY, and her daughter married, Nancy longed for the old Broadway showgirl days now that she was no longer employed by Mr. Logan.

"You don't find it strange Dickerson said nothing to you?" I asked.

"MIGHTY BOY! It was him, old slew foot! Wait!" The old showgirl came alive.

"What?" Cordelia asked.

"I called him old slew foot behind his back because of the way he walked with his feet pointed out all the damn time, like he was loping over Texas. But that night he shuffled straight footed for some reason, liking to take the carpet up with his walk. Don't mean a thing now. Poor Mr. Logan's relatives arrive here tomorrow to make the final arrangements."

81ST STREET AND YORK AVENUE

"Must have come through the service entrance. As God is my witness, I only saw Dickerson leave past me. He was looking straight ahead," Carey, a fair-haired young man, said. A B-17 veteran juggling college on the GI Bill, he wore a green-gray uniform as a doorman. Carey was one of the lucky ones, as the lifespan of a B-17 crewman was short during the war. "What could I do?"

"You did your best, dear. You have vitality," Cordelia consoled him, causing Carey to blush as evening mellowed in with an East River chill in the air.

"But when he left, you're sure it was him?" I was starting to hear the slap of my belt on a mare that had left this world—not good for Dickerson.

"Sure I'm sure. One thing that… Good evening, Mr. Elroy," Carey said, pausing to open the door for a portly man in a dark suit who tipped him a quarter.

"Like I was saying, one thing after he left and all hell broke loose; we had to have the service elevator fixed. Something about the weight, the Otis elevator guys complained. I told this to the homicide bureau cops, you know."

"Thanks, buddy." I showed my appreciation to the portly man by slipping Carey five bucks.

"You know, maybe you should hang around. The cabbie who used to pick up Dickerson swings around here about this time—around the same time Logan got his neck wrung. Colored guy named Jasper, you know," Carey said.

"Jasper?!"

"Yup, you know him."

"Maybe. Thanks." We walked back to Black Betty, got in, and waited.

"I think I know this Jasper character, though I could be wrong," I said to Cordelia.

"So far, except for the shuffling, and Dickerson not speaking to Carey, this affair looks barren, Madison." Cordelia wore the same type of outfit from the other night, but it was all sensual black, with a wide red leather belt, a leopard skin pillbox hat, and a matching leopard skin clutch bag. She pulled out a small compact and applied a little ruby-red lipstick, using the glow from the streetlamp to help her. I tried not to stare.

Twenty minutes later, a yellow Checker cab pulled up in front of Logan's apartment building.

"Jasper! You old fare jockey, how goes it, brother?"

Startled for a moment, Jasper reached inside his jacket. He was a shade of chestnut, sporting a typical cabbie cap, Eisenhower jacket, dark pleated pants, and dark shoes, pulling up alongside us.

"Hell, what are you doing around here, zebra?! I reckon you should be up along Riverside Drive or Harlem, doing your strange private dick work!" Brother Jasper still had a hearty laugh.

"I'll pay you a sawbuck if you park and talk to me and my partner about the murder in the building where you pick up fares." A former torpedo for gangster Bumpy Johnson, Jasper had gone straight. Instead of breaking legs, he was breaking for red lights, much to the relief of some underworld rivals. "Let me park, brother, and I'll be with you."

"Who's the fox? It sure isn't Seneca Sue." Jasper was spellbound as Cordelia exited Black Betty.

"Cordelia Lovemilk; she's helping me on the Logan murder case."

"Hello, Jasper." Cordelia was cordial, and that was all.

"Sorry for calling you a fox, ma'am, but gosh, you sure are a good-looking woman." Jasper seemed locked onto Cordelia's quiet brown eyes. I had to focus him back on me.

"Jasper, I need to know what happened the night of Logan's murder."

"Yeah, well, not much at first. On slow nights, I stop by Logan's building to pick up a fare or two, and every now and then, it would be that Dickerson mug. Didn't know he was a writer until he had his face splashed all over the *Daily News,* the *Evening Post,* and the *Sun.* If it's not Willie Shakespeare, Countee Cullen, or Cowboy comics, don't bug me when it comes to reading. Like I told the cops, he had become an irregular regular; don't know if that makes sense. But that evening, his lame ass paid me no mind. Doofy man got in the back of an old green Streusel's bread truck, like he was sick and all."

"How do you know it was Streusel's?" Cordelia asked before I could. Jasper was more than happy to answer her.

"After driving a hack for so many years, you tend to pick up on things in traffic, Cordelia. Is it okay if I call you Cordelia, ma'am?" She nodded. Jasper smiled, and Cordelia let her stoical look fade into a smile, batting her eyelashes in response. "You could still see the lettering stenciled under the green paint. Plus, I know their make and model—a Ford A. Also, an odd item for you two is the fact that he got in the back of the truck by laying on a board while two guys pushed him in. I told the flatfoots, but they figured they had Dickerson dead to rights and didn't need any more facts. Plus, they don't like a Negro trying to tell them how to do their jobs."

"What did the two guys look like?" I asked.

Jasper was at it again, searching Cordelia's eyes while pulling his collar up against the top-shelf wind that jumped off the East River and onto East 81st.

"Jasper?" I nudged him, even thinking of telling Cordelia to wait in the car, but she was my even-Stephen partner.

"Oh, both wore glasses. One was sandy-haired; the other had black hair—a bowl cut, we call it. Sandy had a red and black bow tie; the other I can't remember. Both had what you all call… ah, lab coats! By the way, who are you and Cordelia working for? Why do you all have a penny in this bank?" A few autumn leaves trickled down between us from the almost naked tree we were standing under.

"We work for his defense counsel," I said.

"We are trying to get to the truth," Cordelia added with a come-hither smile.

"Good luck, brother and sister, because I think doofy man's gonna get the chair if you ask me," Jasper chuckled and insisted I come to his cab for a private conversation.

Shortly thereafter, Cordelia and I headed to my apartment crosstown. Once there, I rummaged through the icebox for something for us to snack on while Cordelia sat on the sofa, flipping through a copy of *Collier's* magazine that Sue had left on my coffee table.

"So all involved have Dickerson pegged at the scene of the murder," I said, my voice bouncing around inside the icebox.

"But Cydell Amaro felt the AFWA was behind it. Howard Eggmont was at the Potluck; maybe he was going to use the heat ray gun on Amaro. But now he's gone underground." Cordelia was now behind me, peeking to see if I had any luck with my food search, the warmth of her body pressing against my vampire coldness as phantom hands uncoiled her hair muffs and redid them into long braids again.

"And he's never had a real address all the decades you've known him?" I passed her a plate of cold fried chicken, some leftover mock Francis Sweeny mincemeat pie, celery stalks, endives, a wedge of Parmesan cheese, and a bottle of orange juice. For myself, along with the pie, I had a link of blood sausage. From my lower right desk drawer, I fetched a bottle of Bombay Sapphire gin and two glasses. I doubted that Cordelia drank, but I left the second glass on the desk anyway. Alas, no tonic water, but then again, no real Francis Sweeny, either. I placed a tea tin holding hyssop leaves for the morning on the kitchen table.

"I cannot lie to you, Madison; I've never known him to have a stable place." Cordelia conjured one of the black leather guest/client club chairs to hop up near the front of my desk so she could sit as we feasted on our late-night snack.

"If we can locate the truck, I think we can end this affair." I chased the meal with a glass of gin and juice.

"And how do we do that?" Cordelia asked between bites and sips of gin straight.

"Streusel's probably sells their old trucks as they put new ones into service. They should have information on the buyers."

I looked up Streusel's Bread Company in the Yellow Pages and phoned their main number. Unfortunately, they didn't start operations until 4 a.m., and the records department wouldn't be open until 9 a.m., according to the night watchman who answered the phone and was glad to talk to someone at such a lonely hour.

"I'll take the couch, and you can sleep in my room, or I can give you the keys to Sue's place upstairs," I volunteered.

"Madison, I think we can sleep in the same bed without incident." Cordelia wanted companionship. For the rest of the night, I wore blue pajamas, and Cordelia wore a red striped pajama top I loaned her. Seeing that I could produce a magenta mist with my left hand to light my Old Golds, Cordelia showed me how to play tic-tac-toe, her X's comprised of lemon neon yellow mist and my O's a warm magenta glow in the darkness of my bedroom until we drifted off to sleep.

—

"Yes, uh, thank you Louey. Right. Thanks." Cordelia hung up the phone just as I entered from the kitchen with two steaming cups of hyssop tea. I wore a double-breasted blue suit. Cordelia was dressed in an olive-green day dress borrowed from Sue's closet upstairs.

"That was Louey from Strusel's record department. We're looking for a man named Umberto Hedderman. Strusel's Bakery is out in Williamsburg, Brooklyn," Cordelia said as she adjusted the red belt on her waist.

"Okay, we'll ride out there and look the address over and then come up with a plan of action. Oh yes, before I forget..." I handed her a piece of paper with Jasper Davis's phone number scribbled on it. "Jasper asked me to give you this during our 'private' conversation. He's a nice guy for a mortal, Cordelia. Likes to listen to Willaim Grant Still and the other long-haired composers you like. He's a good guy; maybe give him a chance." Ambiguous as the situation was, I felt they were a good match. Better to lose her to Jasper than have Sue rip my throat out.

"I purposely abstain from dating mortals, both male or female. I've only dated as a cover to move around in society. But I'll consider it, Madison." She folded the paper and slipped it into her clutch bag.

The address on South Third Street turned out to be an old bootlegger warehouse. The red neon sign of the Domino Sugar Factory glowed further down the street, its main luminosity hitting the East River.

It was a lonely 3 a.m. We were parked across from the warehouse, facing Hewes Street.

"Truck's coming," Cordelia whispered.

A green cargo truck parked for several minutes, during which time a man in a white lab coat jumped out and unlocked the two wooden high-arched warehouse doors. This provided me an opportunity to slip into the street shadows, close enough to sneak in behind the truck and into the warehouse while Cordelia waited in Black Betty. Large pale wooden crates rose from floor to ceiling, helping to conceal me.

"How long is the calibration going to take, Sanderson?" the driver's partner nervously demanded.

"It's come down to us or the AHSCC, Hedderman, proving science over witchcraft and emotional folklore! We must!"

"I can't do a damn thing without the right tools," Hedderman yelled.

"Hold your potato while I peel mine!" Hedderman, the electronic genius, shot back. Sad blue eyes, a thick face, and a Moe-styled haircut—he dismissed Sanderson with a hand wave. Kneeling behind a crate, close enough that the two would hear my heartbeat if I had one, I gave a silent laugh. I couldn't help but wonder what the next possible genre war would be. Westerns versus romance novels?

A number of workbenches lined the wall, each separated by packing crates. The benches were crammed with cathode vacuum tubes, wiring, large resistors, tools, and cannibalized radio parts from the last war. I crouched lower as Hedderman walked by my crate. The delivery truck, now parked in the middle of the warehouse, faced two tarp-covered objects; their outlines suggested they were seated.

"Help me with the tarps, Sanderson." Pushing a tool cart up to the tarp, Hedderman handled a modified Army surplus walkie-talkie while Sanderson fumbled with tools on a workbench. "Never mind. I'll do it myself!" It seemed that Hedderman was a nuts-and-bolts science journal man with neither time nor patience for science fiction writers. He pulled the covering back, revealing a seated A.Q. Dickerson and a Cydell Amaro lookalike, both staring off into space. I figured A.Q. Dickerson to be robotic, especially since Jasper had tipped Cordelia and me that he'd witnessed Sanderson and Hedderman placing the fake Dickerson in the back of the van on a board, likely using some type of metal roller track and gurney. The Amaro robot's origins were harder to pin down.

Stepping back, Hedderman flicked a switch on the modified walkie-talkie, and a loud hum emanated from A.Q. "We still got a hum coming out of A.Q." As the horror author robot hummed with life,

Hedderman adjusted control knobs in sync with its actions, guiding it toward my hiding place.

"Hold it, you two!" I yelled, jumping up, Luger in hand.

"The hell you say!" Hedderman immediately adjusted the controls.

"Drop the remote, science man!"

"The hell I will!" he snapped back.

"I said drop it! Now!" The A.Q. robot was advancing on me. I aimed at Hedderman's hand holding the control, but a wrench flew from Sanderson, knocking the Luger from my hand and across the warehouse floor, sliding away from me. The A.Q. robot put me in a bear hug so tight that it threatened to squeeze the life out of me. My only fear was how many volts this thing worked with because I was about to use my left-hand mist to break free, which might also do some serious nonregenerative harm to me.

As I struggled, Hedderman and Sanderson jumped into the delivery truck and backed out of the warehouse, smashing the doors open. A magenta aura began to form around my hand. My air supply was running out. I grabbed hold, and we ignited. The explosion sent A.Q. robot parts across the warehouse, the concussion somehow activating the Cydell Amaro robot, which jumped up and performed a mad mambo-like dance before collapsing in a heap of plastic, rubber, and metal. My suit sleeves were aflame as I ran to the warehouse entrance, but not before hearing chaos erupt outside. I saw an upright member of the Alligatoridae family reaching into the driver's side window of the delivery truck as it swerved along South Third. Before I could take a step, the delivery truck crashed, flipping end over end in a flaming mess. Somehow Cordelia—who was now an alligator—was thrown free of the vehicle.

"Are you alright, Cordelia?" She didn't recognize me, but after a few seconds she began to revert to her natural human form, naked as day, focused on the wreck like a seasoned gunslinger surveying a kill. While I beat out the small flames on my sleeves, I dashed to Black Betty and grabbed Sue's extra change of clothes from the trunk, which we carried for those occasions when she transformed to her Lycan alter-ego. Although I knew she'd understand, Sue was nonetheless going to be sore about the ripped-up day dress.

"I'm okay," Cordelia panted as she quickly dressed, hoping no one would see us.

"Help me! I... I need a doctor!" Sanderson crawled toward us on his knees and elbows, his burnt arms and hands glazed red.

Hedderman was still in the truck, unreachable and burning to a crisp.

"I'll tend to him, Madison. You should find a phone booth and make some calls." It was a sound plan. I searched for a phone booth and pulled a fire alarm box on the corner of South Third and Hewes Street along the way.

—

The robot Amaro was just that—a robot. Cydell Amaro could not be found. Sanderson confessed to the following: Amaro wanted to take over the AHSCC, pushing Logan out, but as an alchemist, he was weakly skilled. He therefore decided to use science as a means, believing the pulp fiction magazine business could prove lucrative. He formed a clandestine alliance with the AFWA, met with Eggmont, and they arranged for Hedderman and Sanderson to build an automaton fixed up to resemble A.Q. Dickerson, intending to kill Logan and, thus, pinning the murder on the real Dickerson. Amaro played the concerned friend and even helped fund Dickerson's defense. But he hadn't counted on Edwards retaining our services. Edwards was a mere pawn in the affair. Eggmont and Bosch, struggling over a heat ray gun, had an accident when they dropped it between them.

The meeting with Amaro had been a setup—the heat ray gun had been meant for Cordelia and me. Amaro also failed to count on being double-crossed by the science boys. Sanderson and Hedderman planned to bump off Eggmont using the Cydell robot so they could slurp up his position in the AFWA. With each organization having hundreds of members, I wondered why it didn't occur to them to simply take a vote. Go figure. For a man of his talents, Sanderson missed the electric chair and was whisked off to a certain government agency to perform electronics work, as relations between the USSR and the US were cooling. Logan wasn't the type to receive Christmas cards from people anyway, if you know what I mean. Sadly, a body found in a garbage dump in Queens matched the Potluck waitress—a missing college student named Bonnie who happened to be at the wrong place, with the wrong people, at the wrong time.

—

"Here you are, love." While no one was looking, Cordelia used a low-level mist from her right index finger to light my Old Gold hanging from the corner of my mouth. "Matched you, Maddy," Cordelia purred.

We stood in front of 16 Court Street after visiting Edwards to collect the second half of our fee. While there, the exonerated A.Q. Dickerson and a relieved Roberta thanked us. Murdering Cydell Amaro had stepped back into the shadows; this mortal world was no longer fun for him now that the two pulp genres had reached a truce, for what it was worth.

"Madison, it's been fun and vital! Thank you." Cordelia extended a hand. Before we could shake hands, she pushed forward, grabbing me by my trench coat lapels and planting a kiss on my cheek, narrowly missing my cigarette. Under her coat she wore a sexy red deep-plunge evening dress that implied she was ready for a night on the town.

"Hey! What's the idea stealing a kiss from my woman?" Jasper teased as he pulled up, nattily dressed in a dark suit.

"Can we give you a lift to Riverside Drive?" Cordelia offered. "Jasper and I have to kill time before heading to Club Café Society in the village; Pearl Primus is tonight's headliner."

"Thanks, but no. I'm parked on Jay Street. You two go enjoy yourselves." Thus began a passionate mortal-immortal romance.

CHRISTMAS EVE

Snow covered the ground outside our place on Riverside Drive. Our tree was up and decorated; the roast duck had finished roasting and was in the oven. Yams, blood pudding, cranberry sauce, fresh mincemeat pie à la gangster, and expensive truffles were on the stovetop. On the kitchen table, a bottle of Veuve Clicquot Brut was chilling on the windowsill in the New York evening air, soon to be uncorked.

"Oh, we've just one hour until Christmas. Why can't you wait, Maddy?" Sue was, as usual, wearing the top of my green-and-red-striped PJs, what we called X-mas pajamas; I wore the bottoms. She was a beige beauty. All was right in the world tonight for us. Confessing my feelings to Sue about Cordelia, Sue confessed she was not surprised, as Cordelia had surfaced similar "erotic flusters" in her, too, when they served together in the 6888th Mail Battalion in France during the war, culminating in a salacious night in Sue's upstairs apartment following their return to the States. Yet Sue said she was still a blockhead for me.

"Come on, let me open just one gift," I mock pleaded as she rubbed my stomach; we were in bed. All things paranormal—although tonight was kind of paranormal—were far from our minds right now, except for Santa. Sekhmet, back from her little mysterious vortex hiatus, was curled up at the foot of the bed, napping.

"Who in Hades is that?" I yelled in response to the phone ringing.

"Something's not right with Cordelia," Sue automatically sensed. She answered the call.

"Cordelia, what's happened?!" For what seemed like an eternity, a backward whispering voice spoke, followed by Cordelia.

"HE'S… OOOOOOH… DEAD. JASPER! OUT THE SHADOWS, MY LOVE. DEAD. I MADE A MISTAKE!" Sue tried to understand Cordelia's cryptic rant, but the line went dead.

"Maddy, we've got to get up to the Bronx." A look of foreboding washed across her freckled face. Sue threw on blue jeans and galoshes and grabbed her .32, while I dressed in a sweater, galoshes, and my .44. Winter coats draped over our arms as we carried our occult aid chest between us, which held assorted items just for occasions like this. After Sue scribbled a note instructing Sekhmet not to touch the food on the stove, and leaving her a duck leg in her food bowl, we hopped in Black Betty and sped up to Bronx County.

We pulled up in front of Cordelia's house. The gray-cast Christmas early morning reflected how Sue and I felt as we made our way into the mansion while snow flurries started up again. The rich scent of dried blood had replaced the strawberry incense. The house was a crime scene.

"Oh, Maddy," Sue said, sadness filling her voice. Splayed out on the living room floor was the body of Jasper Davis, his face mutilated by blunt force. Where his mouth should have been, Zoltar's tulip, Xelma's veils, and Bickerdyke's lavaliere were stuffed into the bloody, cracked-tooth entrance. The carpet was soaked through and saturated with Jasper's blood. On one side of his body lay Maldade Lovemilk's blood-covered staff, while on the other, in an open ring box, was a sparkling engagement ring I assumed was for Cordelia.

Sue and I began a search of the mansion, which turned up no sign of Cordelia. Out in the backyard, the grass now covered with a thin layer of snow, was an empty grave, shattered coffin wood around it, and the soil cast about as if possibly Hugo, resting in it, had dug himself out as opposed to someone digging him up. Was this Bataille's doing? Was it Cydell's attempt to get back at Cordelia, or was it the act of another former jaded lover? If Cydell Amaro or Cordelia was behind Jasper's murder, they could kiss their underworld asses goodbye once I caught up with them.

"Maddy, the only way we'll find out what happened is for me to…"

"Go ahead, love," I told her. Sue was referring to her and sometimes my dealings with the infinity pull, aka conversing with the dead, as she'd done in '38 during the East 55th Street Affair in Cleveland. Sue knelt down near Jasper's body, extracting the bloody gifts from his mouth. She cupped his head in her hands and concentrated. Jasper's eyes blinked open, and he emitted a garbled scream. In a whisper, Jasper revealed the name of his killer.

Sue's outburst provided the answer. "MADDY, OH NO! HELP US! IT WAS…"

THE
SCHUYLER
AFFAIR

1954

MARCH

The seventh floor of an apartment building overlooking Plaza de Zocalo in Mexico City, the residence of Gustavo Hernandez, playboy, polo player, wild cat oil driller, and thrill-seeking gem thief. His bludgeoned body splayed out on the floor of his spacious living room carpet, stained with blood and stained Old Parr's whiskey.

Pieces of a cracked and broken tumbler once used to contain the spirit and meant to brace Hernandez's terror from ruthless visitors were scattered next to his body, which was clad only in underwear. His torso was caked in red from a gash running horizontally across his neck, a coup de grace following a tortuous beating with his own pallet sticks.

In a corner of the apartment, a HiFi record player's needle bounced and skipped against the outer grooves of a 45 RPM record and repeat-played "Cerez Rosa" at a loud volume. No neighbors complained—they knew of Gustavo's rumored ties to crime and did not want to risk his wrath. The music snuffed out any noises within the room as two gloved men snuffed out Hernandez. In another corner, a candle lit as a shrine to bandit Jesus Malverde, his ceramic image a mute witness to what had transpired in the room. Job finished, one of the killers—a large man in a dark-colored turtleneck and suit—sidestepped Hernandez's body, a soon-to-be-crime-scene outline, to switch off the HiFi while the other killer, thin in build, stood near a coffee table waiting for an appointed time on his Japanese-manufactured watch. He dialed an unlisted number on Hernandez's phone. Bloody rubber shoe booties and gloves were placed in Casa Ley bags that would accompany the killers upon their departure.

"*Si?*" a monotoned voice asked, answering the phone call.

"*Ella tiene el sortiga.* She has the ring, and it fits!" the thin man announced.

"*Find her! Ahora!*" The voice was irate. "The ring must be found!"

"*Pero como?*" asked the thin man, as the big man approached him from behind to listen in on the conversation. "She could be anywhere in the city. *¿Qué podemos hacer?*"

"*What can you do?* I know people in New York who can help."

"*Nuerva York?*"

"*Si, Nuerva York.* For now, burn the apartment. Burn it to the ground."

"*Pero…*"

"Do as I command!" the voice on the other end said and racked the receiver.

APRIL

We were set to check out Sonny Rollins at the Village Vanguard that night and then drive up to Harlem to the Prelude Club for drinks and more bebop. With no full moon that evening, I felt relaxed, meaning it was up to me whether I would undergo a Lycan transformation. As for my Maddy, the night belonged to him as long as he sipped some hyssop tea to cool himself down. It might sound corny, but as occult detectives, danger was our beat. Here was an affair.

Our Riverside Drive apartments still doubled as a place of business, but the Art Deco furnishings of our Upper West Side dwellings had given way to Isamu Noguchi aesthetics in both our spaces. We had purchased what you might call his-and-hers Philco swivel television sets with earnings from our last paying affair—his in one corner, mine upstairs since sometimes we couldn't agree on programming, especially since Maddy was a Giants fan and I was a Yankees fan. Sekhmet added to the sports tension, being that she loved "Dem Bums" from Brooklyn.

When I came into Madison's apartment after shopping, I brought an outfit that was going to make me look boss at the Vanguard that night—or "hot to trot," as we used to say: a nice blue evening dress along with some Jezebel earrings. But at the moment, I wore a red and green plaid dress suit, red heels, and a red beret covering my now-blond, poodle-clipped hair, fuzzy and short. Maddy sat behind his desk (the one piece of furniture he refused to part with), dressed in a chocolate pinstripe suit. Before I could say hello, the phone rang. He answered and switched on the Jordaphone so the caller's voice could be heard over a loudspeaker and Maddy could talk hands-free. Maddy waved a hand for me to take a seat.

"Madison, it's George Schuyler. Please don't hang up," the voice on the other end begged.

"Okay, George, what's this about?" Madison hadn't heard that voice in years, not that he wanted to.

"It's about my daughter."

"You mean little Philippa?"

"She's not little anymore, Madison," a weary George warned. "She's 23 years old and a grown woman. Maybe too grown."

"She's still considered a prodigy?"

"Madison, she's a concert pianist." George was impatient.

"Alright, George, what can I do for you? What's your beef?" Madison did not like this man.

"Someone is trying to destroy my Philippa and her career."

"Who's the someone?"

"I don't know; that's why I need you and that partner of yours to help me. Philippa can't get a proper night's sleep. She's been having nightmares since she moved into her own apartment. Whoever they are must not have known she's moved because Josephine has been receiving threatening phone calls and mail directed at her at our apartment."

"Where is she now, George?" Madison took notes on a yellow legal pad with a pencil that had been well chewed upon by Sekhmet.

"She's headed to see Josephine at our apartment on Edgecomb Avenue. You remember the address from the old days, Madison. She's headstrong. I'm out of state on a journalistic assignment, but I will phone Josephine and tell her to persuade Philippa to wait for you when she comes by to pick up her mail. A retainer fee will also be there for you two."

"George, I want you to be square with me. Why me? You badmouthed good friends of mine, calling them Reds and the like. You wrote a blind item column in the *New York Negro Gazette*, stopping just short of calling me a commie and Sue a 'half-breed fake,' to use your nasty words, while I was in damn Korea fighting for my country and getting shot at by actual commies. Again, why me? And what if I say no, you bum?"

"I love my daughter, and I don't want the police involved, Madison. I love my daughter. Please!" George Schuyler's voice cracked into sobs over the long-distance connection.

"Okay, George. Okay. We'll take the case. We'll head over now."

"Thank you, Madison. Thank you."

Maddy ended the call as I walked across the room and sat on the corner of his desk.

"Sue, I know what you're going to say."

"Well, I'm still going to say it: How could you, Maddy?" He flashed his cute fangs in an effort to diffuse my anger. "I mean, of all the nerve! He gossips about me in the papers, saying I'm full of bunk and hokum, yet you take the case. Why?" I demanded an answer. Okay, the fang thing was kind of working, but that wasn't the point.

"He's a desperate man, Sue."

It was hard to argue against parents trying to protect a child.

"We'll see what's going on when we arrive and speak with Josephine."

"As long as you don't mention Sonny Rollins, I'll be okay," I told Maddy. Missing the Rollins set really stung.

We got ourselves together, hopped into our 1953 model aqua blue and white Metropolitan, and drove up into Harlem and over to Sugar Hill, our old Packard, Pierce Arrow, and "Black Betty," all having bitten the dust some time ago.

When we arrived at the Schuylers' apartment building, around the corner from Philippa's apartment, the edge of a chilly spring night loomed over Sugar Hill, one of our old stomping grounds during the Harlem Renaissance. This turf had an elegance to it.

———

"Madison and Seneca, you remember my daughter, Philippa," Josephine said in a Texas accent that had faded after so many years of living in New York. Her blond hair was styled in big victory rolls, and she wore plump, dangling jewelry popular from the 1930s in an unfitted lime-green day dress and matching pumps. This former pinup girl was now a classical music stage mom and very limpid when it came to protecting her daughter.

"Hello, how do you do?" came a voice from a figure stepping out of the kitchen of the cozy apartment decorated in bell pepper green and warm orange. I couldn't lie; I had pegged the babydoll as a rival as soon as I set eyes on her, with her ogling of my Maddy. But I also sensed a troubled life and a tragic future from this young lady.

With faux bobbed raven-black hair, a light sand complexion, dark eyes, and a round, soft, baby face, Philippa exuded a sensuality in a tight-fitting white angora sweater. A dark blue pencil skirt, navy silk stockings, and dark blue high-heeled shoes complemented this young lady's beauty. Following behind her was a brown-haired young man in horn-rimmed glasses, his face in need of a blemish stick, dressed in a tweed college professor suit—very bookwormish.

"Philippa, if I may say, heed your mother's concern," said the young man with puppy love in his eyes.

"No one asked for your opinion, Cicero," Philippa said. "Josephine and George feel my life is in danger, but I assure you I'm fine." She strode past us into the living room, not taking us a bit seriously. She did, however, stop and size Madison up briefly, which, for her to be just mortal, made my Maddy—Mr. Cosmic Vampire—a bit uncomfortable.

"Your parents are concerned and have your well-being and safety in mind. You have to take their phone calls and letters seriously, Philippa," Madison warned.

"What letters? What phone calls?" Philippa demanded, astounded.

"Oh my god. Letters? Phone calls?" Cicero echoed.

Josephine pleaded, "Philippa, we did not want you to get upset and lose focus on your music. We thought you were having really bad nightmares that you could not construe after returning from Mexico. When we received the letters and telephone calls…" Josephine tried to take hold of Philippa's hand to comfort her, but the young pianist pulled away. "I want to see these letters!" Philippa exploded, hands on her hips.

"Philippa, this is serious. This is not a game. I… I… do care," said Cicero meekly.

"Cicero, go home! Your work is done for the day, and if you wish to return tomorrow rather than being let go, I suggest you leave now!" The look in Philippa's eyes showed me babydoll meant it. Cicero bade us farewell and, with a taut "Good night, Miss Schuyler," left crestfallen, a valise filled with sheet music in hand.

"Philippa, please, tomorrow afternoon you owe Mr. Lynn an apology!" Josephine pleaded more forcefully.

"We'll show you the letters in due time. Right now, you have to trust Sue and me," Madison said, redirecting the conversation back to her problem.

"Let's speak to you in private at your apartment, honey," I said in my best sugary voice.

"Maybe I can trust you two better than George and Josephine, but in an hour, I have a meeting with someone at my apartment," Philippa fumed, grabbing a trench coat laying on the family sofa. Josephine handed three envelopes to Madison: one contained our retainer fee, and the other two, neither bearing a return address, had been mailed to Philippa.

"Here is your retainer fee, Mr. Cavendish. Miss SunMountain, I would also like to apologize for the red leanings George wrote about you two in the *Gazette* in '52," Josephine said, not making eye contact with us, knowing George was guilty as sin.

"But you see the times we live in," she added, hoping we would feel better about his reckless red-baiting.

"That can be discussed at a later date, Josephine." Madison spoke with diplomacy while I simply stared at her, bewildered.

"Let me guess: You're paying them with my concert earnings, on top of them being fellow travelers, too?" Philippa cut in.

"Philippa, stop it this instant!" Josephine had reached a tipping point. Her Texas accent was back in full force.

"Come on, honey," I said, ushering her out the door with Maddy.

"Listen, young lady," Maddy said as we stood outside on the sidewalk, "your parents hired us to do a job, and that job is to protect you until further notice. So you might as well get used to us being around. Understand?" Maddy held Philippa's left arm firmly, which was good for her since I personally wanted to beat some sense into her. Philippa seemed to enjoy the attention.

"If you say so. I'll go along with this for now." She smiled, squinting her eyes at us like a defiant child.

"And who was that young man you got condescending with?" I asked.

"That's Cicero Lynn, a Charles Ives Institute scholarship student. He's been doing intern work for me since my return to the States. Now he has a mushy crush on me. Tries to stick to me like glue. Sadly, he is of the milquetoast variety, which I find reprehensible," Philippa said offhandedly.

Philippa's new apartment, furnished in a mix of antique furniture, artwork from South America and Africa, all took a backseat to a sleek black Bechstein piano that consumed half of the living room. On a corner table a black Crosley phone was at the ready for conversations. Her bedroom gave one the impression that she couldn't let go of her childhood. Indeed, her wallpaper, comforter, curtains, and pillowcases were adorned in caricatured images of royalty, such as kings and queens, printed in hues of purple, pink, and yellow.

"I'm having a reading of my immediate future via tarot cards tonight and must insist that you two do your bodyguarding in my living room while Senora Borrero and I conduct the reading in the kitchen, please."

My stars, this woman-child could be curt.

"Sue's familiar with the tarot, you know," Maddy said, with a side glance.

"You do tarot readings?" Philippa asked for validation. We were sitting in her living room after having been given a brief tour of the apartment by a young lady who fiercely relished her independence from her parents but longed for her prodigy days, or so it seemed to me.

"Yes, I do. Maybe in the future I can do yours, honey," I told her, not wanting to contradict another reader's work.

"No, I don't think so. Ouida Borrero will more than suffice. She works in lowbrow entertainment, but she is fabulous at reading," Philippa said. "Earlier this month, we met at a recital I played at Cooper Union's Great Hall."

Philippa's mood perked up when her intercom buzzer came alive. Buzzing the woman in, Philippa shooed Maddy and me into the living room. After a minute or so, there was tapping at her door.

Entering the apartment was a woman taller than me, her hair styled in the Italian look that was all the craze lately. It could be no one else but Ouida Borrero. With golden-brown skin and an angular face, a beauty mark near her left eye signified her ambition. Under a white fur swing coat, she wore all black: a tight sweater along with a leather pencil skirt and fishnet-captured legs in stilettos. Under the scent of her perfume, I sensed her blood and felt it pump, which I was sure she picked up from me. If not Lycan, then she had to be one of my human/beast relatives, only more ancient than me. My Maddy picked up an aura, too, but defensive in nature, he would tell me later.

"Holla, everyone," Ouida exclaimed as Philippa hurriedly hung up her coat. They sat at the kitchen table. From our vantage point on the couch, we could only see Philippa.

"They're my bodyguards," Philippa now boasted in response to a whispered question from Ouida.

Ouida began the reading. "You, honey, have the Five of Wands. I see a failure of a project due to a friendship or a quarrel," she said, placing the first card down on Philippa's Haitian red-and-white-checked tablecloth. Philippa sat across from her with a look of silent awe on her face.

"In your home and with your family, I see worry and loss of energy," Ouida continued, "says the Five of Pentacles. In business, a chestnut-haired young man, generous of heart yet naïve, will be involved in your music," she spoke, revealing the King of Cups.

"You must mean Cicero Lynn; he's a recent intern or gopher from the Charles Ives Institute, assisting and learning—a bit too provincial for me," Philippa said. "The King of Wands seems to feel a dark-haired man, honest, faithful, and open, who seeks your love."

I didn't like the fact that after placing the card down and sharing the card's vision, Philippa looked in the direction of the living room where Madison was reading the newspaper and winked at him. My Maddy, with a flick of his wrist, folded the newspaper more firmly, trying to ignore Philippa. For a second, as a werewolf, I thought of standing up on the couch and marking my territory on Madison as a warning to Miss Schuyler, but I didn't think my Maddy would approve.

"Oh, I guess that must be Simon Yeates; he's my new booking agent for South America," Philippa said, trying to look innocent. The cards ran up to the left and then to the right at an angle, forming one side of a diamond-shaped pattern, with the opposition card at the top.

"Five of Swords: you're going to have anxiety and danger." Even in the living room, I felt that card, but I couldn't sense what it foretold at the time. "Two of Cups says love and friendship; maybe you will come across a lover while on tour and it will help your finances," proclaimed Ouida.

"Maybe not." Philippa winked, looked out the kitchen to the living room again.

"Your intellect will bring you good fortune the Six of Pentacles has revealed, and your outcome will be…"

Ouida softly placed the last card down on the table.

"The Three of Swords says you will need to part with something, like a ring or bauble, due to faithfulness and love gone wrong."

I was concerned about the presence of the Five of Swords.

"All in all, Philippa, you have to be careful with whom you love and who loves you, and you must get rid of the ring, yes? Has anyone made a gift of a ring to you lately?" Ouida warned and asked, the cards in front of her arranged in a diamond shape.

"I think you've missed the mark. No gift of a ring. I'll be fine," Philippa reassured, rising from the table to retrieve her checkbook. As Ouida stood to pull on her fur, Madison and I looked at each other, wondering about Ouida's ring foreshadowing.

"Well, I must be going. Sue, right? Can you walk me downstairs? I need your help; I don't know which side is best to catch a taxi back downtown, 145th Street or Edcombe Avenue, yes?" Ouida asked while placing a personal check from Philippa into her purse and then inside her black leather hobo bag. Philippa seemed perplexed by Ouida's request and merely shrugged.

"Sure, honey, my pleasure," I said to Ouida. We had to wait until we were outside in front of the building, as a tenant shared the elevator with us.

"So it seems, Susan, we are related, yes?"

"Are you Lycan, Ouida?" I asked anxiously.

"No. I am Ahuizotl. What one would call a water beast. Aztec canine in nature, many centuries before you were born," Ouida answered matter-of-factly.

"I'm Lycan. Of the cosmic horror variety," I replied, earning a look of awe from Ouida.

"I also sense curandera in your blood, Sue."

"If you mean Shamanic, I got that from my grandfather on my father's side of the family." That gift sometimes conflicted with the lycanthrope in me to the point that certain ancestors shunned me whenever I conducted vision quests.

"Sue, Philippa is soulful yet naive and, based on the reading, I see she has gotten herself in a dangerous situation. Maybe you can help egress her from it, yes?"

A checkered cab approached and slowly pulled up to us. Before I could answer Ouida, she pulled a business card out of her purse.

"Think about it."

"See you, amiga."

Ouida hopped in the taxi and was off. Back upstairs, I opened the door and found Maddy fanning Philippa, who lay prone on the couch unconscious.

"Madison Prescott Cavendish, did you bite her?!"

"I didn't put the bite on her, Seneca Sue SunMountain or, when the day comes and I marry you, Mrs. Cavendish. She asked to see the letters. So as to let her see the gravity of the situation, I let her read them. It's like this, Sue: Missy opened the envelope, unfolded the letter, and read the note, comprised of letters cut from a newspaper. The first letter reads, 'Hello, you little mulatto witch. No matter how much you pound those piano keys you're still a little monkey shit and not equal to a white woman. Your boot-licking black ape of a father and your sick, perverted pinup girl mother can't save you. Give the ring back, you live. Keep it, you die!'"

"Maddy, that's terrible!" I said.

"But wait, there's more. The second letter reads, 'I'm going to finish you, you half-breed bitch. You're going to kneel before us and die like in your nightmares, for I have the POWER!' After reading the letters, Philippa quietly folded them and then screamed in a way that raised the hair on the back of my vampire neck and, jumping up off the couch, I caught her before she hit the floor," my Maddy explained.

"And they say reading isn't harmful," I said.

—

Morning found me stuck with Philippa in her apartment. Madison had left to pick up a change of clothes and to make a long-distance call to Brazil to find out if our friend, Coffin Joe, had any dope on Ouida since Joe had underworld connections in Latin America. Cicero Lynn was due around noon to help Philippa transcribe some music. Before he arrived, I had to settle an issue when the time came.

"Miss SunMountain, can I ask you a personal question?" Philippa was seated on a gray divan, her pianist fingers—the tools of her profession—clasped in her lap, across from me on the couch.

"Shoot, Philippa," I replied. The time was at hand.

"Are you and Mr. Cavendish an item?" Philippa had a hopeful look on her face.

"You mean, are we circling?"

"What? Excuse me?"

"Meaning, are we married? Philippa, no, we're not. But listen, honey, not only are Madison and I business partners, we're also boyfriend and girlfriend. I have dibs on him and a bond that most everyday mortals—uh, I mean people—wouldn't understand, so you may as well chill your chat when it comes to him. Or, to use a colloquialism kids and beboppers use these days: 'Daddy-O is in my serious lockdownsville.' Get it? Or dig it? Whichever floats your boat."

"Yes. I apologize, Miss SunMountain."

"Call me Sue," I said. A troubadour of the classical music world, yet she seemed lonely—that was the feeling I got from her.

"Okay, Sue. I guess since I returned from Mexico, I've been looking to get back into dating too fast. A bad bunco of a relationship will do that, don't you think?" The melancholy look on Philippa's face made me start to see her in a different light.

"Was it someone you met in Mexico?"

"Gustavo Hernandez. We got into a whirlwind romance; he had me doing things that better judgment should have whispered to me not to. The last time I heard from him, he said he would come to the States to win me back after our breakup, but I told him I've moved on. I guess Gustavo was or is behind the letters and calls," Philippa confided.

"Well, if it's him, Madison and I will see to it that he doesn't bother you anymore. In the meantime, do I or do I not sense Cicero having a honey bunny infatuation for you?"

"Cicero only entered the picture recently. He's not worldly; his backbone is soft like the inside of a cannoli because he'll do anything I ask, which tells me he's weak. I like a strong man."

"Give him a try, sister."

"I don't know," Philippa said, sounding perplexed, yet still maintaining her hauteur.

Around noon, Cicero arrived, and I must say he did show some backbone by the flash of consternation on his acned face when he saw me. Starting with Chopin's Études, Philippa went through her paces. I was captivated by her playing.

At 3 p.m., she took a break for tea, cheese, and crackers, which I had to endure silently, craving some bacon or a few hotdogs—minus buns and condiments. By 6 p.m., Philippa was finished for the day so as not to annoy her neighbors by playing into the evening. Ushering Cicero out the door, Philippa was borderline rude as she turned down his offer to practice on a Koestler Harmophone that he'd recently repaired.

—

Madison returned a short while later, now in a gray suit. While handing me a blue pantsuit, blouse, and other unmentionables to change into, he complained that when he connected to Coffin Joe's number, all he got for his long-distance charge trouble was someone on the other end picking up the receiver and laying it down on a table, the song "Solfeggio" playing in the background over and over again. So, with no word from Coffin Joe, we spent the rest of the night listening to Philippa recount incidents she'd experienced during her world tours. We also deflected various questions.

"I have to admit that I find it strange—or maybe a blessing—that you two look so young while George and Josie have aged," Philippa said, trying but failing to keep from batting her eyelashes at my Maddy despite our earlier conversation. So much for seeing her in a different light.

"I do have a faint memory of seeing you as a child," Maddy said. We had first met the Schuylers back in '25, before Philippa was born, at a soirée given by hair the care heiress, A'Lelia Walker, at her mansion, a foreboding edifice known as the Dark Tower, located on 136th Street.

"If we look young, it's simply a result of clean living," my partner lied, chuckling as he nursed a cup of hyssop tea brewed from tea leaves he brought from home. Madison had also stopped at a delicatessen to get me a link of hotdogs, which I munched raw, much to Philippa's silent approval since her diet demanded everything raw. A bowl of wheat germ and cottage cheese was her dinner.

After clearing away our meal, Philippa was off to get ready for bed, a crime noir paperback in one hand and a raw carrot to munch on while reading in the other.

"Madison, a few things about this affair bother me," I said, as we tried to get comfortable in her living room; I had the couch while Madison took the divan. "She claims she knows nothing about a ring. If that's what her mysterious antagonist wants, then she should stop fibbing and hand it over. And far be it for me to digress, but why does Philippa still call her parents by their first names instead of Mom and Pop or something?" I envied people with families. Both my parents were dead by the time I reached eight. As a result, my only family member was the grandpa who raised me.

"I have not the faintest idea why she does that, Sue." Madison was in the chair, his suit coat off, adjusting both his painted tie and the holster that held his .44.

"I don't know; maybe they're just atomic age formal with each other," Madison chuckled. "But what I do know is we have to get to the bottom of this ring thing—it's the key to everything."

I wanted to wrap up this whole affair. I had taken my .32 out of my clutch bag and stashed it under a cushion I was resting my head on. Had I known we were going to spend the night at this piano brat's apartment, seemingly in perpetuity, I would have told Madison to bring Sekhmet up here in secret. But as long as she was in her little octo-kitty vortex or sensed that a Dodger game was airing on Channel 9, her world was ducky.

"They just don't seem happy around each other," my Maddy admitted, wishing we at least had that option with our own daughter, Simone, who, after birth, had slithered off to parts unknown back in 1919—a subject we seldom mentioned, even though we both hoped that one day she would return. I drifted off to sleep while Maddy took the first watch.

—

The sound of fingernails scratching around the doorknob to Philippa's bedroom woke me from a snug slumber. The door slowly opened, and Madison, already standing, placed an index finger to his lips, signaling me to be silent. The only light left on in the living room was an ambient lamp on a corner table, one table leg propped up by a stack of sheet music, one of many concerto pieces stuffed into bookcases along the hallway leading to the pianist's bedroom. The dim light picked up Philippa, stiff-legged, walking down the hallway in a carnation pink chiffon nightgown and pink slippers, her hands balled into shaking fists and a sleepy but assertive look in her eyes.

Making her way past the living room, she fumbled the apartment door lock open, stepped out into a quiet hallway, and staggered toward the elevator.

"Sue, follow her onto the elevator while I run down the stairway to the lobby to make sure nobody's waiting to grab her," Madison whispered to me.

After Madison dashed off, the sound of the elevator bell pinged, and the doors slid open as Philippa and I stepped aboard. She stood facing one of the corner walls like a child being punished. When the elevator door opened, she turned around, and we exited, heading toward the lobby and onto 145th Street. I saw Madison running to the corner after a black Crown Imperial that had just screeched off. I began to wonder how we were going to get this lady out of her trance. If I had done it to her, I could bring her out, but who or what was doing this to her? An idea occurred.

Summoning up a magenta mist just ever so gently in my right palm, I grasped her hand, and Philippa jolted, yelping and collapsing to the ground, befuddled by her surroundings. Good thing this part of 145th Street was void of people at this early morning hour. Madison helped me get her back into the lobby and up to her apartment. He said when he got downstairs, two men—one heavyset and the other thin, both resembling pugilists and wearing vicuña overcoats and fedoras— were in front of the building and seemed to be waiting.

Intrigued, Madison started toward the mysterious two, but not before the men ambled quickly into a limo and zoomed off. We got Philippa back into her fourth-floor apartment and tucked her into bed. We both stayed up on watch, waiting to see if the two men would return, but the only unwanted guest was a hungry mouse peeking its nose under the threshold of the apartment door in search of a bite.

—

"Good morning, Mr. Cavendish and Miss Sue," Philippa said. She looked as fresh as a daisy, dressed in a nice olive dress, a black belt, flesh-colored stockings, and matching olive heels. Meanwhile, we were wrinkled in our clothes, in need of some coffee for me and some more hyssop tea for Maddy due to his topsy-turvy vampire proclivities of being up during the day. Philippa remembered nothing of the earlier sleepwalking incident.

"I want to apologize for my rude conduct these last few days. I understand the two of you are here to help me. I wish George and Josephine were more forthcoming about the letters and harassing phone calls. After having my phone installed, I hoped they wouldn't be overzealous in phoning me during practice, to the point of leaving the receiver off the hook."

"It's all right as long as we're on the same page. We don't want to crowd you," Madison said as I stifled a yawn.

"Would the two of you like breakfast? I can cook breakfast, you know," Philippa said, anxious as a child wanting to show an adult that she could perform grown-up tasks.

She made Maddy and me a supreme breakfast. While we didn't want to give any hint of oddness, we let her prepare some poached eggs, coffee, toast, and orange juice. She didn't partake of the food but instead munched on cheese, crackers, washed raw carrots, and tea with honey.

The Corsley kettle phone jumped to life with Philippa's first call of the day.

"I really must get some practice in. I guess that must be Josie phoning to check up on me." The caller on the other end wasn't Josie. After a few hellos, Philippa screamed, letting the receiver slip from her hands. Retrieving the phone, I continued with the hellos.

"Tell that little mixed-breed tart she's in peril if she doesn't hand over that ring!" barked a voice.

The connection ended. Philippa was on the couch, not crying but catatonically staring off into space.

"Philippa, we're going to try something, honey," I said, though she seemed unresponsive. I had an idea.

"Philippa, come on, pretty face. We're here to help you. Come with us into the bedroom." Of course, when Madison said that to her, she moved. Guiding her to her bedroom, we got to work. A dream quest, in contrast to a vision quest, is hard enough, but a joint dream quest could be damaging to the conductor of its mind if not done right. Once we got her to focus, Philippa lay on her bed, and I lay next to her. Grasping her hand, I began to concentrate on entering her mind. Her eyelids slowly blinked closed. Her shallow breathing signaled that it was now safe to enter her mind to search for the whereabouts of this phantom ring and why it was so important.

A barrage of images surrounded me like relentless waves in an ocean storm:

> *Philippa as a child during a wartime Christmas: celebrations, toys from Gimbel's. Through a frosted mind's eye, I saw a once-happy family with an us-against-the-world outlook because the parents were of different skin colors. Homemade gingerbread houses melted forward into visions of Mexico: romance*

with Gustavo Hernandez, polo-playing playboy and thief. The romance turned into a vulgar batch of photos featuring her and Gustavo in the act, now hidden in the bottom of her closet. He wanted to use them to make money in the Tijuana Bible market in Los Angeles or San Francisco's Tenderloin smut industry, maybe even blackmail Philippa with the negatives if he got desperate. An invitation to join a satanic church located in caverns under the Chapel of the Blessed Guadalupe: Philippa got cold feet and told the taxi driver to turn around as she pulled up to the front of the chapel on a dark, moonless night, with a robed Gustavo waiting in the cavern below. Fleeing back to the States, she unknowingly transported the stolen ring and negatives that Gustavo had hidden in her practice keyboard, meant to be retrieved at a later date.

"It's the Abraxas ring!" I yelled, bolting up from the bed. Like a psychic stray bullet, my eyes connected with Maddy, who was sitting in the corner at Philippa's mirrored vanity desk. Rising, my love and partner walked to the other corner of the room and pried open the top of the keyboard. After a moment of digging, Madison produced the Abraxas ring, dark blue with ruby-red onyx streaks, which, if given the exact Gnostic incantation, could summon Abraxas to appear and do one's bidding—for a price—along with the dirty negatives.

I staggered to Philippa's closet and retrieved the photos from the bottom. Not just vulgar, but more like hardcore Denmark pornography. After tearing up the humiliating images, I sent them on a voyage down the toilet while Maddy, with a left-hand palm glow, burned the negatives to ashes.

"Okay, so what do we do now?" I asked, wiping sweat from my brow while Philippa fell into a sound sleep.

Rolling the potentially upheaving ring around in his hand, Maddy said, "We'll wait for another call and get this thing out of our private eyeballing jurisdiction. The last thing we need in the Big Apple is Qlippoths and spirit Nagas running around going apeshit in the streets under Abraxas's directions!"

As usual, my Maddy was stone-cold correct.

—

"Miss SunMountain! Mr. Cavendish! Where is Philippa?" Cicero asked, holding a dozen roses wrapped in cellophane in one hand and his valise in the other.

"She's asleep but will be up in an hour or so," I answered.

The classical music student eyed us with suspicion but then

shrugged and parked himself on the couch to wait. That hour or so stretched to about three in the afternoon when Philippa, subdued in mood, entered the living room to tend to her craft.

Right before Cicero was to leave for the evening, the Corsley jingle rang, and I picked up.

"You have the ring. I can help you, amiga." Ouida's voice was a cold whisper.

"Okay, Ouida, let's deal. We give you the ring, you leave the poor child alone," I offered.

"*Trato!* We have a deal."

"Madison and I will be at your workplace at 8 p.m."

"I should be finished with my first set by then, amiga. You come alone, my *loba* sister; leave your bloodsucker."

Ouida hung up.

Although Maddy knew I could handle myself, he was still iffy about me going to Ouida's place of employment, the Times Burlesque Playhouse on 42nd Street near Times Square. So, with Cicero nervously volunteering out of love (after Maddy gave him a redacted story about a smuggled ring out of earshot of Philippa) to stay with Philippa, I headed down to Times Square at 7 p.m.

—

Pulling the Metro up in front of the Playhouse, I crossed my fingers, hoping I wouldn't get a parking ticket from some quota-hungry police officer. Bright lights from the playhouse's marquee fought for the attention of tourists amid movie houses, chess and checker shops, mystery-meat burger stands, arcades, and Hubert's Museum along 42nd Street. Though the lights were neon and artificial, I wasn't about to take any chances. I slipped on my rose-tinted shades to avoid a Lycan hiccup during transformation. The last thing I needed was to be loping down the Forty-Deux with cops and WeeGee, his camera in hand, cigar in mouth, trying to snap pictures in pursuit.

"Hey, freckles, what can I do for you?" asked a little, receding red-haired man, pausing from his tuna sandwich and black coffee. He was stationed in the playhouse ticket booth kiosk.

"I'm here to meet with Ouida Borrero," I said, pointing to a black-and-white lobby poster of Ouida dressed in faux Aztec priestess Ixiptalli garb, along with other performers and a card trick expert cum organist named Cloverdale lining the lobby walls.

"Who? Sorry, I don't... oh, Damares. You want Damares Tabla, I guess. Yeah, she mentioned that she was expecting a visitor. Hey, Fritz!" He briefly opened the back of the kiosk. "Let freckles... sorry, I mean, let this young lady inside. She's here to see Damares!" he yelled to a Tor Johnson-looking boulder of a man in a mauve-colored suit guarding the entrance.

"Up the stairs there, knock on the second door to your right with the foil silver star on it." He pointed toward the staircase. The big man might have looked like Tor, but his accent screamed East New York, Brooklyn.

The place was a haze of light blue tobacco smoke. The human blood scents I picked up were laced with cheap rye, watered-down bourbon, and a few Knickerbocker beers as I stopped to peek inside the main room. Whirling through an obtuse version of "Night Train" was, I assumed, a silver-haired, crusty tuxedoed Cloverdale on a Hammond B-3 organ, helping a woman named "Pinky" in a pink bouffant and a tiny bit of silver fabric do a bump and grind. "You know you've got the gams for a job here, lady," said the big man sneaking up behind me. For a New York minute, the offer crossed my mind, but I moved along.

Before I knocked, I heard a fire exit door creak open and then close down the other end of the hall. I heard the sound of women giggling from the other side of Ouida/Damares's dressing room door.

"¡Hola! Come in, amiga, come in!" Ouida yelled, pausing from her giggle fit.

A vanity desk's mirrored reflection showed Ouida in a tangerine terry cloth bathrobe seated on a couch, sharing a Lark with a young buxom woman, rusty-haired and wearing only a pair of pasties and dark high heels. I turned toward them.

"Sue, Cherri. Cherri, Sue. Sue's a private investigator." We both silently nodded at our introductions—me because I was in a bit of a rush to get the deal over with, and Cherri, perhaps in her little mind, thinking I was here to get it on with Ouida.

"Cherri, you'll have to excuse us, yes? Sue and I have business to conduct. Cherri, after work, what will it be—Horn & Hart? White Tower on 14th? Or back to my place, *dulce chica*?"

Ouida gave one of Cherri's pasties a little pluck, making it briefly spin, eliciting a giggle from the dancer. Theirs appeared to be a *Boston marriage*.

Before rising off of Ouida's lap, Cherri gave her a soulful kiss, their lip movements syncing with Cloverdale's encore of "Night Train" downstairs amid the hoots and hollering of two sheets-to-the-wind sleazy customers. In a melodramatic emote, Cherri didn't answer until she paused in front of me. "Your place, *mi dulce mamá*," she said, rolling her eyes at me as she exited the dressing room. *Thou goest, for thou knowest not who thou art messing with,* I thought to myself.

"You have the ring, Sue?" Ouida's demeanor shifted from bubbly to cold and businesslike.

"Ouida, I trust you as a sister cryptid. I must have your word that Philippa will not be harassed or harmed anymore. It was one of your own members, Gustavo Hernandez, who stole the Abraxas ring," I pleaded. That's right, pleaded, because, at the end of the day, Philippa was only guilty of falling in love too quickly. As I placed the ring in Ouida's hand, we were interrupted as the dressing room door opened.

Ouida and I froze as two men—one heavyset and the other thin, each with brawler-scarred faces—entered with guns drawn.

"*El anillo, ahora!*" the big man shouted.

"Of course," Ouida answered.

My heart sank. "I trusted you, Ouida."

"Here… here is the ring, fools!" Ouida made as if to surrender the object, then suddenly stepped back, crushing the ring with a bare hand. Blood spilled forth as Ouida struggled to endure the pain through clenched teeth.

At that moment, all hell—though in this case, all Abraxas—broke loose.

"*Ayudame!*" screamed the big man as both thugs dropped to the floor in spasmodic pain. Their skin began to change before our eyes into grotesque reddish leather as the fluids in their bodies were sucked out and splattered onto the walls like an abstract Jackson Pollock drip-style original. Ouida and I stumbled back against the vanity desk and witnessed the two men's demise as they were transformed into crystallized red dust. Their clothes and two easily concealable .22s were all that remained.

"Okay, Ouida, what's the deal? I thought those two were your socios?" I asked, tending to Ouida's mangled hand with a torn sheet I had found in her costume closet, ripped into strips as a makeshift bandage. With her good hand, Ouida lit up a Lark.

"Sue, I am sorry. It was Gustavo you mentioned who placed Philippa and her parents in danger. You see, at this moment in Mexico, there is a three-way struggle between the Catholic Church, the Aztec legacy led by curanderas, and those like Gustavo and the red polvo at your feet—members of the Alreves Church, secretly established by one of the twelve friars during the time of Cortés. Not content with destroying our culture, they still peruse us, but we now come after them equally. The border with the United States and Mexico means nothing in this struggle."

Ouida blew a smoke ring into the air. She was right, of course. Borders meant nothing because when the time came, and another cosmic entity like the one that infected my Maddy and me back in 1914 returned, the question of this planet's existence would be moot, with us taking control of this hot mess called Earth.

"When you said, 'We now come after them,' who did you mean?" I asked.

"Pinky. You saw her downstairs, yes? Her real name is Bonita Suárez. We have a following here in New York, like they do."

"Do you know who their contacts are?"

"No. They are *rojo polvo* too by now." Ouida rummaged around in her closet for two Bohack's supermarket bags while I left and returned to her dressing room with a broom and a dustpan, not that it was going to be any help with the walls.

Ouida helped as best she could as I swept up the former henchmen into the grocery bags, now their urns, I guess you could say.

"You go now, *amiga*. Philippa is out of this picture, but if she somehow enters again of her own doing, you and I will be at odds."

"Until next time, Ouida," I said, heading out of the dressing room door with the paper bags, but not before Ouida rested her right hand on my shoulder.

"Until next time, *mi dulce loba*. Maybe by then you will have dumped the *sangre crédulo*," Ouida said as I turned around for her kiss. To me, she and Cherri were just fine and didn't need me forming a love triangle with them.

Outside, I tried to get the Bohack's bags into the wastebasket on the corner, but the big man's bag tore open, spilling onto the sidewalk. I said a quick shamanic prayer over it, ditched the other bag into the wastebasket, and recited another prayer for calmness after finding a parking ticket wedged in the Metro's hood. Piss! Damn it!

—

"We've got a problem, Sue," Maddy said, ushering me into Philippa's apartment.

"She didn't turn into red dust, did she?"

"What?"

"I'll tell you in a few. What's her problem now?" I asked, looking around but seeing no sign of Philippa.

"Well, you see, Cicero abruptly departed, fear of the situation getting the better of him. This left Philippa and me sitting on the couch. With her combination of chatting while inching closer to me, and me, after being cooped up in this place, let out a hissed yawn and unintentionally bared my fangs. Understandably, Philippa started to bug out, like she was in Korea or something and, well, you know the drill." Maddy grinned. I couldn't get mad at that smile; he knew this.

"Don't tell me she screamed and fainted again?"

"Yup. She's in the bedroom."

"Okay, dear. New plan of action. But let me tell you about the Times Playhouse first."

—

Back in her bedroom, I once again connected with Philippa's mind. This time, I planted a post-hypnotic suggestion that she would recall nothing of the events of the past several days. I also placed in her mind negative thoughts about Madison Prescott Cavendish, private detective, and positive thoughts bordering on love for Cicero Lynn. A girl's gotta do what a girl's gotta do.

With Philippa's life back to normal, our services were no longer needed. We received the second half of our fee the following day. But when we came by to pick up our check, Philippa and Josie, both worried, asked if we could go see what was going on with Cicero, who hadn't shown up for his internship.

We traveled downtown to his apartment on West 27th Street in Chelsea. After a few knocks, Maddy used his magenta glow and lock-picking skills to open the door. Cicero's apartment was strangely naked of furniture, as if no attempt had been made to move anything in. On a kitchen counter was an unused one-way American Airlines ticket to Mexico City. As we entered the living room floor, I gasped.

"Maddy, look…"

Next to a valise were Cicero's remains in the form of a pile of red crystal dust mixed with a tweed suit, loafers, and horn-rimmed glasses. "So much for the internship," my Maddy said.

THE
REVELL
AFFAIR

1967

The eruption of Detroit was still a few months away.

HARLEM: SUE

I love Harlem. Decades ago, we would swing through Walker's Dark Tower, the Savoy, the Apollo, the Renaissance Ballroom, or Attucks Hall for our Mignonette Society affairs. We'd hang out at that flat of a Renaissance friend like Zora Neale Huston or attend a rent party for Nancy Prophet. On a good night, you would also find us in a hooch joint or a buffet flat; this is how we stomped. But my real joy was going to a simple restaurant either before or after a night out. Wilson, Floyd, & Jimmy's Fish Fry & Chop Suey Emporium on 129th Street was an alternate place for a client to get a hold of us for an "Affair" back in the day, but I really dug Three Sisters Restaurant on 116th Street and Lenox Avenue. Those church sisters could burn!

Standing in line waiting for my takeout order, I feel euphoric, but I try to block out the fact in my mind that Harlem is headed for rough times, rougher than the decades my Maddy and I had jitterbugged and be-bopped through. Heroin has intensified its crawl into the community, wrecking more lives than any throat-ripping werewolf or blood-thirsty vampire could achieve.

A hefty-bodied, hair-netted woman of various shades of brown wearing long-hemmed white nurse-type uniforms, protected by aprons stained with BBQ sauce, swiftly moves back and forth behind the counter. The dress hem's length reminds me of another life when I was a seamstress back in 1910. I'm also reminded that I'm older than these stern-looking women and their mothers (most likely, though one could not tell). My hair in a black beehive style, I'm feeling neato in an orange blouse, orange above-the-knee skirt, orange pumps, and, of course, a groovy tangerine leather coat that are working for me today, baby.

"How much, sister?" I ask as I'm handed my order, consisting of BBQ and a can of Tab for me, and fried whiting, fries, and a fresca soda for Sekhmet.

"On the house, ma'am," says the young brown, sugar-toned cashier, who also sticks a business card in my hand along with the brown paper shopping bag containing my order.

"What?" I ask, but she's already disappeared back into the kitchen to help hurry along more orders for the evening dinner rush. I consider waiting for her to return but happen to look down at the business card. It shows the phone number and address of Scat Johnny hoodoo, a community leader who once put a price on Maddy and my heads, blaming us for the death of Zoe Churel in 1927. That is until he discovered it was Zoe's own trick bag messing with a jive Jinn that had got her laid out. The issue was settled.

I pause to wonder what he might want from us now. Sliding in behind the steering wheel of my Root Beer Hue Duster, I flop a back issue of *Ramparts* magazine from out the glove compartment down on the passenger seat and place my dinner on top of it so as to not get any fish grease or BBQ sauce on the passenger seat. A second later, I zip off toward Riverside Drive and 107th Street. I think about what Maddy will have to say about Scat's outreach, but I know I'll have to wait to tell him since my Maddy is currently over in Nam.

HILL 558 NEAR KHE SANH COMBAT BASE: MADISON

"What you say?" I ask, stirring from my daylight hibernation.

"I said, 'You're up, Major,'" replies Lieutenant Holman, reaching out to shake my arm in the humid darkness of a forward post bunker. I'm not really asleep. Who could rest with all this noise? Not far away a firefight rages in its intensity, tracer rounds bouncing red light up and down hills. The firefight is between our grunts of the 2nd Battalion, 3rd Marines, and the Vietcong 6th Division with a sprinkle of the PAVN's 325C Division. We're rocking and rolling between Hills 558 and 950, separated by the Rao Quan River, a forward position from Khe Sanh Marine Combat Base.

"Alright, Lieutenant, I'm up. Get on the PRC-77 and radio the operations commander in this sector to quiet things down after ten minutes so I can ply my trade once I cross over to the VC side. Let them know Yankee Reaper (my US Army Signal Corps code name since the

Great War) will be in the field. Once I'm finished, I'll cross back over in the morning to this bunker location. Make sure to give the exact coordinates. If I end up either north or south of here, just tell them to challenge along the perimeter, and I'll yell out 'Apollo.'" An ode to the Apollo 1 crew who lost their lives earlier this year in a cabin fire ignited during the launch rehearsal. "If I take any kind of fire, well, you know what to do," I hiss, then yawn.

Yes, Lieutenant Holman knows about my rejuvenation process, which at first had unnerved him; that's what he got as communications specialist 4 for seeking a promotion by volunteering for the US Army Signal Corps Clandestine Paranormal Section. But soon a cornucopia of items unnerved Lieutenant Porter E. Holman, a ruddy, hawk-faced, raven-haired Georgian: Civil Rights, talk of more team expansion in Major League Baseball, the Women's Rights Movement, and the big nerve shaker… taking orders from a superior, half-Black vampire like me, burned his biscuits. He kept it on simmer and, in truth, is still terrified of me. The first time he witnessed me coming rice paddy water drenched back into a bunker, my fangs dripping blood one predawn, the poor peach's head shrieked, and he blacked out.

"When it hits the ten-minute mark, crawl out of here, Lieutenant," I ordered as I lazily gathered up my gear.

"Sir, wouldn't it be better if I returned and supervised your crossing back to our lines? The battle lines keep worming around the hills tonight; the firefight is very fluid. A lot of fresh fish, quick-trigger jarheads on the hill," warned Holman.

"No, they shouldn't be a problem. Got to get on the good foot. Now, start communicating. Scramble it, or whatever it is you do on the seventy-seven, then hump it back to HHC's bunker. I've got work to do," I say, as I heft myself up and over our bunker's sandbags, down the hillside, hopping over tripwire.

"Good luck, *Bela Wayne*," I hear Lieutenant Holman mumble under his breath, a not-so-subtle reference to the late celluloid horror star and the dippy Western shoot 'em-up actor.

Yeah, Yankee Reaper alright. From the Great War to World War II and Korea, I've been slaughtering the enemy off and on the field in service to my country. During peacetime, I've done shamus work back home with my lovely Lycan wife. Tonight, I'm on loan to the Marine Corps. I'm one of Uncle Sam's best-kept secrets. The US Army Signal Corps, with the help of the CIA, hid me so deep you couldn't even find any references of me in the *Pentagon Papers* unless you knew where to look, and God forgive you if you did. Rounds of mortars, AK-47s, M-

79s, Claymore mines, and M-16s reach a crescendo at the ten-minute mark. The VC and PAVN personnel keep firing but, in bewilderment, cease firing, too. Now the awkward silence is just as deafening as the battle moments before.

I'm not squeamish when it comes to killing. Quite the contrary. I use whatever means are necessary, and this includes burying my fangs into a neck, my infamous folklore legend carrying over into these present times.

I descend Hill 558 through scented leaf evergreens and thick grass, a break from sloshing through lower-region wet mangroves. But I have a strange vibe tonight, as if I'm being watched. The first trio of VCs passes me. I get behind them and, with a bayonet knife, slit their throats so quickly they haven't time to feel the burn one feels when cut. Their blood sprays out on each other, and they go limp like cut-string marionettes, squirming as they try to clamp the lacerations with their hands. I can see in darkness, so I witness the blood soaking. Two men and one ponytailed woman in black pajamas approach and then quickly move away from them. From the corner of my eye, I see a shadow descend, vulturelike, over their bodies, and I hear slurping sounds.

I continue, disemboweling a VC here, plunging my bayonet into a PAVN soldier's head there. Now, I let loose on a hillside of the enemy, strafing them with my M-16. Again, in the darkness comes a loud slurping sound. I travel across the Rao Quan River toward Hill 950. The work is making me thirsty, seeing all this blood. I witness two VCs running up Hill 950 parallel to me in fear; something overhead is following them. Quarter moonlight through the trees flashes for a second a ghostly vision, a robed, flowing, dark-haired, milk-hued woman in what has to be the most extreme lotus yoga position I've ever seen: legs bent up so her toes are fitted in her nostrils with fingers inserted in her ears. She floats.

I shake my head back to lucent sanity after what I've seen and follow the two VCs. I use my vampire creeping and leaping skills to appear suddenly in front of them. I get the vibe I'm providing sustenance for the competition. My M-16 tears the VC to shreds. The entity, whatever it is, floats off. I'm sure now that it's not a Batut tut or rock ape that's been roaming around the countryside ripping up VCs and dropping rocks on the helmets of US and SEATO personnel. Finally, with a body count of about thirty-plus, I've plugged up this gap in between Hills 558 and 950 for more Marines to flood in and hold it down until I have to answer the bell another night, like Muhammad Ali. My olive tiger camouflage uniform is dark as the night from blood and waxy vampire and cosmic magenta sweat, which permeates from my body. On my way back to the bunker, I see a VC. His face is soaked in jungle sweat and tears as he crawls atop the grass, trying to reach safety. His right foot is missing, and he leaves a bloody trail on the grass. Looks like he may have stepped on one of his own VC toe popper mines. I grab him, prop him up into a sitting position against a tree, and mumble, *"He'n mon xau,"* which means "Sorry" in his native tongue, and then puncture his jugular vein. The warm, rich life nectar—rather, what remains since his right leg is bleeding out—is my reward for tonight. Those back in DC, the suits and brass buttons leading from afar, demanded a body count, so I give them a body count. I stroke the hair of this poor amputee to calm him for my final act. I wipe crimson spittle on my grimy sleeve, then snap his neck with my hands so he can't come back as the living dead. I've already, as requested by the Pentagon East MACV in Saigon, created a small cadre of undead VC and PAVN vampires roaming uncontrolled in the North above the DMZ and don't need anymore. You would be surprised at how many strange operations the US government has us Black contract people running in this country. But what was that, hovering over my little blood orgy?

—

Dawn arrives. I put on a pair of green-tinted shades and overshoot my bunker position. I stray up to another one. It's manned by nervous young Marines who, no doubt, are wondering who or what the muck-covered creature is steeping into the range of fire armed with an M-16. I yell out, "Apollo!" when challenged. They reply with a full side of friendly fire cutting into my chest. As I fall to my knees, two thoughts enter my mind: One, this is a breach of strict field discipline. Two, I'm getting tired of this forlorn shit we're doing in this country.

I sink to my knees and plop forward to the ground, where I wait for Holman to arrive with my body bag so he can zip me up. A shame; I was looking forward to a nice shower and a bit of rest after regeneration.

RIVERSIDE DRIVE, MANHATTAN: SUE

I return home to a relaxing shower, change into a black night gown, and have at my sister's dinner. Then, once settled in, I dial up Scat. But first I have to give Sekhmet her dinner. The sound of swift typing on a Remington tells me she's in Madison's apartment, not mine upstairs. Now that Madison and I are married, the keys that would otherwise be under our perspective mats now hang on our keyrings.

"Hey there, sassy sister. You got my food?" asks Sekhmet.

I must declare: No matter how many times I've seen our Sekhmet, our familiar, in human format's been awkward for me to dig it. A leggy darling, maple wood in complexion with her hair a short natural, Sekhmet looks groovy in my green daisy flower print dress and sandals. I make a mental note that Maddy and I must get this chick her own wardrobe, more sooner than later. A slight scar tissue in the shape of an X on her forehead hides a third eye and is the only hint of her true self. She held things down at home while we went back and forth on affairs until we felt she was ready to handle one on her own. Leaving Sekhmet to retype an old file, "The Dickerson Affair, 1946," and to enjoy her writings, I head one flight up to my crib and pick up the phone.

"Scat Johnny, it's Susan Cavendish. What it be like, baby?" I ask, curled up on the couch with the television volume turned down.

"Hey, Sue! How you be, lady? How that man of yours, Madison, doing?" Scat's deep and sultry voice scared many a man and stroked the passions of many a woman.

"We jumped the broom in '66, Scat," I say. "Right now, Maddy's over in Nam."

"Hells bells! Well congratulations, Missy!" Scat seems tentative. "Nam! Damn mortals' war jive seeping over too much into our domain these days! Shit!"

"And how you and Lucy doing these days?" Lucy was his common-law hoodoo queen.

"That's why I want to rap with you, Sue. Can we parley this call into a meeting at my place?"

"Now?" You know how it is when you just don't want to get up and go back out. But with business being a bit slow, I'd prefer a retainer for this affair in the making than to touch our bank account or that cache of gems we had from 1927 courtesy of Rollo Ahmed from "The Rollo Ahmad Affair."

"Now," Scat insists, "I'll pay you double the—what you call it, a retainer?"

"Okay, Scat. Give me about an hour or so and I'll be up there. Where's your pad located again?" I slip out of my nightgown, ready for Scat to surrender the address. The end credits for *Bewitched* flash on the television screen.

"I'm at 532,116th and Lenox Avenue, apartment 01R. Act like a mortal when you arrive on the block, but watch your back and purse, baby," warns Scat.

"Okay, solid, Scat."

"I'll be waiting, Sue. Thank you kindly because I really need your help."

Scat ends the call. Jumping into a blue jean denim suit, gray sweatshirt, scarlet-red PF flyers, and no purse, I let Sekhmet know I'm heading out. I hop back in the Duster for the drive over to 116th Street to the hoodoo master's pad.

—

Soon, Buffalo and Newark are going to erupt. If this year is the Summer of Love, it has a funny way of showing it.

The address is a tenement building situated near the corner of an open-air heroin market. Pushers and junkies slipping in and out of buildings while being berated by people in the neighborhood tired of the dope fiend circus. The building itself is well-kept outside but tired-looking within. Inside the paint-chipped lobby hallway, a transistor radio tuned to WWRL competes with an argument between a husband and wife over how to spend the meager check he's brought home filters down from the second floor. A dying lightbulb reveals that the bright red door in front of me is apartment 1R, the number and letter seared onto the door as opposed to the gold stenciled characters adorning other nearby doors.

Four mice, their fur primary colored, scramble across my red PFs. I step back, startled. I'm not scared, I just don't like surprises. Yellow, green, and blue mice chase a red mouse. Before I can knock, a voice calls out, though perhaps it's in my head.

"Come in, Susan, come in," Scat says. On his silent command, the door unlocks and opens. Once I'm in, it closes and locks.

The room is… unique. Zebra-skinned carpeting covers the living room, overkill with faux zebra-skin mod-designed furniture. The room is also decorated functionally with Santeria, Yoruba, and other West African items of art and worship. Coconut incense fights with an okra-shrimp gumbo stew simmering on a stove in the kitchen. The smell of tobacco juice in a spittoon in one corner of the room attacks my nose. A human skull-shaped white transistor radio floats back and forth across the room, playing Aretha Franklin's "Respect." Johnny Scat sits on a sofa with a rare edition of the *Demon Box of Ebril: Fact or Hoax*, posthumously printed by the E. Abbott Logan estate. His hair is dark, conked, and straightened. Scat, except for a high-bridged nose, favors soul singer Clarence Carter. Sunglasses tinted silver, white alpaca sweater, dark pants, and black suede Count Marcello loafers minus socks enhance Scat's looks as a cool conjure man.

An immortal originally from New Orleans, Scat was an underling to Black Herman, Harlem magician and hoodoo leader. Prior to that he studied under the LaValles, an old black Knickerbocker voodoo family whose origins date back to the times of New Amsterdam, now New York, before switching back to hoodoo. But by cutting loose from Black Herman, Scat had started his own hoodoo family. The upshot occult rumbles lasted for the next twenty-five years before finally ending in a truce brokered by hoodoo supreme Sandy Jenkins. I hope he didn't call me for aid in breaking it because Maddy and I were allied with Black Herman.

"Have a seat, *la loba feroz*," says Scat, smiling and patting the sofa cushion next to him for me to sit upon—and calling me by the corny street name that folks and creatures in the underground named me, which, translated from Spanish, means "the big, bad she-wolf." I wave him to slide over to the end of the sofa closest to that damn spittoon 'cause I can't take the smell. Maybe I should tap the Chemical Bank account Maddy and I share or sell a gem instead of stepping into this gig.

"You know, with that hair and your looks, you could be a fourth freckled Ronette," says Scat. Like I haven't heard that line before.

"I'm thankful for the compliment, Scat. But Scat, baby, let's get down. Down to business, that is."

"Susan, I love my wife. Lucy started out as my assistant, but it be funny how love and business mix sometimes. I sure you know. Shoot, look at you and Madison. A werewolf and a vampire. As the King of Cool, Dino Martini, once sung, 'Ain't that a kick in the head?'"

"Me and Maddy are groovy, Scat." I'm not so sure about that. Lack of poo-tang for a man aboard and the lack of joyful process for a woman at home might drive them to the edge and into Cheat Town chauffeured by Loneliness.

"You know, Lucy is a side woman playing rhythm guitar in Lady Bo's Summit."

"Really? I met Lady Bo on the West Coast when she was playing as a side guitarist for Bo Diddley."

"Yeah, sho'nuff. Hot damn, Lucy got some T-Bone Walker licks in her. They do gigs up and down the East Coast these days." Scat beams proudly.

"And?" I cut to the chase.

"And she's cheating on me." Scat reaches over to the coffee table in front of him to get a plug of Big Kick chewing tobacco to pop into his mouth, but I grab his arm. He gives me the courtesy of leaving the plug on the table. "She used to come right home after gigs and slide right in bed next to me, call me 'daddy sweet,' and give me all of her love until dawn. But lately she been coming in after sunrise and going straight to bed. Shrug her shoulder off of me when I touch her like she be pissed."

"You sure and bona fide? You haven't done anything for her to stray, like cheat yourself?" If life has taught me anything, it's that stories are like coins. They all have two sides.

"Shit, I'm working overtime casting spells for clients, plus casting spells on these no-good drug dealers while trying to maintain things for her. It's a whole lotta shit going up here in Harlem, Susan. Both me and Black Herman have been losing members to this skag shit out here. Some of our people have been falling into using or selling. Remember Trudy, my lieutenant?" Scat's voice is becoming uptight.

"Yeah, the petite brown girl. Dresses mannish in sharkskin suits and pork pie hats?" Not my style, but if that's what floats her boat, more power to her.

"She gone. Trudy left my family and started selling skag on her own. One night she was standing on the corner and a trio, one man and two women, all cold-gangster-looking in suits, snatched her up. Trudy hasn't been seen since. I sense she's dead." Scat shakes his head. "I taught Lucy all I know; I keep her in comfort, and you mean to say she's jiving around with another man on me?!"

"You sure Lucy's not messing with skag instead? You sure you not using cheating as a cop-out for her skin popping?" I ask.

"I don't think so," Scat says, wavering.

"Scat, I don't see why a man with your mojo can't see who the backdoor man is with your psychic third eye."

"She blocks me out, is why. She's that good now."

"And you mean to say none of your folks can't follow her?" The skull radio floats around the perimeter of my beehive hairdo, then heads across the room.

"Listen, Susan, I've got members all over town, people you wouldn't know are part of my hoodoo family. A city councilman, gamblers, teachers, pimps, SNCC members, bus drivers, and even a few brothers on the corner selling religious newspapers. Shit, look at the church sister who passed my business card to you. Lucy knows all of them. That's why I contacted you, because the two of you have never really hung out. She may not be able to sense your private eyeballing and stalking her. Get me?" Scat's mood is turning dark.

"Sorry, Scat, I won't *stalk* her. Just trying to find out whose bed she laying in or whose apartment she shooting up in." Although if I had agreed, Scat would have loved to let me give her some wolf bites. "You sure she's not shacking up with Black Herman? Or what about the

Lukach Joe family down in the east village?" The skull radio is headed back toward us.

"Lukach Joe! Why that roly-poly little cracker Cajun know better than to cut in on me!" Scat eyes the tobacco plug, then me. I shake my head no.

"Anybody else down there I should look into?"

"She was hanging out with that cat, Jimmy James, leader of the Blue Flames band, but he's cool with me. Besides, I think he's left for London. That brother is out of this world," Scat says, which we both know is putting it mildly.

Our mutual friend, Jimmy James, aka Jimi Hendrix, is another person Madison and I met in '65. Jimi's Blue Flames played at our wedding. He was out of this world in that he and others like him—such as Sun Ra, Phil Ochs, Nina Simone, and Knott's Berry Farm owner, Walter (so L-7 he had to be from another planet) Knotts, to name a few—were here on vacation or to experience this ball of confusion named planet Earth and would someday return to their prospective solar systems.

"Tomorrow night, she's playing with Lady Bo down on West 14th Street, a club named the Cherry Lama. Damn kids and their club names these days. Show starts at nine," Scat says.

"Where is Lucy now?" I ask as I shoo away the transistor radio, which has been hovering too close for comfort despite playing "Respect."

"She went downtown to Manny's Music Land to pick up some strings for her Vox. Is this good for you?" Scat leans near me. Ew. That tobacco chew smell! Goes into his pants pocket and pulls out a torn piece of a Chinese takeout menu with an offer scribbled on it. I look at the number and nod. Scat reaches into his pants pocket again and pulls out a wad of bills held in place by a blue rubber band. His thumb licks out my fee and he hands over the tobacco-stained bills. I brace my nose and stomach, slipping the money into my denim jacket pocket. You better believe I'm going to spray Aqua Net or anything I can find to purge the smell on those bills.

"What are you going to do if I find out something?"

"You never mind, let me handle that," Scat says, turning his gaze away from me.

"Don't hurt her, Scat," I growl, hoping to get through to him. He responds silently by standing up and ushering me to the door.

"Thank you kindly, Susan," he finally says.

Once outside the flat, I watch as the four primary-colored mice scurry along the wall and then vanish under an opening in the staircase. From within Scat's apartment, I can still hear the skull radio as it belts out the final bars of "Respect."

SAIGON: MADISON

The heavy rotating blades of a CH-21 roar over my head as it flies north from Saigon. I don't know or care to know its destination. I'm in the financial district of Saigon along the Kinh Ben Nghe waterfront of the Song Sai Gon River. I feel numb as I wonder what it was I saw on the hill the other night. Just waiting for Lieutenant Holman to return with a debriefing memo After Action Report we have to deliver to the Pentagon East MACV in the American sector, at which point we'll go our separate ways for R&R.

The lieutenant will, no doubt, head to Tu Do Street to carouse and me back to my hotel room where gin, tonics, and loneliness await. We are to meet across the street from the Hotel Carvalle, a few blocks down from my temporary residence, the Hotel de Commandant, to make any North Vietnamese infiltrators (which the city is chock-full of) work for their pay. Hazy traffic zips along. South Vietnamese citizens in cars, on mopeds, and on bikes form a virtual moving mass of Non la hats that flows down the Rue. I emerge from the Hotel Carvalle and make eye contact with the lieutenant. In front of me, a woman dressed in olive fatigues and lugging a portable typewriter exits the hotel. Damn if it isn't Philippa Schuyler! She stumbles down the hotel steps and loses her hat.

"*Xin chao xinh dep*," I say, helping her to her feet and handing over the Beetle Bailey forage cap.

"*Cha'o*," Philippa says in a formal tone. Her lisp still intact, and her once-sensual black hair now reddish-brown in color. I eye her figure, which is now more buoyant than the vivacious young pianist of 1954. Her face still retains its baby-soft appearance, but her eyes convey a dark world-weariness as if her spirit is trying to keep up that supercharged, youthful zest she once held.

"Can you see what just occurred? I'm so clumsy!" she stammers. "Don't I know you?" She scrutinizes me and the nameplate on my uniform. "Good lord! Madison Cavendish? It can't be!"

"Ah, yes, and no." This is crazy. I should not be doing this. Susan and I should have kept up with her career. "My name is Major Madison Cavendish Jr. You must be thinking of my father." Here we go. The lies will start as a squirt and grow into a deluge. "You're Philippa Schuyler, right?" I ask, trying to make my gin-and-tonic-and-cigarette-scratched voice sound young and peppy.

"I never knew they had a child," she says, ignoring my question.

"I was born at the start of WW II, but they sent me to the West Coast to live with my me-ma, Grannie Lola, in Pasadena." Kiss the stars. I'm a good liar.

"Really?" Philippa searches for my eyes through my sunglasses. The sun isn't too intense, so I oblige her by removing them to show my blues.

"I met your parents by way of George and Josephine. Your parents were bodyguards for me during an incident back in '54." Squatting down, she snaps open her Smith Corona carrier and checks the typewriter for damages. I reach into my uniform breast pocket and flick an Old Gold from the pack. She takes a few pigeon-toed sidesteps to dodge the smoky path as I light up, bumping into Saigon residents trying to make uncertain days normal in the city. She still calls her parents by their first names.

"Where are your parents now? I see you've picked up one of your dad's bad habits. I hope not his left-leaning political views, too." It seemed Susan had done a sufficient job of posthypnotic suggestion on that spring night back in '54. Philippa still holds a contemptible false memory of me—or, should I say, my father. Unaffected is her arrogant snideness, which she still possesses. I want to blow a cigarette smoke ring in her face in response to her snotty remark but decide against it.

"I may be LBJ all the way, but I'm no red diaper baby if that's what you're insinuating or insisting."

"Where are your parents?" Philippa asks again. The press ID card attached to her fatigues makes it clear she gets her kicks and a paycheck asking questions as a journalist.

"Ma's in retirement in Pasadena. Dad passed away," I lie.

"Sorry to hear about your father. I'm on assignment for a newspaper back east in the States." Philippa gazes around into traffic, I guess for a solution to her transportation problem.

"Major Cavendish," Lieutenant Holman drawls as he pulls up in a dull green, white star-stenciled CJ-5. "Ready, sir?"

"Lieutenant, a change in plans. I'll take the AAR to Pentagon East MACV. I have to drop this young lady off along the way. You do need a lift, right, Miss Schuyler?"

"Yes, why thank you, Major," Philippa winks, clearly loving the "young lady" comment.

I pull Holman out of earshot while Philippa loads her journalistic gear into the back of the Jeep and hops in. "Listen," I tell the lieutenant, "after your R&R, I need for you to see what you can find out about vampires in this country; he's got me doing Renfield work again." Holman rolled his eyes. "Find out if the Pentagon East MACV is doing any Black contract work that we don't know about. I'll do some looking into myself. And don't ask why, just do it, please."

The lieutenant snaps a salute, then catches a *xe'om* to Tu Do Street where, somewhere, a woman in a miniskirt and bourbon shots chased by a 33 beer awaited him and his Army pay, away from the horrors and bullshit of a Major C. Cavendish. I merge the CJ-5 into traffic and we first head to the press liaison center on Le Lou Street so Philippa can settle a beef she's having with MACV about access to Black GIs who've been complaining about their treatment, then northeast to the PPT/Voice of America radio complex—she has an interview scheduled with one of the officials there. During the ride she asks more questions, and I tell more lies. We stop in front of the gates of the PPT/VOA. I ask for a dinner date at my hotel for 7 p.m. She agrees to the date but emphasizes the fact that I'm many years younger than her. She finally relents because I had acted like her knight in shining armor. My mind flashes back to the wallpaper depicting caricatures of kings, queens, and knights in the bedroom of her apartment in the Sugar Hill section of Harlem. In that same moment she touches my hand and kisses my cheek but draws back as if a left-hand magenta glow had pinched her, hopefully not getting a taste of my flashback.

After she leaves, I rest my head on the Jeep's steering wheel and sink into deep thought over my actions. I would have stayed in that position all day if not been for the arrival of two MPs in blue helmets who stop to check on me.

NEW YORK CITY: SUE

The Monterrey Pop Festival may have tried to take us to new heights, but NASA actually did.

I throw my blue turtleneck sweater with the white horizontal stripes on the bed and opt for a solid black alternative to match my jeans. I want to throw on some mod stuff, but in this business, functionality matters. Thus, I step out into the night in a sweater, jeans, my good old red PFs, and a dark three-quarter peacoat. I've got some spending bread, a small compact mirror, and my rose shades. I leave the .32mm behind. Sometimes nocturnal light is okay; it's like a form of catnip in that it mellows me out. But in some cases, if full Hecate, it causes a case of the spells, or, as Maddy and I often joke because we like to stay up to date with "Hip" for this decade, I become "Spelladelic."

I arrive at the Cherry Lama thirty minutes before showtime, and it's good that I have my shades. The strobe lights make my eyes wolfy itch. The psychedelic decor is cool; the music is a far-out groove via DJ, but the go-go dancers would benefit from a lesson on how to shake and shimmy from this old flapper. Peggy takes the stage and is followed by the rest of the band. She's dressed in a black leather pantsuit, hot-pink ruffled blouse, and black suede moccasins, handling a sunburst Gibson six-string. I'm in the back of the club near the bar out of Peggy's eyesight, but I have to put up with a sake-tipsy, orange Nehru-suited Japanese poet who's sprouting Yukio Mishima wannabe haiku, which is not so bad but isn't the right time. I try to tell him. I need to focus on Lucy. He's infatuated with me and with his cute self.

Golden-brown complexion, flip hairdo, oval faced, her intense brown eyes, behind mint-green French cat eyeglasses, Lucy Revell is plugging her mint-green Vox into an amp behind her in the club shadows. Stage lights power on and light the stage. Lucy wears a minidress, plastic earrings, and high heels the same color as her Vox. Her attire, along with a pair of black fishnet stockings are wowing the straight men in the crowd. The remaining band members take their places. Thump Cominski, who would later go on to be one of the best session drummers during the age of disco, is on percussion. Chatty Cathy, a wiry cornsilk blond from Milwaukee, and the Calypso brothers, Kent and Keith, who are as much from the Caribbean as I'm from Albuquerque, alternate lead and backup vocal duties. A cat named Lee, a Sly Stone knockoff, is on keyboards, and a brown brother named Manny from El Barrio keeps Thump with him in the rhythm pocket on bass. The band has been transitioning from the mod look to full-throttle hippie style recently in stage and street outfits. Through the haze of cigarette and funny cigarette smoke, which give the stage lights a bluish tint, the band kicks off with a cover of the Beatles' "Eight Days a Week." Cathy and the brothers do some serious harmonizing. I'm grooving to it. I'm also getting a contact high from the latter half of the smoky haze. Lucy's jiggling along to her strumming and cord changes. Since they're a cover band, the rest of the set consists of some older stuff mixed in with what's current on the Billboard charts. Between songs, Peggy chats with the club crowd and does some stiff comic shtick with Cathy and the brothers. The Summit ends the night with a cover of the Supremes, "The Happening." I finish my glass of sake, courtesy of Mr. Haiku. I smile at him and say we have potential, peck him a kiss, then bid him *oyasuminasai* as I slip his telephone number into my jacket pocket. I head to the ladies' room. Once outside, it's time to earn my pay.

Thirty minutes later, the Peggy Jones Summit exits the Cherry Lama. After a round of hugs, Peggy and most of the band head east on 14th Street While Lucy heads west along 14th toward 12th Avenue carrying her guitar case. Thump, sucking on a cigarette, is the only band member headed in a northerly direction.

This part of Manhattan is home to the meatpacking district, warehouses, highline freight tracks, the Westside Highway, various hookers, and beyond that, the Hudson River piers. I try to stay my distance a block behind Lucy in the shadows as she turns uptown. Now she's under the High Line headed to a hot-sheet motel called the Love Bug Inn, a whitewashed brick standalone building with a cartoon ladybug and bubbling hearts painted on the side exterior. According to people in the know, love had little to do with the place. It was a place where straight and crooked tricks were turned, and the lovebugs found in the rooms were, big surprise, bedbugs. As Lucy makes her way from under the High Line to the inn, a thick, calloused hand reaches out to me, swings me around, and thumps me inside and up against a grimy brick wall alcove supporting the High Line. The rose shades fling off my face.

"Don't move!" my male assailant commands in a whisper. The putrefying cologne of Kool cigarettes, muscatel wine, and a brunt sweaty heroin aroma from his hand covering my mouth and nose ignites my gag reflex.

"Can't… breathe," I gasp, voice muffled. My face scrapes the facing the wall.

"Struggle and I will cut you the fuck up! You hear me, spic bitch?" he threatens. Despite inaccurately identifying my ethnicity, I quickly nod in compliance. "Scream and I will cut you *the fuck up!*" He continues to threaten me. His eyes reveal a buzz from a recent fix, so much so that he doesn't even notice as I slip out of my PFs. *Dealing with this skuzz is going to be good sport.*

"You know what I am going to do, baby? I'm going to screw you, and you're going to pay me for it. And then I will kill you. How's that for kicks?"

I feel him dry-humping me as a switchblade point menacingly snags into my sweater. I could take him right now and send him into eternity, but I want to have some fun. "I'll… I'll give it to you for free, baby! I'll even give you my night's bank I made from tricking, but please don't cut me. I'd rather take an ass whipping from my Mack Daddy la Maddy than be carved for sure!" I beg in my best fake junkie hoe whine. "Oh, come on, baby, you don't want to kill me! Please!" Kiss the stars.

As Madison would say, I'm an expert liar.

He releases the hold on my neck and sorts through my coat pocket, pulling out a wad of bills. "Is this all?"

"I have more in my bra. Let me slip off this coat off so I can get it, baby. Then we can get down to business… and pleasure."

"Go ahead, but I'm warning you…" He's tentative but lets my coat slip between us to the ground. As he fumbles with the top button of my jeans, I reach into my bra and pull out my compact. I flip it open, catching a few strands of full moonlight coming through the High Line rail tracks overhead. This is my freedom, my justice, and my damnation.

He has pockmarked cheeks. Pockface shrills a shocked scream. I whirl around and rip his left arm from his shoulder socket. It tears loose with a loud, wet crunch. He drops to the ground in shock. His dingy, pale, belted trench coat and dark suit are turning crimson red in the moonlight. His feet, covered in worn-out froggy-doo canvas sneakers that have seen way too much asphalt, start to twitch. He flays his blade and tries to stab at me, screaming, futilely, for help from God while blood spurts over the garbage-covered ground. He screams at me—*bitch this* and *bitch that*—before he begins pleading for his life. My dark pupils turn a bestial shade of hazel. Muscle mass morphing rips my clothes apart, fur bristling up through the pores of my skin to form a sleek gray, silver, magenta-streaked, fur-covered pelt. Kicking my peacoat and PFs to the side, I stare at the severed arm still in my grasp. Because I can, I smack him in the face with his own detached hand. Color me ferocious. I want to say something jovial, but my face and mouth have contorted to a canine appearance. The best I can do is a deep grunt as I growl "Spelladelic love" before starting my snack.

To be honest, his stringy flesh didn't have too much of a dope flavor, meaning that he must have been chipping. Calming down to human form after having my fill, I locate my peacoat and PFs, find an open fire hydrant to wash up, and stroll to a less-barren part of 17th Street. I can't raise my arm too high to hail a taxi because my coat covers only so much of my bare nakedness, but there are worse problems. Just ask Pockface.

SAIGON: MADISON

I'm in the lobby of my hotel. It's after seven and Philippa hasn't yet shown up for dinner. The Hotel de Commandant lobby is low on foot traffic this evening. Dressed in my civvies—a single-breasted blue suit, blue-striped shirt minus a tie, a .44 holstered under my suit jacket—I'm ready to head to the bar for a gin and tonic when, peripherally, I see Philippa entering the lobby, no longer in fatigues. Susan, forgive me, Philippa is stunning. Shoulder-length reddish-brown hair. Bright metallic green Ao Dai dress with white blossom print patterns, the Dai, of course, slit up to her thighs to reveal white pajama-like pants and green high heels. Nervous, I run my fingers through my slicked-back, midnight-black hair, take a deep breath, and walk over to greet her.

"You're looking provocative this evening. You are such an item," I say, as a red-jacketed waiter scoots between us.

"*Ch'ao*. You don't look too bad yourself, Major." She gives me a light horseplay punch in the arm, then places her hands in mine. For a few seconds I feel her consciousness blink into mine.

We descend the stairs and reach the hotel dining area. The same waiter who cut in between us earlier now escorts us to a table.

"So, what are your duties here in Saigon, Junior? You don't mind if I call you Junior? You can call me Phil," she says.

"Okay, Phil. I'm with the Army Signal Corps. Can't go into details 'cause it's classified. I recently returned from Khe Sanh."

"I've heard rumors that things were hairy there in a creepy way. Grunts seeing strange things in the air flying around at night. Some say ghosts, others say UFOs. Did you see anything like that, Junior?"

"Nope. Not a thing, Phil. You'd have to ask the higher-ups at Tan Son Nhut."

"You know full and well the DAO will just deny everything. Nothing for nothing, people both north and south have seen this whatever-it-is all over the place. Once I get a break in my assignment I intend to see what I can learn. I see a story in this. Great for folks back home to read other than a steady diet of war, don't you think?" Philippa smiles.

I offer a fake smile, knowing she's wading into a dangerous area, not unlike the satanic order Susan and I saved her from back in '54. Maybe it was a bad decision that Susan blocked it out of Philippa's mind back then.

"Don't be so delusional, Phil. You can't really believe that bunk." I start to grow impatient waiting for a server to show up with menus to provide a distraction from our conversation. "I'll level with you. One night in Khe Sanh, while I was laying out comm wire I saw a UFO land. Its hatch door opened, and a Nordic-looking alien emerged. Extending a giant hand, he greeted me." I watch the tension and release build up in Philippa's eyes.

"What did he say?" she asks anxiously.

"He locked eyes on mine and said, 'Sock it to me!'"

A flash of anger shoots across Philippa's face but is soon replaced by laughter at my use of a background lyric from Aretha Franklin's "Respect." She reaches across the table with both hands to hold mine, then shudders at the coldness of my hands.

"Are you married, Junior? Just asking; don't mean to pry."

"Yes, her name is… uh… Portia." Where is that waiter?

"Well, at least you have someone to go back to in the States. I have no one. Only a shoebox full of love letters from bad relationships. Soon I plan to get my concert pianist career back on track. Music is my one true love."

Finally, the waiter arrives. After some deafening silence, we order. The drinks, a gin and tonic for me and a rare, she said, 33 beer for her, arrive first. Over the next hour we talk openly while consuming nem, bun xao shrimp with nuoc cham sauce, and taro mochi for dessert. We discuss the war, home, her career, my vague career, her father's ill-fated op-ed column criticizing Dr. Martin Luther King Jr, her parents letting her know that my father (i.e., me) was part Black, her trials and racial tribulations in "Passing," me not freaking caring about trying to "Pass" (the one truth I reveal tonight) anymore. For the rest of the evening, we put our anxieties and depressions to the side and enjoy each other's company.

"I saw a piano in the hotel barroom," she says, rising from the table and taking me by the hand. I signal the head waiter to charge the meal to my account. We return to the lobby and walk down the few steps into the subdued light of the barroom, where an upright piano, well below Philippa's standards, is stationed in the corner. On occasion, a hired pianist would play popular French tunes and heavy-handed renditions of American tin-pan alley songs, but tonight, no one is at the bench. The bartender nods a subtle approval after I rub my fingers together, signaling the universal money sign, pointing to the upright. Sliding onto the bench, Philippa starts off with piano concertos by Ravel and others. She makes a pitstop to do some awkward (for her) pop tunes, including Petula Clark's "Downtown." During a brief rendition of Russian composer Mussorgsky's work, Philippa's back goes stiff and rigid as if someone had pierced her spine. She jumps up from the piano bench.

"You okay?" I grab her as she swoons toward the floor. She shudders again.

"Can I rest in your room for a bit? I suddenly feel ill, Major Madison Cavendish Jr."

The tone of her voice makes me feel leery. "Headache?" I ask.

"No. Just help me to your room." We head into the lobby and onto an ancient, caged, baroque-looking elevator that creeps along up to my room on the third floor. Once inside, I feel around for the light switch. The lights now on, I turn to see Philippa leaning up against the door.

"Are you okay?"

"I feel better now. You're not actually Madison Cavendish Jr. Don't lie. Madison, I've been having flashbacks every damn time I touch your hands. The last was a moment of pure clarity. I remember that night."

"Yes, Philippa, it's me. If you saw the vision, then you know why we did what we did. Please forgive us. Come sit down. Susan and I belong to a world you can't enter." I escort her to the living room area of my suite, only to have her steer me across to the bedroom, pushing me onto the bed in the room's darkness.

She whispers those three little words to me: "*Em yeu anh.*"

"*Anh yen em,*" I whisper back.

On top of me, she pins an arm under my neck while lightly pounding my shoulder with her other hand, balled into a fist. Her kisses come in wet torrents, tear-moistened cheeks rubbing against mine in a fervent ardor of lust.

NEW YORK: SUE

I press my lips against the glass of the framed photo of Maddy's military photo with continued ardor and kiss it. The photo shows him, unsmiling, in his dress greens, an Army Signal Corps insignia patch on his shoulder. I pull back and whisper to the image, "Isn't it time you came home, Maddy?" I sense what is going down over there, but right now I must go to work. My jeans suit ruined courtesy of the other night's incident, this time I choose a full-length black leather coat, cow neck, suede boots, and jeans. Oh yeah, now the 32.

Before I forget, Pockface's name was Phil Defante, a small-time hood and Richard Speck wannabe who was slipping back and forth between New Jersey and Manhattan, preying on women, implicated in but never tried for a murder in Hoboken.

Earlier today I was summoned by Muckensten to the Office of Special Concerns headquarters in Long Island City, Queens. He suspected I killed Defante.

"Play nice, please, Susan," he teased after I explained the

circumstances that led to Defante's demise.

Muckensten nodded and repeated his previous suggestion to play nice.

"You know me, Chief. I play the hand I'm dealt. Always have, always will. You know where to find me if you need me."

Opening my apartment door, Sekhmet startles me as she stands in the doorway. Damn it, she still has her catlike ways.

"After last night, don't you think you need backup, Suzy? Dig like a checkmate Charle?" says Sekhmet, pushing me back into my apartment. Lawdy, this feline is just as persistent in human form.

"I'm cool, darling. I can TCB on my own."

"Please, Susan. I'm sho'nuff you can, but pretty please, I would feel better having your back." Not waiting for me to say yes or no, Sekhmet moves past me into my bedroom and rummages through my closet. She picks out and changes into my maroon sweater and white PFs. I've got to get this familiar an Alexander's credit card.

We head to the offramp on the Bronx side of the White Stone Bridge, having crossed from Queens, where the Summit has a gig at a club right off the 59th Street Bridge. Lucy has hopped into her and Scat's Buick black deuce and, a quarter after, again splitting from the rest of the band. We follow with Sekhmet, making sure to cast a spell over the Duster so that if Lucy looks in the rearview mirror at the Duster, she'll see different vehicles and divers behind her. Indeed, she looks back at various intervals and sees either a thick George Halas-looking Chicago businessman driving a sky-hued Savoy with his pet beagle by his side, two nerdy Smothers Brother-looking guys driving a Mr. Softee truck laying down that soft addictive jingle, or a Latino family in a gold Impala, with kids happily bouncing up and down in the back seat. We lag back as the duce approaches the front of the Whitestone Motel, a kitsch rest stop catering to businessmen and spousal cheaters. In the distance, the Throggs Neck Band Ferry Point Park near the motel makes for a lonely area this time of night. We wait for several minutes before stepping in, enough time to let Lucy settle in her room and wait for her paramour. I get a room next to hers, both facing the front of the hotel from a fussy black pompadour-wigged motel manager, his stripped bell-bottoms clashing with a striped shirt worn over a black turtleneck, winking at Sekhmet and I as a couple. At the sound of Lucy leaving her room, I peek out the door. She gets an RC Cola from the soda machine and steps outside. Ducking back in my room, I go to the window. Lucy is headed to the parking lot. She returns with a dark-skinned man in a red rose-colored sharkskin suit. Her type of man is etched in stone because damn if this brother don't look like Scat Carter. Arms interlocked in love, they enter the motel. Once they're in the room, Sekhmet hops on the bed and faces the motel room wall with Lucy's room on the other side. In a lotus position and with her eyes closed, Sehkmet concentrates her psychic third eye to do some peep show spying on their balling. Well, as sure as the night, it isn't Scat, and when I confront Scat, he isn't going to like hearing this. Quietly, we leave the motel. The sleeping motel manager is too busy letting the late show on his portable television behind the front desk watch him, so I quietly leave the keys on his desk on the way out. Back in Queens, then west to the 59th Street Bridge so we can return home, I think to myself that if I knew what I knew now, thanks to Sekhmet, this affair would be over before it started. Slapping the steering wheel, I plan to have a sit-down with both Scat and Lucy tomorrow.

MADISON

I awake from a restful sleep, feeling as if someone has slapped my face. I turn to my right, expecting to see Philippa, but instead there is only a vacant spot on the bed. What was supposed to be a night of hot vampire-human sex had ended up as a platonic night of sleep, far away from the war outside. She's gone now. Levitating up to a standing position then slipping my shades on, I pull the hotel curtains back to reveal a sunny Saigon midday. A folded piece of hotel stationary rests atop the dark wood nightstand, hotel pen on top to ensure it would be noticed. I unfold the paper and gaze at the handwritten note.

> *Dear Madison,*
>
> *I did not want to wake you. I'm headed to Khe Sanh, then a humanitarian mission in the Da nang sector over the next few days.*
>
> *I'm in love with you. With the visions of that night in 1954 resurrected in my mind, I love you and am not afraid of what you are. I wanted to become a part of your life back then and still do now, although I will be damned in the eyes of my faith. To lay next to you was so wonderful, passionate, and heartfelt. I want to give myself to you forever. I must see you when I return. Maybe if those strange sightings in Khe Sanh are occurring up here in Da Nang I can get a story. We must talk.*
>
> *Love,*
>
> *Philippa*

I no sooner finish reading the letter than the sound of fists begins pounding at my room door, accompanied by the voice of Lieutenant Holman. Ignoring the urge to punch him, I straighten out my suit then snatch the door open.

"Major, I have orders here saying our R&R is rescinded and we have to report to MACV HQ in one hour. The situation at Hill 950 is back, and it's become more intense," Holman, bleary-eyed from an overabundance of Tu Do Street, explains. "They said you have work to do tonight." Holman offers a sympathetic look.

"I'll meet you downstairs!" I grumble and shut the door.

Ten minutes later, we're outside. Lieutenant Holman is already fitted in his tigers. His gear is stowed in the CJ-5 next to a lance corporal he's driving to the pickup point.

"Did you find anything on what I saw?" I ask. Lieutenant Holman pulls me out of earshot of the corporal.

"What you saw that night was a *Ma Ca'rong,* as the people of this land call it. One of your own kind, this is the real deal in both the north, south, and the DMZ, not that fucking bullshit the Army psychological operations team has been trying to pull with 'Operation Wandering Soul' on par with you and that toothy gang you created and sent north. Major, can I have permission to be candid and speak off the record?"

"Please do, Lieutenant."

"'Wandering Soul' was basically GIs humping around the jungle at night with a freaking tape deck, playing the supposed spirits of VC dead moaning to their comrades to surrender. I didn't need a tape deck to hear the dead from both sides or an 'infinity pull,' as my dear wife, who's more attuned to such things, calls it."

"Shoot," I say.

"Sir, after this go-around in Khe Sanh, I'm putting in for a transfer. I done three tours, two with you, and I'm played out. Enough for this Georgia boy. Under your command, I've seen a lot of weird shit that I hope I'll be forgiven come judgment day. Because of you, I've come to respect Black folk. I've got your back, Major, I shit you not. But I'm done. I want to spend my last days in the Signal Corps, maybe behind a desk at Fort Meade. After that, I heard NASA needs security personnel. Or maybe I'll start a church or open a bar, maybe a church bar. A church bar. Wouldn't that be a kick in the head, as old Dino Martin likes to sing." Beneath a calm exterior, Holman's voice is peppered with anxiety.

"Cool. Fair enough, peach head. Let's get going," I say, after a few moments of silent introspection drowned out by Saigon's hustle and bustle noise.

SUE

The hustle and bustle of those same primary-colored mice in Scat's tenement lobby doesn't surprise me this time. Matter of fact, I chase them under the staircase and catch one to the shock and terror of some little girls playing on the staircase. Slipping the little critter in my orange outfit purse, I knock on Scat's door. From within the apartment, a heavy argument is in full swing.

"That you, Susan?" Scat asks, after a few raps on the door. He opens it for me like before, with Lucy close behind him.

"What kinda surprise Scat said you got for me?" Lucy says, a lemon-lime swirl nightgown hanging loosely over her otherwise naked body. Scat is wearing a silk robe adorned with a zebra print.

"I don't know how you and Lucy get your kicks, but I can't be wasting my time like last night. Y'all got to get it together."

"What you be talking about, Susan?" Scat demands.

"What I'm talking about is this." Pulling the mouse from my purse, I dangle it by its red, furry tail. "Show Scat, Lucy, or I'll go wolf on this little critter and have a snack. This is la loba feroz talking to you." I hate saying it because, in truth, it's really Sekhmet who wants to snack on the mouse, so it's best she stay in the Duster.

"Okay, okay," Lucy says. Her style of conjuring isn't a bewitched nose wiggle but the lifting of her cat eyeglasses off the bridge of her nose and dropping them back down. With that, a red puff of smoke storms up from the paisley carpet, and after a quick dissipation, a double of Scat Johnny stands in a rose-colored sharkskin suit. It stares blankly at Scat and squeaks.

"Oh, hell no, Lucy! Why?" says Scat, walking around the quivering mouse which he inspects.

"You've been neglecting me, Scat," Lucy says. "You only want to get down when you feel like it. No romance at all these days."

"But you see, I be damn busy, woman. What you want?"

"I want love, Scat. I want it to be like before," Lucy pleads. "Also, take a break from that tobacky chew. Shit has your breath stinking around the clock."

"Scat, take a break," I suggest. "Take Lucy to Paris or something. Y'all need to TCB—that is, take care of business. Get on the same page and love, baby, love. And try to go cold turkey on the chew."

"What about my hoodoo family?" Scat asks, looking into Lucy's eyes and moving toward her.

"If the family falls, they fall. Lucy's your queen and you have to maintain her," I answer for Lucy. "Lucy, Peggy, and the Summit can hold it down while you're on hiatus."

"You think so?" Lucy asks.

"I know so, baby."

"Okay, it's set," Scat concedes. "We going on… what you call it… hiatus? Now turn red Scat back to red Mickey Mouse so I can squish his ass!"

"Nooo!" Lucy and I both yell.

"Just joshing!" Scat smirks, but I knew better. As soon as Lucy does her glasses trick, I quickly bend down and scoop up the red mouse. Already Scat and Lucy are slobbering, sucking face and pulling at each other's clothes which is a cue for me to split. On the way out I deposit Mr. Haiku's phone number in Scat and Lucy's kitchen trash. Out in the hallway, the red mouse (now back to brown) leaps out my hand and slips through a crack under the stairs with the rest of its buddies.

MADISON

Slipping through an opening in our concertina wire and down Hill 558, plugging the gap between the hill from VC and PARN has turned into a siege that's been grinding for a week. The corporal who had hitched a ride with Holman and me didn't even get through his first night, his body by now on the way to Hawaii and then on to Dover Airbase. A downpour of early monsoon season rain slows my movement tonight, and my killing. I leave behind in the foliage the bodies of five VC. I recognized one as the Hotel de Commandant waiter who had handed Phil and me our menus the other night.

Approximately twenty yards behind me, that slurping sound starts again. Slowly turning around to train my weapon on the *Ma Ca'rong* as if it'll make a difference, I meet up with my past again. Hunched over the VC/waiter is a naked, milky-hued Philippa, the rain instantly washing the blood off her face every time she pauses from lapping up blood. One part of me wants to join her, but just as I begin to raise my M-16, a mortar round launched from somewhere dry ends my debate, knocking us into a black void.

—

Morning. I roll over bunker sandbags into the face of a startled Signal Corps captain.

"Major Cavendish?" You could tell the tawny brown captain was from New York by his accent. Maybe the Bronx.

"Where is Lieutenant Holman?" I ask, chopping a salute at him.

"Sorry, sir, I'm Captain Hulan Brown. Lieutenant Holman took a shrapnel hit, mortar fragments in the arm overnight while you were out doing whatever it is you're doing in the field." His tone made it sound like I was goldbricking somewhere. Maybe snapping his neck may change his opinion of me.

"So, you're my new aide now, Captain?" He nods yes.

"Sorry about Lieutenant Holman, sir. Pentagon East MACV sent me here from Saigon ASAP. At the landing zone, your man was waiting to be med vacc'd out. He asked me to give you this in exchange for a pack of Old Golds. 'It's classified,' he said. 'Put it in his hands,' he said."

Captain Brown hands me the blood-caked manila envelope. In turn, I walk to a corner of the bunker, fish out a pack and matches from my gear, and toss them to a now-smiling Brown, who gives me my space. I begin reading the dossier given to Brown by MACV. Every now and then he glances at me with a *you've got to be shitting me* look on his face. Wait until night falls, Captain Brown. I sit down and unseal the envelope.

The information inside is confusing. An *Associated Press* telex bulletin, reporting that classical pianist, author, and journalist Philippa Schuyler had been killed—along with young passengers and a US Army crewman—in a helicopter accident off the coast in the Da nang sector, with more details to come.

My mind reels. How is this possible when I saw her last night? To know I was the last man to lay beside her was a hurt consolation. I'm supposed to be timeless, but right now I feel old. I hope to put a hold on my Black contract and head stateside. I need Susan and a break. Was Philippa attacked by the *Ma Ca'rong*? How could she be in two places at once? Or was she possessed by it all along? *Tan biet*, Philippa.

SUE

A closed-circuit camera feed wired to a television monitor stationed in the reception area of Pan Am's headquarters shows the passengers disembarking from the New York Airways helicopter shuttle from JFK International Airport to the Pan Am building roof. My Maddy took a connecting flight from Honolulu to Detroit, then home to New York.

I'm decked out in a royal-blue caftan. I say goodbye to the beehive, get my hair half combed/back up. Sekhmet stands next to me, decked out in a floppy hat, minidress, and knee-high boots, all purple, which she purchased all on her own from the cut of bread I gave her for her help at the motel. The elevator doors slide open, passengers rush off and greet loved ones. Maddy is the last to exit in his dress greens. He awkwardly switches between his hands two gray Samsonite luggage cases and a dozen roses.

"Over here, Mr. Major!" we yell, and quickly approach him. We kiss in more than a New York minute, finally coming up for air. Maddy gives Sekhmet a peck on the cheek. She replies with a purr and a lick on his nose.

"Glad you're home, Major," I declare. It's been too long for me.

"And I'm glad to see you and Miss Kitty, Mrs. Cavendish," my Maddy says, his arms around our waists.

"Tonight, we're going to the Purple Manor Club on 125th Street for jazz and to watch a Grandassa fashion show our Sekhmet wants to attend. Then, except for answering the door for Chicken Delight or Henry's Hamburgers, we're going to TCB for the next few weeks, baby."

"Fair enough," my Maddy chuckles.

THE TIFFANY AFFAIR

1973

"The boss wants to see you in his office," said Millie Holstein, tapping me on my shoulder as she glided by my desk, her mail cart loaded down with dull apple-red file folders and mail for the twenty private investigators that made up the Cavendish Agency.

"About what? I haven't finished my report yet," I huffed after a sip of Tab soda.

"Listen, if I knew I'd give you the lowdown on the get-down, but I don't," Millie told me, and I believed her, a nice kid from Rego Park, her amber hair Partridge Family, straight and sleek, and on her form a moss-green miniskirt topped by a red wool sweater, and Earth shoes on her feet. With a sigh, I stood up from behind my desk, smoothed out my pleated blue mini dress, and headed to Mr. Madison Cavendish's corner office while looking around for Hulan Brown for support, who was nowhere to be found.

My name's Everina, and this is my story.

The late '60s, as many know, were a turbulent time in the US, but for me it was a time for a sister to find herself. I had disappointed my parents, Erine and Sharon Dawson from Bed-Stuy Brooklyn, by not attending Cleveland University in Ohio or majoring in chemistry and using Aunt Stella's home in Glenville as a base as planned. Instead, I'd detoured to Reno, Nevada, where I landed a gig as a dishwasher. With my gift of gab and my dark chocolate legs, I soon parlayed myself a job as the first showgirl of color in the King's Castle Casino, partying along the way with celebs like Lola Falana and Stu Gillian. I then got a gun permit and became one of the King's Castle gambling room security guards. My nickname was "Semisweet" because, as a guard, I played no games. But by 1971, I was restless and homesick for Brooklyn, so after promising to take some classes at CCNY, to my parents' relief, I changed my hair from a perm to Bantu knots and headed back east.

"Have a seat, Ms. Dawson. May I call you Everina?" Mr. Cavendish was rubbing fish food into the open top of a large hexagon aquarium for his Koi, who took regal nibbles at his offerings. A collection of old texts, which I felt would bore me, were set neat in bookcases behind his desk, and glancing at the top of his desk, I spied an old, dog-eared file folder labeled *The War Memorial Affair.*

Okay, none of my beeswax, I said to myself, and sat down in a chair in front of my boss's desk.

"Okay here's the deal: I need for you to fill in for Hulan on an insurance fraud case. He's working with the vendor, upgrading the office to an IBM system, which, by the damn way, is costing me an arm and a leg."

Cavendish looked way too young to be an owner of this company, sitting on the edge of his desk in a forest-green suit and green pinstripe shirt, a Peter Max tie, and, as God is my witness, black sandals. Long jet-black hair draped his shoulders. Hulan said that he served under Cavendish in Nam and that Cavendish was a brother, which, based on his light complexity, could have fooled me, looking at his skin tone, which was ofay city, but I'm groovy with that.

I had a love jones for Hulan. A serious love jones.

Back in Brooklyn I was jobless and living in my parents' basement with no job. A Johnny Staccato rerun aired on the TV, and by the end credits, I knew I wanted to be a private eye.

Picking up a *New York Newsday* the next day, I closed my eyes and blindly picked out the Cavendish Agency to apply for a gig. In their office in the old RKO Building not far from Times Square, I was interviewed by a brown cutie named Hulan Brown, who wore a neat goatee and a mane of black hair like Nick of Ashford & Simpson. I tried to talk my way past my lack of PI experience, which he called me on but hired me anyway. A week later, we went on a cheap date to Nedick's, and a month later we were making love in his apartment in Co-op City in the Bronx. But I was growing perturbed with his disappearing act and being unavailable at night the prior few weeks. It was '73, and I was waiting for the next level in our relationship, which was supposed to be an engagement. "Is that why he disappears halfway into the week?" I wanted to know.

"Sister, I have no idea what brotherman does the rest of the week with his downtime. What I do know is he's on the IBM project; Susan is in London, along with Urraca Vauxhall, working on an art fraud case.

The rest of those cats out front are tied up with other cases. So how about it?”

"Okay, I'm down," I said, tight at the mention of Susan Cavendish, the co-owner of the agency, with her blonde afro and freckles tacked across her face; her and Hulan, along with that weird chick, Nellie de Carlo, who dresses like she should be at the Grand Olde Opry, always seemed to having a ball whispering, as if sharing a damn joke no one else knew the punch line to. To say I wasn't enthralled with them was like asking a raunchy rabbit if it likes to mate.

"Western Insurance suspects a landlord it provides services to is torching his own buildings in the Bronx and Brooklyn using local street gangs. So they have subcontracted us."

"Classic insurance fraud. You want me to catch the arsonists?" I admit to having a cocky swagger to me.

"No, that's for FDNY fire marshals to handle. We're going to ride from property to property tonight, listing fire hazards for Melco Realty to correct. You'll meet me back here tonight at 10 p.m."

"Okay, Mr. Cavendish. Ten it is. This sounds so interesting," I bullshitted him with my bubbly tone. This case sounded boring as shit, but hey, I was going to get paid, and what could be dangerous about driving around all night writing reports?

—

"Everina, reach over in the back seat and grab a few eight tracks. See what you want to hear. We can set the volume low and listen while finishing the Brooklyn paperwork and before checking the building out." said Cavendish, parking his 1970 electric blue Mercury Cougar (which he'd nicknamed "Suzy" after that wife of his) on Tiffany Street, a hard-times neighborhood of tenements and three-story houses dating back to 1907. We had finished Brooklyn and now were wrapping up our work in the Bronx.

Since we were only doing penwork all night, I wore a nice violet polyester pantsuit with a blue popcorn blouse under a denim jacket. Cavendish wore another forest-green suit, but it was leather and sinister-looking. Beneath my jacket in a shoulder holster, I carried a concealed .38, which I nicknamed "Li'l Semisweet," like me.

As mysterious as Cavendish was, he made the job go quickly into the night with his odd sense of humor, talking about how the Bronx used to be mostly farmland, as if he was there back then. Looking down at his choice of music stacked in my hands only confirmed my view of my boss. Methinks that back in NAM, he and maybe damn Hulan may have done some LSD or some other shit.

"You don't have anything more current?" I asked. Various pianists' interpretations of Scot Joplin and Jelly Roll Morton aren't my thing. I managed to find a copy of the Isley Brothers *3 + 3* and pop it into the dashboard tape deck. At 1:32 a.m., Tiffany Street is desolate in the chilly autumn morning.

Silhouettes of tenants—Black, brown, and a white old-timer—could be seen passing their apartment windows every now and then, the blue glow of television sets helping to illuminate them through torn curtains, window shades, and even a bed sheet stuffed into the top of a window. These were poor folk lacking the financial means to move. Southern Bronx can be both paradise and Hell.

———

"Wait! Get down under the dashboard!" whispered Cavendish, pulling the Isley Bros midway into "Who's That Lady" out the tape deck with a suctioned thump. So help me, by the time I dipped down, he was on my side of the Cougar, slipping the passenger door open and crouching down behind it. "Take a quick peek! See them!" he whispered. I figured maybe I was right about the LSD as I glimpsed two brown men crossing the street: one of them carried your generic red and yellow gasoline container. Stitched on the back of their denim jackets in white felt scrolls with black gay '90s font, and in the middle of their jackets a Day-Glo green patch rendering of the Frankenstein monster's head with a yellow lightning bolt slamming into it, letting everyone know they were part of the flying Majestic Bold Ones 169th Street chapter colors. For a second, they looked up Tiffany Street in our direction but kept moving around to the back of the faded brick-hued tenement building.

"Those little shits are going to torch the building with people still in there! Godfery Daniels!" Cavendish's voice was no longer a whisper. He and the situation began moving too fast for me.

My adrenaline was pumping. "Godfery who?" I asked, stepping out of the Cougar and brandishing Li'l Semisweet. We split up and ran around the sides of the tenement again. Cavendish moved too fast for my eyes. Stumbling over loose bricks and garbage, I heard an earth-shaking scream that had prying tenants pull back from their windows, in the overcast dim moonlight, my boss had one MBO dangling up in the air by the neck with one hand. Cavendish's pupils were now a hellish ruby red that was, only a minute ago, a nice ice blue inside the Cougar. Pearlescent fangs extended from Cavendish's mouth as he removed a gravity knife the MBO member had embedded in his neck. He flung it past me as I lay frozen in hypnotic terror.

The poor curly-haired MBO had made a fatal mistake, and now

shit was coming down hard on him. The sound of his neck being crunched by Cavendish still wakes me up shivering at night. At the time, I considered shooting Cavendish, having witnessed his true nature. Before I could decide how to proceed, I was knocked down hard, tackled by the other gang member onto the trash-strewn back of the building.

We grappled with my gun. The sound of two muzzle flashes sent him running.

"Oh dear god! Mama, Daddy!" An electrical shock-burning sensation left me breathless as the two .38 slugs bounced around in my body like molten ping-pong balls. "Get... some... air... girl!" I whispered to myself. I felt a warm dampness spreading on my bra and blouse. "Mama… Daddy… please!" I was dying.

The richness of my blood coughed out my mouth. As I tilted my head to the right, I saw Cavendish approach me, pulling off his jacket. "Godfery Daniels," he hissed, dropping to his knees beside me, biting into his left wrist, magenta-speckled blood spurting out, which his tongue wasted little time in lapping up. Leaning over me, I felt his breath, ice-cold on my neck. A strange scent, a mixture of sandalwood and burnt electrical wiring, was followed by a sharp piercing of my throat; then my body shook into darkness and I experienced a vision colored in various shades of magenta. The clouds, heavens, and sand under my feet as I walked naked on the beach of an unknown world were all magenta. I saw Hulan, naked, emerge from a milky magenta tide. As I ran to him, a cold breeze stole my breath.

My wheezed breathing roused me from the fever dream. A gauze bandage was wrapped around my neck's unholy throbbing, yet something was surging slowly inside me. I struggled to a sitting position. Coming into focus was Hulan's bedroom teakwood furniture. His television was playing *The Mike Douglas Show* with the volume set to low, which indicated it was late afternoon. The sun peeked through closed curtains, stabbing my eyes, but I couldn't feel its warmth.

"OH GOD, WHAT DID YOU DO TO ME YOU BASTARD FUCK?!" I yelled out. Cavendish was sitting in Hulan's wicker chair in the corner of the room, brooding. If I had my .38 I would have wasted him right then and there. I felt like I was losing my mind!

But he was wearing Hulan's prized Joe Nameth jersey. No gun in sight. My body was stiff and I sensed Li'l Semisweet wouldn't make a difference anyway after what I'd witnessed. "Where's Hulan, you bastard?" My shrill yelling caused the gauze to turn into dry-like parchment crumbling off my neck. "Answer me!"

"It's alright, Everina. Hulan will be back soon. For what it's worth, I'm sorry. Hulan loves you so much I had to do what I could to keep you on this side of the veil. You are now in a love supreme with Hulan, to coin Coltrane's masterpiece. A new world has opened its door for you, love, but the world of mortals has now been closed to you somewhat," said Cavendish, a watery tear racing down his cheek.

"New worlds… Coltrane… what the… what the fuck are you talking about?" I cried, but whatever was surging inside me already gave me the answer even as I fought to deny it.

"You know the old vampire films you watched on TV? Well, that's not us. Do you feel it? This is a cosmic piety." I *did* feel it. A new life force was connecting me to the stars beyond, and I, for some reason, now felt I could call him by his first name. Just then, I heard Hulan humming as he entered the crib and headed to the kitchen to deposit something in the fridge. Whatever it was clunked on the top rack as my baby closed the fridge door. I guess he thought it was more important to go to Pathmark than to tend to me.

"Sorry, babe," he said as he entered the bedroom. "I know this has been hard, but I'm here for you now. You've been out of commission for a few days, Madison and I took the time to set things right and did some payback. You know how I roll," my love half-joked as he sat next to me on his bed in that patch blue denim suit I dug the hell out of whenever he wore it. I wrapped my arms around his neck.

"You get it, babe?" he asked, to which I nodded yes, like someone whose body was under control by a horror movie alien. Hulan's body heat triggered a weird craving in my gut.

"I think you both could use some privacy," Madison said and exited the room.

"Where do you fit into all of this? Does this mean we're… we're vampires?" I asked.

"No. I mean, well, yes you are… but…" fumbled Hulan. This was all getting to be too much for this sister.

"What?" I pulled off his neck with a vocal hiss that erupted from out of nowhere within me.

"Everina, calm… cool out, babe. Here's the straight dope: I'm a Lycan, like Susan, babe. But that doesn't mean we can't make it happen," Hulan pleaded. "Also, you're now vampire kin to Nellie de Carlo." Shit, that was all I needed, but at least it explained her freaky deakyness.

"Madison and Susan have been together since being infected in 1914. Susan was my mentor. Back in '71, one ice-covered night, we were returning from a case upstate when Susan's Duster skidded off the road and flipped over. My injuries were internal and I had moments to live.

Before I slipped away, and by the grace of moonlight, Susan saved my life by gnawing into my throat." That explained the whispers between them. "Susan is like a sister to me, and Madison will be like a brother to you," said Hulan. I embraced my love again. "Come on, we've got a surprise for you, babe," said Hulan, taking me by the hand into the kitchen.

"Surprise!" my new mentor and love shouted in unison as Hulan flung the fridge door open. On the top shelf, wrapped in Saran Wrap, his eyes staring at us and his mouth open, was the head of the MBO who had shot me. Before tonight, I would have screamed at the sight of this grotesque scene, but now I felt nothing, certainly not fear or shock.

"Say hello or goodbye to Angel, Supreme President of the Majestic Bold Ones! Say hello, Angel," said Hulan. I glanced to the kitchen counter and saw Li'l Semisweet.

"I'm sure by now you've got the cravings, and for that, I'll make you some hyssop tea. It keeps the blood yearning in check. Has a rough taste at first, but you'll get used to it. Don't get me wrong, we will go on blood hunts, trust me. But only if the contract is sanctioned by Pixie Ramano of the New York City Office of Special Concerns. Mobsters, renegade vampires, thugs, pedophiles, bugging-out wolf pack members, and nasty attitude ghosts that get out of line—we handle with extreme finality."

"That is if Mayor Lindsay doesn't cut the OSC's budget," Hulan interjected. "But either way, we'll make do," he added with a sly grin.

"How does that sound?" asked Madison.

———

Mel Leland, the slumlord who owned Melco Realty, gave up his holdings and ran to Florida after a visit from Madison. Didn't stop the arson in the city, but at least lives were saved that night. I sat my parents down and tried to explain my new world to them, but it just rolled off their backs until one Saturday morning when I staggered into their house with a crimson-stained dress, the taste of mobster blood on my breath. Mama locked me in the basement (with the strength I now had, I could lift a car, but I acquiesced), got her Bible, and went on a prayer bender with Dad until Susan showed up to get me. We all agreed it was best I move out. Sadly, as the years passed, I could only get in contact with them through my cousin Henry, who acted as a sort of unofficial family liaison. The last I saw of my parents was at their funerals, first Mama and then Daddy. Even then, I could only mourn in dark glasses, covering my tears from a distance.

It's now 2024. Susan is my bestie, as they say these days. I'm

Everina Dawson-Brown. My hubby, Hulan, and I own a brownstone in Harlem. Madison is now the CEO of CavenTech, which we use as a front for occult detective affairs of the strange and mundane.

Godfery Daniels! This sister's found herself!

ABOUT THE AUTHOR

JAMES GOODRIDGE was born and raised in the Bronx and now resides in the Yorkville section of Manhattan. He began writing speculative fiction in 2009. After ten years as a visual artist representative and paralegal, James decided in 2013 to make a better commitment to writing. James has since written a collection of *Twilight Zone*-themed stories entitled *The Artwork (I to V)*. He's also contributed to numerous anthologies, including two volumes of *Scierogenous: An Anthology of Erotic Science Fiction and Fantasy* (2017, 2018), *Sweet, Sexy and Special Dark: Blerdrotica Book 1* (2020), and *Funny as a Heart Attack* (2021). James is a member of the Black Science Fiction Society and oversees the popular Facebook group Who Gives You the Write.

SUE
SUNMOUNTAIN

MADISON
CAVENDISH

GRAVELIGHTPRESS.COM